WILDING

Book One of The Traveller's Path

L.A. SMITH

To Julie,
Happy Reading!
Lisa Smith

First paperback edition June 2019

Cover design by ebooklaunch.com

ISBN: 978-1-9990140-1-8 (paperback)
ISBN: 978-1-9990140-0-1 (ebook)

www.lasmithwriter.com

Published by CarpetPage Press

For Mark, who always believed

A note about names, places, times…

Wilding is a work of historical fantasy, which is to say that although there are fantastical elements in it, it is based on a real time and place, namely Northumbria, England, in AD 642.

Historical fiction presents many challenges to writers, and those challenges are even more difficult with a book set in this era, during what is commonly known as the Dark Ages. There is comparatively little surviving written material and artefacts from that time period than there are from others, so there is much that we do not know about this fascinating era.

Because of this, scholars disagree about dates, names, and customs from this time, which presents writers with a dilemma: how do you write about these things with any accuracy?

For me, I did as much thorough research as I could, and for the things that were unknown or conflicting, I made my best judgment on how to present them in the book.

This is a book of fiction, after all. Even so, I have aimed at being as historically accurate as possible. However, those with knowledge of Anglo-Saxon England in the seventh century may see some minor historical details that I have adjusted to fit the scope of this novel. For example, we do not know exactly when Oswald died at the Battle of Maserfield. The generally accepted date is August 5, AD 642, and this is the date I have used in this book. We get this date from the Venerable Bede in his *Ecclesiastical History of the English People*. Some scholars contend that he may have begun counting the beginning of a new year in September rather than January, thus skewing all the dates, which results in Oswald dying in 641 rather than 642.

If you start to research this era in any detail, you will find all sorts of scholarly disagreements like this and might be tempted to throw up your hands. All a writer can do is to research carefully, pick the details they need that fit the story they are telling, do some fictional padding here and there as the story leads, and leave it as that.

Names from this era are also very tricky. First of all, many of them are pretty much unpronounceable to modern readers, unless they have a working knowledge of Old English (and if you do, my hat is very definitely off to you!). Try saying (or reading) Æthelthryth. I "think" it is pronounced Ahh-thul-thrith. On the Irish/British/Celtic side, things aren't much better. What about the name Amargein, which is a male Irish name from this time period? It looks easier than the Anglo-Saxon name, to be sure, but it's not. Because of the differences in how you pronounce Celtic names, this one is actually pronounced aw-VEER-een.

I suspect that most readers would quickly get bogged down in a book in which these types of names were used frequently. To avoid that, when I have named fictional characters, I have tried to use names that, while accurate to the time period as far as I can tell, are also somewhat more recognizable to our modern eyes.

The other problem with names in this era is one that I could not avoid in this book, because they are the names of real people from the time. In particular, the names of the Bernician royal house may present the reader with some trouble — not because they are necessarily hard names, but because they are so similar. Oswald and Oswy were half-brothers (some historians say full brothers). Their cousin Oswine was ruler (or sub-ruler) of Deira, the southern half of the Northumbrian kingdom. Oswald, Oswy, and Oswine. Yes, I know their names are similar, but it's historical fact. I can't mess with it.

Finally, possibly the most problematic of all are the issues surrounding place names and people groups. Of course, over time, place names change. In this book I have tried to use names that were historically accurate to the time. Therefore, the Anglian name of Eoforwic is used instead of York, for example.

People groups are trickier. Today we have the English, the Welsh, the Scots, and the Irish. In seventh-century England, these names would have been meaningless. And in fact it's even more confusing because the Irish at that time were actually called the *Scotti,* but there was no "Scotland." That piece of geography was where the Picts and some of the other northern British and Celtic tribes lived.

I compromised on this. The characters in the book who are native to the time/place will use the proper identifications for the times. But when Thomas, our hero, thinks of the monks, he thinks of them as

Irish. Celyn and Nona he categorizes as Welsh, and Nectan and the Picts as Scottish. The fact that those terms are anachronistic to the times can't be helped.

So is he, after all.

WHO'S WHO

THE FEY

Travellers
Godric—from 1972. Unseelie Fey and harper who travels around Northumbria.
Wulfram—from the present day. Unseelie Fey who lives in Eoforwic.

Fey of the Northern Seelie Court
Nectan—king of the Northern Seelie Fey
Eara—Nectan's wife, Queen of the Northern Seelie Fey
Durst—nine-year-old son of Nectan and Eara.
Domech—Nectan's nephew and his guard/bowman.
Nona ap Albanwr—cousin of Celyn, visiting Bebbanburg from Gwynedd
Brorda—merchant
Emma—Brorda's wife
Conaire Mac Alpin—Nona's betrothed, from Dál Riata
Torht—bone carver of Bamburgh
Hilda—wife of Torht
Strang ap Siric—thegn of Oswy, rival to Nectan for the throne of the Seelie Fey of the North

Fey of the Southern Seelie Court
Selwyn ap Coed—king of the Southern Seelie Fey
Nona ap Albanwr—cousin of Celyn

Fey of the Northern Unseelie Court
Raegenold—king of the Northern Unseelie Fey
Eawyn—Raegenold's wife and queen of the Northern Unseelie Fey

Solitary Fey
Jack Redcap
The Huntsman / The Alder King

BEBBANBURG FORTRESS
Oswy—king of Bernicia, newly crowned in August, AD 642
Eanflaed—wife of Oswy and daughter of King Edwin of Deira
Aethelwin—reeve
Father Paulus—Roman priest who accompanied Eanflaed to Oswy's court
Celyn ap Wynn—exiled warrior from Gwynedd
Father Colm—Irish priest from the monastery at Hii. King Oswy's advisor and scribe
Baldulf—stable master
Brand—a *thegn's* son, fostering with Oswy

BEBBANBURG VILLAGE AND AREA
Dunn—*coerl,* formerly of Stowham
Framric—smith
Bronwyn—Nona's maidservant
Siward—*thegn* at Wulfstam

LINDISFARNE
Aidan—Bishop / Abbot
Father Gaeth—Prior
Brother Barach—Guestmaster
Father Donal—head of scriptorium
Brother Iobhar—head of school
Brother Eadgar—cellarer, in charge of supplies
Brother Eadric—chief healer in charge of Infirmary
Brother Seamas—chief shepherd
Brother Frithlac—one of the monks
Brother Bram—metalworker and crafter of silver implements for the monastery

EOFORWIC (present-day York)
Oswine—half-cousin of Oswy and claimant for the Deiran throne
Wulfram—Unseelie Traveller from the present day
Odda—ten-year-old slave boy, owned by Wulfram

1

Fort Spring, Northern Alberta, Canada
  Present Day

Thomas walked into the quickening wind, snow pellets stinging his face. True to form, Halloween was bringing not only small ghosts and goblins, but the first snow of the season. The cold made him glad for the sweatshirt he wore beneath his jean jacket.

Twilight shadows lengthened around him as children's voices calling *trick or treat* rang faintly from the houses that ringed the scrubby field. He walked across the field, parallel to the thick tangle of trees that bordered its east side. He hunched his shoulders against the bitter wind, trying to calculate the benefits of selling his house. It would provide the money to go back to his university studies, which had been interrupted by his mother's death.

Tommo, don't give up. Promise me. His mother's voice ghosted through his mind, his memory flashing back to that night two months ago when she lay against the pillow, fragile as a bird, her bones showing stark against the thin translucent skin of her face. But her eyes held his, bright blue and shining with fever. *Stay in school. Please.*

He had promised her, of course he had, but when she died the next day, the promise died with her. What did it matter, anyway? Who really cared what he did? His father had died a long time ago, his brother was on the road again. A long-haul trucker couldn't keep his rig off the road for long.

Danny wanted him to join him. Maybe he should. Get out of this

1

town, away from the memories, the sadness. It was mighty tempting. But he had to deal with the house first, and decide about school. He sighed, his breath a cloud in the cold air. He didn't much care about school anymore. Truth be told, he didn't much care about anything.

A movement in his peripheral vision distracted him. A deer—a buck, sporting magnificent antlers, stepping out from the trees. Deer were plentiful in the surrounding wilderness. It wasn't unusual to see one in town, drawn by flowers or gardens or the tender shoots of trees.

But this one glowed with a shimmery white radiance. He stopped to study it. *Albino? Can't be.* Probably the early evening light playing tricks on his eyes. The deer lifted its head, scenting the breeze, its rack perfectly symmetrical.

Suddenly two dark shapes detached from the bushes at the far corner of the field behind the deer. *A couple of kids?* But they moved too fast to be children. Too smoothly. And the shape wasn't right. Human-like, but not quite.

What...? Thomas barely registered their presence before they were upon him. Hard hands grabbed his arms, sparking an immediate flood of sensations.

You are ours...come with us...you will obey...

They wanted to make Thomas theirs, to compel his obedience, to *take* him. He staggered and would have fallen but for their hands—*claws?*—holding him upright, their triumph singing through him. Their satisfaction matched a quick rising eagerness within him to obey. A shuddering horror at the thought blasted through him, breaking the siren song of desire.

"Jesus!" The scream tore out of him instinctively, and with it, Thomas' will returned. He wrenched away with no thought but to escape, launching into a desperate run. He saw a flash of white: the deer, jumping into the trees.

Thomas veered towards the shelter of those trees as well, feeling the creatures at his back, gaining on him now, their eagerness for him beating against him. His feet faltered, the desire to turn and surrender welling up within him again. *Jesus!* He reached the woods and plunged into the trees, thinking only to hide, his breath harsh in his ears.

And then everything went black.

The harsh croaks of ravens brought Thomas to awareness. His head pounded with thudding pain. He cracked his eyes open, immediately squinting against the bright light.

Daytime. He was outside. He could smell smoke. *My head….* The pain made it hard to focus, the stabbing light made it worse. He squeezed his eyes shut again, lying still, trying to pull his scattered thoughts together. *What happened?*

Nothing. He couldn't remember anything.

Panic seized him. His eyes flew open again, barely registering a blue sky, trees. He tried to sit up, but the motion brought dizziness on top of the thundering pain. He sank down again, groaning, nausea flooding through him.

"Ah, you are awake."

Thomas twisted around, his heart bolting into double time.

A man half-knelt beside him. He had a strong face, framed by long dark hair streaked with a bit of grey. A faint scar marred his chin, while another rose from the corner of one eyebrow to disappear into the hair at his temple. "Careful, boy. Rest easy. All is well. You've hit your head, but you are safe." He spoke with a lilting accent that sparked a fleeting sense of recognition, a memory that surfaced but quickly disappeared.

Safe? Do I know him?

He wore a hooded brown cloak edged with blue and red embroidery, fastened at the neck by a swirling silver brooch, and a long deep blue shirt belted at the waist. Thin leather straps crisscrossed on the man's lower legs.

A memory sparked. He had been walking home, crossing Parker's Field. Halloween….

He's wearing a costume. Thomas strained at the flickering memory, but it winked out. He gave up in frustration, looking around him for more clues, his queasy stomach protesting with the movement.

Behind the stranger, a small campfire burned. The trees surrounding them spread branches blazing with autumnal glory, but something was off. The ones bounding Parker's Field had pretty much lost their leaves— it was the end of October, after all. And even before they lost them, those leaves were all gold, not this riot of orange, red, and bronze.

"Where am I?" His voice sounded hoarse and raw, as if he had been screaming. Another flash of memory sparked, but again it snuffed out before he could chase it down.

The man frowned. "You make no sense, boy. Do you not understand me?"

"Of course I do," Thomas rasped. But the man's frown deepened.

"Where am I?" he tried again, slowly and with more enunciation.

The puzzled look on the other man's face cleared. "Ah. You speak strangely, to be sure. But now I understand." The man fell silent, his dark brown eyes wary. "I saw you running last night."

Flashes of memory accompanied the man's words. Halloween. Walking home from...where? A face appeared in his mind: *Dave. Yes.* He had gone to the church to talk to his friend, the young pastor. On the way home, he had taken the shortcut across the field....

His thoughts stuttered to a halt. There was a yawning black hole between that last memory and waking up here.

"Who are you? I don't know what happened. I don't know where I am." He heard the thin edge to his voice and clamped his mouth shut.

"I am the Lord Celyn of Bebbanburg. We are a few days' travel from there." His gaze swept over Thomas. "Do you not remember?"

Thomas eyed the man, fear rising within him like a black tide. None of this made sense. *Did he crack me on the skull and kidnap me?*

He had to get out of here. He pushed himself onto his elbows, but his surroundings swooped around him and his stomach lurched. He fell back.

"Be careful. You must lie still."

Thomas wasn't buying the man's concern. "I don't have any money, if that's what you want." Which was true. His heart sank. He'd even left his cell phone at home because the battery had died. He'd have to talk his way out of this if he could.

Irritation flashed across the man's face. "You fell and hit your head on a rock. I brought you here, away from the road. You have been senseless since."

A raven *quorked* above him, splitting the forest's silence, and with it, another dawning realization: it was too quiet here. Parker's Field was bordered on three sides by roads. He should be able to detect some traffic noise, but there was none of that—only the occasional bird and the rustle of the leaves from the slight breeze.

I brought you here, away from the road. The guy must have taken him into the untamed wilderness that surrounded Fort Spring, just a short drive away from the town. But why?

"What do you want?" he croaked, horrible possibilities opening in his mind, revolving around thoughts of psychopathic killers.

"Calm yourself, boy." The man's accent became stronger as his ire rose. Scottish? No, not quite. Again, a memory skittered around the edge of Thomas' mind, but the man continued to speak, distracting him. "Think you! If I had meant to harm you, I would have left you there for—" He stopped, his jaw bunching, and exhaled through his nose. "You are safe," he repeated.

Another revelation tickled around the void in Thomas's mind. "Left me?" As soon as he spoke, his memory snapped back with crystal-cold clarity. *The deer, those creatures—*

The twin sensations of disgust and desire that he had felt at their appearance flooded through him again, and with a cry Thomas shoved himself upright, with no thought but to escape. But his stomach flipped, everything around him spun, and he fell away once again into darkness.

2

Thomas snapped awake, the fading edge of a dream falling away. *Halloween, Parker's Field, a strange man—*

He looked around, his heart sinking as the dream shifted into reality. Those same trees, their shadows longer now. The campfire burned with a sharp crackle. The stranger rose from where he had been seated beside it, holding a wooden cup.

Lord Something-or-other. Right.

Strapped to the man's waist was a long leather scabbard, with the hilt of a sword sticking out of it. *God help me.* His first sincere prayer in a long time. He tried to get up, but everything whirled, sparkles flitting across his eyes. He gritted his teeth and pushed himself up to a sitting position as the man sat down beside him on a log.

"You are feeling better?"

The man's concern did nothing to erase Thomas' fears. *Who is this guy?*

His head still ached, he still felt dizzy and sick, his muscles were stiff. But he did feel marginally better, and his thoughts were not as scattered. *The deer. The creatures.* His heart jumped, and he took a deep breath. "A bit."

The man offered the cup. "Here. Drink. It will help."

Thomas' thirst warred with caution. Thirst won out, but as he took the rustic cup and lifted it to his mouth, an earthy, sweet, alcoholic smell filled his nose. His stomach lurched. Beer of some kind. He had smelled it often enough to know. But the sweet overtone was odd.

He held the cup back out to the man. "No thanks."

The other man frowned. "'Tis a fine ale, brewed only two days ago."

"I'd rather have water."

One eyebrow lifted. "Don't be foolish, boy. Drink. It is fresh, as I said." His eyes narrowed, and he took the cup back, took a drink, then held it out again. "Think, you. If I had wanted you dead, I could have killed you as you lay insensible. As you see, it is safe. Take it."

The thought of poison hadn't even crossed his mind. But the man had a point. He had a freaking sword.

He had long ago resolved never to touch alcohol, but thirst won over his resolve. *Just a little bit can't hurt.* He accepted the cup and took a cautious sip. He had tried beer once or twice, when he was younger, before his mother's alcoholism had driven any desire for booze out of him. This drink didn't taste much like it. A sweet, flowery note underlaid the earthy flavour of the beer, but it was not unpleasant. His thirst took over, and he finished the rest.

The man's gaze travelled over him, wariness and curiosity evident in equal measure in his eyes. "Who are you, boy? What is the meaning of your strange garments? And why were you running from the demons on the eve of Samhain?"

Demons? He tried to piece together the flashes of memory into something that made sense. "You were there? Did you see that deer, too? It was almost white, with a huge rack."

A sudden fearful comprehension flooded the man's face. "The white stag." He crossed himself. "*Mam Duw.*" He stood and drew his sword in one smooth motion, the tip mere inches from Thomas' nose. "Tell me your name, boy, and the meaning of this. And think you, there is good iron in this blade."

Thomas froze. "Thomas—Thomas McCadden," he stammered. "And I don't know what happened. I was walking home. And then I saw those *things.*" His mouth went dry. *Demons?* He swallowed, trying to continue. "They *grabbed* me—" His words choked off, feeling again the claws on his arms, and worse, the co-mingled flood of desire and horror flooding through him. A yawning chasm opened in his mind, fright almost propelling him in. But then anger flared, bringing him back. "What have you done to me? This is not where I was. If you say you saw me, then either you brought me here or you know who did. You tell *me* the meaning of this!"

The other man frowned, his eyes narrowing, the sword's tip rock steady. "Did you not hear me? I was travelling down the path, seeking a place of shelter for the night. I heard you cry out to the Saviour. God propelled me to seek you out, and I saw you in the grasp of the demons. You cried out again, and with Christ's Name on your lips, you broke free. But you tripped as you ran and fell, striking your head on a rock."

"It doesn't make sense." It was hard to think past the word that kept throbbing through his mind with every beat of his heart. *Demons.* His hand rose of its own accord to clutch the cross that dangled on a leather string around his neck. *What has happened to me? Am I dreaming?*

"Does it not? I ask you plain, then. Have you come from the Otherworld, the land of the *tylwyth teg?*"

Sah-win. Till-eg tay. What's with these words? "I don't know what you're talking about."

The man's eyes roved over him again, and his eyes sharpened. "You are a Christian, then? Tell me true, boy!"

Christian? Thomas' addled brain was having a hard time keeping up. Then he felt the sharp edges of the cross in his hand and realized he was holding it. It had been a gift to him on his baptism from Dave, and even though his faith had waned and stumbled through the darkness that had consumed him since that time, he still hung it around his neck every day.

A talisman, to remind himself of the faith he had once embraced, or an act of defiance. Most days he wasn't sure which.

He eyed the man, trying to figure out what he wanted to hear. *God propelled me to seek you out.* Right. Likely he would be friendlier to a fellow believer. "Yes."

The other man held his gaze a moment longer, but then nodded slightly and sheathed his sword before sitting down. "The white stag, the eve of Samhain. 'Tis a deep mystery indeed."

Deep mystery. The sense of foreboding that had haunted Thomas ever since he had awakened now clamoured for attention. Try as he might, though, he couldn't quite pin it down, could only feel it as if in the distance, like a deep *bong* of a cathedral's bell, far away. "Wait," he said, trying to think through the dizziness, the nausea, the sense of impending disaster. "Tell me again, what you said, before—who you are, where we are—"

The man frowned. "I am the Lord Celyn of Bebbanburg. We are three days' ride south of there."

The sense grew stronger, this feeling that Thomas was on the verge of a great discovery and that this man held the key. "I don't know where that is," he said, helpless. He looked again at the huge trees around them, gnarled and twisting, at the blazing colours of the leaves. He knew the woods around his town of Fort Spring like the back of his hand, and he had never seen this place before. Or had he? The scene chimed recognition within him—if not for this exact place, for ones like it. He *had* seen it before, in books, or pictures, perhaps, or even in his own imagination.

The man spoke again before he could chase down an answer through the foreboding that was growing ever stronger.

"Bebbanburg is Oswy's fortress in Bernicia. A kingdom of the Angles in the north of this isle that the Romans called Britain."

Britain? The word froze Thomas in his spot. His eyes roved over the other man, seeing again his strange clothing, his sword. The revelation rushed towards him. The trees—oaks, and ash and the like. The setting of countless fairy tales and stories, from Winnie-the-Pooh to Robin Hood to King Arthur. He knew those stories like he knew his own heart, and he knew the truth of it: he was there. But *how?*

"Britain—" he said faintly and stopped as a solution presented itself. Crazy, insane, impossible—but as he took in the man in front of him, his clothing, the landscape, it was the only one that fit.

That, or the stresses of the past few months had pushed him over the tipping point into insanity.

He sucked in a breath. "Tell me—" His courage failed him, but he gathered himself and forced himself to continue. "Britain." He swallowed down the bile that rose into his throat. "When? I mean, what year is it?"

The question hung there, between them. Surprise flashed through the man's eyes, and he opened his mouth and then shut it again. "I have not thought of it in some time," he said, and frowned. "My lord Oswald died this summer, and he was on the throne these past years—ten, perhaps? Nay, eight, I would say." He nodded. "The monks can tell you for certain, but I believe it is the Year of our Lord 642."

3

"642." **Thomas didn't** need the older man's answering nod. He could feel the truth of it in his bones. He had travelled through time and ended up in Britain, in the Dark Ages. He tore his gaze from the other man, looked around at the twisting trees, smelled the fresh, clean air. It felt so real.

It can't be. He didn't know a lot about Britain in the Dark Ages, but he did know there is no way he should be able to understand this man. Yet they were conversing easily. *You speak strangely, to be sure, but now I understand.* The man's words came back to him. Those first few moments, Celyn had not understood him, it seemed. But now he did. Why?

The other man broke into his scrambled thoughts. "Where did you come from, boy?"

The twenty-first century. Right. Earlier the man had just about skewered him. If he even tried to tell him the truth, what would happen? A vision of being burned at the stake as a witch flashed through his mind.

But how could he explain it? His clothes, for one thing. "I don't know," he said, hoping he could pull off the lie. His brother always told him his face was a book, able to be read by anyone. *Danny.* He forced away the sudden despair that pierced him and continued. "I can't remember anything. Just that I was walking through a field, and those *things*—" Fear closed his throat. *Had demons brought him here?* The thought made his toes curl.

"Perhaps the blow to your head has stolen your memory."

Thomas nodded. The explanation would work for now, until he could figure out a way to get home.

"You are not from Bernicia, that much is certain. Your garments are strange, and your Latin has an odd sound to it that I have never heard before."

Latin? "I don't—" he stopped. The words sounded wrong, all of a sudden. What he heard coming out of his mouth didn't quite match up with what he meant to say. But why hadn't he noticed before?

"The monastery you hail from must be far away."

Now the other man's words were sounding odd, too. Not quite English, they had an Italian-type feel to them. *Latin.*

The man was speaking Latin, and so, apparently, was he. Even though he knew no other language than English.

He swallowed down the hysterical laugh that bubbled up. All of this was impossible. He began to have a whole new sympathy for Alice in Wonderland. Apparently, he had fallen through a rabbit hole, too.

His thoughts skittered back to what the man said, trying to think through what he knew of this time in history. *AD 642. Right. Before the Norman invasion. Basically the Dark Ages. Super.* Not a lot of civilization. Peasants. Feudal lords? Or did that come after? He looked the other man over again—his embroidered cloak and silver-handled sword—seeing him with new eyes. A certain air of privilege marked him. This man was no rude peasant, but one of the upper nobility. *Lord Celyn,* Thomas remembered belatedly. Of Bernicia.

Celyn was waiting for him to answer. *Monastery. Okay. I've got a cross. Safer to pass as a peaceful monastery-type than some kind of warrior.*

"I suppose so," Thomas said, ignoring the odd dissonance of his words. Concentrating on it made him dizzier than he already felt, so he pushed the problem away. "I don't know much about Bernicia—I mean, I don't know exactly where we are." He took a deep breath, trying to ignore the panic that was threatening to overtake him. Whether this was a dream, or he was suffering some mental illness, or this was really happening, he had to figure out how to fix it. How to get back. Panic wouldn't help.

"You said it is in the north of England...in Britain?" He amended the word hastily, *England* sounding odd to his own ears.

Celyn nodded, frowning slightly.

Thomas pictured the British Isles in his mind, trying to think of some place that this man might know, that was the same now as it would have been in his time.

642. No cities, obviously. He wasn't even sure how many people lived here now. At the most, there might be some small villages or settlements. *Northern England. Think.* "How far north? Are we near Hadrian's Wall?"

"The Wall? We are north of that, and another's week's travel from Bebbanburg."

"Bebbanburg?"

"Where my lord king Oswy holds court, along the eastern coast."

Thomas' rusty history of Britain was kicking into gear now. The Angles and the Saxons, two Germanic tribes, took up residence in Britain after the Romans left. They shared the island with the Celts and Picts, battling it out among themselves for dominion. Try as he might, he couldn't remember too many details, except that eventually the two groups became known as the Anglo-Saxons sometime before 1066 and the Battle of Hastings. And some time before then, the Vikings came calling, too.

Great. Hopefully not now. Panic flared. "I don't understand. How could this happen?"

Celyn's shoulders shifted under his cloak in a small shrug. "As to that, I have heard stories of the Thin Places," he said. "Places where this world and the Otherworld lie close together, where it is easy to travel from one to the other, especially on an *ysbryd nos*, a spirit night, such as the night the Scotti call Samhain."

"Last night." *Halloween. Sah-win.* He filed away the word for future reference.

The other man nodded. *A Thin Place?* The rabbit hole was getting deeper by the second. "And you think I came through one of those? From this Otherworld?"

Celyn half-shrugged again, but his eyes betrayed his casual manner. "The Otherworld is the home of the *tylwyth teg.* And a white stag the sign of one."

The deer, its pale radiance in the gathering darkness at the edge of Parker's Field. Unease skittered down his spine. "Till-eg tay?"

Celyn motioned with his hand, impatient. "The faery people."

Faeries? Once again, Thomas bit back the laughter that bubbled up. The man was deadly serious, that much was certain. *They actually believe in that stuff in this time,* he reminded himself. No wonder the man had drawn a sword on him. *Think you, there is good iron in this blade,* he had said. Iron, anathema to faeries, if Thomas' memory of faery stories was correct. *Not a story to him. He really believes it.*

Would it be better to admit to being a faery, or to deny it? He could see danger no matter what he did. Perhaps it was best to avoid the topic. He shook his head. "Look, I have to get out of here. I don't remember where I came from, but you and I both know I don't belong here." A sudden idea struck him, and he sat up straight. "Take me to the place you saw me last night. Maybe I can figure out a way to go back!"

He pushed himself to his feet and regretted it, as the dizziness increased fourfold and the world swooped around him. He staggered and almost fell but for the other man's strong arms catching him.

"You can hardly stand, let alone walk. You must rest." He eased Thomas back down to the log. "They say the doorways between the worlds are only open at the times of changing. Dawn and dusk. Summer to winter. It would be no use to try it now."

Thomas opened his mouth to protest when he heard a sound, faint but unmistakable: a burst of laughter.

Celyn froze, listening.

Thomas' heart kicked into double time. The last thing he needed was someone *else* to drop by on this little party. He strained his ears to hear anything else, but only a bird's chittering song filled the silence.

"Stay here," Celyn ordered as he rose to his feet. In a few paces he reached the edge of the clearing and melted into the trees without a backward glance, leaving Thomas alone.

Indecision froze Thomas for a moment and then he pushed himself upright, ignoring the dizziness, which quickly faded. It was awkward to be with Celyn, but he'd rather be with the warrior than without him if someone else showed up.

He ignored his aching head and his queasy stomach and forced himself to move quickly, entering the closely spaced trees where the other man had disappeared.

4

As Thomas caught up, Celyn turned back, irritation flashing across his face. He paused, his gaze raking over him, and he signalled for Thomas to remain behind him.

They soon came to where the trees petered out. A grassy meadow stretched away from them, intersected by a faint path that ran to their right and left in front of them. Beyond the meadow, the forest rose up again, the thick trees obscuring anything else.

To their left, the path went around a small hill and disappeared behind it; to the right, it continued through the meadow until it faded from sight among the trees at the far end. A low murmur, coming from behind the hill, and then the sudden snort of a horse broke the silence.

Celyn moved back among the shadows at the edge of the clearing and stood behind a large tree, drawing his sword and motioning Thomas to another tree close by.

Thomas looked over at Celyn and at the sword held ready in his grip. If it came to a fight, he was doomed. He gripped the rough trunk, hard, and waited, his muscles tight with tension. *Maybe I shoulda stayed put.*

But it was too late to go back. Three mounted men came around the hill, moving swiftly and with purpose. They were dressed much like Celyn, with cloaks covering a longer tunic and woollen breeches on their legs. Soft leather boots completed the outfit. Their clothing was of natural colours—browns, greys, and blacks. Each carried a long sword similar to Celyn's at their waist. They were bearded, their hair unkempt.

An aura of grim determination radiated from the men; their eyes sharp on their surroundings as they rode. Thomas willed himself to be invisible.

Heart pounding, he glanced quickly at Celyn.

The other man stood poised, his arm muscles flexed as he gripped his sword tighter, his eyes fixed with deadly intent on the group. He was not happy to see these strangers, that much was certain.

The man at the head of the group stopped, throwing up his hand in a signal to stop. The rest halted behind him, almost right in front of Thomas. They all scanned their surroundings, their hands dropping to the long swords at their waists. Thomas froze, hardly breathing.

The leader was young, probably close to Thomas' age, but there the similarity ended. The hard purpose in the man's gaze belonged to someone much older than his years. He spoke quietly to the men, the occasional word drifting over to where the two watchers stood motionless in the shadow of the trees. Thomas frowned. The words sounded vaguely Swedish or Norwegian. The short conversation ended, and they rode off again, making little noise as they followed the pathway into the woods at the far end of the meadow.

A few moments after the group disappeared from sight, Celyn relaxed, replacing his sword in its leather sheath. He stalked over to where Thomas stood. "I told you to stay put. You are of no use to me without a blade."

"Sorry." He shifted his shoulders, uncomfortable under the other man's hard gaze. "Didn't want to be alone." Celyn frowned, but before he could speak Thomas continued. He didn't need a lecture. "Who were they?"

Celyn's scowl deepened, his hard face darkening with anger. "Mercians." He spat the word, as if it were bitter on his tongue.

"Mercians?"

Celyn's eyes narrowed and he shook his head. "Come, back to the fire. It is not safe here, this close to the path."

It wasn't safe anywhere, as far as Thomas was concerned, but he nodded, and followed the older man back to the campfire, his head pounding with every step. By the time he got back, he sank down on the log with mingled relief and frustration. He had to get out of here, but how could he when he could barely walk a dozen yards?

Celyn sat down opposite him, his jaw clenching as he stirred the fire.

Curiosity distracted Thomas from his dilemma. "Who are these Mercians?"

A dark eyebrow rose at the question. "Mercia is a kingdom southwest of here. Penda of Mercia is an enemy of my king. His men should not be here, so far into Bernicia."

"Spies?" That would explain Celyn's anger, but he had the feeling there was something else, something more personal behind the other man's ire.

"Likely," Celyn said, and added a log to the fire, sparks shooting upwards as he did so.

"Do you know them?"

Celyn cut a glance at Thomas, then stood up abruptly. "I set some snares last night. Mayhap God has blessed us with a hare. Stay here. I will be back shortly."

Before Thomas could speak Celyn turned and melted back into the woods.

Obviously, the other man did not want to talk about it. He puzzled over it for a moment but soon gave up. He half-rose, thinking to explore, but it was no good. The dizziness forced him back down, and he bit back frustration.

God, help me. It was the only thought in his aching head that made any sense, which didn't say much.

5

The crows flew on whispering wings, two black shadows against the deepening twilit sky.

Wulfram calmed his mind as the birds approached. He closed his eyes, shuttering his thoughts from the boy who sat docilely at his feet, whose will he held in an iron grip in his mind.

Not long now, he promised himself, fingering the amulet at his neck as the birds fluttered down before him. *Just a few months more.* A sudden fear pierced him, that he would be unequal to the task ahead. He blew out a breath and dismissed the thought. He could not indulge his fears now.

The task that propelled him to this century was both immense and delicate all at once. Immense in scope but delicate in execution, the web he was weaving was subject to many variables. Fear could easily sidetrack him from his purpose.

He opened his eyes and crouched down, squatting in front of the birds. For a moment, he admired their beauty: the gleaming black feathers, the powerful beaks, the intelligent eyes.

The larger of the two—the male—hopped towards him, cocking its head. Behind it, the female gave a low *quork,* ruffling its wings in sudden agitation.

Wulfram felt the familiar spurt of anticipation as he expanded his Fey senses, looking into the crow's beady eyes.

Even though he had braced for it, the sudden rush of sensation overtook him. For a moment, he lost himself, his mind expanding and contracting to fit the parameters of the crow's alien intelligence.

The sheer bestiality of its existence flooded through him, its innate drive for self-preservation a ravening storm. It was like a bracing dunk in a cold river, a shock that made all of Wulfram's senses come tingling to life.

Time dropped away from him. The bird had no sense of the future or past. It lived in the *now*, unconcerned with time's passing. This, too, had its own seductive charm, the freedom from past regrets or future worries a liberation all its own.

But Wulfram could not allow the crow's mind to dominate his own, no matter the thrill that it gave him. All of the Clan heard the tales of those who lost themselves in their animal brethren; some had even seen it happen. He forced himself to concentrate and began to look through the crow's memories, to see what it had seen.

Humans were mere ghosts upon the landscape of the crows' existence. They flickered in and out of their lives like background actors on a television screen, rarely important to the main story of the bird's lives. But the Fey were solid bright beings that the crows found as fascinating as the shine of gold under the sun.

This was helpful to Wulfram, whose main interest was in the doings of his own people. He flipped through the pictures in the crow's brain, and when he saw one of his kind, he slowed down and took a look.

The crow tried to help him. It thrust its encounters with other Fey at Wulfram eagerly—too eagerly, for the kaleidoscope of impressions became a bright blur that threatened to overwhelm him.

Wulfram gritted his teeth and bore down, forcing the crow to slow down. It *quorked*, a shudder running through it, its beak clattering.

The pictures clarified. He saw Raegenold, the Unseelie King. Wulfram's lip twisted. *Cocky brat.* The king laughed with his queen as they rode through a forest, the sun flashing off his golden armband. The same armband he had given the young king as a gift, Wulfram noted in satisfaction. Raegenold's vanity was an important tool for Wulfram to use. All the gifts and flattery were seeds that would flourish into something useful, when the time came.

The memories wavered, and then Wulfram saw Raegenold's cousin speaking earnestly with a human, who appeared as a blurry outline. But the human moved, made an impatient gesture that Wulfram recognized, along with the arrogant tilt of the head. Penda, king of the Mercians.

Doing his part, speaking into the king's ear. Excellent.

The picture faded, to be replaced by one that caused Wulfram to stiffen with shock.

For a moment Wulfram thought it was another bundle of Fey-pictures, for he saw a confused impression of a figure in the midst of a bright flash. The crow didn't like the peculiar sensation that accompanied the white-bright flare of light, and it croaked in protest as Wulfram looked more closely at the scene. The figure emerged from the flash, stumbling, running, unmistakably Fey.

Wulfram sucked in a breath, recognizing instantly what had happened. He had experienced that flash himself. A Traveller had Crossed.

He watched, transfixed, but the crow's concentration wavered, fear coursing through it. There was something else there, something that overwhelmed the crow, something that it didn't want to look at. It tried to allow the memory to slip away, to show Wulfram something else. Wulfram snarled, grabbing at the bird's attention, forcing it to show him more.

The female crow burst into flight, screeching in alarm, but Wulfram ignored it, wrapped up in the memory he was wresting from the crow's reluctant consciousness.

Two other shapes appeared—from the flash? It was hard to tell. Wulfram squinted, and then an icy spear pierced his gut as recognition came. *The Undying.* The shock momentarily unmoored his grip on the unfolding memory, and it wavered for a moment. But Wulfram quickly recovered and the scene sharpened again. Two Undying, pursuing the Traveller. Wulfram saw their black figures, saw them quickly gain on the Fey.

"Come on, come on," Wulfram muttered under his breath. He was not sure who he was rooting for, the Fey or his dark pursuers. A sudden sense filled him that the outcome of this race was vitally important—a sense of a key turning in a lock, a door opening wide.

The Undying were just about upon the Fey. A dark thrill coursed through Wulfram as he saw their clawed hands reaching for their prey.

He felt the crow's upsurge of alarm, felt it gather itself for flight, and he grabbed it instinctively, pinning it to the earth, hardly feeling its struggles beneath his hand.

And then suddenly a sense of power rushed through the crow's memory. Not Fey power, although Wulfram could see that bright corona coursing through the pursued Fey. A surge of energy, more felt than seen.

Just as the dark creatures reached the fleeing figure and put their hands on him, they vanished completely.

Wulfram blinked in shock, stunned at their sudden capitulation. *They gave up,* he thought, incredulous.

The Fey in the crow's vision tripped and went tumbling, a loose-limbed inelegant sprawl that ended as his head struck hard against an outlying rock, and he went still.

More than anything, Wulfram needed a good look at that Fey, but at that point the fool bird took off in alarm, panic fuelling it. But the bird's training belatedly asserted itself, and it remembered that its Master wanted information on any of the shining ones, so it turned back.

Wulfram saw a shadow-figure, approaching the Fey. A human. But things were becoming dim, the memory slipping away, blackness rushing in around the edges of the picture. Had the Undying come back, while the Fey lay helpless?

Wulfram snarled and bore down, fighting the crow's obstinate brain, bringing his power to bear on the stupid creature. He had to see the Fey's face.

"Master! Master!"

The words were not just spoken: they sliced through his mind like a knife through hot butter. The result was like pulling the plug on the television. Everything went black, and Wulfram was abruptly thrust out of the crow and back into himself with a shuddering gasp, his eyes flying open.

It was the damn fool *boy*. He was hanging on Wulfram's arm, shaking it, his eyes wide with terror. Wulfram roared in rage and struck the boy hard, the heavy ring on his finger splitting the boy's cheek, sending hot blood spurting as the boy tumbled away.

Wulfram grabbed him by the neck of the tunic, hauling him up again, fist cocked to pummel the stupid useless thrice-be-damned *human* into hell where he belonged. He needed to *see* that Traveller!

"Master! The bird! Stop, Master!" The boy was practically gibbering in fear, with blood, tears, and snot flowing down his face. "The bird!"

The words penetrated the fog of rage in Wulfram's mind and he looked down, seeing a still bundle of black feathers beside him.

The crow, dead. Icy fear swept through him at the sight, as those last moments of connection came back to him; his surging power, the feel of the bird beneath his hand as he pressed down physically and mentally on it, forcing it to show him more, the onrushing blackness.

That blackness that obscured the final picture was not the Undying but the crow's impending death.

And with their minds linked together…

A shudder shook him, and he cradled the boy to his chest, taking a few shaky breaths. "Good boy," he muttered, relief coursing through him. He felt the boy's pleasure at his praise through the bond they shared, and he rumpled the boy's hair absently. "Good boy."

He sat still for a moment, composing himself, thinking through what he had just seen. A Traveller, and a powerful one at that, shining brightly in the crow's memory. One of importance to the Undying, that much was certain. Why they had vanished was a question he would give much to have answered. He needed to find that Fey, soon. He looked at the dead crow beside him and shook his head, his lip twisting in disgust, this time at himself. A foolish mistake.

He clambered wearily to his feet, pushing the boy away from him, congratulating himself at his foresight in binding the human to him. It had saved his life, certainly.

He heaved a breath. His power was drained, the exercise with the crow having taken much of his concentration and strength. But there was one more thing he had to do.

Closing his eyes, he brought a small flicker of power to life within him once again. Thankfully, he didn't need much for this particular exercise. His Gift would aid him, his innate ability to commune with the *corbae*. He spread out his arms and summoned them, and they came, beginning with the mate of the dead crow at his feet, which landed on his wrist with a small *quork*. Others followed: more crows, jackdaws, a few ravens, until finally a small flock of birds gathered around him.

They landed on his arms, on his head, at his feet. He pictured the Fey he had seen in the crow's memory—young, graceful, powerful, thick unruly black hair, an impression of the hard angles in his face, the sense of his desperate will. He sent the picture to the birds and commanded them: *Find him. Tell me where he is.*

He released them, and they erupted in a fluttering explosion, winging away from him into the deepening night.

Wulfram watched them go with satisfaction. They would not fail him. They never did.

He turned and walked away without a backward look at the still bundle of feathers on the ground, nor at the boy, who stumbled after him, a dirty hand pressed to his bleeding cheek.

6

Thomas awoke from troubled dreams with a start, with Celyn's hand on his arm.

"Wake up, boy." Celyn was a dark shadow crouching beside him, backlit by the smouldering fire. "I need some sleep before the morrow. Keep watch. Wake me if anything happens."

Thomas got up, stiff with cold and bruises, and sat down on the log by the fire. He put his hands out to warm them, glancing at his watch to see the time, and froze.

His watch. He glanced over at Celyn, to see if the other man noticed, but he lay still as stone, wrapped up in his cloak, presumably asleep already.

Thomas peered at the watch. *5:20.* Upon closer inspection he realized the second hand was not moving. It must have stopped at the exact time he went through the Thin Place. *Appropriate.* He stripped it off his wrist and put it in the chest pocket of his jean jacket. *Good thing I didn't look at it earlier.*

He poked at the fire with a longer stick, watching the sparks rise and hearing the faint hiss as the wood burned. The flames were mesmerizing in their dance upon the logs, and before he knew it, he found himself nodding off.

Alarm drove him to his feet. *Gotta stay awake.* He had seen a small stream earlier, not far from the campsite. A short walk would wake him up. Besides, he was thirsty.

The woods were dark, but it was easy to find the stream by the sound it made. He stood on the low bank, looking down at the water, which glimmered under the moonlight. Just below the bank there was a flat, pebbled area that extended a few yards to the water. He waited for a moment, making sure all was clear, and then made his way down the bank and crossed the stones, crouching down to dip his hands in the cold water and lift it to his mouth. He paused again, wondering about bacteria, but with a mental shrug he slurped the water from his hand. Bacterial infection was the least of his worries. *At least there's no pollution.*

The water tasted fine, but it was cold, numbing his hands. He wiped them on his jean jacket and began to stand, and in that instant, heard a sound behind him, distinct from the burbling music of the water: the soft scuffing of leather on the rocks.

He dove to the side, twisting to see behind him, and caught a glimpse of a man, moonlight glinting off the sword in his hand as he swung it in a wide arc where Thomas' head would have been. The man's snarl of frustration mingled with Thomas' yelp of surprise as the sword whistled through empty air, causing the man to stagger a few steps forward to gain his balance as Thomas scrambled to his feet.

For a shocked moment Thomas thought Celyn was attacking him. The man growled some terse words at him, and sudden recognition flooded through him: it was the leader of the men they had seen earlier.

As Thomas scrambled to his feet, he heard the sharp whinny of a horse and the clash of steel. Celyn had been attacked as well. But he had no time to think as Mercian raised his sword and Thomas turned and ran.

He clawed up the bank, his attacker close behind. Ahead of him, the ring of steel on steel and the grunts and guttural curses grew louder. He crashed through the trees into the clearing, skidding to a halt.

A figure lay on the ground, motionless. Celyn and the remaining Mercian clashed swords with deadly intent beside the downed warrior.

Taking advantage of surprise, Thomas sprang at Celyn's attacker and crashed into him, tackling him in his best football form, just as the man behind him broke free of the trees, sword raised. Celyn intercepted the newcomer's vicious swing, the two swords ringing as they met.

Thomas and the Mercian went down in a heap, the man dropping his sword from the impact. Triumph surged through him, but he didn't stand a chance against the other man's greater strength and skill. The man quickly gained advantage over him as they wrestled on the ground, and before he knew it, the man had his hands around his throat, the face above him distorted in rage.

He bucked and twisted, clawing at the warrior's arms and face. But his strength sapped away as the edges of his vision began to dim. Panic surged and he dug his thumbs into the man's eyes.

The Mercian snarled and heaved him up, then slammed his head down on the ground. It was an effective tactic. Blackness flared, the man's face dimming above him. His arms weakened and his hands fell, even the brief spike of fear fading out as he fought for air. *Jesus...*

From far off he registered a crushing weight, then, blessedly, he could breathe. He sucked in great gasps of air as Celyn's face appeared above him, orange-lit from the fire beside him. "Thomas!"

Celyn helped him to sit up as he sucked in deep breaths. He glanced beside him, to see the still form of his attacker lying on the ground, and beyond it, the other two Mercians, lying motionless as well. "What...?" he rasped, then stopped. It hurt to swallow, hurt to talk.

"They're dead." Celyn seemed unhurt, but he was breathing hard, and he spat into the ground beside him.

A shudder seized him, then another. *Pull yourself together.* He ground his teeth and tried to concentrate. "They were the men from the road," he said, his voice hoarse and ragged.

Anger flitted over Celyn's hard features. "Penda's men. Yes."

Thomas' teeth clattered as another full body tremor shook him, his thoughts a mushy whirl in his mind. *Shock,* he thought, dimly.

Celyn retrieved the blanket and dropped it around Thomas' shoulders. "Come to the fire."

Thomas swayed briefly as he stood, leaning on Celyn for the few steps it took. He sat down, nausea twisting his stomach, grateful for the warmth of the flames. Celyn retrieved his sword and sat down, wiping off dark stains that gleamed red in the firelight.

Three men, dead, just like that. And he could have died, too. His stomach lurched, and he forced himself to think of something else. "How did they know we were here? And why try to kill us?"

Celyn looked up at him, then bent back to his work.

The brief glance clicked the answer into place. "They were looking for you. They knew you were around here somewhere."

Celyn looked up again, his eyes narrowed. "Perhaps," he acknowledged.

"Why did they want to kill you?" Another thought struck him. "Are there more?"

Celyn snorted in grim humour. "Oh—there are more who wish me dead." The closed look on his face told Thomas that was all he would learn, for now.

Celyn might be dead now, if I hadn't been here to help. Thomas pushed his hand through his hair, disconcerted. What would that mean for the future? Maybe Celyn was meant to die here, and he had stopped it. *Or maybe these men died because I was here, and they were supposed to live.*

Is that why the demons had brought him here? To change events to suit their purpose? Cold pierced him at the thought. *I have to get out of here.*

As if he was reading Thomas' mind, Celyn spoke up. "We must leave as soon as the day dawns. Others may come, looking for these." He gestured at the bodies.

Cold panic washed over him. "I can't. I have to go back to the Thin Place tomorrow, try to get home…" He fell silent, unable to explain his urgency.

Celyn shook his head, impatient. "Think you. You came here on an *ysbryd nos.* Likely you cannot go back again except on another one."

"*Ees-breed…?*"

"I told you before. A spirit night, when the worlds are close together. Like Samhain."

The chill inside Thomas grew. "And when is that?"

"Candlemas. Or if not then, the summer solstice."

Thomas shook his head. He didn't know when *Candlemas* was, but the summer solstice was too far away to bear thinking about. "No. I can't wait that long." He forced down his panic. "You said yesterday it was better to wait until dusk, the time of turning." Celyn nodded. "So what about dawn? Isn't that another time of turning? Between night and day? I could try tomorrow morning. If it doesn't work, I'll—" He sucked in a breath. "It has to work. I can't stay here."

Celyn looked at him steadily for a moment, then sighed. "Very well."

Thomas ignored the skepticism on the other man's face. A thought struck him, a welcome distraction. "What language was that word? *Ees-breed…*"

"*Ysbryd nos.*" One dark eyebrow rose. "'Tis the language of my people, the Cymry."

Thomas sat back, nonplussed. Celyn's accent, the unfamiliar words: it all snapped into place.

Cymry. He saw his mother's face, smiling. *We Welsh, we are the Cymry. The People. That's what we call ourselves.* She did not have the accent, only traces of it around the edges of some of her words, as she had come to Canada as a young child. But her brother, Thomas' uncle, did, and it was the memory of his voice that niggled at Thomas as he heard Celyn speak. "My mother, she is—was—" Grief pierced him, closing his throat. He swallowed painfully. "She was Cymry, too. She died last summer."

"May God rest her soul," Celyn said, crossing himself.

Thomas wanted to retort that his mom had wanted nothing to do with God, but stopped himself. He nodded instead.

Celyn leaned forward. "*Ach chan Gwynedd?*"

Thomas frowned. "I don't understand. She didn't know the language, except for a few words. She moved away from there when she was a young child."

"To where?"

Canada. Thomas again stopped the word before it could escape, and shrugged instead. "I don't remember." He glanced over at the bodies, looking for another topic. "What should we do with them?"

"Commit their souls to God, if He will have them. But 'tis likely they are pagans, and their souls consigned to hell."

"Pagans?"

"The Mercians follow Thor and Woden, as does their king." Celyn rubbed his face and yawned. "For now, I must sleep. Wake me before dawn. I will take you to the Thin Place. If you are unsuccessful, we will leave together."

It will work. Still, he had to ask. "To where?"

"I go to Bebbanburg, but the monastery of Lindisfarne is close by. I will take you there, to Bishop Aidan and the monks. The bishop is the wisest man I know, blessed by God. He will be able to help you, and you will be safe there."

Safe. Right. Thomas hunched down beside the fire as Celyn wrapped himself back up in his cloak.

He let out a deep breath as silence fell, broken only by the small sounds of the leaves rattling on the branches as a breeze blew through them, and the crackle of the fire. As he watched the sparks float up and extinguish in the dark, he tried to compose a prayer to a God who seemed indifferent. Tried to think of something he could bargain with to ensure that he could get home.

7

Celyn tugged his knife from the holder on his belt and thrust it at Thomas, hilt first. The path where they had seen the Mercians was empty now, the trees in silent vigil along its length.

"Take it," he said. "It may not be of any use, but if the demons appear again, at least you will have a blade."

A chill ran through Thomas at the thought. He hadn't thought of that possibility when he insisted Celyn take him back to the place he had found him.

Why did they appear in the first place? Did they want me to come here? If he was some kind of demonic tool, all the more reason to get out of here as soon as he could. He swallowed and took the knife from the other man, gripping the bone handle tightly. Even though he doubted it would be much use against those dark creatures, he felt better having it in his hand.

"If we come across anyone, it is best if you do not speak. If we are attacked, run."

The chill inside of Thomas deepened. "Attacked? Do you think there's more Mercians around?"

The older man lifted one shoulder in a slight shrug. "I don't know what to expect, boy. I didn't expect to find you last night. All I know is that it's best to be prepared."

He turned and stepped onto the path and headed across it, towards the woods that lined the clearing beyond the path. Thomas followed behind. The night's sleep had done him good. His head still pounded, but with less intensity, and his thoughts didn't feel quite so scattered.

Be prepared. A memory of a long-ago night at the Scouts Hall flitted through his mind. Somehow he didn't think the Boy Scouts had this situation in mind.

A breeze kicked up as dawn crept closer, the shadows brightening imperceptibly around him. It blew in short gusts through his hair, a cold bite to it that reminded Thomas of the snow-kissed breeze that he had walked into on Halloween night. His stomach clenched.

Celyn stopped when they reached the trees. Scanning the ground intently, he walked back and forth along the tree line for a few moments, and then stooped to examine something closer to the ground. "Here. This is where you came out of the trees."

Thomas frowned, trying to make sense of it. He had encountered the demons in the meadow at home. But Celyn said he saw him here, with the demons in pursuit. Perhaps they had grabbed him twice? Once in the meadow at home, where he had gotten free and run towards the woods, just as he remembered. Then he had hit the Thin Place—*bang*— and he had come through, and the demons followed? And then they grabbed him *again,* and events unfolded as Celyn had seen?

He realized that Celyn was looking at him expectantly. He shook his head. "I don't remember."

Grey clouds scudded across the sky as the wind kicked up and whipped Celyn's cloak against him. "The sun is almost up. Come."

He plunged into the trees, Thomas following close behind, a strange excitement seizing him. *Home. I can do this.* Celyn stopped when they reached a break in the trees that marked a small clearing. Thomas came up beside the other man, his breath catching in his chest as he saw what lay ahead.

The trees lining the clearing were massive and obviously old. As Thomas looked around, something inside him sparked to life at the musty forest autumn smell. At the sudden swirl of leaves and sway of branches in the wind, the dark bulk of them standing fast in the early dawn's light. This was a quiet place, an old place. *A Thin Place.*

He took a few steps into the clearing, turning slowly around, the knife falling forgotten from his hand as memories flooded through him.

He'd felt this way before, on a hike in the mountains with friends, climbing until the trees were left behind and they were scrabbling over rocky boulders and scree that slipped under their boots. They had turned a corner in the trail and stopped for a rest. His friends sat down on the rocks, pulling drinks and snacks from their packs. But Thomas felt an unnameable tug and wandered off the trail a short distance, to a flat rock that thrust up solidly from the mountainside. He had clambered up on top and sat down, facing down the mountain the way they had come.

And been captured the way he was captured now. Captured by the cold mountain breeze blowing in his face; the tall peaks that surrounded him, thrusting white and sharp against the cloudy sky; the thin whistle of a marmot. The sound of his friends' voices, laughing and joking, fell away, to be replaced by a song that thrummed under his feet and sang on the wind. He had newly come to faith then, and it was as pure a form of worship as he had ever experienced.

A sweet spot. That's what he called them, for lack of a better name. He had come across a few others, here and there. A lake up north, where the northern lights crackled and spun above him. A stand of birch that shone white in the summer sun. Standing on a rise in southern Saskatchewan, the wide prairie around him defining the edges of the world. Sweet spots that tumbled through his mind as he stood in the darkening glade. His eyes drifted shut.

All at once he was seized with a longing so fierce his knees almost buckled. It called him to surrender, to allow himself to be swept away until there was none of him left. But even as it touched him, he rebelled. It was so like the compulsion that he had felt in the hands of the demons that fear surged through him; snuffing the delicate buoyant joy he had felt only moments earlier. At the same moment of loss he realized his error, that the demonic compulsion had been asking something very different from this pure surrender.

But it was too late. He gasped, the enraptured feeling fading even as he grasped at it. He opened his eyes to see the massive trees standing sentinel around him once again.

A Thin Place. He raked his hand through his hair, shaken, the exultant call to surrender dissipating to silence, certainty filling him that he'd missed his chance.

He squeezed his eyes shut again, seeking to find that thread of joy, but it was no use. It was gone, no matter how hard he looked. He was stuck here.

He opened his eyes, despair filling him. *Now what?* Stay here and keep trying? Every morning and night, until he got it right? But what if it didn't work? How could he survive on his own? The wind tugged at his hair, the feel of it sharp against his face. The temperature was dropping steadily. It was November 1, and winter was coming. He couldn't even start a fire if he wanted to. He had never been great at it, even with a flint.

He went to put his hands in his pockets and remembered the knife. He picked it up from where it lay at his feet, feeling foolish that he had dropped it. *Good thing the demons hadn't shown up.*

Fear beat at him with black wings that he tried to push away as he forced himself into motion on stiff legs to where Celyn stood, a mere shadow against the darker mass of the trees.

He would have to go with the other man for now. The Welshman had seen his wild flight from the demons, understood his strange dilemma. And he seemed inclined to look out for him, at least. Others might not be so understanding.

The Mercians, for example.

But he was going to have to be careful. Even in Celyn's company, things could go terribly wrong.

As he reached Celyn's side, the man placed a hand on his shoulder. "The way is closed, as I said." There was rough sympathy in his voice, tinged with fear, and for a moment, Thomas wondered what Celyn had seen as he watched. "For now, you are here. And if God wills it, you can try again another time. But for now, we must go, I have no desire to be here if anyone comes looking for the Mercians."

Thomas clenched his jaw and nodded, too full of emotion to speak. This was insane, impossible. He couldn't make sense of any of it, only that somehow he had to survive until he could try again.

A thought struck him as he trudged on wooden legs behind Celyn to the edge of the trees once more.

This can't be the only Thin Place here. I know what they feel like now. Maybe I'll find another one, closer to where I'm going.

He sucked in a breath, resolution filling him. He would find one, stay out of everyone's way, and wait for the next *ysbryd nos*. Then, please God, he would go home and leave this nightmare behind him.

8

"It is the bone-fire, at Wulfstam," Celyn said, peering at the thick plume of smoke on the horizon. Thomas rode one of the Mercian warrior's mounts, a docile mare he had named Missy. The two other horses were tied to their saddles with lead ropes. Celyn's mount, a big brute of a stallion, was none too happy about it but had accepted the extra horse after some stern words from Celyn. Missy was happy enough to have the other one follow her, thankfully. He had been riding a time or two on his uncle's farm, but was no expert by any means. If either horse bolted, he had no chance.

They had been on the move for half a day, stopping only to let the horses drink. Nothing had disturbed their journey except for this telltale smoke, which had stopped them in their tracks when they rounded a corner and spotted it. "We are a half day's ride away. We will be there just as sun sets, God willing." He looked at Thomas. "You have not told me all. That is your right, and I suppose you have your reasons. Your story is one I would not believe unless I had seen the demons with my own eyes. But know this: what you do not tell me is that which I cannot protect you from."

Thomas felt his cheeks flush and clenched his jaw. Was it that easy for others to see he held secrets? "I understand," he said finally.

Celyn waited for a moment, and then, when it was obvious Thomas would not say more, spoke again. "We need a tale to explain your presence to tell the Lord Siward."

"Siward?"

"A *thegn* of Oswy's. A Christian, but a hard man. You must be wary around him. His eyes are sharp and his ears, sharper. He is called Wolfsbane, for it is told that he fought off a wolf with his bare hands, one that almost tore his throat out before he killed it with his knife." Celyn must have seen the skepticism in his face, for he snorted. "Aye, I know. It seems to me the scar on his throat is more likely from a rope than a wolf's teeth, but it is not worth my life to speak of it." He thought for a moment. "I will tell him that I came upon you, injured and with your memory lost. We will not speak of the demons, nor the Thin Place. If you must speak, be careful what you say. Most do not speak Latin, but all know a few words from the monks. Some know more than a few, including the Lord Siward. It is best if I do the talking for both of us."

"Do we have to stop there? Why don't we just sleep in the woods, like we did last night?"

Celyn grimaced and shook his head. "The Mercians came from this direction, and Siward's men watch the roads. I must find out what they know of them."

This time and place held events and undercurrents that were beyond his knowledge. But he had no choice, now. He had to understand what was going on here if he had any hope of survival. "You think this Lord Siward might be working with them against your king? That maybe he sent the Mercians after you?"

Celyn's eyes narrowed. "We do not know such a thing," he said, his voice sharp, "and you would be wise not to say it, lest you find your head separated from your body."

"But you don't trust him."

Celyn's mouth thinned. "I trust him to do what is right for Siward, at all times."

He urged his stallion forward, ending the conversation. Thomas kicked his mare into motion, unease rippling through him as he thought of the night to come.

Rain fell steadily as they rode, and Thomas was glad of his cloak, which kept him warm at least. They had cobbled together some clothes for him, from the bags on the dead Mercians' horses and from Celyn's supplies. As much as he hated wearing them—besides the fact that they were dead men's clothes, they didn't fit quite right—he had no choice. His own clothes he had stuffed into his bag attached to his saddle. He would need those for the journey home. Despite the risk of someone seeing them, he had not left them behind. They were a promise to himself that he would make it back.

He also wore one of the Mercian's knives at his belt. He wasn't sure if he could use it if it came right down to it, but he felt slightly better with it bumping against his thigh as he rode.

After a couple of hours, as the day waned, Celyn reined Arawn to a halt at an intersecting path. The stallion turned and snapped at the extra mount following him. Celyn tugged at the reins, speaking sternly to his horse in Welsh, exasperation in his voice. The sun was nearly down, although they couldn't see it through the clouds.

Once Arawn settled down, Celyn turned to Thomas. "This will take us to Wulfstam. The road will be watched. Be careful what you say."

Thomas nodded. As much as he did not want to have to try to fit in among these new people, he would be more than happy to get off his horse. His head pounded, he felt dizzy, and his legs ached. He wanted nothing more than to lie down in a dark room somewhere.

The wind picked up as they turned down the path, sending gusts of rain against them. He huddled down in the saddle. He supposed he should be grateful that they wouldn't be sleeping in the open, but his anxiety about the unknown didn't give him any room for gratitude.

Missy tossed her head, protesting his tight hold on the reins, and he tried to relax, breathing in a deep breath of the cool air. He let it out again, feeling only marginally better. The whole litany of everything that could possibly go wrong kept jangling through his mind.

Soon they came to a bend in the path, and the small settlement came into view. A fence around its boundaries hid most of it, but through the open gate he could see a few huddled buildings with whitewashed walls and thatched roofs. The roofs came down in sloping eaves past the walls of the buildings, almost to the ground. He glimpsed the large bone-fire behind them, burning in the midst of a barren field.

As they approached, a figure detached itself from the deepening shadows by the gate. Celyn reined in his horse, and Thomas stopped just behind him, feeling slightly sick.

The man greeted Celyn in the same language Thomas had heard the Mercians speak, and they had a brief conversation, Celyn gesturing at Thomas as they did so.

After a few more words, they rode through the gate, and once through Celyn dismounted. Thomas stifled a groan as his feet hit the ground, his stiff legs protesting.

Another man watched, hand on his sword, his eyes sharp as he looked

Thomas over. Thomas nodded at the two men in greeting, trying to calm his thudding heart. The gate guard said a few words to the other man, who took Missy's reins and the lead rope of the other horse from Thomas. The guard took Celyn's horses, and the two men led the beasts towards a large pasture where a few others whickered their greetings to the newcomers.

Once they were out of earshot, Celyn turned to Thomas. "Your fear marks you." he said. "Commit yourself to God. All will be well."

He turned and walked away, leaving Thomas no choice but to follow.

9

A few dogs barked as they walked along the main path, but they saw no people, the dwellings shuttered against the night and the rain. They approached a long hall, music filling the air as they grew closer. It sounded like some kind of celebration, from the raucous noise that came from within.

"What's going on?" Thomas asked.

Celyn glanced at him. "They celebrate the end of harvest."

A few steps led up to the large double doors at one end of the hall. Celyn opened the door and stepped inside. Thomas took a deep breath and followed, willing himself to look calm.

The torches along the walls lit the interior with a fiery glow, competing with the hearth fires to lend warmth and light to the smoky darkness within. A few people turned to look at them as they entered. The smell of food, smoke, sweat, and ale hit Thomas' nose, a sharp contrast to the cool, rain-washed air outside.

A man approached, his face lighting as he saw Celyn and said a few words, clapping the Welshman on the shoulder as he greeted him. Celyn unbuckled his sword from his belt and hung it by the door on a hook. He did not remove his knife, however, so Thomas kept his on his belt as well.

Which suited him just fine. At least he had something to defend himself with, if things went badly here.

He shoved that thought aside and looked around, trying to get his bearings.

There were about fifty people in the hall, men, women, and children alike, seated at long tables that filled the room, as well as at benches that lined the walls. A large fire burned in the centre of the hall. Along one wall, a smaller one with banked coals smouldered, over which hung an iron pot.

Most people had finished eating, and dogs chewed contentedly on bones beneath the tables. Here and there men were playing at dice, families laughed together, and a small knot of lively women and children danced to the music being played by a man playing a guitar-like instrument at the far end of the hall.

Thomas followed in the Welshman's wake as they made their way to the front. People looked up as they passed, and many nodded at Celyn, but Thomas couldn't help but notice a general lack of warmth in their greetings. Aside from the one man who had met them at the door, the people seemed ambivalent about Celyn's presence. But even that guarded reception was better than the narrowed gazes that swept over him. He was glad he had Celyn as a buffer. If he had come alone, he probably wouldn't have made it through the gate.

A raised platform stood at the end of the hall. On it was a long table at which the *thegn*, Lord Siward, and his family sat, and beside them stood the musician, his head bent over the strings as he played. Thomas' gaze skipped over him, and then skittered back as the musician raised his head and finished the song with a flourish, a crooked grin upon his face.

An odd tingling sensation and a sudden flash of recognition washed over him. Thomas frowned. The man had long dirty blonde hair tied back with a leather thong, and he wore a green tunic edged with embroidery. He looked to be in his early thirties, with bushy eyebrows and a large, hooked nose. For the life of him, Thomas couldn't think of whom the man reminded him, but he felt as if he knew him. Which, of course, was crazy.

He looked over at Thomas, but then bent down to listen to someone who was trying to get his attention. But in that split second when their eyes met, Thomas saw surprise pass over his face. Thomas watched him for a moment longer as he began a new song, but the musician ignored him, focussing instead on the man who had requested the song. He had no time to think further of it as Siward rose and stepped down the few steps of the platform to greet them.

Celyn had told him that a *thegn* was a wealthy nobleman, a lord in this society. And this man certainly looked the part. He was in his forties, a strong man with no fat on him. Firelight glinted off his reddish blonde hair, worn straight and cut short at the nape. His tunic was finely woven and edged with decorative embroidery, and a golden armband wrapped around one powerful bicep. A large jewelled brooch pinned to his tunic added to the impression of wealth.

The scar that Celyn had mentioned marred his neck, shiny in the firelight.

His pale blue eyes were sharp and assessing as he looked Thomas over, and then dismissing him, he turned to Celyn. "Greetings, my Lord Celyn, and welcome."

He must have spoken in Latin, as Thomas understood him, but as he continued to speak, the rest of the words were a jumble, with a few words jumping out at him here and there. It was disorienting, for it felt as if he might just be able to understand if his head didn't ache so much and he could concentrate better. His name jumped out, and then he realized that they were looking at him, waiting for him to speak. Thomas looked at Celyn helplessly.

"*The Lord Siward gives you welcome,*" Celyn said, in Latin.

Celyn had coached him in the proper Anglian words in reply. "Thank you, my lord," Thomas said, nodding his head respectfully. Hopefully he hadn't mangled it.

Siward's eyes opened slightly in surprise, but he nodded. He turned to Celyn, and with a few more words, gestured up at the table on the platform.

Thomas watched him, remembering Celyn's earlier misgivings. He looked for any sign that this man had betrayed Celyn to the Mercians. He seemed friendly enough…on the surface at least.

But as the *thegn* looked at him again as they sat down across from him, his pale eyes unreadable, a shiver of fear snaked up Thomas' spine. He had no doubt this man would throw anyone under a bus for his own gain. *If they had such a thing as buses.*

A young man appeared at Siward's command and took their cloaks from them. Siward's wife sat beside him, an older woman with dark hair who nodded at him coolly. Beside her sat a young woman, clearly their daughter, for she looked much like her mother, but with long blonde hair under her head covering. She looked at him and smiled, a dimple appearing in one smooth cheek. Thomas flushed and nodded in reply, wishing he were anywhere but there.

A young man sat beside Siward, who Thomas assumed to be the *thegn's* son. Arrogance marked him, and he did not try to disguise the hostile look he gave Celyn as the Welshman sat down.

Thomas glanced at Celyn, to see if he had noticed, but he continued his conversation with Siward, ignoring the son.

Siward's wife saw the look her daughter gave Thomas, and she turned to her, speaking in sharp tones. The girl nodded at her mother and got up, casting Thomas another look under her lashes as she hurried away.

Thankfully. The last thing he wanted was to be flirted with by a daughter of a powerful and ruthless warrior.

Servants arrived with wooden trenchers laden with roasted meat and fresh bread dripping with creamy butter. Thomas was momentarily stumped as to how to eat it as there was no fork, but he followed Celyn's lead and soon got the hang of pinning the meat with his knife and tearing off bits with the bread acting as a kind of holder in his other hand, like using pita bread to scoop up food from a plate.

It was surprisingly good, and he was starving. It was his first real meal since before this whole thing had started, and he ate in a state of near bliss, the unintelligible conversation flowing around him.

When he was full, he pushed back the wooden platter and took a drink. Ale again. His lips twisted. His mother had been a raging drunk when she died. He had vowed never to touch the stuff, but it's not like they had water on tap here. He took a drink. It tasted good enough, and only vaguely alcoholic. *Maybe it's not too strong.* He put the mug down, wiping his mouth. He would drink enough to quench his thirst, but no more.

The musician glanced at him, but looked away quickly when he saw Thomas notice. Thomas frowned. *What is it about him?* He watched him for a moment, appreciating the skill with which he played his instrument. He had a good enough voice, and the people seemed to enjoy the performance.

A pang hit him as a memory surfaced of his father, playing his guitar with the same easy skill. He had played with the same confidence this man exhibited. Perhaps that was what had sparked recognition. He puzzled over it for a moment longer, but soon gave up.

It didn't matter anyway. They would be gone tomorrow.

10

Thomas's eyes flew open, vague dread and wisps of memory from a dark dream chasing through his mind as he oriented himself to his surroundings. It was dark. The fire had burned down to coals, which did little to cast light other than a reddish glow. Memory flooded back. He and Celyn had been invited to bed down in the *thegn's* hall.

All at once he longed for clean air. He needed to clear his head, needed to get outside, away from this close, smoky place, rank with the smell of dogs and unwashed bodies. He rose, and Celyn stirred at his movement.

"What is it, boy?"

"Just need some fresh air. And the latrine."

Celyn grunted and rolled over, but lay still, his breathing deepening again.

Thomas made his way carefully through the hall, skirting dogs and sleeping men. Two boys—slaves, he presumed—sleepily watched the banked hearth fire. One looked up as he passed, but only for a moment. Thankfully none of the dogs sounded an alarm, although most of them stirred at his passing, lifting a head to study him as he walked by. In their eyes Thomas saw more curiosity than he saw in the boy's.

Reaching the door, he eased it open and stepped outside. The guard stood by the door, a black shadow in the night, his eyes hard and wary. He spoke a few words to Thomas in the Anglian tongue, his voice low.

"Latrine," Thomas said, hoping the word would make sense. The man frowned, then grunted, indicating with his head where Thomas should go.

Thomas nodded and stepped down the stairs, taking a deep breath to calm his nerves. The night was cool, the air scrubbed clean by the rain, which had stopped. The various buildings that made up the settlement were dark shapes in the night around him. *AD 642*. He shook his head, unreality stealing over him again.

Smell led him to the appropriate building, a small hut located behind the main hall. Inside, the stench was almost overpowering, the latrine an open trench. Thomas hastily did his business and stepped outside again, pulling the door shut behind him. He stood silently for a moment, breathing in the blessedly fresh air.

Out of the corner of his eye he saw a silent, dark shape round the opposite corner of the hall, and Thomas froze, the memory of the shadowy demons jumpstarting his heart. But it was only a dog, the white tip of its tail waving slowly back and forth as it stopped and looked at him with interest.

He crouched down, extending his hand towards it. "Hey there, boy." The dog approached slowly, eyes glinting in the dark; a medium-sized dog, black with white on its chest and the tip of its tail. It sniffed at the extended hand carefully, then moved closer, tail lowering as its manner changed from wariness to acceptance. Thomas stroked its rough fur, grateful for its companionship in the dark night.

I wonder if anyone is looking for me yet. He stood up abruptly, dismissing the thought. He couldn't think about that, not now.

"'Bout time you got up, man!"

Thomas whirled around, seeing a figure coming around the corner of the shadowed building. But it wasn't just the sudden appearance that froze him in place; it was that the words the man spoke were unmistakably English.

11

It was the harper. "*We are long parted,*" he said in a low voice, and then paused, looking at Thomas expectantly, his shaggy eyebrows raised.

English. He spoke English. "Ehh…*qui*…?" Thomas stopped, aware that the word was wrong, but he couldn't find the right one, no matter how hard he tried.

The man grinned. "I knew it! A newbie! Take it easy, man. This is your lucky day. We'd better go for a little walk. We've got lots to talk about, and it wouldn't be good for the locals to hear us and come investigate," he said, glancing back meaningfully at the darkened village as he took Thomas' elbow and began to walk away from the cluster of buildings around the hall.

"But…*ego*…" Thomas sputtered. The right word wouldn't come. The stranger pulled him along, putting his finger up to his lips, the dog trotting contently beside them.

The man looked to be in his late twenties or early thirties. Shaggy eyebrows accentuated deep set eyes. He wore soft leather shoes, woollen leggings, a long tunic, and a cloak for warmth, its bright colours reduced to black and grey in the dark.

They stopped in the shadow of a smaller building near the edge of the village, a hut of some sort. Beyond it the empty pasture stretched into the distance, the bone-fire still smouldering but mainly out now. "So…when are you from?" he asked.

Thomas tried to gather his scattered wits. "*Ego…qui…*" He stopped in frustration.

"Oh, right, I forgot." The stranger stepped forward and gripped

Thomas' shoulder, looking deep into his eyes. "Just relax, man. Don't think about it. You'll switch easier that way. Breathe. Relax."

The dog settled down on his haunches, looking from one to the other in interest.

"Now tell me your name—just that."

"Thomas. Thomas McCadden."

A gleam lit the harper's eye. "Now, as quickly as you can, without thinking about it, recite *Twinkle, Twinkle, Little Star.*"

"Twinkle, twinkle, little star, how I wonder what you are. Like a diamond—" Thomas stopped abruptly. His difficulty had ceased. "Who are you?"

"Well, here, I am Godric. That'll do for now." He looked Thomas up and down. "So, you haven't been here long. When did you jump?"

Being pulled from one incomprehensible situation to another was hard on his aching head. Thomas forced himself to focus. *Jump* must mean the leap from one time to another. "Two days ago," he finally managed, working it out. It felt as if he had been trapped here forever. "What's going on? Why am I here?"

The other man held up a hand. "Hold on, man. I know you've got lots of questions, and I'll get to them. But me first." Seeing Thomas' frown, he added, "Just trust me. Like I said, this is your lucky day."

Trust him? As if he had any choice. Thomas raked his hand through his hair, frustrated. "Fine."

"So. When and where did you come from?"

"Canada. 2019."

Godric's eyebrows raised, and he gave a long, low whistle. "Cool," he said thoughtfully. "A long one." He gazed at Thomas for a moment, then added, "I'm from the U. S. of A. California. 1972."

1972? "How is this possible? How long have you been here?"

Godric's shaggy eyebrows lifted, and then he frowned. "Wait a minute. You really don't have any idea of what is happening here, do you?" His eyes travelled over Thomas, up and down. "That story the Welshman told Siward, that's true? You don't remember anything?"

"Not exactly. All I know is that I was home, and then those things appeared, and I ran, and then—" Thomas waved his hand, helpless. "Here I am. I don't remember how."

Godric blinked at him, several emotions chasing over his face. Astonishment...and fear? Thomas couldn't be sure in the dim light. "Things?"

Thomas swallowed, the night around him silent but for a dog barking on the other side of the village. The dog at his feet perked its ears, looking in that direction.

He couldn't speak of the demons, not here, not in the dark shadows with night pressing on them. "You know," he said, his voice low. "Isn't that how it works? Didn't you see them, too? When you came—I mean, jumped. And the white stag?"

Godric looked at him as if he'd grown an extra head. "My God, you're a wilding!" His gaze skimmed over Thomas again in horrified fascination.

"What do you mean? I don't know what you're talking about. I just want to go home! Do you know how? I went to the sweet spot and tried again, but it didn't work. Is there another one around here?"

Godric held up a hand again at the barrage of questions, shaking his head. "Wait. Just chill out, man; just hang on a sec." He took a deep breath, squaring his shoulders, eyeing Thomas warily. "Okay. Here it is. You're not what you think you are. Not exactly human, for one. You're a Traveller, one of the Fey. Like me." Seeing Thomas' face, Godric grimaced. "Oh hell, this isn't coming out right."

Not human? Was this guy crazy? Questions swooped around his mind in a whirl. *Get a grip. Crazy or not, he's the only one who can tell you how you got here. And how to get home.* "What are you talking about?"

A half-smile ghosted on Godric's lips, and was gone. "You are Fey. Like me. One of the fairies, if you like. That's one of the names the humans have for us. But I don't recommend you use it around any of us."

"Right. Tinkerbell. Sure. As if I wouldn't have noticed before now. I mean, in case you haven't noticed, I don't have any wings."

Godric shrugged, an amused expression on his face. "No reason for you to notice before now. The Gifts of the Fey only show up at maturity, right about your age, which I'm guessing is what, nineteen?"

Thomas shook his head, impatient. "Twenty."

Godric nodded, spreading his hands. "See?" His smile faded. "But I would guess that you have noticed something, even so." He cocked his head, considering. "Let me guess. You're lonely. You don't fit in. Not many friends, right? And that feeling you get in the morning, when the sun is rising, or at night, at sunset? Like the world is holding its breath, and you can't breathe either, 'cause you know something is coming, something big, something that fills you up with a joy so sweet you can almost taste it? You've learned not to talk about the way the sky looks in the morning, or how you feel when the rain falls, or when you hear a robin sing." His voice was low, intense. He snorted slightly, studying Thomas' face. "Oh yeah, you've noticed."

It was true. He had never quite fit in anywhere. Could it be that this man was right? He shook his head, dislodging the spell of the harper's words. He wanted an explanation, but not this one. A crack in time he somehow stepped through. Or ley lines. Something outside himself. "I didn't exactly come from fairyland. I came from Canada. My parents were ordinary people. And I wasn't adopted."

Godric waved a hand. "There is no *fairyland*. That's a human story. We live amongst them. Hidden in plain sight, right? Everything you've heard about the Fey is just camouflage. Some truth here and there, a way for us to deflect attention. No Tinkerbells, man. We don't have wings, we can't fly. But we do have Gifts. Healing. Glamour. Speaking. Wards of weather and animals. And Travelling. Time-travel. Which is how you're here," he added, pointedly. "You Travelled." The shaggy eyebrows rose again. "And your parents…well, it happens, man. Genetic crapshoot. Every once in a while a human couple will have a Fey child. We try to find them, to rescue them, but we don't get them all." He stopped suddenly; regret flashing across his face, and something else. *Fear?* He waved his hand, his gaze sharpening on Thomas again. "Obviously, you were missed."

Thomas' head was starting to ache again. "I don't understand."

Godric snorted. "It's a trip. I get it. Don't worry. You'll figure it out. You just have to accept that the world is not what you think. There are not just humans here. And we've been here just about as long as they have."

We. They. "Just about?"

Godric nodded and looked him over. "You're wearing a cross. You know the Bible?"

"The Bible?"

"Yeah. You know, Genesis, Moses, Jesus…"

"I know what you're talking about. But what does that have to do with anything?"

"Everything, if you wanna hear one of our stories that explains where we came from. Do you know the story of Noah? The Flood?"

"Of course."

"Back before the Flood, there was wickedness and all that, right?" Godric's teeth flashed white in a mocking grin.

That smile of his was getting on Thomas' nerves. "Yeah, so?"

"It says that, 'the sons of God came in to the daughters of men, and they bore children to them.'"

"The sons of God," he said, the story coming back to him. "The fallen angels. The—" He was about to say *demons,* but the word stuck in his throat.

Godric spread his arms wide. "Bingo. Here we are, their descendants. Back then, we were called the Nephilim. Now we call ourselves the Fey."

A cold chill washed over Thomas as he remembered the shadowy shapes, the hard, clawed hands on his arms. He rubbed his arms to dispel the feeling. *They came for me because I'm like one of them?*

Despair speared through him. No wonder God didn't answer his prayers.

He was cursed.

The dog at their feet stiffened and suddenly sprang to its feet and disappeared around the building. They exchanged a glance, and Godric stepped swiftly to the corner of the building and peered around it.

"The guard," he said and looked back at him. "You'd better get back to the hall. He didn't see me leave, but he'll be wondering where you went. I'll find you tomorrow, and we'll talk some more."

Without further words he too disappeared around the corner.

Thomas stood frozen for a moment. He wasn't sure exactly what explanation he had expected for his crazy adventure, but what Godric told him certainly wasn't it. He forced his feet to move, his gut churning.

You just have to accept that the world is not what you think. Godric's words echoed through his mind as he walked back to the hall, greeting the guard, who gave him a narrow-eyed look, and wrapped himself up in his cloak once again.

Fey. Traveller. Nephilim. The words swirled around his mind, stirring up confusion, fear, and despair as he stepped inside. He closed the door behind him and leaned back on it for a moment, shutting his eyes.

Now what?

12

"Are you not hungry?"

Thomas glanced at Celyn, startled from his reverie by the other man's words. He flushed and looked down at the mush, some sort of porridge, that cooled in his bowl. It didn't taste half bad, especially with the addition of thick cream and honey, but Thomas had hardly touched it.

Apparently it was another couple days' ride from here to Bebbanburg, as long as the weather cooperated. It might be awhile before he had a chance to fill his stomach. He forced it down, even though his gut was in knots.

Fey. Nephilim. The meeting with Godric in the night was like a dream, the memory of it even more bizarre in the light of day. The whole thing made no sense. But he was here, after all. And that was what scared him most, for it meant that what the harper had said must be true.

If he could believe him.

Celyn pushed his bowl back and got up. "I must have a word with the Lord Siward. We will leave this morn, so don't go far." His look of warning made Thomas' cheeks flush as he nodded his head in agreement. *As if I have anywhere to go.*

Celyn gave him a narrow-eyed look but turned on his heel and left Thomas alone, much to his relief. Celyn wanted to speak with Siward about the Mercians. Thomas, on the other hand, would take the opportunity to speak more with the harper.

He extracted himself quickly from the dimpled smiles that Siward's daughter kept throwing his way, his cheeks flaming again at the suspicious scrutiny of her mother.

He threw up his hands helplessly at their questions, glad he could not converse, and soon they ignored him as they finished their breakfast and then got up and left.

Thomas shook his head at the girl's pantomimed invitation to go with them. Thankfully her mother intervened, speaking sharply to her daughter and marching her out of the hall, ignoring the pleading looks the girl gave her.

The hall was almost empty, and Godric was nowhere to be seen. After giving the others a few moments to get away, Thomas stood up and went outside, wondering where he should begin to look.

He stood on the steps of the hall, scanning the village in the morning's murky grey light. The rain had stopped, but it looked as if it could start again at any time, and the air was cool. He could see a few people here and there—chopping wood, hauling water, feeding animals, or sitting on their porches, doing repairs on tools or clothing.

A small boy, perhaps seven years old, came around the corner of the hall and stopped, eyeing Thomas with unabashed curiosity. Others as well were beginning to notice him standing outside the hall's door.

He stepped down the stairs and started walking, hoping he would come across the harper, when suddenly the hairs on his neck lifted as he felt something, a small pressure in his mind. *The bone-fire.*

He stopped and looked around, startled. It was Godric's voice, he was sure. But the harper was nowhere in sight, only an old man sitting on the porch in front of his hut, whittling a piece of wood.

The bone-fire. The whisper spoke again in his mind, and Thomas winced, his flesh crawling. "All right," he muttered, shaking his head, trying to dislodge the odd sense of pressure. He squeezed his eyes shut. "All right!"

The pressure vanished, snuffed out like a candle at his fierce reply. Thomas opened his eyes, shaken, to see the old man looking at him with curiosity, the knife stilled in his hand. *Great. Just great. Way to be inconspicuous.* Thomas nodded at the man, his face hot, and hurried towards the bone-fire.

He had not quite made it to the pasture where the large fire smouldered when Godric stepped out from between two closely spaced huts. He smiled at Thomas and nodded at another woman who passed by. He took Thomas' elbow.

"Come, friend. There is...something for you...to see...I show you..." His halting Latin trailed off as he pulled Thomas with him behind the huts,

stopping at the fence that enclosed the pasture behind the buildings. Beyond the fence, some small shaggy cows were dotted here and there, contentedly chewing cud or nibbling at the grass.

Godric gestured at the animals, saying quietly in English, "Look like you are appreciating Siward's fine herd."

It took a moment for Thomas, mentally shifting language gears, to understand this fully. But once he did, he looked over at the cows, and nodded, trying to look impressed.

"What was that?" he asked, darting a glance at the harper. "In my head. How did you do that?"

Godric shrugged and leaned on the fence. He looked over at Thomas, amusement in his eyes. "Just one of the Gifts, man. It's called Speaking. A kind of mental telepathy, I guess. Great with the chicks, if you know what I mean." He winked at Thomas, then sighed. "Aw, come on. Don't look like that; it's no big deal."

Stories of the Fey chased through his mind, stories that warned of the fairies and their tricks. *Some truth here and there, a way for us to deflect attention.* Godric's words from the night before flashed through his mind. How could he believe anything the harper said? But what choice did he have? Frustration at his circumstances flashed into anger. "Don't do it to me again."

Godric's eyes narrowed slightly. "You can't stop me. I'll use my Gifts if I need to. Just like you will, once you get it figured out."

"Just keep out of my head."

Godric shrugged and waved a hand. "Whatever. It's no big deal."

"It is to me."

"Fine."

Thomas let out a breath, irritated at being distracted from his questions. They didn't have much time. But before he could speak, Godric turned to him.

"I've been thinking about what you told me. Must have been quite the trip, man." He looked Thomas over. "Those things you saw. The Undying. We Fey see them from time to time. Best to keep away. They're nothing but bad news."

"It's not like I had an option. I told you, they grabbed me." His skin crawled at the memory. "Why did they do that?"

Godric shrugged. "Who knows. Best not to think about it. Dwell on it too much and they might come looking for you." He shook his head, dismissing the topic. "This Celyn. How did you find him?"

"He found me. He saw me running away from the demons, and then I fell and hit my head." Thomas was about to tell Godric about the Mercians but stopped himself. For all he knew, the harper might be in league with Siward, a part of some plot. And if he was, he didn't want to know. "He took me to his campsite and took care of me." He raked a hand through his hair, wincing as it tugged at his still healing bruise. "He thought I had been kidnapped by fairies and escaped through a Thin Place on Halloween. I guess he wasn't half wrong."

Godric grunted, noncommittal. "He must be a Sensitive. There are some humans like that. They can sense us, but they don't know what we are, really. Be careful around him. And whatever you do, don't tell him anything I've told you. Or about me."

"Of course not. I'm not stupid."

Godric snorted. "We'll see about that. So. He must have spoken Latin to you first. That's why you can speak that language. It's one of the Gifts we Travellers have. We will be fluent in the first language we hear within moments; it helps us fit in. But don't worry, you'll pick up the other ones quickly, too. Handy, that. It makes things easier."

One mystery solved, although it opened up plenty more he didn't have time to explore. Easier for what, for example. Why exactly did the Fey jump through time, anyway? He set that aside. He had more important things to know.

"What are these Thin Places, anyways? How do they work?"

"We Travellers call them a Crossing. It's where we jump from one time to another. We don't need any help to do it. Just your luck you stepped into it when you did."

"Right. Real great luck, to end up stuck here."

"Could be worse places, man. Trust me on that one."

"So how do I get back?"

"Same way you got here. Find a Crossing spot and jump."

"I tried that. Didn't work."

"Really." There was a hint of respect in the other man's voice. Then he shook his head, his teeth flashing in a brief grin. "You are one lucky dude, you know that? To try it again so soon, not even know what you were doing—you got balls, I'll give you that. But don't worry about it. There are quite a few around, once you know what to look for. You do know what to look for, right?"

A sweet spot. Thomas nodded. "But do I have to go back to the same Crossing to get home? And why did I come here, in particular?"

The harper shrugged. "Any Crossing will get you home. As to why here, I dunno. Just the way it goes. It's a crapshoot, every time."

Thomas frowned, trying to understand. "Crapshoot?"

Godric waved a hand. "That's what makes it fun. Normally on your first jump you should go with another Traveller, someone who knows the ropes. Otherwise, you could end up in la-la land. Happens sometimes." He leaned towards him, his eyes intent. "Stick with me, man. I've got more to teach you. We Travellers help one another. Like I said, you're lucky I found you. Some wildings jump and never know what happened to them. They end up dead, or worse, sooner or later."

Thomas didn't want to know what *worse* was. "So do you know if there's a Crossing near here?"

"Yeah. Pretty close. I could show you. We could leave tomorrow. I'm supposed to play for the *thegn* again tonight."

Dismay dashed his hope. "I'm supposed to go with Celyn, later today. I can't stay behind and then leave with you. How would I explain it?"

"Where's he taking you?"

Thomas shrugged. "To some monastery. Linda—something."

Godric snorted. "Lindisfarne. The monks. Typical. You are better off with me."

"Can you meet me there?"

Alarm flashed over Godric's face. "Nah, man, that's not for me. Or for you, either. It's not a great place for a Fey. Just sneak away from him, tonight, while he's asleep. When he wakes up in the morning, he'll be glad you're gone, trust me. He can go on his merry way without having to babysit you. Not that he strikes me as the merry type." His teeth flashed in one of his mocking grins. "I'll wait for you at the intersection of the road. And then we'll kiss this century goodbye."

Sneak away? Before he could ask how to do that, Celyn came around the corner of the building, his eyes narrowing as he saw the two of them.

The harper executed a flourishing bow as Celyn came to a halt. "Good day, my Lord Celyn. A fine day it is."

Celyn nodded at him, a faint frown on his face. "Gleeman. I have need of Master Thomas." He turned to Thomas. "We must leave, ere the day gets too old. Come now, your horse is being made ready."

Thomas glanced at Godric and nodded at him, then turned and followed Celyn, fear churning his gut. He couldn't shake the niggling feeling that there was something about the harper that wasn't quite right, and he wasn't sure he could trust him completely. And how exactly was he supposed to get away from Celyn that night?

He set that concern aside. He would figure it out. He had to. If everything worked out right, Godric would show him how to get home. He would be gone from here soon, maybe tomorrow.

Home. The thought was a burning cinder, thawing him from the inside out.

13

"Wake up, boy."

Thomas jolted awake as Celyn's hand shook his shoulder gently. Their small fire danced nearby, the only light in the sea of darkness all around. After a long day of travel, they had found shelter for the night in the ruins of a Roman way station, its broken-down wall and partial roof providing some relief from the rain.

Godric. Thomas sat up, suddenly afraid that Celyn had let him sleep through the night. "What time is it?"

"Just past midnight, I would say," Celyn answered with a yawn. "All has been well. But if you see anyone, don't reveal yourself. Wake me at once. Anyone travelling at night is an outlaw, or worse. Trust no one."

Thomas nodded, glad for the darkness that hid his face, certain that his plan was written there for the other man to see.

Celyn wrapped his cloak around himself and stretched out beside the fire. "Wake me at dawn," he said and closed his eyes.

Now that the time was at hand, doubts plagued him. It was on the tip of his tongue to tell Celyn everything. The thought of sneaking away in the dark, which had sounded so logical earlier, felt cowardly now that the moment was upon him. And Celyn was relying on him to keep watch. What if something happened?

Thomas took a deep breath, forcing himself to relax. Celyn knew how to take care of himself. He would be fine. Telling the Welshman what Godric had said was impossible.

He'll be glad to get rid of me. That's what Godric thought, too, but it brought him no comfort. He sighed. No use dwelling on it now. He was going home.

Excitement flared, and he stretched, working the stiffness out of his limbs. An echo of the headache that had plagued him since he woke up in this century still lingered, but he felt ready to tackle the journey back.

He glanced at Celyn. *Best to wait until he's deeply asleep.*

He wrapped himself in his cloak and sat by the fire, stretching his hands out to warm them, listening to the rain patter and drip around him. *Not a great night for a ride.* He grimaced, forcing his thoughts away from all that could go wrong.

God, help me. It was the only prayer he could manage these days. It would have to be enough. He didn't have any other.

He took another steadying breath as he looked back out into the night. As he let it out, it misted in front of him, and he watched it dissolve in the rain.

Surprisingly, it was relatively easy to sneak away once Celyn fell asleep. The sounds of the rain and wind masked any noise he made.

He rode all night, most of the time with his heart in his throat, expecting to hear Arawn's hooves thundering after him at any moment. But as the hours passed with no sign of Celyn, he began to relax. Just before dawn, the rain eased, and he found himself slumping in the saddle, his eyes falling shut.

He straightened up, alarmed. *Better have a nap before I go any further.* Godric said he would wait. Besides, Missy was tired too, her head drooping as she walked.

A little further down the path a large oak some yards away from the path offered drier ground under its spreading branches. He quickly tied Missy to another tree nearby, gave her some of the oats he had brought, and wrapped himself up in his cloak, lying down under the oak.

I'm going home. He blew out a breath, forcing away the eagerness that filled him at the thought. He had to have rest or he would drop out of the saddle.

As soon as he closed his eyes, the exhaustion he had been ignoring swept over him, and took him away into sleep.

A small sound woke Thomas, and his eyes snapped open. He froze at the sight of a long length of glittering steel stretching above him. A sword, its tip pointing at his throat.

Celyn. Thomas' heart tripped into double-time as his eyes met the

Welshman's.

"Think you carefully, now. Give me the truth, or you will die. Understand?" Celyn hissed the words, his eyes hard.

The shock of seeing him robbed Thomas of speech. He blinked once, then nodded carefully, trying to avoid the razor-sharp point at his throat. The other man loomed over him, the long blade of his sword pinning Thomas to the ground as effectively as if he had skewered him there. Beyond Celyn, he could see the oak's autumn coloured leaves waving in the breeze, backed by a clear blue sky.

He had slept a few hours at least, it seemed. *Idiot. Shouldn't have stopped.* But there was no time for recriminations.

Celyn spoke again, his voice flat. "You are going back to Wulfstam."

"Yes." His voice came out as a croak.

"To meet with the gleeman."

Dismay flooded through Thomas. *How did he know?* "Yes."

A snarl twisted Celyn's face as, quick as lightning, he leaned over and grabbed Thomas' tunic at the neck, hauling him to his feet and slamming him hard against the oak. The sword pressed flat against his throat, holding him in place. Celyn's other hand held his shoulder in a steely grip, shoving his shoulder into the tree.

Sparkles danced in front of Thomas' eyes, and he heard Missy's whinny of alarm faintly, through the buzzing in his ears.

"Why?" Ceyln hissed the question as he pushed the sword against him harder, causing Thomas to crane his chin up in order to avoid the sharp edge. "The both of you in league with Penda, is that it? What are you planning? Speak, boy, now!"

"What?" Thomas struggled to understand through the fuzziness in his head. *Penda? The Mercian king?*

"You met with the harper at the holding. You left me in the middle of the night to come back to him." The pressure on his neck increased as Celyn leaned closer, his face hard with anger. "Tell me true, boy: what are you plotting?"

Plotting? His blood roared in his ears, and he noticed with detachment that the scar that snaked from Celyn's eye up to his temple was white against the flushed skin of his face. Blackness danced around the edge of Thomas' vision. He would faint if he could not get Celyn off him soon.

"Speak, or I will gut you like a fish," Celyn snarled. "I don't know who you are, or what you are, but whether you are faerie or demon, or even blessed St. Peter himself, I will not allow you to harm Oswy, do you understand? Tell me the truth, now!"

Thomas had no doubt that Celyn was in deadly earnest, but he couldn't reply even if he knew what to say. He plucked ineffectively with numb fingers at Celyn's arm which held the sword across his neck. "I…can't…" he gasped out.

Celyn's face twisted in disgust, and he pushed himself away, containing his anger with a visible effort.

As the pressure against him eased Thomas sucked in a breath, but it didn't help. His knees weakened, and he leaned over, his hands on his thighs, not wanting to pass out. His head pounded in time with his heartbeat, a percussion of pain. Slowly the blackness receded, and he lifted his head, eyeing Celyn warily. If he straightened up completely, he thought he might just fall over.

Tell me the truth. Celyn's words echoed in his mind. He took a deep breath, trying to think through his pain and panic. What could he say? If he answered wrong, he'd be dead.

In the tree above him, a bird began to sing, and the lilting trill of its song steadied him. The bird could be singing over his death for all he knew, and if it was…well, so be it. Not a bad thing to hear as your last sounds on earth. The sky was blue, and the red and gold of the leaves exquisite against its expanse as he looked up. *Not a bad thing to see, either.* He took another deep breath as he looked back at Celyn. "It's not what you think. Yes, we met. But not for some—" he waved his hand "—plot against your king." He gathered his strength and pushed himself upright. Everything swooped around him, and he closed his eyes.

"Look, can I sit down? My head—" Suddenly his stomach lurched, and he leaned over and retched, sinking to the ground as his knees gave out. His head felt like a herd of elephants were gambolling around merrily inside. *Post-concussion syndrome*, he thought, holding his head in his hands. *Too many knocks on the head. This is not good, Tommo, not good at all.* He heard an exasperated snort and a rustle of leaves beside him. He cracked his eyes open to see Celyn's boots and lifted his head carefully. He would give everything he owned for an aspirin.

Celyn squatted beside him, his sword back in its scabbard, Thomas saw with relief. But anger still flashed in his eyes. "If you were not plotting rebellion, or murder, why did you meet with him in secret? And why go back to him?"

"Because he can help me get home!" The words burst out of Thomas, and Celyn drew back, startled. "I don't care about your king, I don't care about this place. I just want to go home!" He stopped, trying to control himself. *You gotta do your first jump home with someone who knows the ropes. Otherwise, you could end up in la-la land. Happens all the time.* Godric's laconic voice filled his head. Urgency seized him. He had to persuade Celyn to let him go. It was his only chance.

"And how can this gleeman help you? What does he know of where you come from? You are not making sense."

In for a penny, in for a pound. His queasy stomach roiled. "Because he came through a Thin Place, like me."

Celyn's eyebrows shot up, his eyes widening. He opened his mouth to speak, and then thought the best of it, snapping his mouth shut. Clearly, whatever he had expected Thomas to say, this wasn't it. "A Thin Place," he said carefully. "Like you."

"Yes."

"God's Blood, boy!" Celyn's jaw clenched. He pushed himself up, whirling away from Thomas, his hands fisting. Thomas tried to imagine what the other man was thinking, but he gave up. He hardly knew what to think about it all himself.

Celyn muttered something in Welsh and turned back. "This Godric, he is from your home?"

"My country. Yes." *Close enough, anyway.*

"And he was also taken by the *tylwyth teg* and escaped from the Otherworld?"

Thomas shrugged helplessly, wondering how to answer the man. It was as good an explanation as any. "I suppose. We didn't talk about that."

"God, have mercy." Celyn crossed himself quickly. "This is devilry, or worse."

"Look, I know this whole thing is strange. I don't understand it either, I've told you that. All I want to do is to go home and forget this ever happened. But to do that, I need Godric. He said he could show me how to get back." Celyn frowned, but Thomas continued before he could speak. "Let me go back to the village. Godric is waiting there. Just forget you ever met me. It'll be better for both of us." He didn't need to fake the sincerity in his voice.

The Welshman shook his head, scowling. "As to that, it would be better for me, perhaps. But you would go to your death, that I can promise you." He squatted down in front of Thomas again, exasperation mixed with anger in his face. "Truly, you know nothing, boy. As God is my witness, I don't know what to do with you. Yet as much as I have asked

God to be relieved of this responsibility of caring for you, He refuses to let me go."

Thomas struggled to follow his meaning. "I don't think Godric means to kill me. Why would he?"

"Nay, not the gleeman, although I do not trust him and his tales. It is the Lord Siward who would seek your blood. He suspects you and the gleeman both of treachery. I had to promise I would watch you carefully just to persuade him to let you go. You can be certain he is watching the gleeman as well. If you showed up there and met with this Godric again —" he broke off. "Nay, you cannot go back."

Fear pierced him. He struggled to rise, black spots dancing around the edges of his vision. "I have to go. It's my chance to get back home!"

Celyn stood. "Listen to me, and listen well. My loyalty is to God first, and then to my lord, King Oswy. You go to the gleeman, and you will die. If I take you to him, I will be aiding in your death and so failing in the duty God has given me to protect you. And to take you to the gleeman would give Lord Siward more cause to mistrust my oath to Oswy. I will not allow that to happen. You will come with me to Lindisfarne as God desires, and then you will be Aidan's problem—may God have mercy upon him. And if you do not forget this gleeman and come willingly, I will truss you like a pig and throw you on the horse. Do you understand?"

There was no doubt that Celyn would do as he said. And in his weakened state, Thomas couldn't stop him. Bitter despair crashed over him as he saw his chance to get home disappear in the face of the other man's resolve.

Celyn's fists clenched. "Answer me, boy."

"I understand," Thomas managed to say through clenched teeth. Celyn nodded once, then stalked back to where their two horses stood idly munching grass. He swung himself up on his black stallion effortlessly and looked back at Thomas with a flat stare.

It took Thomas a couple of tries before he could mount, the pounding in his head increasing, his nausea almost overwhelming. But he managed it, his jaw clenched with effort. Once he was ready, Celyn nudged Arawn forward, back onto the road. Thomas followed on Missy, having only the energy to concentrate on staying in the saddle.

Godric knew where he was going. Maybe when he didn't show up, the harper would come looking for him.

It was the only hope he had left.

14

The large raven hopped a few steps away from Wulfram and then launched itself into the air clumsily, black wings beating strongly at the air. Wulfram stood, hands on hips, watching absently as the bird flew away, his mind filled with the information he had gleaned from it.

The young Traveller whom the raven had spotted earlier was now heading northwards in the company of a human. The shock of finally seeing his face had etched it into his memory. Dark unruly hair, angled cheekbones, clear grey eyes.

He knew that face, or one very similar at any rate. The likeness was clear and unmistakable. And with that knowledge more questions arose about the Traveller, questions Wulfram would very much like answered.

He tamped down his impatience. Surely those answers would be coming soon, thanks to the plans *he* had made, to his boldness in seeing what had to be done, and not shying from it, no matter the cost to himself. Or to others.

Like Godric. A memory flashed through his mind—the harper, striding away from his holding, the shadow of the Undying clinging to him. A shadow the harper did not sense. *Yet.* Wulfram thrust aside the discomfort the memory brought. The harper was obstinate. He had made his choice and would have to live with the consequence.

He still puzzled over the meaning of the young Traveller's arrival. But he was confident the answers would come soon enough. His birds would keep watching, keep reporting to him. And soon the harper would find him, bring him to Wulfram.

Wulfram felt a spurt of excitement. It was all starting to come together. This new Traveller was another piece that he could use.

C'mon, Corb, you can do it. You can't stop there. The wind brought him his brother's voice, and Wulfram closed his eyes, chasing the memory. They had been on a trip together; where was it? Suddenly it snapped into place.

Bran looked down at him from where he clung to the rock face above him. They were on the side of a mountain, roped up, the summit one hour's push from there.

It was crazy that Corbin was there at all. He was never one for heights—which Bran thought hilarious, because they linked with their birds and flew with them all the time, exhilarating in the flight together.

But that effortless soaring on borrowed wings was different entirely from this precarious attempt. A slip, a mistake, and he would be falling, no wings to catch the updraft, no matter the ropes that held him. He couldn't get past the feeling that this would be how it would end one day; useless fingers grabbing at the air, his body broken after a long spiralling descent.

But Bran loved to climb, and more than anything else, Corbin loved Bran. So he set aside his fears and followed him, determined to share with his brother in all that he did. That was how he found himself frozen into immobility on the side of a mountain, the wind plucking at his hair, seeking to toss him off the mountain's face.

This was not a particularly high mountain or a difficult ascent—more of a scramble, really, which is how he preferred it. There was only one section on this climb that required ropes, and they were just about through it. Above his head the rock thrust out, the line to the top taking a sideways jag. He had to traverse the cliff horizontally for a few metres, and then—once past the upthrust rock—pull himself up the last section to the summit. Naturally Bran just about skipped his way through it, whistling all the way.

Corbin only had to get reach over to the handhold Bran just vacated and then move his foot over, and then do the same thing again, just a few times more. Then they would move up again.

But he couldn't do it. He hesitated too long, allowing fear to take over. The handhold seemed impossibly far away. He couldn't make it. And the small rock where Bran had put his foot was crumbling. It had held for Bran, but how could it hold for him? He looked around, searching for a shadow against the grey rock, a small fissure he could jam his toes into. But here was no other place to put his foot, unless he backtracked a bit, went down the cliff face a little ways, tried from there.

His fingers were starting to cramp. He was going to have to move, soon. But he would fall, he knew it, and then the rope would catch, and his weight would drag his brother off the mountain as well. His heart seized in his chest. The thought of being responsible for his brother's death was almost worse than the idea of dying himself.

Cold sweat trickled down his back, his breath coming short.

And then Bran looked over and saw his plight. An easy smile split his face.

"C'mon, you can do it. You can't stop there." He looked away for a moment, hauled himself sideways again, and then looked back expectantly.

"The rock, where you put your foot—it's steady?" Corbin heard the shakiness in his voice, but he couldn't help it, as much as he hated this weakness, hated exposing it to his brother.

But Bran didn't tease him, as he might have done if they were on solid ground, and Corbin felt a surge of gratitude.

"It's good. But move your hand first. You saw where I put mine?"

Corbin swallowed and then nodded. He tried to move his hand, but it was no good. As soon as he moved his hand, his balance would shift, and he would have to move his foot, or fall for sure.

"Maybe I should go down a bit. That rock looks shaky."

"It's fine. Come on, Corb; trust me. Don't look down. Just look at me. It's okay."

Corbin looked at his brother and saw the bright power in him, felt his steady presence. His green eyes were solemn, the Unseelie mischief so often present in them quieted for now.

As always, Bran's confidence boosted his own. He was always better with his brother, always braver, always readier to take the risks that needed to be taken.

So he moved his hand, and then his foot, feeling the blessed solidity of the rock under his boot, and then his confidence returned. Soon he crouched on a narrow ledge beside his brother, taking a breather before they tackled the last ascent.

Bran's crooked smile lit his face. "See? I told you it was okay. Don't second guess yourself. You'll just get stuck. It's best to keep going. And don't worry. I'm here to catch you. That's what big brothers are for."

He gripped Corbin's arm then, and their eyes met in a shared moment of togetherness that made Corbin feel like he could do anything.

Sudden tears filled Wulfram's eyes as the memory faded, the loss of his brother piercing him anew.

Despite his fears, it was Bran who died falling—choosing to jump from the burning tower, his body tumbling over and over again through that bright September sky. Almost twenty years ago now, but just as vivid in Wulfram's mind as the day it had happened, when he had stood watching in horror, choking on smoke and ash, screaming out his brother's name.

He had been Speaking to Bran just before, frantically telling him all that was happening down below, trying to find a way to get his brother out of there. But the flames were advancing, his brother trapped. Wulfram saw the clear intention in Bran's mind just before his brother shut him out, had known exactly what he would do.

I'm going to fly, brother. Sometimes that last thought from Bran woke him up at night.

Wulfram's fists curled, his rage at the injustice of it striking to life again. The whole country had mourned along with him, but he had been oblivious. After all, it was the humans and their fatal mismanagement of their affairs that had brought about his brother's death—and not just his. The extermination of the whole race of the Fey could be laid at their feet.

But he could change it all, he and the rest of the Travellers, those who were bold enough to break free from the hidebound Rule that hampered them.

He could change it. It was a path fraught with difficulties, almost too many to count. The way ahead was uncertain. But he would not get stuck. He would keep going; he would not second-guess himself.

And in the end, when he Crossed back, he would meet his brother, see his lopsided grin, and know that it had all been worth it.

15

"There," Celyn said, pulling Arawn to a halt as they rounded a corner in the road. "Bebbanburg."

Thomas squinted in the direction of Celyn's pointing finger, shielding his eyes against the glare of the sun reflecting off the ocean waves on his right. A dramatic upthrust of land, crowned by a large building, jutted up from the horizon. Smoke drifted up from the structure as well as from the walled village, which huddled at the bottom of the rocky hill.

He took a deep breath, trying to calm his racing heart. The thought of meeting the King of Bernicia tied his stomach in knots. The ten days that had passed since his failed escape had not served to decrease his anxiety at the thought of his arrival at Celyn's home. If anything, it had only increased.

The journey took longer than it should have. The lack of sleep, stress, and the lingering effects of his injuries suffered after his jump finally caught up to him, and they had to stop frequently to let him rest. Once he had started feeling better, the weather turned against them. Two days were lost to a tumultuous rain, but today the sun shone bright and the temperature was mild, much warmer than it would be back home. Thomas shifted in his saddle, remembering the snow that he had walked through in Parker's Field with a pang of homesickness, which he quickly suppressed. He could not focus on that now.

The delay gave him the chance to adjust to the Anglic language, which he asked Celyn to speak instead of Latin. As Godric predicted, he picked up on it quickly and could now understand most of what was said, and speak it passably, according to Celyn.

Which was good and bad. Having proven the truth of Godric's claim made it hard to dismiss the harper's other statements. Namely, that the Fey were real, an ancient race hiding among the humans, and that he was one of them.

With all of his heart he wanted to deny it, but every morning when he awoke and realized he was still in this misplaced century, Godric's claim crashed over him again. It was the only explanation he had, and until he could find another one, he would have to accept it. But he didn't have to like it.

Celyn kneed Arawn into motion, and Thomas gathered the reins and urged Missy to follow, dread growing in his gut. Now that the moment was upon him he felt almost numb. All his prayers had fled from him, except the one that kept running through his mind like a mantra. *God, help me.*

Less than an hour later they were riding up to the gate in the wall that protected the small settlement. Guards stood on either side of the gate, armed with swords and wearing light chain mail.

Missy tossed her head in protest at Thomas' tight hold on the reins, and he took a breath and tried to relax as he looked around.

They were not the only ones wanting entrance into the village. As they approached, a commotion erupted at the gate. A family of peasants had been blocked by one of the guards. The other stood with his hand on the hilt of his sword, keeping a watchful eye on the group.

The spokesperson for the peasants, a short, burly, dark-haired man with overhanging brows that made him look like a Neanderthal, stood with his chest thrust forward, his face inches from the guard's. One hand gesticulated vigorously, poking at the guard's chest or waving angrily in the air as he spoke. The other caressed the handle of the axe that was thrust in his stained leather belt. The guard was trying to get a word in edgewise, with no success that Thomas could see. As they rode up behind the group, the peasant's wife turned and eyed them boldly, her gaze travelling over them, and she sneered, turning back to her family.

Thomas had quickly learned that their horses, along with Celyn's sword and richly embroidered cloak, marked them as part of the upper class in this society, judging by the respectful nods and awed manner in those they had passed on the road. This contempt was unusual, but Celyn ignored the woman, looking intently at the guards.

"My Lord Celyn!" The guard who was not occupied with the peasants strode towards them. His blonde hair gleamed almost white in the sun. "God be praised! You are back!" Genuine delight laced his words. Thomas had no difficulty in understanding him, and one of the knots of tension within him eased just a bit.

With this exclamation, the group turned as one to look at them. Even the mule that was loaded down with lumpy bags swivelled a lazy ear in their direction.

"We was 'ere first. Wait yer turn," the wife said, her voice laced with scorn. "Just because yer 'igh-an'-mighty—"

"Shut up, woman!" the beetle-browed man interrupted, looking over Celyn shrewdly. The woman shot him a venomous look. A small child who was clamped to her leg let out a high-pitched screech that stabbed through Thomas' skull like an ice pick.

Another child, around seven and with long thin blonde hair, examined them solemnly with wide blue eyes. She clutched a rope attached to a goat, which began to bawl loudly.

Thomas winced, feeling his headache creeping back.

"See, m' lord," the man continued, raising his voice to be heard over the racket and addressing his remarks to Celyn, "the king, see, 'e said as I could come 'n see 'im, like, as I got skills 'e could *use*, 'e said, and this one 'ere—" he turned and shot the guard a vicious look from under his brows — "'e says I gotter wait, like, until the king *summons* me, but I told 'im, see, I *told* 'im—"

"ENOUGH!" The flaxen-haired guard's voice cut through the burly man's speech, stopping it abruptly. "Step aside and allow this man to pass!"

Celyn held up a hand. "Hold, Uhtred." He turned to the peasant. "Your name, and be quick."

The man shot the guards a triumphant look, then turned back to Celyn. "I be Dunn, recently of Stowham," he stated with some dignity, the effect of which was ruined by the goat who at that moment left off bawling and nipped at the man's filthy tunic. "Gerroff, ye beggar!" he bellowed, yanking his tunic out of the goat's mouth. He shot a foul look at the young girl, who shrank back and pulled at the goat's rope in order to stop it from taking another inquisitive nibble.

Arawn neighed shrilly, shifting on his massive hooves, and Celyn spoke into the sudden silence that followed. "You say the king has asked for you?"

Dunn nodded. "Aye, m'lord. Like I said, I have skills."

"What skills?"

The other man's eyes shifted under his brows. "Well, m'lord, not me, *exactly*, see, but this one, she's the one 'e needs, and she couldn't come without her family, like.*" He shoved the young girl holding the goat forward. The girl, her eyes widening as all eyes shifted to her, shrank back as she looked up the height of the stallion to Celyn seated on top.

The girl's fine long blonde hair lifted from her shoulders in a sudden breeze that came off the nearby ocean and her clear blue eyes filled with tears. Under the grime, her features were delicate. Thomas tried to imagine what the king would want with this girl. With a sudden knot in his stomach, he thought of one possibility and looked over at Celyn in alarm. He couldn't allow this girl to be given to the king as some sort of consort, could he? With a sinking heart, he realized that perhaps he could. Perhaps this kind of thing was done all the time.

Celyn frowned. "What of her?"

"She picks eggs, see. She can climb up and down them cliffs, bring the king 'is eggs every day. She's half bird herself, that one. She'll just about fly if she has to."

"I see. And who is your lord? He has allowed you to leave your lands?"

Dunn flushed. "I serve the *ealdorman* Baldred. The harvest was poor, see, and 'e bade me come to the king and bring my daughter, so as to perform the service I had promised."

Thomas frowned, piecing together the words with what he had learned from Celyn. This man must be a *coerl,* nominally a free man, but in reality beholden to a *thegn* or *ealdorman,* who must be this Baldred. The *coerls* worked their land on behalf of the upper classes, giving them rent and service whenever asked, in turn for the lord's protection against raiders or outlaws.

Looking at Dunn's defiant stance, Thomas wondered how much of his story was true. Had the king actually asked them to come? Or had it been a passing comment, one the king would have forgotten the moment they rode away? Thomas thought likely it was the latter, but couldn't blame Baldred for wanting to wash his hands of Dunn and his contentious family. Just a few minutes in his presence was enough for him.

Seeing Celyn's narrowed eyes, Thomas thought that probably the

Welshman had come to the same conclusions.

Celyn let out a breath and looked at the guard, who watched this exchange with a scowl. "Let them in. I'll explain it to the king."

Uhtred's eyebrows rose, but he gave a small nod. "If you wish, m'lord." The skeptical tone of his voice left no doubt that he thought this was a bad idea, but he turned to the other guard and nodded. They stepped aside, allowing the family to pass.

A brief squabble occurred as the *coerl* and his family pushed past the guards, the goat bawling noisily all the time. Dunn gave the mule a vicious kick to get it going, and finally the way ahead was clear.

Uhtred watched as they disappeared past the gate, then looked up at Celyn, a wry smile on his face. "I do not envy you your conversation with our lord king," he said. "That man is an ogre and will likely cause trouble ere the winter is over."

"And that trouble on my head and all, aye, I know," Celyn said. A smile ghosted over his face, quickly gone. "As for that, you can thank me later, that it is my head and not yours."

Uhtred grinned. "Indeed, I will, my lord. God's blessing on you. It is good to see you back."

Celyn nodded, and kneed Arawn into motion. Missy ambled behind, Thomas nodding at the guards as he rode past, feeling their eyes on his back.

The settlement was much the same as Siward's village, but bigger. The buildings were the same whitewashed wattle and daub, and animals roamed here and there much like those in Wulfstam.

Ahead of them, Dunn's family stopped, husband and wife hissing at each other in a heated argument. They were speaking too quickly and using too many unfamiliar terms for Thomas to follow, but as they approached, the argument was ended by Dunn, who suddenly slapped his wife, hard, the retort loud.

She staggered back a couple of steps, a hand to her face, glaring at her husband. Dunn ignored her, turning and plodding down the road once again, the children trailing after.

The wife, seeing Thomas and Celyn approaching, raised her chin, the red mark on her face blazing through the dirt, then lifted her skirts and followed her husband without a backward glance.

Thomas clenched his jaw. "Nice guy."

Celyn glanced at him. "He is a brute," he agreed. "But his children will not starve this winter. The rest we leave up to God."

Thomas grimaced. God didn't seem to care too much in his opinion, but he kept it to himself.

16

Celyn's home in the village was a small dwelling, neat and tidy inside, as reluctant to give up clues about its owner as the man himself. Except for one: the Welshman lived alone. This in itself was telling.

He had tried to ask Celyn about his home and his family on their journey, but he had not gotten far. The only thing Celyn had told him was that his wife and child were dead, and then he would say no more.

A dark grief shadowed the man, one that Thomas had yet to find the words or the courage to ask about. But he couldn't help but speculate that the story behind that grief would explain why Celyn lived as an exile here in Bebbanburg, instead of serving the king of Gwynedd.

Some borrowed clothes, and a brief wash with cold water drawn from a well, revived Thomas. At least he would meet the king looking halfway decent.

Celyn looked him over. "Only speak if you are spoken to," he reminded. "Follow my lead." He placed a hand on Thomas' shoulder. "Do not fear, boy. God is with us."

They left their horses with the amiable stable master Badulf, who looked Missy over with keen appreciation, assuring Thomas she would be in good hands. Just past the stable was the path that led up the rocky upthrust to the king's hall. Once they reached the top, Thomas looked around, his stomach fluttering with nerves.

The area on top was bigger than Thomas expected. The large hall dominated the scene; it, and a wooden church, were the biggest buildings in the complex. In the clearing in front of the hall, a group of men were clustered around two men who were engaging in a practice fight with wooden swords. Shouts of encouragement from the watching men met their ears, and the *thwack* of the swords meeting cracked loudly through the air.

People greeted Celyn courteously enough, with a nod or sometimes a smile and a spoken "Good morn, my lord," but it was evident to Thomas that there was the same wary distance between the Welshman and the people of Bebbanburg as there had been at Wulfstam. There was respect there, certainly, but not a lot of warmth. Celyn acknowledged the greetings with a polite nod, his face giving away nothing. If he was disturbed by the less than effusive welcome, Thomas could not tell.

As they walked up to the group gathered in front of the hall, a ragged cheer broke out. The fight was over, and several were congratulating the victor, a dark-haired man whose muscular frame was streaked with sweat and dirt. His teeth flashed in his face as he grinned, accepting the praise of the men gathered around.

Others helped the loser up off the ground. Some of his stringy brown hair had come loose from the rest, which was tied back with a leather strip. A large bruise was forming on his cheek, and he held his side carefully as he arose. A thick beard covered the lower half of his face. But he didn't seem bothered by his injuries and smiled in response to the good-natured ribbing of the men.

Despite their casual manner, Thomas knew these men would kill him without a single thought if they suspected him of being dangerous to their king. A cold shiver of fear touched him at the thought. *I know the future. I'm more dangerous than they could ever imagine.*

The trick would be to hide the truth as much as he could. The story of his lost memory would help, but how long could he pull that off?

The victor glanced over as they approached, his smile fading as he saw Celyn. The loser of the fight turned at the same time. In contrast to the dark-haired man's hostile stance, his face broke into a smile. He had a wide face, with a broad nose and mismatched teeth.

"Lord Celyn! You are back, God be praised!" He strode out to meet them, coming to a halt in front of Celyn and grasping his shoulders warmly.

A rare smile appeared on Celyn's face in response. "God's blessing on you, Lord Wynstan."

The dark-haired man stepped forward, a hard glint in his eye. He was close to his own age, Thomas guessed. His long chin kept him from being classically handsome, but there was a certain brash recklessness to his face that Thomas suspected some women found attractive. Although it was cool outside, he was sweating freely after his exertions in the fight. "So, you return. The king has been impatient for your news."

Thomas looked at Celyn, trying to see the reason for the sudden tension. The Welshman's smile faded. "As to that, my lord, you had best make way so I can report to him."

The young man held Celyn's gaze. "Of course, m'lord. Far be it from me to stand in the way of your *duty*," he said, with a slight sneering emphasis on the last word, and Celyn's eyes narrowed slightly.

"Enough, Brand. Let him be," Wynstan said.

The young lord ignored him and turned to Thomas, looking him up and down.

Thomas felt his face flush. His borrowed clothes didn't fit right and his cloak was stained and dirty from travel. He felt like the misfit he was, truth be told.

"Who is this" Brand asked, looking back at Celyn. "Have you brought us another *waelisc?*"

Someone snorted.

Sometimes the meaning of new words filtered through a split-second later. As it did in this case. *Foreigner.* It was evident from the sneer on Brand's face that it was meant as an insult.

"He is none of your concern," Celyn replied, his voice even, and he began to walk past, shouldering his way through the knot of men.

Brand bowed, sweeping his hand in a flourish towards the door of the hall, a mocking smile on his face.

It reminded Thomas for a fleeting moment of Godric. But he set that thought aside as they walked up the steps that led to the big wooden double doors of the hall. He couldn't let himself get distracted.

All around the doorway, carvings in the wood frame swirled and twisted with masterful, riotous skill. A banner mounted on a pole over the door flapped in the sea breeze that lifted up the hill from the ocean. It was red, with a stylized gold and blue beast embroidered on it. The guards at the door nodded at Celyn and opened the doors for them as they reached the top step.

He took a deep breath as he followed Celyn inside. *Don't mess this up, Tommo.*

17

The inside was impressive, both by its size and the richly appointed decorations. But Thomas took in the details quickly, his eyes skipping over it all as he looked to the back of the hall, where a man sat on a large stone chair carved with the same designs that decorated the hall's door.

"It is the Lord Celyn!" someone called out.

The king looked over, and his eyes widened as they lit upon Celyn. He sprang up and hurried down the few steps that led to the raised platform, striding towards them as they divested themselves of their cloaks and hung them on pegs by the door, along with Celyn's sword.

The king had shoulder-length blonde hair, and a neat reddish beard. Another man followed in his wake, who looked young but was balding, with curly black hair that came to an abrupt halt on top of his head at the level of his ears.

Thomas took a deep breath, trying to settle his fluttery stomach as Oswy stopped in front of them and Celyn dropped to one knee, bowing his head. Thomas followed suit, feeling awkward and uncertain.

"Lord Celyn!" exclaimed the king. "Praise be to God! I have prayed daily for your safe return, and here you are. God be thanked! Rise, friend, and be welcome!" The warmth in his voice was unmistakable, as was the faint Irish accent that sounded odd on the Germanic Anglic words.

Celyn rose smoothly to his feet. Thomas stayed on one knee, uncertain of the protocol. He schooled his face into neutrality, looking over the king with interest.

Oswy had a narrow, open face, alight with obvious intelligence. The two men greeted in an enthusiastic bear hug, and after a couple of thumps on the back, Celyn pulled back. "Good it is to see you, my lord king. I have much to tell you."

"And I am eager to hear it, my friend," Oswy replied, his face breaking out into a smile that faded as he glanced over at Thomas. "But who is this?"

"This is Master Thomas. I found him on my travels. He was injured and has lost all knowledge of his past. I am taking him to the monks."

"I see," the king said, a faint pity in his hazel eyes. Thomas felt another knot ease inside of him. Pity was better than suspicion. "Rise, Master Thomas. You are welcome here in the name of the Lord Christ, who bade us welcome strangers on his behalf. You will find succour with Bishop Aidan, I am sure. His healer, Brother Eadric, is well known in these parts. He will be eager to see you. He likes nothing more than an opportunity to unravel a mystery. Is that not so, Father Colm?"

"O aye, 'tis so, indeed," the priest said as Thomas rose to his feet. Curiosity filled his face. "Truly, you remember nothing?"

"No, Father." Thomas said. "Nothing before I met Lord Celyn."

"You are a Christian?"

Thomas flushed, realizing that he was fingering his cross, and he let it go. *Actually, I'm some sort of demon-human hybrid, and I have come to you from 2,000 years in the future.* He thrust that thought aside as quickly as it popped into his head, hoping nothing showed in his face. "It would seem so."

He caught the quick glance Celyn shot him but ignored it. The answer might not have been the best one, but it was honest at least. Where he did not have to lie, he would not. Easier, that way, not to get tangled up.

"He speaks Latin fluently. He has had some training in a monastery, to be sure," Celyn said.

Surprise flashed across the priest's face, and he opened his mouth to reply, but Oswy interrupted. "I'm sure these two are tired after their journey, and I am eager to hear Celyn's news. We will continue this after they have had some refreshment."

"Of course; please forgive me, Lord Celyn," Father Colm said, bowing his head slightly in deference. As he did so, Thomas saw that the monk wasn't balding, as he had thought. His hair was shaved from ear to ear, in an odd sort of tonsure. The monk straightened up. "Come."

They followed the king and Father Colm to the back of the hall. There were others gathered in the hall, sitting at tables or on benches against the wall. Curiosity sparked in some faces as they passed, and a few men greeted Celyn with a nod.

Sunlight streamed in through unshuttered windows, bringing the fresh sea air into the smoky interior. A group of women gathered around a loom in the light by a window, the sunlight winking off the gold and silver embroidery that decorated their clothing.

A long wooden table sat beside the throne, and as Thomas sat down beside Celyn on a bench across from the king, he took a deep breath. *So far, so good.*

Father Colm did not sit but instead stood beside the king, and indicated to a young servant boy to bring Thomas and Celyn some ale and food.

Celyn quickly summarized their journey and when he was done, Oswy sat back, his face troubled. "Penda's men. A disquieting bit of news, indeed. Where were you exactly when you saw them?"

"A day's ride south of Wulfstam, my lord king," Celyn answered.

The king frowned. "Siward's lair?"

Celyn nodded. "Yes. Siward says his men saw the strangers but lost them in the woods when they pursued them."

"And you believe him?"

An image of the *thegn* came to Thomas' mind, with his calculating eyes that missed nothing. A pragmatic man, one who was most interested in pursuing his own best interests. One whose loyalty could perhaps be bought. Had Penda been soliciting support from Siward? The thought had obviously occurred to Oswy.

Celyn thought Siward didn't trust him, and Oswy didn't trust Siward. A frisson of fear snaked through Thomas. This was a dangerous time and place. He was way out of his depth. *I've got to find some way to get home. Soon.*

"As to that, I believe he spoke the truth," Celyn said.

Before the king could reply, the door to the hall flew open with a bang against the inside wall. The bright sun backlit the figure who stood in the door, making it impossible to make out any features, but from her slim form and long dress, it was evident that the newcomer was a woman. She looked around, impatience in her manner, and then picked up her skirts and hurried straight towards the king.

"Celyn!" she cried. "*Ach'ma!*"

Thomas froze, his heart skipping a beat as he looked first at the woman and then back at Celyn, who half-rose from the bench, a startled look upon his face. The king sat relaxed upon his throne, a smile half-hidden behind his hand as he stroked his beard.

The woman sank in a low curtsy before the throne, her head bowed.

"I told you I had some news for you, my friend," Oswy said, clearly enjoying the Welshman's expression of surprise. "Rise, Lady Nona, and greet your cousin."

The woman rose gracefully to her feet. She was young, closer to his own age. Her light green tunic was decorated with a wide band of white embroidery along the sleeves and the bottom edge. Round golden brooches held the tunic together at each shoulder. The narrow sleeves and bottom edge of a dark green dress of a fine material, perhaps linen, was visible beneath the tunic. She wore a white veil, which covered most of her hair at the back. In the front her hair hung loose, framing her face in dark, tumbling curls. She ignored Thomas, all her attention on Celyn as he stepped off the platform, a warm smile lighting her narrow face.

Thomas was glad for her disregard of him, for it gave him a moment to compose himself.

Judging from his previous experience, there was only one explanation for the strange tingle he felt all along his nerves, the odd feeling that he knew this woman from somewhere.

The woman, Celyn's cousin, was unmistakably Fey.

18

"Nona!" Celyn exclaimed, gripping her shoulders. "*Clod I Dduw! Ond pam wyt ti yma.*"

Thomas sat frozen on the bench as Celyn enveloped the young woman in a hug, lifting her bodily off the ground and spinning her around as she laughed.

Finally, Celyn released her and she glanced at the platform, and their eyes met. Her eyes were a clear green, almond-shaped, and they widened as she saw him. It was only because he was expecting it that Thomas saw the reaction before her gaze skipped back to the king.

"Forgive me for the interruption, my lord king," she said with a smile, her voice a pleasant alto, holding the same Welsh lilt as Celyn's. "I heard of my cousin's arrival, and it has been so long since I have seen him."

"Of course; it is no matter. I would not begrudge my Lord Celyn a reunion with his family. Come, join us." Oswy indicated the bench upon which Thomas sat. "This is Master Thomas, whom Celyn has rescued on his travels. Celyn was telling us of their adventures when you arrived."

Nona looked at Thomas, who flushed as the Fey-sense tingled along his nerves again. She nodded at him with polite interest and then Celyn took her arm, helping her up the stairs to the platform. He sat down beside Thomas again, and Nona sat next to Celyn.

Thomas realized his hand was fisted on his thigh, and he unclenched it, trying to act as unconcerned as the woman. But wild thoughts careened through his head all the same. *She is Fey. And Celyn must not know it. Maybe she knows how I can get home.*

"What brings you here, cousin?" Celyn leaned towards the girl, his eyes intent on hers. "Is all well in Gwynedd?"

Before she could reply, the king spoke. "Your lady cousin is to be married," Oswy replied. "To Conaire Mac Alpin of Dál Riata."

Celyn drew back, shock flashing across his face. "But Cynric is your betrothed!"

Nona flushed and lifted her chin. "He died, a year past, at his king's side in battle."

"God rest his soul," Father Colm said, crossing himself quickly.

Nona glanced up at him, her dark brows drawn down in a frown. "He would not appreciate your prayers, Father," she said with some asperity. "He was no friend of Christ. Likely he went to his death screaming Woden's name."

Father Colm drew back, startled at Nona's frankness. "Then God has favoured you, my child. Conaire Mac Alpin is a good Christian man, and a prince of Dál Riata." Father Colm looked pleased, although Thomas thought he saw a hint of exasperation on Nona's face.

"At his king's side?" Celyn's voice was hard, his eyes like flint. "Where?"

Nona's jaw tightened, and she glanced at Oswy, who looked on impassively. She looked back at Celyn. "'Twas a skirmish, only; 'tis possible you were not there."

"And 'tis possible I was. Tell me where it was."

Thomas grew cold as he realized the difficulty: As he was now for Oswy, Celyn had been one of Oswald's sworn men, fighting alongside the king. It was possible he had been involved in the battle that killed the man.

Nona's cheeks were flushed. "He rode out with Penda when Oswald raided into Mercia, in the fall last year."

"Ahh." Father Colm frowned at Oswy. "That was when your brother took Penda's cousin as hostage. And then got a ransom for him, so he did."

Thomas' heart sank. It was obvious from the look on Celyn's face that the Welshman had been at that battle, too.

Nona laid a hand on Celyn's arm, concern etched on her face. "Do not be troubled. It is well with me, truly."

"Your cousin holds no ill will towards you," Oswy said before Celyn could speak. "She had said so to me already."

But Celyn ignored him, his eyes fixed upon Nona. "Well with you? You have been pledged to Cynric since you were but a babe."

"Indeed. And I pray for his soul every day. But I cannot stand against God's will, and nor should you."

Celyn's jaw clenched. "All the same, I am sorry to hear of it." Shouts from the outside filled the silence that followed; the practice bouts had resumed. Celyn ignored the noise, his gaze sharpening on his cousin. "Conaire of Dál Riata. Surely Penda would see you wed to one of his *thegns?*"

"Surely he would," Nona replied, her chin lifting. "But my father has his own mind."

Penda? Thomas frowned, trying to keep up. Why would Bernicia's enemy have any say as to this Welsh girl's husband? The answer came to Thomas in a flash. Because her father must be one of Penda's men, vowed to the Mercian's king's service. And perhaps not just Celyn's uncle, but Celyn's father, too, and the rest of the overlords of the kingdom of Gwynedd. Which would mean that Celyn had broken ties with his family, his people, and had come to Bernicia and vowed himself to its king.

Celyn had said the Mercian warriors who attacked them might have been looking for him. Now Thomas understood why. Celyn was a traitor to the Mercian king. And here in Bernicia, he would be seen as an outsider who had broken a pledge to his former king. His frosty reception began to make more sense.

Breaking that pledge was not something Celyn had done lightly. Thomas knew him well enough to know that. Whatever propelled him here, far away from his family and his home, to the service of his former king's enemy, must have been catastrophic.

He glanced at Oswy, another thought striking him. *Why trust the oath of one who was known as an oath-breaker?*

His speculations were cut short by a sudden commotion from outside. Voices were raised in alarm, and suddenly the door to the hall slammed open once again.

"My lord king!" It was one of the men who had been watching the fights outside. "Come quickly! It is Aldred—he has been wounded!"

The king cursed and sprang off his throne, the rest of them following in his wake as he hurried through the hall and outside into the bright sunlight where a small crowd was forming around a man lying by the steps to the hall.

As Oswy dropped to one knee beside the man, all conversation ceased, leaving only the steady thrum of the waves in the background, accented by the sudden mournful cry of a seagull, wheeling overhead.

Wynstan knelt beside the wounded man, pressing a bloody cloth against his side.

As Thomas came to a halt, joining the onlookers, Nona stopped beside him. He glanced at her, a small quiver in his stomach as the odd tingle washed over him again. As if sensing his eyes on her, she looked at him, then quickly looked away towards the man on the ground.

Dirty blonde hair matted with sweat lay lank on the wounded man's brow. He tried to lift himself up to see the extent of his injury but sank back with a cry.

"Easy, Aldred. Lie still." Wynstan's words were soothing, but his eyes betrayed his worry.

"How bad?" Aldred's question came out as a harsh gasp.

Wynstan shook his head. "Hard to say," he replied, but Thomas caught the quick glance he exchanged with the king.

It was easy enough to see what had happened. A sword lay nearby. Grouped around the wounded man were many of the men Thomas had seen earlier, mock-fighting. Something had gone wrong during the practice fight. Thomas frowned. *Why would practice swords be so sharp?*

The king looked up. "What has happened here?"

The men looked at each other, but no one spoke for a moment. Finally, Brand stepped forward. "My lord king, it was a mistake. My slave has mistakenly sharpened my practice sword. I did not know, I swear."

Oswy's eyes narrowed. "Did you not."

Brand held the king's eyes steadily, but his jaw bunched. "The slave will be punished, I assure you."

"My lord king," the injured man gasped, reaching up to pluck at the king's tunic. "It was an accident. He speaks true."

"Come now," Oswy said. "Save your strength." He looked up at Brand, who stood stiffly in front of him. "Go to the hall. I will speak with you later."

"Yes, my king," Brand replied, and then paused as if to add something else. Thinking better of it, he abruptly turned on his heel and left, shaking off the hand of one who tried to stop him.

Father Colm kneeled down beside the king, crossing himself as he did so, his lips moving in silent prayer. "Let me have a wee look, my son," he said, his voice gentle, and Aldred nodded, his eyes falling shut.

The priest nodded at Wynstan, who carefully pulled the bandage back from the wound. Fresh blood flowed, adding to the stain that had already darkened the man's tunic. The priest frowned and glanced up at the king, their eyes meeting in silent confirmation.

Thomas didn't know much about medicine, but he knew enough that this wound would be a serious one in his own time, never mind here, where germs, bacteria, and the importance of sanitation were unknown.

Celyn's face was bleak, mirroring those of the onlookers. Some crossed themselves quickly.

Aldred was young, probably about his own age. And likely he would die in agony, a raging infection taking over his body. He could help, tell them about sanitation, get them to use clean bandages at least. But how to do that without revealing the reason why? *I don't have a choice. There's no way I can tell them.* Despair pierced him. Keeping the knowledge to himself could result in this man's death, and there was nothing he could do about it.

"We must get him inside," the priest said.

Oswy nodded and glanced up at the surrounding men. "Bring a bench," he commanded. "We will take him to my chamber." Several men hurried away in the direction of the hall.

"We must get word to Lindisfarne," Father Colm said. "We will need the skills of Brother Eadric." He cast a look at the sky, judging the time, then shook his head. "The tide is up now. He cannot cross until later tonight."

Oswy laid a hand on his shoulder. "Until then he is in your hands, Father."

The priest looked troubled. "In God's hands would be better, so it would." He sighed. "I will do what I can, but Brother Eadric has far more skill than I."

"I could help, my lord king. I have some skill as a healer," Nona said.

Oswy looked up at her in surprise.

Celyn nodded. "As to that, she has helped many among my kin. Her skills are well known among us."

Relief flooded the priest's face. "I would be glad of any assistance, to be sure."

Nona nodded. "Of course. I will get my herbs." She dropped in a hasty curtsy in front of the king and turned to Celyn. "Father Colm and I could use your assistance, cousin, and your friend as well, if you so wish," she added, glancing at him.

Thomas nodded. Perhaps he would get a chance to speak with her if he went. She nodded back and hurried off.

Thomas' eyes followed her as she left, his heart filling with a strange hope—hope mingled with fear. Godric had told him one of the Gifts of the Fey was Healing.

Perhaps Aldred had some hope of surviving the wound after all.

19

"I must go tell the king how Aldred fares," Celyn said, the gusting wind making his cloak flap against his legs. He looked up at the sky, which was filled with rapidly approaching dark clouds. "Looks like rain. Go back to my house, and I will meet you there later."

Thomas hesitated for a moment as Celyn strode off, leaving him alone. He had no good reason to stay behind with Nona and Father Colm to watch over Aldred, so he had followed Celyn outside. And he could not think of any excuse to go back. His hopes of speaking with the girl alone had evaporated once he realized the priest would stay with her as they cared for the wounded man.

I'll find another time to talk to her. The wind gusted again, but he welcomed the salty air that blew the stink of blood, and worse, out of his nostrils. He took a deep breath, trying to settle his stomach.

It had been quickly apparent why Nona wanted their help. She cauterized the wound with a hot iron as the rest of them held Aldred down. He would not soon forget the man's screams, the stink of the hot iron, and the sizzling sound.

He clenched his jaw and turned away from the buildings, heading towards the edge of the rocky outcrop, hoping that a walk would clear his head.

As welcome as the wind was, it was cold, and he pulled his cloak around him more tightly as he reached the edge. Below him the ground fell away in grassy humps to a long sandy beach, agitated waves breaking hard against it. The sea was a steel grey that mirrored the clouds that filled the sky. Thomas gazed at the endless expanse of water that melted into the horizon; he could hardly tell where the ocean ended and the sky began. It was like standing on the edge of the world. He felt a knot within him unravelling at the immensity of it, a loosening of some of the shackles of fear and anxiety that held him in their grasp since he had crossed through time and space.

To his left, curling out from the shore in the distance, was Lindisfarne, the tidal island where Celyn intended to deposit him among the monks. The euphoria faded away at the thought. He could not fathom how he would manage there, cooped up with a bunch of chanting monks.

As much as he didn't want to be thrust into the monastery, as much as he would rather be just about anywhere else, his options were limited. Where else would he go? He could hardly refuse the option to be healed of his supposed memory loss. At least at the monastery they were used to taking in strangers and those who had nowhere else to go; and physically, he should be somewhat safe, there. Or as safe as anyone could be in this crude century.

And Godric said he would find him there.

But maybe Nona could tell him how to get home, or introduce him to another Fey Traveller besides Godric. The thought brought a sudden spurt of hope.

A narrow stretch of sand edged the water where the waves pounded below. Looking at it, he was suddenly seized with the desire to get down there and explore.

He found a faint path and started down. Rocks and boulders jutted out from the steep slope, and he had to be careful as he descended. At the bottom he paused, looking around, and began to walk along the sand, just out of the reach of the booming surf.

The beach was empty of life except for the wild antics of the seagulls as they pitched and swooped against the gusting wind. He walked for about ten minutes when a sound reached him above the pounding of the waves. His head snapped up, ears straining, and he heard it again: a high, thin scream.

He whirled around towards the direction of the scream and began to jog back, scanning the landscape for the source of the voice.

A flicker of movement caught his eye, and he stopped momentarily, squinting against the rain that had started to fall. His hair blew in his eyes, and he impatiently pushed it aside and saw the movement again.

A little girl was plastered against the outcrop below the fortress, about two yards above the beach. Her cloak was the same greenish colour of the bracken that grew among the large tumbled stones. Her long blonde hair, whipping this way and that in the wind, was what had caught his attention.

Where the girl huddled, the outcrop jutted out sharply towards the sea. The incoming tide churned below her, the sand already covered by its relentless progress. She bent over and tugged at her leg, and the problem became clear. She must be stuck. And just above her was the tide line. If she couldn't get free, she would drown.

She can climb up and down them cliffs; bring the king his eggs every day. She's half bird herself, that one. Dunn's words came back to him, and the pieces clicked into place. Obviously the *coerl* wanted to waste no time in proving to the king his family's worthiness, even though it meant sending his daughter out into a storm.

Thomas began to run as he saw the waves crashing closer to the girl. *How long before the tide comes in?*

Her head turned towards him and she saw him. He was close enough now to see her delicate features, her face pale and frightened.

"I'm coming!" Thomas yelled as he stopped. The waves at the bottom prevented him getting to her from directly below. He would have to go back up the path and cut across to her. He turned and sprinted back to where he had come down to the beach.

He clambered up the slope and stopped directly opposite her, a cold hand of fear gripping him as he studied the ground between them. It was going to be tricky, with the waves surging higher, and other rocks poking out here and there, slick with water from the spray. He could easily fall, or worse, get his own foot caught.

He quickly undid the brooch that kept his cloak shut at his neck, placing it carefully beside him on the path, securing it from the wind with a large rock. The last thing he needed was to be pulled off balance by the wind tugging at his cloak as it blew.

After a couple of hesitant steps he grew more confident. The borrowed shoes he wore, whose soles consisted of a few extra layers of leather stitched on the bottom, proved surprisingly helpful in the task. Not having a hard rubber sole meant that he could flex his toes and grip the uneven surface, and it was easier to feel that surface underneath than it would have been if he had been wearing his sneakers.

But it wasn't easy. Thomas was breathing hard when he reached the girl, who was clinging to a large rock that thrust out beside her, her blue eyes wide as they met his.

"Help me, good master!" The girl's voice was thin with fear. Her foot was wedged into a small crevasse that opened up beside the rock. She pulled frantically at her foot, but it did no good.

"Don't worry," Thomas said, edging a bit closer, gripping the slippery rocks that jutted out from the hillside beside him. The girl might have passed this way easily, but it was tricky with his larger feet.

A few more steps and he reached her. He crouched awkwardly beside her, swiping the stinging salt water from his eyes, along with the rain, which came down heavily. They were both getting soaked. He cautiously grasped the girl's leg, feeling along it until his questing fingers found her foot. He could feel her shivering as the wind brought another wallop of rain and spray against them.

"C'mon, c'mon—" Thomas' mutter accompanied the girl's small whimpering breaths as he probed with his fingers along her ankle, tugging experimentally. A smoky, wet woollen smell permeated her clothes, filling his nostrils. Suddenly he managed to turn her foot slightly in its prison, and she was free.

A sharp cry burst out of the girl as she put her full weight on it.

"Can you walk?" He would carry her if he must, but it would be tricky with the wind and those wet rocks…

The girl placed her foot down, trying it again. She bit her lip, obviously in pain, but nodded.

Thomas let out a breath. "We must hurry. Hang on to me if you need to!" The girl nodded, and then Thomas turned away and began the tricky navigation back the way he had come.

Thomas' feet were freezing and going numb, making it harder to find a sure path, but they made it to the wider path that led upwards, where he turned and helped the girl over the last part. She stumbled a bit and Thomas stooped down, catching her in his arms.

"It's all right. We're safe now," he said, feeling her shiver.

She pulled back and looked at him. Thomas was struck again by her blue eyes, which caught his in a wide-eyed gaze. She lifted a small hand and placed it on his cheek. "Why are you sparkly?" she asked solemnly.

Thomas frowned, wondering what she meant.

"Hey!"

Thomas looked up. The stocky silhouette of the *coerl* Dunn was outlined against the grey sky as he looked down at them. "Gerrout of there, you fool! The tide's comin' in!"

No kidding, genius. Thomas released the girl, who scrambled awkwardly up the path, hampered by a slight limp. Thomas stooped down to pick up his cloak and followed. The wind felt doubled in strength at the top; a wild gusty force that seemed determined to knock them back over the edge.

Dunn shot Thomas a vicious look, then grabbed the girl's arm in a harsh grip, leaning down to put his face close to hers.

"I tol' you to get back sharpish, like. Just a lil' look-see, I tol' you. Yer ma's that worrit —" The words were accompanied by a sharp shake that twisted the girl's arm, causing her to cry out.

Anger flared and Thomas stepped forward, fists clenched. "Hey, that's enough!"

Dunn straightened up, his beetle brow drawn down in a scowl. "Stay away from my girl, ya filthy *waelisc*," he growled, his finger poking in Thomas' chest. "Or I'll speak to the king, I will!"

He whirled around and stomped off towards the hall, his head down against the wind. His hand still firmly clamped his daughter's arm, and he dragged her along behind him, her small feet skipping and tripping as she tried to keep up. She turned once and looked back at him. Her eyes met Thomas' briefly and then she stumbled after her father, disappearing around the corner of the king's fortress.

"You're welcome!" Thomas yelled after him, disgusted, and then shivered. He was completely soaked through. He threw his sodden cloak around his shoulders and hurried back towards the warmth and security of Celyn's house.

20

A **warm glow** of firelight leaked around the edges of the shuttered window of Celyn's small dwelling. He opened the door, expecting to see the Welshman, and froze in surprise as Nona rose to meet him instead. She was alone.

"We are long parted," she said.

The words didn't register for a moment, distracted as he was by the Fey-sense, the tingling shock that danced along his nerves. But as a slight frown appeared on her face, he realized she was waiting for a reply. *Parted?* Godric's face flashed through his mind. The harper had said the same thing.

A cold gust of wind brought a splat of rain against his back and reminded him that the door still stood open behind him. He took a step in and shut it, closing out the tumult of the wind and rain. "I don't know what you mean."

Nona's eyes widened as she looked him up and down. "God in heaven above," she breathed, shock flashing across her face. "A wilding."

Again, he recalled Godric using that word, but he had been distracted by other questions and had not pursued it. Judging from Nona's reaction, maybe he should have.

She took a breath, visibly collecting herself, a cool distance in her eyes that wasn't there before. "You are soaking wet. Don't you have the sense to come in out of the rain?"

Thomas flushed, but ignored her question. "What do you mean, a *wilding?*"

Nona opened her mouth to reply, but then shut it, looking him over again, wariness in her eyes.

Great. Obviously nothing good. Thomas took his cloak off and ran his fingers through his hair to try to bring it into some kind of order, taking a deep breath to collect his thoughts. "Look, I know what we are. But I don't know much else. So anything you can tell me would be helpful."

Nona lifted a black eyebrow at that, and he was suddenly reminded of Celyn. "Indeed," she said. She let out a breath, collecting herself. "Get yourself dry. I will wait outside while you change. But hurry. We have much to discuss, and not much time. Celyn will be back soon."

She grabbed her cloak and stepped outside, and Thomas hurriedly changed his soaked clothing. Moments later they were sitting across the hearth fire from each other. He held out his hands to the welcome warmth, trying to calm his fluttering stomach. Now that the time had come, he was not entirely sure he wanted to hear what she would say.

"I have never instructed a wilding before," Nona began, "although my father did, once. He told me it was a most difficult task. But I shall do my best, for all our sakes."

The superior tone of her voice grated on Thomas' nerves. Irritation replaced his anxiety. "So start by telling me what a *wilding* is. And what do you mean, that we have been parted, or whatever you said. I've never seen you before."

"'Tis the Greeting between one Fey and another. One says, *we are long parted,* and the other replies, *but never far apart.* And as for a wilding, that is what you are. A Fey who has been through the Quickening without any teaching." She made an impatient gesture at his blank look. "The Quickening is the time of maturity for a Fey, the time when our Gifts are made evident. It happens between the ages of eighteen and twenty years, usually accompanied by sickness."

Thomas remembered the low-grade fever and aches he had suffered over the past few months. He had put it down to grief. "I see."

"You are a Traveller, that much I can surmise from your story and from the look of you. You do not fit here, as much as you try." She let out a breath. "And evidently Celyn stumbled across you." Her lips thinned. She did not look too happy at the thought.

Irritation flared again. *I'm not that happy about it myself.* He opened his mouth to speak, but she held up a hand, stopping him.

"This will be easier if you tell me what has happened, how you came to be here. But be as brief as you can. Celyn is sure to come soon."

Brief. Right. "About two weeks ago I was walking along minding my own business when—" He stopped. He couldn't speak of the demons. Besides the creepy feeling the memory brought him, he suspected Nona may not be as understanding as Godric. He took a breath. "I don't know exactly what happened. I woke up here. Celyn found me. I tagged along with him, I mean, what choice did I have? We were just about killed by some Saxon warriors, and then we went to a village where I met another one like us. A Fey, I mean. Godric. He's a Traveller too. He filled me in on some things, but we didn't have much time together because I had to leave with Celyn. I told Godric I would sneak away from Celyn and come back. But your cousin found me before I could get back to Godric, and I had to come here with him." He shrugged. "So here I am."

He sat back, his arms folded over his chest. Nona had listened carefully, her dark brows knitting in concentration at first, but as he spoke they raised higher on her forehead, leaving her goggling at him as he finished.

"Saxon warriors," she said faintly. She blinked once and shook her head slightly, regaining her composure. "Never mind that. We will speak of it later." She took a deep breath. "So, the other Traveller, this Godric, told you that you are Fey."

He nodded.

"What did he tell you, exactly?"

"That we are the descendants of the Nephilim. That we carry the blood of demons, and share some of their powers." A chill washed over him. Speaking it out loud gave it finality, made it real.

She arched an eyebrow again. "Is that all he told you?"

"Isn't that enough?"

"No. That is only the beginning of the story of the Fey. There is much more."

He grimaced. "More than enough for me. I just want to get home and get my life back. I don't plan to ever Travel anywhere again."

"It's not that easy. Think you, you are Fey, whether you like it or not. You will be noticed. And you are fortunate that you know the truth. Most wilding Travellers who Cross untaught are soon dead, or wish they were, or so it is told. You should thank God for His mercy."

"*Thank* God?" He snorted. "God and I aren't exactly on speaking terms right now."

Anger flashed in Nona's eyes. "Then you will be Unseelie, or worse, before the year is up. They will not hesitate to use your ignorance."

Worse? The two Courts, Seelie and Unseelie, dark and light…those stories were true? He felt he was lost in a maze, with no way out. And the further in he went the less chance he had of escaping. He shook his head. "I have no idea what you are talking about. And it doesn't matter anyway. I just want to go home."

Nona stood, her fists clenched. "Don't be foolish! The Unseelies are there, too. They will find you, and through your ignorance use you to wreak such harm that you will wish you were dead, but they will deny you that solace. You will become their creature, their pet, their tool, and thank them for it. Now that you know the truth, you cannot go back to what you were. That is not a choice you have. You must understand who we are, who *you* are, to have any chance at all to resist them."

He wanted to deny it, but she was right. There was no going back to what he was before this strange adventure began. *You will become their creature.* An echo of the compulsion to obey that had accompanied the demon's touch rippled through him, and he suppressed a shudder with effort.

"Fine. So tell me then."

Nona sat down again, composing herself. "'Tis true that the first Fey, the Nephilim, were cunning creatures of demon-power, wreaking havoc on the earth. The state of the world before the Flood was largely their making. God's anger burned, and the earth drowned." The rain pattering outside complimented her words. "But the Nephilim were not all destroyed. One seduced a wife of one of Noah's sons. She was with child by him, secretly, before they got on the Ark. She bore a son, and through him the demons planned to continue their plan of subjugating the humans to their rule. But hidden this time. They planned, and bred, and whispered, and plotted. Their numbers grew, slowly, because we are not a fertile race. All the while they encouraged the humans to set themselves against God. But not all of the Nephilim agreed with this. There were some who regretted how we had been used by the evil forces against the humans, against God. There began to be a division amongst us."

A shadow crossed Nona's face. She stood and began to pace back and forth as she told the rest of the tale, as though the events described propelled her into motion. Her hands clasped at her waist, her fingers entwining. "A great leader arose at that time, he who is called Nimrod. He was a Fey of great power, who longed for the former glory of the Nephilim. He became a king of men, and beguiled them, leading them away from the fear of God. It was through him that the idea came that the humans should build a huge Tower, the likes of which the world had never seen. Nimrod planned that all should worship him there. The Scriptures say that the Lord would not allow this and so scattered the people and confounded their speech, so that they could not understand one another."

The fire burned low now, murmuring beneath her words as a muted accompaniment. Thomas felt chilled despite its warmth.

"There was a terrible war between Nimrod and his followers and the children of men. Nimrod gathered with him the Nephilim with all their powers and the humans they had persuaded to their cause. But some of the Nephilim fought on the side of the humans, to aid them against their dark brethren. Many died, human and Fey alike. In the end, the humans won, with the help of Nephilim. The Nephilim were left divided between those who wished to aid the humans and those who sought the supremacy of the Fey. Nimrod's son became the leader of the Unseelie Court. They are tricksters and schemers, always taking risks, always chafing against the humans. The Seelie Court is made up of the descendants of those who aided the humans. We live in harmony with the humans as best we can."

Nona sat down again. "This is but a short version of the story. But it should suffice for now."

"So why are we called the Fey? Where did that name come from?"

"After the battle, the Nephilim went into hiding. The very word, Nephilim, faded away, only to be used in tales of a time long ago. Our numbers were few, but we began to craft a way to survive. We developed a Rule, which tells us how to live circumspectly among the humans. And we gave ourselves a new name: Fey. It means "one who is about to die," for we are fated to fade away from the earth. It is as God wills. But in the meantime, we hide. There is in every human a dim memory of us, and of the havoc we wreaked upon them. They hate us and will not rest until we are wiped out."

Thomas struggled to understand. "I don't get it. My parents were normal. How come I'm—"

The door opened, and Celyn stepped in. He frowned slightly, looking at them both. "I have been looking for you, cousin. Bronwyn sent me to fetch you. Aldred needs you."

"Of course." Nona rose and put her cloak on. She looked back at Thomas and inclined her head. "Good eve, Master Thomas."

Thomas stood and nodded back at her. Celyn held the door open for Nona, giving Thomas a sharp look before he followed his cousin outside.

Thomas sat down, his thoughts whirling as he stared into the fire. The flames murmured and licked at the wood, their destructive fervour a fitting counterpoint to his tumultuous thoughts.

21

Celyn left early the next morning, instructing Thomas to stay put, which suited him fine. The weather was still foul, matching his mood. But being alone was not ideal. The story of the Nephilim and his place in it—that he was one of them, one of the Fey—it all jumbled together in his mind as he paced back and forth in Celyn's small house.

By midmorning he was ready to face both the rain and other people. Both were preferable to being stuck by himself with only his disorderly thoughts for company. And besides, if he went to the hall, he might find Nona.

He lifted his cloak from the hook at the same time a knock sounded on the door.

"My Lord Celyn, are you there?" It was a child's voice, high and thin. He opened the door and saw a young boy, whose eyes widened as he looked at Thomas.

"He's not here. What is it?"

"The Lady Nona, she sent me to fetch her cousin, but the fence is down and everyone gone to chase the cattle, and I can't find 'im anywhere, but she's sent me for 'im and will be terrible angered if I don't bring 'im she said."

Thomas sorted through the jumble of words as he swung his cloak around his shoulders and fastened it. "I'll go see what the Lady needs. She is with the Lord Aldred still?"

The boy nodded, looking worried, and Thomas crouched down to look him eye to eye. "Don't worry. I'll explain to the Lady that you could not find her cousin. She will understand. And I will help her with whatever she needs."

Relief flooded the boy's face. "Thank you, good master," he said, bobbing his head, and then he scampered off without a backward glance.

"Master Thomas! But where is Celyn?" Nona rose at his entrance, standing beside the bed where Aldred lay sleeping. Some of her hair had escaped from her head covering and lay in black ringlets on her cheek. She looked tired.

"They are all out chasing cows or something. A fence broke."

Nona glanced at her maidservant, who had followed Thomas into the king's bedchamber. "Master Thomas will aid me with the Lord Aldred. Add the comfrey now to the poultice, and then it must cool. I will call when we are ready."

Casting a quick glance at Thomas from under lowered lashes, Bronwyn nodded at her mistress and went back into the other room, where the poultice had been heating over the hearth fire, sending the scent of honey and herbs to the smoky interior of the king's dwelling.

"How is he?" Thomas said, into the awkward silence that had fallen between them. There were so many questions circling in his mind, but now that he was face-to-face with her, his tongue was tied.

She grimaced, looking down at Aldred who lay unconscious, his face flushed. "He has a fever, but that is to be expected. By God's grace, he will recover." She touched Aldred's forehead, her face troubled despite her confident words.

"You healed him yesterday, didn't you?" He spoke softly so as not to be overheard by Bronwyn in the next room. Something had happened while they bowed their heads together in prayer after the cauterization and dressing the wound. He had felt something odd, a strange flutter of his senses, and had opened his eyes to see Nona with her hand on Aldred's bandage, unnoticed by the others whose eyes remained closed in prayer.

"Yes, of course. It is my Gift." Nona's voice matched his as she answered, and then she added, speaking more loudly, "Come, help me move him so that I may undo the bandage."

Thomas glanced back at the open door, then back at Nona, and nodded, understanding. *Not the time to speak of it now.* He stepped closer, gently rolling Aldred onto his side and then back again as Nona began to unwind the cloth around his torso that kept the bandage in place.

As he leaned over the wounded man, he caught a scent of lavender, wafting from Nona's hair as her head bent close to his. His cheeks flushed, and he clenched his jaw, trying to ignore the Fey-sense that caused his heartbeat to pick up a pace. Not just the Fey-sense, if he was honest. She was beautiful, with an untamed spark in her clear green eyes that brought to mind a falcon riding a thermal high above the prairie.

And just as unattainable, he thought. *Focus.* He looked down at Aldred, forcing his mind back to their conversation. He couldn't waste his time mooning over her. "Shouldn't he be better, if you healed him?" He pitched his voice low once more.

Nona glanced at him, her black brows drawing down in a slight frown. "My Gift will aid in the healing, no more. If the wound or illness is too severe, I cannot do more than ease their suffering. I cannot overcome God's will."

She looked back down at Aldred, unwrapping the cloth that held the bandage in place in quick, efficient movements, but Thomas could see the tension in her as she worked. If she failed and Aldred died, it would not reflect well on her, and by extension, on Celyn.

He clenched his jaw, biting back words of advice. The worry of changing events he shouldn't change squelched his desire to help. But if Aldred died, and he hadn't said anything, could he live with that? *It wasn't my choice to come here. Anything I do, or don't do for that matter, could change the future. And maybe saving this guy is the reason I'm here.* He spoke before he changed his mind again. "Have you changed his bandage?"

Nona glanced at him. "Nay, not yet. There is no need. It will do for some time."

He shook his head. "Change it, every time you put a new poultice on. Keep the wound clean as you can." Her brows drew down in a frown, but he spoke again before she could object. "Listen. You'll have to trust me on this. It will make a difference for him, for anyone you treat with any kind of wound. Wash it out as best you can. Use water that has been boiled. Keep the wound clean, and change the bindings a lot."

She eyed him skeptically for a moment, then shook her head slightly. "We are told to heed the Travellers, and so I will think on what you say."

It was as much a concession that he could expect, and better than nothing.

They worked in silence a moment longer, and then Nona glanced at him. "How do you fare?"

The unexpected question disarmed him, and he answered before he could think about it. "I don't know. Confused, mainly."

"Of course," she said. Sympathy tinged her words. "Celyn says he hopes to leave for the monastery tomorrow if this weather clears."

"Yes." The word didn't come out as confidently as he hoped.

Nona gave him a sharp look. "It troubles you? Why? Surely even in your time the monks offer sanctuary to those in need?"

"I don't know. Probably." He sighed. "I've told everyone that I have lost my memory, because I fell down a hill and hit a rock. Which is true, but not the lost memory part. But that story won't hold for long. And I know nothing about this place, this time—" He broke off, fear closing his throat, and he shook his head, thinking of all that could go wrong.

"I have heard that Bishop Aidan is a compassionate man, and wise. They will treat you kindly, never fear. Things will get better as time passes; the longer you are here, the more you will become accustomed to our ways."

Her sympathy only made his anger flare. "I've already been here long enough! I have to figure out how to get home, not get cozy with a bunch of monks. I don't want to stay long." He raked his hand through his hair. "Do you know of any other Travellers who are close by who could help me?"

Aldred moaned, restless in his fever dreams. Nona looked down at him, laying a hand on his forehead, and then looked back up at Thomas, a slight frown on her face. "I've heard tales…" she said, thinking, and then shook her head. "I am not sure. I will see what I can find out. But you are right. You need to find someone who can teach you about the ways of the Fey."

"Can't you?"

"It is too difficult for us to be alone. And I have little knowledge of the Travellers." She hesitated a moment, then opened her mouth to continue, but was prevented by Bronwyn, who poked her head in the door.

"I am sorry, my lady, but the poultice, it does not smell right, not like the last time."

"I will join you in a moment," Nona said, and Bronwyn nodded and withdrew.

Nona looked back at Thomas helplessly. "There is not enough time now to speak on this." She let out a breath. "There is only one way. You must see the King of the Northern Seelie Fey."

Thomas drew back. "King?"

"You are in great danger because of all that you do not know. Indeed, it is only by God's grace that you have survived thus far. Your tale of the other Traveller you met worries me not a little. He will be telling other Fey of you, and if I am right, the Fey he will be telling are Unseelies. And they will come looking for you. The Seelie King will help you, protect you. He will find you a Teacher, one who knows how you can get home."

The Seelie King? No thanks. He shook his head. "Godric is probably on his way. He said he would meet me at the monastery if I didn't meet him. I'll be careful, don't worry."

Nona's eyes flashed. "You should not go with him. He is dangerous. You cannot trust him."

The truth was, he didn't trust Godric, with his Gift of Speaking and his sardonic smile. Not by a long shot. But he wasn't going to admit that to her. "I don't trust anyone here," he retorted. "I don't even know if I can trust you."

A flush rose on Nona's cheeks. "The Seelie King needs to know that you are here, for the good of all the Fey," she said, her voice even. "And you need his help. I can see that, even if you can't. I will send him a message on the morn."

Thomas glared at her for a moment then threw up his hands. "Fine. I can't stop you. If he can help me find another Traveller other than Godric, great. I don't care who gets me home, just as long as I get there!"

She opened her mouth as if to say something but obviously thought better of it, for she shook her head slightly and closed her mouth again, brushing a black curl off her face. "The king is a Pict and lives in the North. Winter has come early there, so it is likely we will not see him for some time. But in the meantime, think you, you must be careful. Do not leave the monastery, except to come here when you must."

"Yes, mother," Thomas muttered, but nodded his head anyway at her sharp look. This girl was getting under his skin, and he wasn't sure why.

"My lady?" Bronwyn called again from the other room.

Nona sighed. "I must go, and you as well. I will likely see you before the morn, but if not, be at peace. God has not abandoned you." She left him then, without a backward glance.

Thomas blew out a breath. Half-remembered stories gave him the impression that the faerie folk on the whole were sneaky, creepy, and not to be trusted. The last thing he wanted was to meet their king, surely the most sneaky and creepy one of the lot.

Yet Nona was Fey, and as much as she irritated him, he didn't get the same vibes from her as he had from Godric. Maybe that was one of the differences between Seelie and Unseelie. Maybe this king wouldn't be so bad. And maybe he knew someone who could help him get home.

Find a sweet spot, and go. Despite Nona's fears, he felt certain that Godric spoke the truth about that. While he waited for Godric, or this king, he could do a little scouting around, see if he could find a Crossing. Once another Traveller showed up, either Godric or anyone else, knowing the location of a nearby Crossing would make his return home all the quicker.

He took another breath. He could do this.

He had to.

22

The next day dawned bright and clear, the rains gone. After an early morning breakfast at the hall, Thomas and Celyn started along the path that led towards the monastery. Lindisfarne sat on a tidal island, which meant the tides released it from its isolation from the mainland twice a day. According to the tides table Father Colm consulted, the way would be clear for a couple of hours before noon.

The rain had cleared, but the sky was overcast and a cold wind blew off the ocean to their right. The beach was long and empty, but they rode along a worn trail through the marram grasses that studded the sandy soil inland of the beach, here and there skirting soggy areas where the ocean waters made a deeper incursion into the mainland.

To their left the land rose in gentle hills to the horizon, their slopes unclear in the morning half-light, dissolving into the grey sky. The wild beauty of the place made the cold stone of fear easier to bear.

After about an hour and a half, they came to the gleaming stretch of sand that connected Lindisfarne to the mainland, marked with tall poles of wood along the way.

Celyn pulled Arawn to a halt and turned to him. "The monks will give you shelter for as long as you need it. Bishop Aidan is wise, well acquainted with Christ. He will be able to help you."

"I doubt he can help me get home." The words slipped out before he could stop them.

"As to that, you may be right, but perhaps that is not the only help you need." Celyn held his gaze a moment longer, then turned and nudged Arawn into motion, scattering the seagulls and other ocean birds that picked at the debris on the glistening sand.

Thomas sucked in a breath and let it out. "Let's go, girl," he said, lifting the reins and kneeing Missy to get going, a sense of inevitability falling over him now that the time was upon him. *God, help me.*

The irony of that particular prayer was not lost to him. A short gallop across the wet sands brought him to where Celyn waited at a gate that interrupted the low wall surrounding the monastery complex. He took another steadying breath. *I suppose if God is anywhere, He is here.*

The Guestmaster, Brother Barach, met them at the gate. His wide, friendly smile and enthusiastic welcome untied one of the knots in Thomas' gut.

They deposited their horses to the care of an affable monk with such a thick Irish accent that Thomas could hardly understand him and dropped off their belongings at the guesthouse.

Beyond the stables and the guesthouse, a low earthen embankment Barach called the *vallum* encircled the monastery proper. The buildings were a far cry from the Gothic stone monuments Thomas had pictured. They were much like the buildings he had seen elsewhere, mainly of wattle and daub but some, like the small church, constructed out of wood. But it was orderly, and a sense of peace permeated the place.

"These are where the monks live?" Thomas asked as they walked by small buildings that were laid out in rows. There were about twenty of them, but Thomas didn't see any of the monks outside. The place seemed deserted, in fact.

"Aye," Brother Barach said. "Two in each. We share a dwelling with another brother, or with one of the students we teach at the school. In this way each has an *anam chara*, as God provides."

The phrase was not Latin or Anglic, and Thomas looked to Celyn for explanation.

"Soul-friend," Celyn said. "*Periglour,* in my tongue. A teacher of the Way of Christ to another, and who receives his confessions."

"All who follow Christ should have someone to share the journey, no?" Barach said, with a smile.

Thomas shrugged, uncomfortable, thinking of David, the pastor at his church and the closest friend he had, and a sudden wave of homesickness rushed over him. "I suppose," he said, thrusting the memory aside with an effort. He couldn't dwell on it now.

They veered towards one of the buildings, and just as they got close, a monk stepped out. He looked to be in his mid-thirties, with a lean, inquisitive face. But any severity in his expression was swept away by his smile as he recognized Celyn.

"My lord! God be praised, you are back!"

"As to that, it is good to be back, Father Gaeth. I see you are recovered, thanks be to God! He has answered my prayers."

"Yes, it seems I am not fit for heaven, yet."

Looking closely at him, Thomas could see the gauntness that emphasized the monk's high cheekbones, and the shadows under his brown eyes. In fact, his whole body looked frail, the bones pressing hard against the skin on his wrists where they were exposed under his tunic.

"As for heaven, I leave that to God," Celyn replied. "But it seems that He has use for you here yet. None could do the job as Prior as well as you."

"That is not true, my lord, and you know it. Away with your flattery then; it is not good for my soul." The monk dismissed Celyn's comments good-naturedly, with a wave of his hand, and looked at Thomas with curiosity.

"This is Master Thomas, whom I met on my travels. He has had some difficulties and has nowhere else to go, for now. He seeks shelter here among you, if the bishop allows."

Compassion filled the monk's face. "Ah. Do not worry, my son. Our bishop will not turn down your request, I am sure of it." He looked back at Celyn. "Will you stay with us awhile, my lord?"

"The night only. I will leave on the morrow."

"Then I shall see you tonight in the dining hall." He looked back at Thomas. "God bless you." He hurried off, putting the hood of his cloak up against the chill in the air.

Barach knocked on the door. "My lord bishop?" he said, opening the door and peering inside. There was an indistinct answer from within, and the Guestmaster looked back at them. "Come."

The gloom inside was only alleviated by the hearth fire and one small window, which did not let in much light. Thomas' first impression of the Bishop of Lindisfarne was of a shadowy slim figure rising from the table that was situated behind the hearth fire.

"Celyn! Praise be to God! *Fáilte ar ais!* Come in, my friend, come in!"

The voice was rich with warmth and good humour, the words liberally laced with an Irish accent that gave them a pleasant sound. As Aidan came around the table, Thomas eyed him curiously.

It was hard to tell his age from his lean, bearded face, although

Thomas guessed he was older than Celyn. The odd tonsure made him look older, with the way his hair was shaved from ear to ear across his skull. His thick black hair was cropped neatly at the back of the neck, but it was curly, with some silver glinting here and there as the firelight caught it. It was a strong face, not classically handsome, but interesting.

He wore a dark coloured tunic, belted at the waist with an intricately embroidered belt. A large silver cross lay against his chest, hanging from a thick silver chain. The cross was in the same Celtic style as the large stone one that stood outside the church, with a ring around the intersection of the stem and arms. And it also was carved with the same swirling patterns that decorated the one outside. A large blue jewel was set into it, winking here and there as the firelight caught it.

Celyn dropped to one knee, and Thomas followed. "Good it is to see you, my lord bishop," Celyn said. "May God bless you and keep you."

"No, *a chara*. Rise, rise." Aidan reached down and pulled Celyn to his feet. "Kneel not to me. I have told ye—this honour is for Christ alone."

"And for you, his bishop," Celyn said, with a hint of stubbornness. "Far be it for me to not acknowledge it."

Aidan turned to Thomas as he rose to his feet. "And who is this that ye have brought me?"

Thomas had prepared some words of greeting, but they died on his tongue as the bishop's eyes met his. They were set deep under his brows, an unusual golden brown. But it was not the colour so much as the intelligence and depth of expression they held that stilled Thomas' words. This was a man who had seen hardship and prevailed; who had known sorrow and joy and whose character had been honed to a keen edge because of it; who both expected men's loyalty and deserved it. All this he saw in Aidan's eyes, and more.

Thomas had never experienced charisma before he met the Bishop of Lindisfarne. The force of it stilled his tongue. He could not say anything even if he tried.

"This is Master Thomas," Celyn answered, "whom I discovered on my travels back to Bebbanburg. He seeks shelter here for he has nowhere else to go."

Aidan's eyebrows rose on his face, and curiosity flared in his eyes as his gaze skimmed over Thomas, lingering for a moment on Thomas' cross before meeting his eyes once more. "I am eager to hear the story, so I am. But be assured that any brother in Christ is welcome here, on God's island."

Thomas found his voice at last. "Thank you, my lord bishop."

Aidan cocked his head slightly—in reaction to Thomas' accent, Thomas presumed. He looked Thomas over again, more carefully this time, obviously puzzled. "Have we met before? There is something familiar about ye."

Thomas shook his head, opening his mouth to deny it, when a sudden thought froze him. He was a Traveller, after all. Could he, at some time in his own future, travel back to Aidan's past and meet him there? Meaning this could be Aidan's second time he had met Thomas, without Thomas having any knowledge of it now? It was a possibility he had not considered before, and the unpleasant speculations it brought to mind tangled his thoughts up in a knot. But Aidan was waiting for a reply, and so he forced his thoughts from those disturbing speculations. "I don't think so. But I am not sure—" He snapped his mouth shut before he could say more.

"Thomas has suffered a blow to his head and his memory is faulty," Celyn said, coming to his rescue. "'Tis one of the reasons I brought him here, that God could heal him."

Sympathy and understanding flooded Aidan's face. "Ah. Sorry I am to hear it. Brother Eadric has great skill in healing. With God's grace, he will be able to help ye. I will think on it further, so I will. Perhaps if I can remember if we have met, it might help ye as well."

"Thank you, my lord," Thomas said, trying to pull himself together, hoping that the bishop was mistaken. How on earth could he explain it?

"Brother Barach, you must take our guest to the kitchen. I am sure he is hungry. And ask the novice, Chad, to bring Celyn something to eat as well, for I have matters to discuss with him here."

The monk nodded. "Yes, my lord bishop."

Aidan turned back to Thomas. "Go with God, Master Thomas. I look forward to hearing more of your tale, so I do."

Thomas nodded, glad for a reprieve. But as he followed Barach outside, he had a sneaking feeling that no matter how much he prepared for another meeting with the Bishop of Lindisfarne, it would not go as smoothly as he would like.

Seagulls wheeled far overhead, and a sudden longing filled him to be able to lift up on wings and fly away with them from this impossible situation.

23

A week after his arrival, Thomas stood on the north end of the island, where the land reached out into the sea in a couple of narrow points. Jagged cliffs fell away from where he stood, down to the churning water below. There the waves battered against the rocks, smashing against them in a wild surging rush of foam, the sound of them thunder in his ears.

Lauds, the morning prayer service, had just ended, and he was alone. He squinted against the bright dawning of the day, grateful for a respite from the rain that had fallen every day since his arrival. Although it didn't look as if the fine weather would last, if the clouds scudding in over the ocean were any indication.

Thomas took a deep breath of the salty air, knots of tension easing within him as he gazed at the vast expanse of water and sky, the wind whipping at his hair and cloak.

Bless the Lord, O my soul, and forget not all His benefits. The monks' voices, blending together in harmony as they chanted the psalm, echoed through his mind. The rigorous schedule of services the monks held to every day was too much for him, so he didn't go to every one, but he particularly liked Lauds. Being in the church among the flickering candles and chanting monks as the sun rose over the horizon gave him a thrill of joy every time, a sense that all would be well.

The solemn formality of the services was far different from the easygoing church services he used to attend, before his mother got sick and his faith began to waver. But he was growing to appreciate the reverence of the monks' worship, and the way the words of the recited Scripture and formal prayers gave words to the longings and fears that he was unable to articulate himself.

In fact, to his surprise, life at the monastery was growing on him. Steady rhythms grounded his days, rhythms of sea and tide, toil and prayer. The rugged beauty of the place suited him, the temperamental wind and crashing waves a mirror to his roiled emotions.

And so, when he wasn't in the infirmary enduring the ministrations of Brother Eadric, or attending services, or assisting the monks in one task or another, he walked the coastline, finding the constant susurration of the waves a soothing backdrop to the questions that tormented him.

Questions he still didn't have answers to, such as why he was there and how he could get home. A little bit of exploring brought no luck in discovering another Crossing either at Lindisfarne or in the surrounding area. But he hadn't gone too far away, afraid of getting lost.

He pushed the hair out of his face and took a deep breath, letting it out in a sigh. He turned to head back to the monastery and saw Aidan, picking his way towards him. Anxiety pierced him. *Great.*

It had been quite easy to avoid Aidan; the man was busy, after all. Thomas had hoped that he would be forgotten in the daily rounds of the bishop's work. Apparently not.

Christ have mercy.

The words of the *Kyrie* ran through his mind as Aidan stopped beside him, his hand lifted in greeting. "Good morn, my son, and God's blessing be upon ye. Ye be finding your way around, I see. The brethren tell me ye often walk these shores."

Thomas quickly learned that the monastery was a hotbed of gossip and speculation, no matter that Aidan tried to discourage idle chatter. He shrugged. "It helps me to think."

"Yes," Aidan agreed. "I often find it so as well. God's Creation has a way of speaking which goes much deeper than words." He admired the view for a moment, and then turned to Thomas. "Brother Eadric tells me that your memory is still lost in the mists."

He flushed. Eadric was kind and well-meaning. His dedicated attempts to help him retrieve his memories filled Thomas with guilt. "Yes."

"Well, perhaps it be for the best, for now. It could be that God is shielding ye from that which could harm ye."

"I suppose," Thomas said, looking back out over the ocean to escape Aidan's penetrating gaze. He could see the black head of a seal, bobbing in the waves, and then another one. Then they both disappeared smoothly under the surface of the water, gone without a trace.

"It troubles ye," Aidan said.

Thomas glanced at the bishop, and a sudden longing to reveal all washed over him. He swallowed, and let out a breath. "I just don't understand any of this," he said, choosing his words carefully. "Why I am here. How to get home. It's like a nightmare I can't wake up from."

Aidan studied him for a long moment, the wind whipping their cloaks around their ankles. "What do ye know of the *peregrini?*"

The word, an Irish Gaelic one, was unfamiliar to Thomas, even though he was starting to pick up a bit of the language here and there, as it was often spoken among the monks. "Nothing."

"Those who choose the way of the *peregrini* are those who follow where God leads, so they do." The bishop looked to Thomas expectantly, to see if he understood, and Thomas nodded. Aidan tucked his hands in the sleeves of his cloak to keep them warm and continued. "There are three ways for the *peregrine* to show his devotion to God. Three types of martyrdom, of relinquishing yourself to the will of God." He paused, a small smile on his face. "The first be the green martyrdom. We learn the joy of obedience under its easier yoke: setting ourselves apart for God and travelling within familiar boundaries. Stretching our faith and yet comforted by the sights of our home country."

The sun was suddenly covered by the clouds, and Thomas felt a splat of rain against his cheek. Aidan cast a look at the sky. "Come. The rain will be upon us soon enough. We will talk as we walk back."

Thomas turned his back on the sea and fell into pace beside Aidan, whose long strides were brisk. He was almost as tall as Thomas himself, a rarity in this time.

Aidan continued his explanation as they walked. "Secondly, there be the white martyrdom, where the *peregrine* leaves his home to follow God to a foreign place. There he is driven to the only familiarity he knows, and that is the love of God, the fellowship of Christ and all the saints. My brothers and I are on that path. 'Tis a hard one, so it is, but with many joys." He shot a keen look at Thomas. "It seems to me that God has brought ye to us as a *peregrine*, on the path of the white martyrdom, in a land that is not your own."

"But I didn't choose to be here," Thomas said, anger edging his words, the unfairness of it a sharp edge in his heart.

Aidan stopped, and turned to face him, his face solemn. "Celyn has told me how he found ye, of the demons that chased ye, and the fears he has as to where ye be from. It is a mystery, and I am not sure he has the right of it, but until your memory returns, we cannot know for sure."

Shock froze Thomas to the spot. Celyn had not told him this before he left. *Aidan knew?* But he saw no condemnation in Aidan's face, and he let out a breath. "I don't know what happened." At least that was the truth. "Those things chased me, and grabbed me, and then I woke up here."

The rain fell harder, the soft pattering muting the cries of a seagull that flapped by overhead. Aidan put a hand on Thomas' shoulder. "Do not fear, my son. There is an answer to this mystery, and we will find it. It is not your choice, but God's, that brings ye here. Your task is obedience. Your past is lost in shadows, and the future uncertain. Ye must seek Him now, where He can be found." He squeezed Thomas' shoulder. "God will reveal His purpose to ye when the time is right, so He will. Until then, ye must seek Him in prayer, look for the truth to be revealed."

Aidan held his gaze for a moment, and then he turned and continued on his way again, the falling rain obscuring his figure until he disappeared.

Thomas watched him go, waiting for his heartbeat to return to normal. At least Aidan wasn't going to throw him out. *Yet.* He shook his head, dismissing the thought.

Your past is lost in shadows. That was true enough, but not in the same way that Aidan meant. It wasn't lost in the shadows of memory, but of time and space, a vast shadow that blocked the way from here to there.

It was not your choice, but God's. The bishop was right. He couldn't do anything about his circumstances, not yet anyway. But he did have a choice to trust God, or not.

He thought of his mother, her face gaunt on the pillow, her eyes bright with drugs and fever. *I'm not worried about you.* Her voice a mere whisper, the cancer taking all her strength. *You have your religion thing. It will be a comfort to you. Don't lose it because of me.*

But he almost had. His mother's death had shaken his faith, badly. And this bizarre adventure was straining his already thin trust almost to the breaking point.

Another seagull cried over his head, and he looked up, tracking its flight as it dipped up and down, fighting to stay on course as it flew headfirst into the wind towards the sea, until finally its outline melded into the grey of the clouds and it disappeared.

A grimace twisted his mouth. *Okay, God, I get it. I'm flying into the wind, struggling to stay aloft. Help me. Show me the way.* But he wondered just how much further he could get blown off course before he found his way home.

L.A. Smith

24

BEBBANBURG
  DECEMBER 20, AD 642

"Thomas! God be praised!"

Thomas turned from his task of unsaddling Missy, relief washing over him as he saw Celyn entering the stable.

Thomas grinned, glad to see the Welshman. Oswy and his war band had recently returned from a skirmish against a neighbouring kingdom, but the monks had not heard yet the details of who might have fallen against the Alt Clut. Thankfully, Celyn looked unharmed. "We heard Oswy had returned. I'm glad you did, too."

A shadow passed over Celyn's face. "Aye. But Domnall Brecc of Dál Riata is dead."

The monks had taken a dim view of the king of the Alt Clut's winter campaign to strike at Oswy, but they were equally certain that Oswy himself had been partly to blame. And for it all to end in the death of the king of Dál Riata, Oswy's ally who had ridden out with him, had made their disapproval even sharper.

It was all to do with the local kings and boundary disputes, and feuds that had gone on for centuries, in some cases. It was hard for Thomas to sort it all out, especially as he was wary of asking too many questions and looking more ignorant than he should be.

He understood the times better now, but he still didn't grasp all of the subtle details of the ties of kin and clan that bound the people to one another, nor all of the obligations and societal expectations that everyone else took for granted.

One thing was very clear, though. There was an undercurrent of uncertainty at the monastery towards Oswy, which stemmed, in the main, from Aidan. A wary reserve coloured Aidan's voice when he spoke of the new king, a lack of wholehearted approval that was subtle, but definitely there.

"Yes, we heard." He hesitated, unsure of how much to say. "Aidan was troubled by the news." *Angry* might be a better word.

"Indeed. Oswy has lost his foster-brother and a solid ally. Dál Riata will still back him, all the same. Domnall's co-ruler Ferchar will not easily cast aside Bernicia." Celyn shrugged, dismissing the subject, and looked him up and down. "You are well? What brings you here?"

Good question. It was hard to explain the restlessness that seized him, and he could not very well tell Celyn of his need to see Nona and to talk with her about the Fey.

"I needed a break," he said finally. Which was true, in a way. The intensity of the monks' devotion and the discipline of their lives became overwhelming at times, the vigour of it both attractive and daunting.

"Master Thomas! You be back!" Gadd, the stable master's son, stepped in, a smile wreathing his face as he approached. He patted Missy's neck. "I thought I recognized this 'un. Leave her to me, good master."

Thomas nodded. "Thank you." He turned to Celyn. "Your cousin asked Brother Eadric to send her some healing herbs that she needed. I have brought them with me. Is she around?"

Celyn's eyebrow rose. "Ah. She mentioned something about that. Come. I think I know where to find her."

Thomas picked up his leather bag and followed Celyn out of the door of the stable, squinting as the light from the winter sun, fully risen now, met his eyes. His breath steamed out as vapour in the cold air. Ahead the smoke rose steadily from Oswy's hall, but Celyn did not head that way. He glanced at the bag slung over Thomas' shoulder. "You are staying overnight?" he asked.

"I hope to stay a few days. Over Christmas, if I can." The thought brought a pang, the melancholy he tried to keep at bay threatening to surface. Christmas was only a few days away, and he was still here, stuck in this time. Despite careful searching, Thomas had not found a Crossing spot on or near Lindisfarne. And there had been no sign of Godric.

He wanted to look around Bebbanburg, see if there was one close by Oswy's fortress. He had half a mind to try the jump back on his own if he found one, regardless of Godric's warning. He had to get back. The thought of what his brother was going through at home, looking for him, rose up in his mind, but he pushed it resolutely away. Those thoughts did him no good.

Celyn smiled and clapped Thomas' shoulder. "Of course. In truth I was thinking of coming to the monastery to see how you fared, but God has brought you to me instead. Come. My lady cousin will be anxious for what you bring, I am sure."

Thomas nodded, his spirits rising at the thought of the Healer, a frisson of the same excitement coursing through him that he felt this morning as the sun rose over the horizon. He decided then to come to Bebbanburg, to find a way to talk to Nona, to get some answers, the decision falling fully formed in his mind before he was barely awake.

Maybe she has found another Traveller, or someone else who can help me. Maybe I can get home before Christmas after all.

They found Nona brewing up a poultice in the cookhouse. As they entered, Thomas threw up an arm to his face against the noxious fumes that emanated from a bubbling mixture in a pot and hastily stepped outside again. "I'll wait out here."

Celyn shot him a sour look and entered the building, shutting the door behind him.

Thomas heard a murmured conversation, and then Celyn's voice, raised in anger, followed by a sharp reply from Nona. A moment later the door flew open and Celyn strode out with a determined stride, a cloth wrapped around his hands as he carried the pot around the corner of the building.

"Celyn! Come back!" Nona flew out of the building, then stopped short at seeing Thomas, her anger replaced by shock. "Thomas!"

Thomas momentarily forgot what he was going to say at the sight of her. The tingle of Fey-sense was part of the reaction she elicited from him, but not all. He forgot how beautiful she was. He swallowed, reining in his scattering thoughts. "We are long parted," he said, his voice low.

Nona let out a breath and pushed a curl that escaped her head covering back into place. "But never far apart." She glanced around. They were alone, but for a woman herding waddling ducks in their direction, who was too far away to hear them. "You heard it, then?"

Thomas frowned. "Heard what?"

"The Call, to the Gathering," Nona said, impatience colouring her voice.

"What do you mean?"

Nona opened her mouth to answer but closed it again as the woman drew nearer. "Come with me to the hall," she said, taking his arm. "We will talk on the way."

Thomas gritted his teeth at the quickening of his pulse at her touch. *Focus.* They passed the woman and once she was out of earshot again, he looked down at Nona. "What Call?"

Nona let out a breath. "Answer me. Why are you here?"

Thomas frowned. "I wanted to come, to see if Celyn was all right, and Eadric said you needed some herbs—" He stopped. That was true, but what about that surging excitement he felt this morning, that still bubbled around the edges of his mind?

Realization slammed home and he stopped dead, shaking her hand off his arm. "You said the Call. That feeling, it's a Fey thing?"

"Keep your voice down," she hissed, then took his arm again, forcing him to keep walking. Thomas swallowed, his stomach twisting into a knot as she continued. "The King of the North has Called a Gathering. It is tonight, at solstice, under the full moon."

Tonight? The excitement and anticipation he felt turned sour. He concentrated on that fizz of expectation; it was like a bright thread snaking through his mind. His stomach flipped in reaction. With gritted teeth he concentrated on that bright thread. *Enough,* he thought fiercely at it, and it disappeared.

"Thomas!" Nona's voice snapped him out of his reverie, and his eyes flew open. He blinked at her in confusion—he hadn't realized he had closed his eyes, nor that he had stopped walking again. He raked his hand through his hair, shaken.

They were in front of a house, and a man who sharpened a knife on a whetstone looked at them with a frown.

Thomas nodded at him. "Good day," he said, forcing a rueful smile on his face. "Too much of the king's ale last night," he said. "I feel it this morning."

The man smiled, the suspicion on his face fading away. "Oh aye, indeed. Too much of that, young fella, and ye be no good to the Lady." He smirked and winked at Thomas.

Thomas felt the flush on his face as he nodded back and hurried along, pulling Nona with him. "I don't want them in my head," he said, once they were out of earshot.

She scowled at him. "Don't be foolish. 'Tis no harm in it. It is from the king's Speaker." She sighed at the look on his face. "We'll speak more inside," she said, gesturing at the hall, and Thomas had no choice but to follow.

They found a pot of *briw*, the Saxon pottage, steaming away on one of the smaller fires that were alongside the walls of Oswy's hall. A stack of wooden bowls was arranged on a table beside the fire. The hall was mainly empty, except for an older man snoring away beside the main hearth fire.

A slave girl brought them some bread as they took their full bowls to an empty table, and Thomas tore a piece off, dipping it into the bowl to scoop out some of the hearty soup. "This Gathering, what's it for?" He pitched his voice low, so that no one could overhear.

"To meet together," she replied with a small shrug. "We meet on the solstices, and at other times when the king sees the need."

The king. Thomas put his bread down, his appetite suddenly gone. "You told him about me."

"I said I would." Nona frowned at his look. "You must meet him. You need his help." She hesitated, then continued. "And perhaps there will be another Traveller there."

Hope flared. "Godric?"

"No, this is a Gathering for the Seelie Fey. Even if he wanted to, he would not be allowed."

"You don't know that."

"I do," she said, scowling. "He is Unseelie, I am sure of it."

Thomas shook his head, unwilling to argue the point. "So why would they let me in? I'm not Seelie."

Nona drew back. "You must not say such a thing!" She collected herself and continued. "The king wants to meet you. There will be no difficulty."

Just then Celyn entered and headed towards them. Nona grimaced and leaned towards Thomas. "Meet me after sundown behind the hall, tonight. Wear your finest clothes."

Thomas could only nod before Celyn joined them, and he finished his meal in silence as the two of them conversed, forcing it down past the twist in his gut.

25

Thomas stood at the cliff's edge behind Oswy's hall, listening to the boom of the surf, the night painted in black and silver around him. He wrapped his cloak more closely around him, to shut out the ever-present ocean breeze. His breath gusted white as he waited. It was cold, and getting colder.

He couldn't help but be affected by the dark beauty of the night: the streak of silver on the water as the moon rose and the pale sands of the beach stretching out towards Lindisfarne, which was lost in the darkness along the curving shore to his left. The shimmering anticipation returned full force, and no matter that he tried to shut it out, it remained, lending a sharp edge to his anxiety over the coming Gathering.

He felt Nona before he saw her, the Fey-sense tingling over him, and he turned, seeing her lithe form step around the corner of the hall. She looked ethereal in the night, rimmed in a faint moonlit glow as she approached. His heart leapt in his chest as he saw her smile in greeting. It was getting harder for him to care that he should not develop feelings for this girl.

He raked his hand through his hair. *God, have mercy. Christ, have mercy.* The *Kyrie* steadied him, and he blew out a breath.

"Thomas," Nona's voice, husky and soft, came to him on the wind. She stopped before him, her fair skin luminous in the moonlight. She seemed a part of the night, belonging to it just as the stars and the moon did. Despite his resolve, his stomach flipped as her eyes met his. "Is it not beautiful?"

A sharp wind blew up the cliff from the sea, snatching the cloak from his fingers, setting it flapping behind him, and a wild exuberance filled him, born of the Call and the nearness of the Fey girl. He grinned. "Yes," he said without thinking, captured by her eyes. "Beautiful."

A slight flush stained her cheeks at his reply. She was betrothed to another, and he would be leaving her forever the first chance he got. But no matter how much he scolded himself a fool, he could not help the quickening in his pulse whenever he was near her.

He forced himself to remember what they were doing, why they were there, and the remembering brought an entirely different flutter to his gut. "So where do we go?"

"As to that, you tell me. You are Fey. Listen to the Call. Listen to the wind."

"I don't..." his voice trailed off as he suddenly realized what she meant, as if her words unlocked the meaning.

She stepped closer to him, her hand lifting to his cheek, her eyes solemn. "There's no need to be afraid. It will not hurt you. All Fey can hear the Call, and know where to go. Just listen." She lowered her hand, waiting.

He couldn't say no, caught as he was in the spell of the night and her intoxicating presence. But even so, he struggled for a moment, battling the memory of the demons and the feel of their hard claws upon him, the sweeping desire that almost took him away. *God, have mercy. Christ, have mercy.*

He pushed aside his anxiety, trying to ignore the voice that told him there was no mercy for him, a descendant of the Nephilim. He steadied himself and then, resigned, turned his attention towards the burgeoning sense of excitement that clamoured within him.

And just like that, he discovered Nona was right. A whisper of a voice threaded through the anticipation he felt. *Come.* He turned towards his right, instinctively seeking out the spot that fell into place along with the word. *There.* He couldn't see it, exactly, but he could feel it, the spot a lodestone in his mind. It was some ways away, in the midst of the crowded trees that were a black silhouette of shadow in the night below them, past the village that huddled against the bulk of outcropped rock upon which Oswy's fortress stood.

He met Nona's inquisitive glance and let out a breath. "Okay. I've got it. Let's get this over with."

26

After about an hour Nona suddenly stopped, laying a hand on Thomas' arm. "Wait."

He looked down at her, startled out of the reverie that had gripped him as they travelled through the moon-painted night. "What?" She dropped her hand from his arm.

"There are things I must tell you. I would not have you unprepared —" She broke off, looking away for a moment, her hands twisting together under her cloak.

"What things?"

Nona looked back at him, and he saw a settled resolve on her face that replaced the anxiety of a moment ago. An owl hooted softly nearby, then fell silent. "There will be great interest in you tonight. You must be ready."

He frowned. "Interest? Why? Because I'm new?"

"Yes, but it's more than that. There are always new Fey at a Gathering; it is one of the purposes of it, to meet other Fey that are in the area. But you are a wilding, and a Traveller, and the Blood in you is strong."

"Blood?"

She made an impatient gesture. "You are a Fey of some power, 'tis evident. You will see tonight, when there are many Fey together. You will feel, and see, the strength of their Giftings, and how some are stronger than others. Usually the strongest Fey are those whose parents are both Fey and who come from a long line of Fey, with few human ancestors. We call these the Full-Bloods. I would say you were a full-blooded Fey, if not for the fact that you are a wilding, untaught. That would not be if your parents were Fey. You have no knowledge of the Rule or our ways, but you have Travelled here and survived." She sighed. "On top of that, you are unmarried, and not unattractive. You are a mystery, and we Fey love puzzles. For all these reasons, you must be careful tonight."

Not unattractive? Thomas set aside that comment, to think on later. "I wasn't planning on making a big scene, believe me. I'll just stay in the background, meet this king, and then we'll get out of there."

Nona stared at him for a moment, then shook her head again. "Just stay close to me," she said. "Let me speak for you as much as I can."

It was a logical suggestion, but Thomas' ire rose, just the same. *Why does she want to treat me like a child?* Even as he thought it, he knew he was being unreasonable, but he couldn't help his irritation even so. "Fine," he muttered. "Let's not stay too long. Meet the king, see if there are any other Travellers there, and go."

Nona gave him a long look before replying. "We will not leave before it's over. That is the way of a Gathering." She turned and continued to walk, cutting off any more argument.

Thomas blew out a breath, releasing his irrational anger. They were close now. Thomas could sense it, and more than that, he could hear music floating faintly through the night on the breeze as it stirred the bare branches of the oak beside him. His stomach clenched in anticipation, and in fear. *She can stay as long as she wants. I'm not going to stay all night.*

A short while later they came to a small stream frozen hard in the winter's chill. Thomas stopped by a tree that leaned out over the stream and looked for a good place to cross. The ice would be thin at spots, and he didn't want to get his leather boots wet.

His skin prickled, and his head came up. He froze as a shadow detached from one of the trees across the stream, the moonlight revealing a cloaked man, his breath streaming out in a pale cloud. He was Fey, and the source of the Call. And not only the Call. Thomas' hackles raised as he felt a small brush of the stranger's mind against his own, deeper than the Call…and more insidious in its purpose.

Fear and anger blazed to life within him, and he reacted instinctively with a hard mental shove against the other Fey's questing intrusion, a low snarl escaping him as he did so, taking a step out from under the tree.

"Thomas!" Nona's low gasp brought him to himself. His knife was in his hand, but he had no memory of drawing it. He saw a flicker of movement behind the other man as another Fey stepped out of the shadows, a tautly strung bow lifted to his shoulder, the arrow notched and trained on him.

He ignored the bowman. The real danger was the Fey who had tried to use his power to push into his mind. He could feel Nona's rigid tension behind him, but he ignored it. "The power of Christ aid us," he muttered, hardly aware of the words. It was part of a prayer Celyn had recited more than once as they travelled together to Lindisfarne, and it sprang to his lips unheeded, a shield against his fear.

The other Fey raised his hands and drew his hood down, revealing a face with strong cheekbones and a sharp chin. His dark hair was tied back at the nape, and his eyes glittered coldly in the moonlight. Thomas' nerves tingled as the Fey-sense danced along them. *You will see, and feel, the strength of their Giftings.* Right. This was one strong Fey.

"Are ye Unseelie, stranger, that ye close yourself from me?" He spoke with a Scottish accent, in a thin, hard voice that held a hint of affront. "Know this: ye canna be allowed passage to this Gathering if ye claim allegiance to that Court."

"He is no Unseelie," Nona replied before Thomas could answer. She stepped up beside him. "Nor am I." She glanced quickly at Thomas, tension tight in her face, a warning in her eyes.

Thomas' ire returned, fuelled by fear. Did she expect him to allow the other Fey to muck around in his mind without a protest? If so, she would be disappointed. His gut-level distaste for the touch of the other man's mind against his own trumped all other considerations. If they refused him entry to this Gathering, so be it.

The narrow-faced man's eyes flickered over Nona, then he dismissed her, turning his gaze back to Thomas. "Come ye in peace, then, to this Gathering of Nectan, King of the North?"

"Sure. If you stay out of my head."

The Fey eyed him coldly. "Ye ha' been Called—" he began.

"Not the Call. The other."

The other Fey's eyes narrowed as he swept his gaze over Thomas once again. Thomas' fingers tightened on his knife, and he took a breath, his heart hammering.

Nona quickly stepped in front of him and curtsied. "My lord, please forgive my companion. He is a wilding Fey, and this his first Gathering. He meant no harm. He is new to our ways."

The man frowned. "The wilding! So ye must be the Healer from Bebbanburg."

Nona rose and dipped her head gracefully. "Yes. I am Nona ap Albanwr, loyal servant of King Selwyn ap Coed of the Southern Seelie Fey."

The man's cold gaze returned to Thomas. "Your name, then, wilding, and from whence ye came."

Thomas heard scorn in the other Fey's voice as he spoke the word, *wilding.* "Thomas McCadden," he said. "I'm a Traveller, and I've come from a long way, and time, from here."

Silence fell, broken only by the sound of music, closer now, and around it and through it, the murmur of voices raised in excitement. The other Fey gazed at Thomas for a long, measured moment, and then looked back at Nona. He bent his head. "Ye be welcome here, Lady. My king will be eager to hear the news of the Southern Court." His gaze shifted to Thomas, his eyes hardening. "Take care, wilding. Ye will be watched."

He gestured at the bowman, who lowered his bow, standing at vigil as before.

Thomas nodded at the Speaker, his stomach flipping in nervousness. *Now or never,* he thought. *Let's get this over with.* He turned and extended a hand to Nona, to help her across the frozen stream, his fingers tingling at the contact, feeling the eyes of the Speaker and the bowman upon him all the way.

It was a relief to walk into the line of trees beyond, out of their sight. It was a narrow band of trees, and Thomas could see shapes flickering in the moonlight in the clearing beyond. Music filled the air, the sound lively and inviting, the hum of voices a muted counterpoint.

Now or never, Thomas thought, as they paused at the tree line. He nodded in reply to Nona's glance, and, with his heart in his throat, they stepped into the clearing where the Seelie Fey Gathered under the silver light of the moon.

27

It was hard to focus on one thing. The distracting fizz of Fey recognition tingled over him every time his eyes lit upon the figures in the clearing, whether they were in the shadows along the trees or dancing with abandon to the intoxicating music, dazzling in the light of the fires that burned along the edges.

The bubbly anticipation inside him swelled. He caught his breath, feeling a smile tug at his mouth, and just like that his anxiety fell away, swept aside by a sudden lightness, lifted by the music that thrummed through the moonlit glade. His heartbeat quickened, and his fingers drummed against his leg in time with the complicated rhythms, a sudden longing for his guitar seizing him.

Get a grip. Don't forget who you are, he reminded himself. Another thought followed. *But who, exactly, is that?* He raked his hand through his hair, his fingers trembling slightly, feeling as if he were on the edge of a precipice.

His gaze snagged on a woman dancing with exuberance, looking up and laughing at a tall Fey with a long, lean face, who looked down at her with what could only be described as rapacious interest.

Thomas frowned, watching as they glided through the dancers. As they swirled into view again, he asked, "Who is that?"

Nona peered, and then her lips thinned as she caught sight of the woman Thomas indicated. "The human woman? I do not know her."

Human? Looking closely, he realized she was right. The woman did not elicit the same Fey-sense as the others did. "But why is she here? Isn't this supposed to be secret?"

Nona shrugged slightly, faint distaste on her face. "She is a Sensitive.

The music drew her, or he Charmed her. She will revel with us this night, and remember it as a pleasant dream come morning. There is nothing to fear from her."

The couple whirled close enough for Thomas to see the slightly glassy look in the woman's eyes, the odd stiffness in her movement, at least compared to the graceful Fey. The lean-faced Fey bent his head down to her, murmuring something in her ear, and she shuddered, her eyes closing briefly.

"Looks to me like he has more than dancing on his mind." The sight made his skin crawl. She was caught like a fly in a web. A willing fly, it seemed, but was she?

A gap in the dancers revealed a tall Fey standing by the large fire in the middle of the clearing, and Thomas' breath caught at the sight, the others forgotten.

The leaping flames glittered off a golden circlet on his head, and a thick gold torc encircled his throat. He had dark hair and a swirling tattoo on his face that Thomas, from where he stood, could not quite make out. Their eyes locked from across the clearing, and for the second time that night, Thomas felt the brush of another's mind against his own.

Once again Thomas reacted instinctively, mentally shoving against the presence in his mind. The king's chin came up, and Thomas saw him take a step towards him. Sudden fear spiked through Thomas as he belatedly realized what he had done. *Probably not a good idea to make him mad.*

At that moment a woman spoke to the king, and he turned to converse with the newcomer. Thomas blew out a breath, grateful for the reprieve.

"Welcome, my lord, my lady!" A small woman rushed over and curtsied in front of them. "We are long parted!" She had a breathy voice, her golden hair floating in wisps around her face where it had escaped her head covering.

"But never far apart," Nona said, with a smile.

The newcomer turned to Thomas and looked him up and down, her eyes widening slightly as her gaze returned to his. "You are new to these parts, my lord?"

The address threw him off; among the monks and the people of Bebbanburg he was Master Thomas, for he had no family, no lands, no kin. And although he had put on his cleanest clothes, he was not dressed nearly as fine as the rest of the Fey Gathered here, with their sparkling jewels and cleverly embroidered clothing. It was odd that she would address him with a title normally given to the nobility of this society.

He was saved from answering, however, as the music suddenly ceased and the clearing fell silent except for the crackle of the logs in the fire and the low whisper of the branches of the trees as they swayed in the slight breeze.

The Fey King stepped onto a log and stood easily balanced there, his arms crossed over his chest, surveying the crowd.

"All hail Nectan, King of the North!" The cry came from a man beside the king. The crowd erupted in a flurry of cheers.

Most of them, at any rate. A small knot of Fey stood off to the side, separate from the crowd. They watched the king in stiff silence. One in particular, a man with dark hair and a sour expression on his face, crossed his arms, his gaze sharp upon the king.

"Who's that?" Thomas asked quietly, indicating the man.

Nona peered at the dark-haired Fey, frowning. "I am not sure," she replied. "But I suspect it is Strang ap Siric. His family ruled the Northern Seelies for many years before Nectan was crowned, two years past. It is said he will challenge Nectan at the summer solstice Gathering, if he can convince enough to follow him."

Thomas frowned, puzzling out the meaning of Nona's words, but there was no time to ask further questions. The king held up his hand, and silence fell once more. "We are long parted," he said, his voice ringing through the clearing.

The crowd answered in a low murmur: "But never far apart."

"My brethren, Kin of the Blood," Nectan said, his clear tenor voice carrying though the clearing on the cold night air, the Saxon words coloured with a Scottish accent. "Welcome. Most of ye are known to me, but there are a few who are not. Come forward, now, and be presented to this Gathering of the Northern Seelie Court." His eyes scanned the crowd and came to rest on Thomas.

Heads turned, and Thomas felt himself flush under the scrutiny. Nona exchanged a quick glance with him, and then they stepped through the crowd to stand in front of the king. Nona curtsied beside him, and Thomas went to one knee, bowing as he had learned to do, his gut clenching.

God, have mercy. Christ, have mercy.

"Rise," the king commanded. The Fey King was older than he had appeared from a distance, probably in his forties. Light touches of grey glinted in his auburn hair, catching the firelight here and there. Fine lines fanned out from his copper-coloured eyes and etched grooves at the corners of his mouth. The dark tattoo, Celtic in style, which covered one side of his face and curled up over his left eye, gave a fiercely barbaric cast to his features.

Despite the signs of age, however, there was no hint of weakness about him. His shoulders were wide, the arms that crossed over his chest heavily muscled beneath his tunic. He stood balanced upon the log with unconcerned grace and easy confidence. He shone and shimmered in the firelight, and not only from the crown and jewellery he wore. Thomas' Fey recognition screamed along his nerves with an almost unpleasant intensity.

Nona had told him that among the humans this man was Nectan, metalsmith and trader. But here he was every inch the warrior king.

"Greetings, my lord king," Nona said, her voice calm and clear. "I am Nona ap Albanwr, Healer. I come from Gwynedd, a loyal servant of King Selwyn ap Coed of the Southern Fey. I am betrothed to Conaire mac Alpin of Dál Riata, a Fey of your Court." She took a small breath and continued. "I bring with me Thomas McCadden, wilding Fey and Traveller."

A low murmur from the Fey behind Thomas rose up at Nona's words.

Nectan's narrowed gaze touched lightly on Thomas, and then the king turned back to Nona. "Be welcome here, Nona ap Albanwr. 'Twas good news to hear of your betrothal. I give ye my congratulations, and indeed, my blessing. 'Tis a pity the winter storms blow hard upon Dún Alt. Surely Conaire waits in impatience for spring."

Nona flushed, casting her eyes down. "As do I, my lord," she murmured.

Nectan turned back to Thomas, his amber eyes hard. "So. Are ye a child then, Thomas mac Caden, that this woman speaks for ye?"

Thomas clenched his jaw against the retort that sprang to his lips. Someone in the crowd behind him tittered. "I meant no disrespect, my lord king. I am new to this place, and to the ways of the Fey."

"Aye. The Lady has named ye a wilding, and a Traveller." The king paused, his face unreadable. "This is true?"

"Yes."

"Or are ye both Unseelie impostors, come to make mischief among my Court? I canna tell, for ye have closed yourself from me, have ye no." It was a flat statement, not a question.

Nona sucked in a quick breath, and her eyes darted to Thomas.

"I am sorry, my lord," he said, his mouth dry. "I don't know your ways.

I Crossed here on Samhain, by mistake. I was pursued by two creatures; I didn't know what they were, but I'm told you call them the Undying." The Fey King drew back at this, and Thomas heard a shocked gasp from the crowd, and some exclamations. The king held his hand up, and the crowd quieted. Beside the king, the Speaker's nostrils flared, his hand tight on his sword's hilt.

"Finish this story, and be quick," the king said.

"The last memory I have before I Crossed was them grabbing me. But it's foggy. I hit my head here, after I jumped through. But I remember them touching me. I remember what that felt like." Thomas' skin crawled, the memory crystal clear for a moment. "When someone Speaks in my head, it makes me feel the same way."

The king's Speaker gave an exclamation of disgust and drew his sword in a quick motion, the firelight glittering off its edge as he held it rock steady, pointing at Thomas. "My lord king! Surely you cannot allow this wilding—"

"Hold!" Nectan threw up a hand and stepped off the log, stopping inches away from Thomas. They were close to the same height, but Thomas was a bit taller, and so the Fey King had to lift his chin slightly to look Thomas in the eye.

"And without any training, or knowledge, ye closed yourself from us," Nectan said, his voice soft. His eyes looked to be lit by a lambent fire from within as he looked Thomas up and down again. "'Tis no wonder the Undying seized ye. Ye would be a mighty tool in their hands, wielded without mercy against us, or against the humans. But not many have the ability to tear themselves away from the Undying's touch. How is it that ye were so fortunate, ye who know nothing of the ways of the Fey?"

Thomas swallowed. "I am not sure," he said. "I don't really know what happened." A memory of Celyn's voice floated through his head. *With Christ's Name on your lips, you broke free.* He shrugged, uncomfortable. "God helped me, I guess."

"God." Nectan's eyes flickered over Thomas' cross. "The Christian god." Thomas nodded. "Then I hope ye gave Him thanks, wilding. Ye would be their plaything but for that aid."

Nectan held Thomas' gaze for a moment, and then he stepped back onto the log, making a gesture to the Speaker, who lowered his sword.

"Thomas mac Caden, wilding Fey and Traveller, you have come to the Gathering of the Northern Fey." The king spoke loud enough for all to hear once more. "Will you now pledge me your allegiance, to swear your fealty to me, and to the Seelie Fey of the North?"

As Nectan said his name, and *wilding Fey*, and *Traveller*, Thomas felt the echo of those words within him, deep inside; it was a strange, hollow feeling.

Beside him, Nona gasped. "My lord king, I don't think—!"

Thomas snapped back to himself, the queer feeling gone as if it had never been, except for the slight wobble in his gut.

Nectan's eyes cut to Nona. "Do ye no?" His voice was colder than the wind, and Nona dropped to a hasty curtsy, her head bobbing low. "Think you this one should pledge to the Unseelies, then?" He turned to Thomas. "What say ye then, wilding? The choice lies before ye now, and I would hear it."

28

Thomas' blood chilled. He understood what Nectan asked of him, after living in this time the past couple of months. A pledge was an oath, freely given, obligating him to service, tying him to consequences that he could not even imagine if that oath were broken. Much more of a commitment than he wanted to make.

"Wait," he said, "I don't understand—"

"'Tis simple, wilding," the Speaker interrupted, his thin voice edged with anger, his hand tight on the sword. "Ye give your pledge to the king, or ye dinna."

Eyeing the Speaker's white-knuckled grip on his sword, seeing the hard edge in Nectan's eyes, Thomas had little doubt of what might come if he refused, despite the king's offering of a choice.

He forced down his panic, tried to think. "I just want to go home. I came here to find someone to help me do that. If there is no one here who can help me, I'll be happy to leave you all alone." He didn't have to fake the sincerity in his voice.

Nectan's muscles bulged as he crossed his arms on his chest. "I wilna help ye unless ye pledge to me." He looked him up and down again. "Or do ye prefer the Unseelies after all?"

Nona straightened and turned to Thomas, fear filling her eyes. "You must pledge to him. The Seelie Fey will help you. 'Tis what you want, no?" She laid a hand on his arm. "Trust me. It will be well."

Easy for her to say. He did need help, that much was true. But he hated being browbeaten into something he hardly understood. He looked back at Nectan, seeing the coiled Fey power in him, ready to be unleashed.

"I have obligations of my own," he said, hoping the king hadn't noticed the slight tremor in his voice. "I won't do something that goes against what I believe in, who I am, no matter what I pledge. And I will leave this place as soon as I can." He took a breath. "If you can accept all that, then I will give you my oath. It's not like I have much choice."

"The Fey find their way between the Blood and the world. Ye will find a path, as we all do, the Travellers especially," Nectan said. "As ye will. I accept your terms. Kneel, Thomas mac Caden, wilding Fey, Traveller."

That odd feeling swept over Thomas again as he knelt down on one knee in the cold grass before the king. He clenched his teeth, willing himself to stay in place, despite a sudden urge to bolt.

The Speaker stepped forward, his eyes sweeping over Thomas, disdain on his face. He looked back at Nectan as if he were going to protest, but the king nodded slightly, and the other Fey turned back to Thomas. "Thomas mac Caden! Ye will repeat the pledge after me, in the sight of the Seelie Fey of the North who Gather here tonight."

An echo of his name whispered through the clearing and among the trees as they swayed in the slight breeze. Time stretched, and slowed.

He spoke the words as instructed, following the Speaker's lead, conscious of Nectan's eyes upon him, and the regard of the Gathered Fey.

Here do I swear, by mouth and hand
By the Earth, the Sky, the Sun and Moon,
Fealty and service to Nectan, King, and to the Seelie Fey:
To speak and to be silent,
To do and to let be,
To come and to go,
To serve and to teach
In such matters that concern this Court;
In need or in plenty,
In peace or in war,
In living or in dying,
Until the King depart his throne,
Death take me,
Or the world end.
So say I, Thomas McCadden, wilding Fey and Traveller.

As he said his name, the sense of dislocation intensified, and he felt something shift within him, a door opening. There was something there beyond that door, something that both thrilled and frightened him. Then it was gone, and he came back to himself.

He shook his head, struggling to harness his swelling emotions as Nectan stepped off the log to stand in front of him, a flash of triumph lighting his clear amber eyes.

"This must be done," Nectan said, and before Thomas could react, the king quickly stretched out his hands and laid them on his head.

The contact sent a sizzling dance of Fey-sense over Thomas, a spark that heightened his awareness of all the Fey into overtime. He gasped, fighting the sensation but losing the fight even as he tried. With preternatural recognition he sensed all the Fey gathered behind him, a feeling that was both exhilarating and terrifying.

Above all, he felt Nectan. His strength, his implacable resolve, his sense of justice, his savagery, the faces of the men he had killed in battle, the compromises he had made to survive, both as Fey and in his human existence. Thomas understood in that moment much more of the Fey King than he could even explain to himself—it was a knowing that went beyond words. He also saw, through the king, a glimpse of the history of the Fey, the long years of exile, the shame of their beginning, the fierce need both of survival and the acceptance of their end.

Even with all that, there were parts of the Fey King that were closed to him, secrets that he held that Thomas could not access.

But Thomas was laid bare. The king's mind blasted through him, knocking aside Thomas' feeble attempt stop him. It was like grasping at the wind.

As suddenly as it began, it was over. Nectan lifted his hands, and Thomas pitched forward, stopping himself from falling flat on his face only at the last second, his stomach swooping and roiling within him, his emotions flayed raw.

What was that? What the hell *was that?*

He heard a low cry from beside him and his head snapped up, causing everything to dip and pitch around him, and he forced his eyes to focus. Nona knelt beside him, raising her hand towards him—

"No!" The word tore from his throat as he flinched away, horror at the thought of the touch of another Fey propelling him back and up onto his feet, but his balance was off and he staggered.

He was aware, dimly, of the Gathered Fey, hearing low murmurs like the buzzing of bees in the background. He righted himself with an effort and heaved a breath, trying to pull himself back together. Flashes of what Nectan had revealed sparked through his head, and he shook his head to dislodge them. *Get out*, he snarled, in his mind. *Get OUT!*

But it was different from the Call; it was not an outside voice, Speaking into his mind. This was knowledge, memories, given to him, and he could not let them go.

"'Twas necessary, wilding." Nectan's jaw bunched, something like sympathy passing through his eyes as he looked at Thomas.

"Necessary?" Anger burst into flame within him. His legs felt odd, but he ignored the feeling, squinting at the king, who seemed ringed in darkness. "You can't just barge...barge..." His tongue was not working properly, either.

Bright spots danced in front of his eyes, and he blinked, the edges of his vision fading.

And then all went black.

29

"In time? You could have explained—"

Thomas stirred, and Nona's voice broke off. He opened his eyes. He felt like parts of him had been jumbled up and tossed around, left lying helter-skelter in the wake of Nectan's intrusion.

Music filled the air. The rest of the Fey were back at their merrymaking, except for Nectan, Nona, and the Speaker. Another male Fey stood close by as well, looking down at him with wary interest.

Nona knelt beside him, worry etched on her face, and behind her, Nectan gazed at him, impassive.

Anger flared again at the sight of the king, and it propelled him to his feet, shaking off Nona's restraining hand.

The Speaker drew his sword, taking a step closer to him, and he saw the Fey power in Nectan swell. It looked slightly different than before, the Fey-sense deeper.

"What was that? What did you do to me?"

Nectan lifted his chin. "'Tis the Knowing. All Fey, after the Quickening, pledge their fealty to their king at a Gathering such as this, and all go through the Knowing. Through it, the king Knows his subject, and the subject Knows him to whom he has pledged. 'Tis our way."

"Your way." Thomas raked his hand through his hair, trying to pull himself together. A sudden thought struck him, and he whirled to face Nona. "You knew he would do this!"

Nona's chin lifted. "Of course, but I thought—"

"Why didn't you tell me?"

Nona's face paled at his anger, but before she could answer, Nectan spoke. "Because she knew ye would refuse it, and she couldna take the risk. She made the right choice."

"It wasn't her choice to make," Thomas snapped, turning back to Nectan. "Or yours."

"It is required for the sake of the Fey, and for your sake, who have pledged to us. Yet ye wouldna allowed it, had I asked. Ye refused the Speaking, no?"

Thomas clenched his jaw, unwilling to concede the point.

Before he could reply, Nectan turned to his Speaker. "Put away your blade, Domech. The wilding will give us nae trouble."

Domech glared at Thomas for a moment longer, then nodded at the king and sheathed his sword.

"I have named ye a Teacher," Nectan continued, nodding at the other Fey, who stepped closer. "This is Brorda Long-shanks, who will teach ye the ways of the Fey, prepare ye for going back to whence you belong."

Hope flared. "You are a Traveller?"

The Fey shook his head. "Nay, there are none such in our Court. I am but a Ward only. But I can teach you the Rule, and other such things you must know." He darted a quick glance at the king, then heaved a breath. "What's done is done, and cannot be changed. You will understand the necessity of it, in time. For now, come get something to eat, enjoy the Gathering."

What's done is done. Right. "Fairy food," he muttered. "Will it turn me into a toad or something?"

Brorda stared at him, then laughed. "Nay, we have not the power for that. But I will eat some first if it will ease your mind." The music swirled around them loudly for a minute. "Come, there is much to tell you, and the telling so much easier over good food and the king's own ale."

Thomas wanted nothing more than to be out of there, but he may as well eat and learn what he could before he left. He nodded. He clenched his jaw as he glanced at Nona, ignoring her stricken look, and followed Brorda. He didn't much care if she joined them or not. *She should have warned me.*

"What use are you as a Teacher if you don't know anything about Travelling?"

Brorda had been about to eat some of the pork that had been carved off the pig roasting in the pit. He paused, the bone in his hand dripping fatty juices.

They sat on a log at the edge of the clearing, which gave them some privacy for their conversation. Some of the Fey darted curious looks at him, but none approached. Which suited Thomas just fine.

"I can teach you the Rule," Brorda replied. "You will need it to survive. And I will ask my kin, and other of the Seelie Fey, see if there be anyone else who might know of Travelling." He frowned. "I seem to remember tales of a Traveller in the North, but that was a few years ago. I doubt he is still here. Travellers do not stay in one place too long. It is dangerous."

"Dangerous?"

"To be too long in a time not your own. Or so I have heard." He shrugged slightly. "I am a Ward. I do not know all of what the Rule says about Travellers."

"A Ward? That's some kind of a—" Thomas broke off, disoriented. The encounter with the king had left behind knowledge that he hadn't had before. Knowledge like the Gifts of the Fey: Healing, Speaking, Travelling, Warding, and the Clan, and what they were.

A Ward could manipulate weather: call up fog or rain or snow or wind in a localized area. In general, they also had a special kinship with the green things: the trees, the forests, the plants. Similarly, those of the various Clans had special bonds with certain animal families, such as the Eagles or Wolves or Foxes or Badgers. All Fey shared all of the Gifts to some extent, but those who were Gifted in one area or another had deeper abilities reflecting their special Gift, or Gifts, for it was apparent that many of the Fey had more than one.

All of this had been part of Nectan's knowledge, all of it lingering now, even though the contact between their minds had been severed. Not all of what he had acquired from Nectan was clear though; some were whispers only, passing glances at things he could barely comprehend.

Brorda opened his mouth to speak, but Thomas sensed the presence of another Fey behind him and he turned.

Nona flushed as their eyes met, but she lifted her chin.

Brorda eyed them, then rose and nodded at the Healer. "Good eve, my lady. You have words to speak that are not for me. I will leave you alone." He looked at Thomas. "I will return later."

"May I sit?" Nona asked as Brorda walked away.

Thomas shrugged. "I can't stop you."

She sat beside him, arranging her cloak underneath her. Despite his anger, he could not stop his reaction to her beauty, seeing her delicate brows arched over her clear green eyes. The faint scent of vanilla tickled his nostrils as the breeze shifted, blowing towards him.

She took a deep breath. "I should have warned you. I am sorry."

"Are you? The king is right. I wouldn't have come, had I known."

She made an impatient gesture. "I knew he would ask for your pledge. But I didn't think he would require it tonight, nor that he would do the Knowing without your permission. That is not the way it is normally done."

The apology in her eyes leeched away his anger towards her, but still, what Nectan had done rankled. "Nothing I can do about it now," he said, clenching his jaw against further words that would not help.

"'Twas for your good." She leaned towards him, her voice urgent. "You are of the Seelie now. Nectan is as obliged to you as you are to him."

"Maybe. I'm a *wilding*, after all."

He couldn't help the sour tinge to his words. The Knowing had given him an understanding of the instinctual fear the Fey had of the wildings, of those who possessed the power of the Fey but were ignorant of it. They had not learned to hide among the humans as all the Fey are taught, and their ignorance had brought disaster and destruction to the Fey more than once in their history.

And as bad as it was to be a wilding, to be one without a Court was worse. He knew now how the Fey felt about those who would not pledge to one Court or another—the horror and outrage the thought elicited. And not only horror. Newly learned sadness filled him at the thought of the Solitary Fey, who had removed themselves from the rest.

Solitary. Traveller. Something snagged in his mind. Something that Nectan had hidden, but he still felt the edges of it.

But he couldn't chase it down, and he shook his head, looking over the crowd gathered in the clearing. The tragic history of the Fey, both what Nona had told him and what he had learned from Nectan, brought mixed emotions. Pride at their survival, and sorrow at their fading from the earth.

He was one of them, whether he liked it or no. *Christ, have mercy.* He was balanced on a knife's edge between his human side and his Fey nature, unsure of which way to fall.

He looked at Nona, frustration boiling up again. She seemed so serene, untroubled by the contradictions he saw. "How do you do it? How can you believe in God, be a Christian, and yet belong to this?" He waved his hand, encompassing the Gathering.

Her brows drew down in a slight frown. "As to that, it is who I am. One of the Fey, Gifted by God as a Healer. I see no difficulty in it. Each of us lives in the world as we must, for we have to conceal our true natures from the humans. So there are Fey who are Christian, and Fey who are pagan. But we all are loyal to the Blood, to each other."

"But doesn't your faith and your loyalty to them ever conflict?"

Before she could reply, the music came to a roiling climax and ended, the Fey laughing and clapping, breathless from their dance. Then a drum began to beat, low and even, throbbing through the clearing.

Thomas stiffened as Nectan strode towards him with a lyre in his hand. The rest of the Fey fell silent, watching their king, darting glances at Thomas. Nectan stopped in front of him. "Thomas mac Caden, wilding and Traveller. Ye have pledged to this Court, and this be your first Gathering. Play us your song now, that we may know ye."

He wasn't inclined to be cooperative, not after everything that had happened. He shook his head. "I don't know how."

Nectan laughed, thrusting the instrument at him. "Play. Ye will find your way."

Once again, he had no choice. Thomas clenched his jaw and took the lyre. But at the feel of the smooth wood, anticipation surged, and he settled it close to him, plucking the strings, his fingers moving as if by instinct.

A pang went through him, remembering his guitar, which used to be his father's. He had worked out the worst of his grief on it after his father died, the music a solace to him when nothing else had helped.

His throat closed, his eyes falling shut as his fingers found the notes, one and then another, and then his head bent down under the ache of loss: of his father, of his mother, of everything familiar.

He gave himself to the music, to the beat of the drum. The music took over, other instruments joining in, and the Fey danced through the night, the song lifting them all.

30

Thomas strode down the beach, tightening his cloak absently against the wind. Up ahead he noticed a commotion—the raucous cries of seagulls as they dive-bombed an object on the beach. They all scattered as he drew closer, a few merely hopping away out of reach, fixing him with their gimlet eyes.

It was a dead animal of some sort, washed up on the last tide. The water had done its work, stripping it of head, feet, and hair, so that all that was left was a mere bloated stretch of skin. Possibly a dog, or a pig, but it was impossible to tell. The seagull's harsh complaints at his intrusion were almost deafening, and Thomas hurried past them, seeking a quieter place to order his thoughts.

Since the Gathering two weeks ago, peace had escaped him, even here at the monastery. His thoughts were too disordered, his emotions still too raw. Christmas hadn't helped; the ache of loss had left him moody and snappish. The one bright spot during the past two weeks was hearing from a *scop* that Oswy had hired for the Christmas festivities that he had seen Godric heading north in the past month.

It was hard after that not to expect to see the harper every day, but Thomas tried to occupy himself with other things in order to pass the time instead of waiting in agonized anticipation.

Brother Barach discovered that Thomas could not read Latin, but merely speak it, so he encouraged Thomas to attend the monastery school. It was something to do at any rate, so Thomas attended classes with the sons of some of Oswy's *thegns* and a few novices. He wasn't much good at it, truth be told, the odd Anglic letters difficult for him to decipher. Apparently, his Fey Gift of languages only worked with speaking a language, not reading it. Another mystery about the Fey that he had yet to unravel.

Brorda spent some time with him, teaching him the Rule of the Fey. *In secret we are born, as secret we must stay. Thus we survive, by the Rule of the Fey.* That was the first Rule, and according to Brorda, the most important. The second—*the wisdom of the Fey comes by doing*—was a little harder to grasp.

To gain wisdom you had to do something, not just think about it. Which made sense, Thomas supposed, but there was a sense of recklessness about the concept as the Fey understood it that made him uneasy.

He heaved a breath, dismissing the thoughts of the Rule out of his mind, continuing down the beach and leaving the screeching gulls behind. He turned and faced the sea, the wind a sharp bite on his face. The grey sky equalled the grey of the waves. He squinted at the clouds, knowing that rain would soon fall.

But it didn't matter. He was alone for once, with some time to think, to be, without the constant strain of trying to fit in among the monks and among those who came to the monastery for refuge, healing, advice, or schooling. Lindisfarne was a monastery, a place for the monks to retreat from the world, but it was a busy place all the same.

He scanned the horizon, looking for a boat. Travelling by water was often quicker and safer, so many people used boats, both on rivers and along the coast. It was possible Godric might arrive on a ship. But no boat marred the expanse of the sea, and he sighed. He looked to the north as he often did when he stood at this spot, thinking about another type of boat: the dragon-boat of a Viking.

In about a hundred years or so, the Viking invasion would begin, and if Thomas remembered his history right, Lindisfarne would be the first place that was attacked.

From the fury of the Northmen, may the good Lord deliver us. That prayer, penned by a monk during the times of upheaval that followed the Lindisfarne attack, had stuck in his mind after he learned it at school. He had been fascinated by the Vikings at the time, but now the thought of what was to come twisted his stomach with dread.

Aidan had chosen the location of the monastery as a place where the monks could withdraw from the world. He did not know that eventually they would need to defend themselves against an attack from the sea.

The monks would die or be carried away as slaves, and there was no way Thomas could hint at this without perhaps substantially changing history as he knew it. He clenched his jaw, hating the familiar helplessness that stole over him at the thought. *What's the point of all this? Why am I here?*

A movement along the beach caught his eye: a figure picking its way towards him. The short, stocky outline and the odd, thumping walk could only be Brother Frithlac. Thomas' heart sank. As much as he had enjoyed the solitude a moment ago, he now wished to be safely anonymous among the others, away from the monk who filled him with unease.

Frithlac barrelled his way through the squawking seagulls, parting them without a pause, and marched up to Thomas, squinting up at him from under his hood. Like most people in this time, Frithlac was shorter than Thomas.

He was skinny, with a square face, his eyes small, his nose crooked where it had obviously been broken. His hair was thin and lank on his head. Thomas guessed him to be about thirty, but he had one of those faces that could be anywhere from twenty to fifty.

"Brother Barach sends me to tell you that the Lord Celyn has arrived and is looking for you." Despite the scrawny look of him, his voice was deep and resonant.

Most of the monks were friendly, but this one was different. Thomas often felt his eyes upon him, and when he spotted him, his face was almost always drawn down in a frown. He had managed to avoid being alone with him so far, but it looked like his luck had just run out.

"Thank you, Brother." He nodded at the monk and moved to go around him

Frithlac grabbed his arm, his small eyes cold. "Why are you here, Master Thomas?"

Thomas shook off his hand. "I came to pray, and to be alone," he added pointedly.

Frithlac scowled. His eyes raked over Thomas slowly. Naked hostility filled his face as he stepped closer, close enough that Thomas could smell the stale sweat stink of him. "You are not hidden from me. I have warned Bishop Aidan about you, but he counsels patience, as he always does. Very well. His love is wide, big enough even to catch you in its net. But I see you, and know you for what you are. I am watching you, *sceadugenga*. Do not think that the shadows will hide you forever." He stepped back. "*God arises; His enemies are scattered and those who hate Him flee before Him. As smoke is driven away, so they are driven; as wax melts before the fire, so the wicked perish at the presence of God.*" Eyes burning with righteous fervour, he crossed himself. "So says the Holy Scripture. God is not fooled by your pretence of holiness. Nor am I."

He turned his back on Thomas and strode away, the seagulls screeching at him as he passed by.

Thomas watched as the monk disappeared around a curve of the beach. *Sceadugenga.* It was an unfamiliar word, but he doubted it was a compliment.

Vikings aside, there were more immediate threats for him to worry about.

31

"'Tis strange, and fearsome, to be sure," Brother Seamas said, crossing himself as he rose to his feet, the ravaged ram's corpse mute testimony to his words. The chief shepherd of the monastery cared for his sheep diligently. Any death under his watch was disturbing to him. This death in particular, even more so.

Thomas was helping Seamas for a few days at Aidan's request, while the shepherd's usual assistant recovered from a badly sprained ankle. Thomas was only too happy to get away from the monastery school, especially since Brother Frithlac was due to spend a few days teaching there. After their encounter on the beach two days past, Thomas had been trying to avoid the unpleasant monk.

Seamas gratefully accepted his help. The care of the sheep was one of the most important jobs in the monastery—they supplied meat, milk, and wool for spinning, as well as the all-important *vellum* that the scribes used in the production of manuscripts.

Thomas enjoyed tramping with Seamas over the island, herding the sheep together at night and attending to the various small challenges that animal husbandry always brings.

Until this afternoon, when they went looking for one of the flock's finest rams and found it dead. The loss of it would be a blow. Luckily, he was leaving behind several ewes that were pregnant with his progeny, so his line would continue, but even so, Thomas knew Seamas had counted on this ram being a mainstay of the flock for many years to come.

Thomas looked at the corpse, unease rippling over his skin. *Fearsome.* The ram, or what was left of it, was lying in the yellowed grass, far away from the rest of the flock that Seamas had gathered together in the sheepfold, located on the other side of the island from the monastery. Only the front half of the ram remained. The back of the animal was entirely missing. The interior cavity was completely visible and mainly empty, except for the lungs. The heart was gone.

Moreover, no blood stained the area around the ram, nor could Thomas see any sign of struggle. The animal's throat was intact, the front legs normal. No predator killed like this.

A sharp whine broke the silence. Seamas' dogs, Fintan and Keely, were circling around them, glancing sideways with flattened ears at them as they did so, approaching no closer than four feet.

Thomas felt the same instinctual revulsion, the same desire to flee. He swallowed it down and turned to Seamas. "Has this ever happened before?"

"Nay. We have lost animals, to be sure, from sickness, wild dogs, or even wolves when we first were established here. But not like this," he said, gesturing to the corpse, shaking his head. He blew out a breath. "It's like the chicken, no?"

The same apprehension he felt was reflected in Seamas' eyes. "Seems to be."

A week ago, a chicken was found with half of the body missing. They dismissed it as the work of a fox, or perhaps a bold weasel. The lack of blood was put down to rain, which fell heavily that night.

But no fox would go after a full-grown sheep in its prime. A wolf could, but what wolf would kill like this, separating half the body with almost surgical precision, and leaving no blood? They had seen the ram this morning, leaving the fold with the rest of the flock. It was late afternoon now, and no rain had fallen. This ram had been killed in the daylight, with none to see.

The dogs whined again.

"What could have done this?"

"As God is my witness, lad, I do not know. But it feels wrong, if you catch my meanin'."

Thomas pushed a hand through his hair and nodded. He looked around, searching for clues, but saw nothing. The hairs lifted on the back of his neck, and he turned around, certain he would see someone watching.

But the clearing around stood empty, the trees silent on its edges.

"Well, we cannot leave him here, poor creature." Seamas sighed.

"Come, lad. We need to dispose of this. Dogs won't have it, if those two be any judge." He squatted down beside the corpse, clearly loathe to touch it, and crossed himself again before picking up the truncated corpse by the front legs.

Thomas walked beside him, the dogs following behind, but not close at their heels as they normally would.

"We'll speak to the bishop about this, but no one else, mind," Seamas said. "I'll leave it to him to tell the others as he sees fit."

Thomas nodded. The monks loved nothing better than a new story or something to talk about, despite Aidan's injunctions to speak only of God and His ways. This odd finding would provide hours of distracting speculation, and perhaps more than a little fear. It was best that Aidan deal with it first, and then tell the brothers once all the details were known.

Soon they came to the water's edge, and Seamas heaved the ram's remains away from him as far as he could. The corpse flew out over the grey water, landing with a splash some yards away.

They watched in silence as it sank out of sight. Relief washed over Thomas as it did so, almost as if a burden he had been carrying had been cast into the waves as well.

The dogs approached, tails wagging happily as Seamas absently scratched them behind the ears. He glanced at Thomas. "The bishop leaves today, after None. I wish to speak of this before he goes. Maybe he has some wisdom for us, God willing."

Bless the Lord, O my soul, and forget not all His benefits...

Thomas stood in the back of the church, the monks' chanting washing over him, the peace he normally felt chased away by the memory of the mutilated ram. He couldn't shake the sense that this was not a random killing, that it meant something. It felt like a challenge, a gauntlet thrown down. But why? Most of the local people seemed happy to have the monastery nearby. But still, he had heard the monks talk of those who still followed the old religion of the Anglo-Saxons, or of the native Druids and their pagan beliefs. Could this be some kind of warning from one of these?

Thomas shifted on his feet, closing his eyes as he joined in on the Lord's Prayer, which concluded the service. As he spoke the words, *deliver us from evil*, the image of the dead ram rose up again, a cold finger of dread touching him.

As the prayer ended, he crossed himself with the rest, hardly realizing he did so. It had become second nature to him now. He crossed himself again, for protection, as the monks did when they were frightened.

Seamas stepped up to Aidan as the bishop approached the door. *"O Bishop, we have an important matter we must discuss with thee,"* Seamas said in the Irish Gaelic often used by the monks when they spoke to each other. Thomas had heard enough of it now for his Fey-gifting to make sense of it. But he had not yet tried to speak it, for fear of more questions from the monks.

"Of course, my brothers," Aidan answered in Latin, with a nod at Thomas. He turned to the Prior, Gaeth, who was hovering anxiously at his elbow, clearly wanting the bishop's attention. "I will leave soon. Brother Cedd will journey with me. Go tell him to make ready."

Gaeth nodded and looked at Seamas. "Do not keep the bishop long, Brother Seamas. He must leave ere the tide turns."

A misty rain was falling, and the gusty wind threw it in their faces as they made their way to Aidan's dwelling. Once there, Aidan lit a couple of candles to chase away the gloom and gestured for them to sit at the chairs by the hearth fire. Once they were settled, he sat across from them, his amber eyes curious. "Is there a problem with the flock, then?"

Seamas quickly told Aidan of their find.

"This is indeed strange, so it is. Ye think it related to the other?"

Seamas nodded. "I fear so, my lord. But who would do such a thing?"

"Yes, who indeed?" the bishop mused, his eyes hooded. "And why? Is there a purpose to it, do ye think?"

Thomas thought for a moment, debating what to say. "It felt like a message."

"But what message could this be?" Aidan asked.

Thomas lifted one shoulder in a half shrug, reluctant to put his thoughts into words. "That you are not in control here. That God isn't in control. Someone is trying to scare you, maybe."

Aidan frowned at him, and then rose, pacing with his hands behind the back. As he did, Seamas quickly make the sign against evil with his fingers under the table, where Aidan could not see.

Thomas glanced at the monk. The bishop had chided one of the monks last week doing for the very same thing, calling it a pagan superstition. Seamas saw Thomas' raised eyebrow, and flushed.

Aidan stopped and looked at them. "I shall tell Father Gaeth. As Prior, he is in charge of the monastery in my absence. He needs to know of this disturbance. Report to him at once if you see anything else that concerns ye. But him only, mind. I must pray, and discover the meaning of this, ere we tell the rest of the brothers."

"If Master Thomas is right, you could be in danger, my lord bishop. Should you no stay here for now, at least until we understand who is behind this?" Seamas spoke urgently. "If someone is trying to disturb the work of God here, how better than to attack you? And you are unprotected out there." He waved his hand, indicating the world outside the monastery's *vallum*.

Aidan raised an eyebrow. "Unprotected? Nay, Seamas. The *thegn* Ulferth has asked me to come and baptize him and his household. This is the work that God asks me to do. I will not cower here behind these walls because of some dead animals, message or no. God will protect me, as He protects all of us. Trust Him, Seamas. He will not allow His work here to fail, of this ye must not doubt. And this work does not rest on me alone. God would use even my death to increase His work here, if it came to that." He took a breath. "But I will pray that this mystery will be solved, and soon."

Seamas bowed his head, chastised, and stood with Thomas. "Of course, my lord bishop," he said, and added, "We will pray for your speedy return, ye may be assured."

Aidan made the sign of the cross over them. "May the God of peace Himself be with ye, me sons, and may His face shine upon ye."

"And upon ye," Seamas replied.

Aidan put his hand on the shepherd's shoulder. "Do not fear. Fear is of the devil. Trust in God. He will not abandon us." He looked at Thomas. "Keep watch and pray, Master Thomas. Your prayers will aid ours, so they will."

Thomas wasn't sure of that, wasn't sure how God viewed him, with the blood of the Nephilim in his veins. But he couldn't very well bring that up, so he nodded instead and followed Seamas outside, into the tossing wind once again.

They headed to the dining hall, where the monk's frugal supper would soon be served, and afterwards, he and Seamas would go back to the flock to watch over them in the night.

A chill ran down his spine that had nothing to do with the inclement weather. He set his jaw, trying to ignore the fear that neither of them would get much sleep that night.

32

Despite Thomas' fears, the night was undisturbed other than the misty rain that strengthened as the night wore on, making it difficult to sleep. The small fire that crackled in the corner of the sheepfold helped some, but not much. The damp rose up from the ground and leached away any small warmth their cloaks and blankets provided, leaving them tossing and turning. Halfway through Seamas' watch during the second part of the night, Thomas gave up and joined Seamas, who leaned on the sheepfold's low wall, looking out into the night.

The monk turned to him, his face indistinct in the gloom. Soon the monastery bell would ring for dawn prayers, and Seamas would join the rest of the brothers at the church, praising God as they greeted the new day. Normally Thomas would attend the prayers with Seamas, leaving the sheep unguarded for the half hour or so that the service took.

But today Thomas would stay at watch so that the monk could attend the required prayers.

"All is quiet," Seamas reported. Thomas could just see the other man's breath ghosting in the dark as the shepherd turned towards him. "Nothing to see or hear."

Thomas pulled his cloak closer to him as a gust of wind slapped the thickening rain against him. "Maybe he just doesn't like the weather," he said sourly.

Seamas chuckled. "Aye, mayhap you are right. Praise God and all His angels for the rain, then."

Thomas snorted. "Amen."

Seamas shook the rain off his cloak, and the closest sheep gave a bleat of alarm. It surged to its feet, bumping into another and causing it to unsettle as well. Seamas clucked his tongue, and crooned soothingly in Gaelic to the flock, the words a low singsong in the pattering rain as he walked among them, touching them here and there, white faces turning to him as he passed by. *The path I walk, Christ walks it. May the land in which I am be without sorrow. May the Trinity protect me wherever I go, Father Son, and Holy Spirit.*

Despite his fears, peace settled on him as he watched, the Gaelic prayer soothing to him as well. The monastery bell broke the quiet, signalling Lauds, and Seamas joined him at the gate once more.

"I'll be back as soon as I can," he said.

Thomas watched him stride away into the misty rain, shooing the dogs back to the sheepfold when they tried to follow.

Fin, the male dog, settled himself at Thomas' feet, whining as Seamas disappeared into the gloom, and the female, Keely, nosed him gently.

"Don't worry, boy; he's coming back soon," Thomas said, ruffling the dog's head gently. Fin responded with a quick lick of Thomas hand. Keely bumped Thomas' arm with her nose, and Thomas petted her as well, grateful for their steady company. They would be able to sense any danger quicker than he.

He glanced around at his surroundings, but saw nothing out of order. The field around him became imperceptibly lighter with every passing moment. But it was still hard to see in the grey half-light, especially with the rain.

All around Thomas he could feel the expectancy of morning's break. Brorda had explained to him about the curious resonance of dawn and twilight for the Fey, the times of changing from night to day, day to night. Their innate Fey powers were strongest at those times. Especially powerful were the equinoxes, when the seasons changed.

His own experiences bore that out. His jump had come at sunset, when his flight from the demons had propelled him into the Thin Place at just the right time. He shivered, thinking of it. Not for the first time, he was glad for the black veil that covered his memories of those moments when he blundered into the Crossing. Once in a while a faint wisp of memory came back: a long, dark void, a feeling of being undone. He didn't try too hard to retrieve it. A glimpse was enough.

As much as he was eager to go home, he knew it was not going to be easy to face that great unknown again.

Home. He sighed, the ache of homesickness blossoming to life in the dawn's half-light. *Danny.* A sharp pang went through him, wondering how his brother was coping with his absence, knowing that he likely thought Thomas dead.

Keely bumped her nose against his hand again, a welcome distraction from his thoughts, and he squatted down. He scratched her behind the ears, where he knew she particularly liked it, and her eyes half-closed in bliss. Fintan crowded close also, the pressure of the two of them leaning against him almost knocking him over.

"Hey, now. Easy, guys. There's only one of me, you know." He smiled, his gloomy feelings dissipating. He heard a snatch of voices raised in song from far off: the service had begun. The monks were praying, chanting the psalms and asking God's blessing on their day's work.

He will give light to those who dwell in darkness, those who dwell in the shadow of death, and guide us into the way of peace.

Suddenly both dogs stiffened, their noses quivering as they looked out through the rain across the field. Thomas rose to his feet slowly, his heart missing a beat. Just then, he felt something. A brief tingle against his skin.

The dogs whined softly, both of them pressed against his legs. He wiped the rain out of his eyes, scanning his surroundings. The few humped shapes of the scrubby bushes scattered in the field were awash with grey and black in the gloomy half-light.

He froze, gooseflesh rippling over his skin. He could just make out a figure standing still about thirty feet away, details obscured by the rain and the gloomy light. From the familiar tingling along his nerves, he knew that the visitor was Fey.

Fin growled and sprang silently towards the figure, Keely following on his heels. The dogs disappeared into the rain as the wind gusted from a different direction, obscuring them. Thomas pulled his knife out, and he took a cautious step forward. But only one step. Suddenly the same surge of power he had felt a moment ago stopped him in his tracks. The dogs barked twice, and then were silent.

Thomas froze, all his senses questing towards where he had seen the figure. He had only glimpsed it for a moment, but that moment was enough. There was something odd about it, something that caused the hairs on the back of his neck to rise.

This Fey was responsible for the mutilated corpses, Thomas was sure of it.

Carefully he stepped forward again, eyes and ears straining, but there was nothing. Suddenly he saw a flicker of movement through the rain, and his heart jumped. But it was only the dogs streaking back, tails wagging as they circled around him, sniffing at him as if to reassure themselves.

The Fey was gone. The dogs would have made more noise, keeping any stranger at bay, allowing Thomas to check him out before they would permit anyone they did not know near the sheep.

But if this Fey was Wolf Clan, and could influence the dogs? Thomas gripped his knife and walked towards where he had seen the figure, just to make sure. He stopped where he thought the Fey had been standing, but there was no one, no telltale tingle that told him another Fey was near.

He did a full turn, scanning the surroundings carefully, but as his eyes fell upon the rocky walls of the sheepfold, his heart lurched in panic. The other Fey had appeared from out of nowhere and had disappeared just as quickly. But where did he go? The spurt of fear kicked Thomas into motion, and he sprinted back to the fold, the picture of the mutilated sheep filling his mind.

The wall was waist high and made of stacked stones. It was not meant for absolute protection for the sheep; a wolf could jump over the wall easily enough. But it kept the animals all together at night, where the shepherd and his dogs could protect them, and it was a safe place to keep the ewes when they were lambing as well.

There was no sign of alarm among the sheep as Thomas skidded to a halt by the gate, his leather boots sliding in the wet grass. He opened it carefully, alert to the possibility of ambush. Someone could be crouching just behind the wall.

But there was no need for caution. The sheep turned mild eyes upon him, the ones that were lying down rising to their feet in the expectation of being let out for the day, as they normally were about this time. He scanned the flock quickly, but it was apparent that all was well.

Thomas leaned against the gatepost, trying to make sense out of it all. Had the other Fey gone through a Thin Place? Could the mysterious visitor be another Traveller? Godric, perhaps? But if that were the case, why disappear so soon? And why would not he, Thomas, also have disappeared through the same Thin Place once he had reached the place where he had seen the figure?

But the Thin Place I came through didn't work the second time I tried, either. He dismissed the thought, blowing out a breath. The place in the field held none of the exultant joy he had felt at the place where he had Crossed. Couldn't be a Thin Place.

Thomas thought through the Gifts of the Fey that he learned through Nectan's Knowing, the deeper knowledge he had gained from the Fey King's touch. Travellers could travel through time and space, through a Thin Place. Travellers like him. He frowned, chasing down a niggling thought. Was it possible to Travel place to place, not through time? A different kind of Travelling?

Thomas' breath caught. He was on to something. *Not like the rest. Different. Alone.* Sudden fear clenched his gut, fear that came from both Nectan's memories and from his own instinct, instinct that crystallized into certainty. The Solitary Fey were dangerous.

The Fey had shown himself to Thomas deliberately, he was sure of that. Had the mutilated corpses been aimed at him, not the monks? His presence here was no secret among the Seelie Fey, thanks to the Gathering. And presumably the Unseelies would know of him as well by now, if Nona's fears were anything to go by. Maybe the visitor was not a Solitary Fey, then, but an Unseelie instead. Neither possibility could be good.

The sheep bleated softly as they jostled towards him, reminding him of his duty. With an effort, Thomas set his thoughts aside. But he would have to find an excuse to leave Seamas and go to Bebbanburg when the tides allowed. He could not tell the shepherd about the figure in the rain, not yet. He needed more information, and he could only get that information from another Fey.

He would have to talk to Nona. Despite the circumstances, he could not help the anticipation that rose at the thought.

She's not for you, he reminded himself, but the words seemed hollow, even to him.

33

It turned out to be easy to get away from his duties. Seamas came back to the sheep accompanied by his young novice, who had recovered enough for work, leaving Thomas free to do as he pleased. Being a guest at the monastery, with no obligations, was handy sometimes. He had to wait for the tide to go out, but by late afternoon he was riding Missy up to Bebbanburg village.

The guard at the gate squinted up through the rain at him. "The monks have sent you, have they?"

"Sent me?"

"Aye, to get supplies from the merchants." He waved at the village beyond the gate. "We sent word to Lindisfarne last night." He peered at Thomas. "But you've got nothing to trade?"

"No, not this time," he said, suppressing a twinge of guilt. He had not told anyone other than Seamas about his trip, wishing to avoid questions.

Merchants. That could mean that Brorda was there, trading pottery he sourced from inland and even from abroad. He kneed Missy into motion. He wanted to see Nona, but he wasn't sure about Brorda. He heaved a breath, setting aside his ambivalence. He would like nothing more than to stay away from the Fey, except for Nona, but any answers about the figure he had seen that morning could only come from them. And maybe Brorda would bring word of any other Traveller he had discovered.

The merchants' wares were spread under temporary tents along the wide beach below Oswy's fortress. Waves lapped rhythmically against their boats pulled up on the shore further down the beach. Sure enough, Thomas spotted Brorda looming over the crowd gathered at his tent, haggling with someone over his goods. It would be some time before he could talk to the other Fey alone, judging by the people crowding the tables, not deterred in the least by the rain that continued to fall.

He turned Missy's head and urged her up the hill. He would talk to Brorda later. In the meantime, he would seek out Nona.

"'Tis too bad the Lady Nona is not here," Brorda said, putting down his mug of ale. "I would like to see her as well. When will she be back?"

"Tonight perhaps, according to Father Paulus. The holding she is at is not too far. Hopefully the child she is attending is not too sick."

Brorda nodded. "Indeed, may it be so." He looked over Thomas with a sharp eye. "You are well then? I've heard word of a Sensitive among the monks. Is this true?"

The Fey liked gossip as much as the monks, it seemed. Although it would make sense that they would keep tabs on any humans who could cause them trouble, Thomas supposed.

"Yes," he said with a grimace, remembering Frithlac's beady eyes.

"Is he a problem?"

"Not really. He spoke to me once, called me something, a word I didn't know." Thomas raked his hand through his hair, thinking, and then the word came back. "*Sceadugenga.*"

Brorda sat back, his eyebrows raising, and he snorted. "*Sceadugenga?* Shadow-goer. Shape-shifter, half-human monster. He has noticed you, for certain." He grew serious. "You must be careful around him. Stay out of his way."

"Yeah, well, even I could figure that out." Thomas tamped down his ire. He resented the way the other Fey treated him as if he were helpless. He may be ignorant of the ways of the Fey, but he was not stupid. He blew out a breath, the reason for his visit to Bebbanburg pressing on him. "Look. I came here to talk to Nona, but since she's not here..." He lowered his voice. "Something's going on at the monastery. Something strange."

Brorda's eyes narrowed. "Something strange? You mean like the death of livestock, decapitated, bodies cut in half, and other evils?"

Thomas lifted his eyebrows. "How did you know?"

"'Tis one of the reasons I am here. There have been reports of such around Bebbanburg, ever since the Gathering. Our king has told me to discover the cause of these events, although it seems likely it is Unseelie work."

King? Thomas was momentarily confused, thinking Brorda spoke of Oswy, then he realized that it was Nectan the Ward had meant. He frowned. "Unseelie?"

"It smells of their work, to be sure."

Great. Maybe Godric after all? Even as the thought crossed his mind, he dismissed it. Somehow, he couldn't believe the harper was responsible. He blew out a breath. "I saw another Fey this morning. Not clearly. Just a figure in the rain."

Brorda's eyes narrowed. "Did he speak with you?"

Thomas shook his head, and quickly recounted what had occurred. "I only saw him for a moment," he concluded. "He was there, and then he was gone. Just like that." He snapped his fingers in emphasis. "He must be a Traveller. But there was no Crossing spot there. I don't know. Maybe he doesn't Travel through time, just place to place. So he doesn't need a Crossing. Is that even possible?"

Brorda frowned. "Perhaps. There are tales among the Fey of such, but I do not know for sure." He took a long drink of his ale and wiped his mouth with the back of his hand. His large hand clenched into a fist on the table. "He is a fool to disturb the humans in this way with these Unseelie games."

"Games?"

"'Tis what the Unseelie do. Tricks, games. Playing with the humans. We can tolerate a certain amount of it, but this is going too far. He must be stopped."

"How?"

A grim smile flitted across Brorda's face. "The Unseelie love to boast even more than they enjoy tormenting the humans. Especially if they can boast to those of the Seelie Court. If the Lady Nona and I go out this eve, he will come to us, I am certain."

"Nona?"

"Safer for the two of us, together."

"And then what?"

"We will start with finding out his purpose. And then, we shall see."

A chill went up his spine at the look on Brorda's face, and he swallowed. "I should come, too."

The Ward shook his head. "No. 'Tis too dangerous for you. You must go back to the monastery."

Thomas waved his hand, impatient. "Tide's not out again until closer to midnight. I won't be able to cross again until tomorrow. And you forget that's he's already found me there. What if I'm the one he really wants? You all seem to think that the Unseelies want nothing better than to get their hands on me. He could come to the monastery again, while you and Nona are off looking for him. How safe is that?"

Brorda regarded him steadily, foreboding filling his face. "Indeed." He took a breath. "Yes, you are right. You will have to join us. But there is time yet before the Healer returns. We will take a walk, you and I, and I will tell you more of the ways of the Fey. 'Tis a duty I have neglected for too long, and there are things you must know."

Thomas nodded, resigned. At least it would pass the time until Nona returned.

34

A half-moon gave faint light along the way as Thomas skirted around the hall, heading for the meeting spot along the edge of the cliff behind it. There had only been time to give Nona the bare details during the evening meal, but she had nodded her assent before Celyn joined them at the table.

Luckily Celyn had not awakened as he snuck out, but he couldn't help feeling jumpy. Celyn had come looking for him before when he found him missing, after all.

The other two were there before him, and turned as he approached. Thomas' steps slowed as he caught sight of them outlined with a faint shimmery glow.

The Quickening reveals much; the Knowing, even more. Brorda's words from the afternoon ran through his mind, explaining why the after-effects of the Knowing kept jangling through him, revealing who he was as a Fey in unexpected ways.

Wisps of knowledge and previously unknown instincts had surprised him over the past few weeks. Odd things, like absently stripping the berries of a rowan tree and eating them, berries that would have made humans sick but burst with fresh sweetness in his mouth, reviving him.

Thomas frowned, trying not to think about it as he approached the other two.

"Is something wrong?" Nona asked.

He took a deep breath and shook his head, setting his tangled feelings about the Fey aside. "No. I just want to get this over with."

Brorda nodded. "I, too, am eager to see this through. Come, let us sniff out this Unseelie."

They headed for the crossroads where the road from Bebbanburg heading east intersected with the one going north to Lindisfarne, which was where Brorda thought the mysterious Fey might seek them out. Crossroads, he explained, were places of possibility, places where Fey power was heightened, especially in combination with a changing time, such as midnight. They did not use the road itself, but travelled parallel to it, using what cover they could find to conceal their presence. Nighttime was dangerous, home to those who survived by preying on others.

After about twenty minutes they came to the intersection. To the west, dark, rumpled hills were silhouetted against the starlit sky. North, the land was shrouded in darkness. An occasional faint boom of the waves from the distant shore broke the silence.

Thomas glanced at Brorda. "Now what?"

"We wait."

Beside the Ward, Nona's dark form glimmered faintly. She glanced at Thomas, then turned to the crossroad, her face intent.

Thomas wrapped his cloak around him for warmth and resigned himself to waiting.

O Sacred Three. A wisp of a prayer floated through his mind, part of a prayer Celyn called the *caim*. A prayer of protection when they settled for the night out in the open during their journey to Lindisfarne. Celyn prayed it while pivoting in a slow circle, his arm pointing outward. Encircling them in God's protection.

It had felt like a bunch of hokum to Thomas at the time, but now, waiting in dark night for the strange figure he had seen that morning, a sudden desire seized him to do the same. He strained to remember the rest of the words. *Our protection be encircling us. You are around our lives, our homes, encircling us.*

A faint pressure pushed the words out of his mind, and he stiffened. Nona's chin lifted, her eyes narrowing, and Brorda slipped his knife from its holder. Thomas reached for his but froze as a white light flared up in his mind. He staggered, suddenly off balance.

"Thomas!" Nona's voice came from above him, which was odd, but as the white light faded he realized he was on the ground, and they were looking down at him in surprise.

Brorda glanced back at the crossroads and froze. "Ah."

The warning in his voice propelled Thomas to his feet, shaking off

Nona's helping hand.

"I'm okay," he muttered, looking past her to where a dark figure stood at the intersection of the roads, rimmed in faint illumination. Thomas shook his head slightly, trying to dislodge the effects of the flash. The others hadn't been affected by it, it seemed.

But he had no time to puzzle it out. Brorda stepped out from the trees. Thomas and Nona exchanged a glance and followed the Ward, stopping beside him, some distance away from the stranger.

He couldn't see any more details than he had that morning. But he had no doubt this was the same Fey he had seen earlier.

"We are long parted," Brorda said.

The Fey cocked his head. "Are we?" The voice was curious, mellow. "A strange greeting from one who bears a blade."

"Step out from the crossroads then."

Thomas saw a quick gleam of teeth as the Fey grinned and took a few steps forward.

The wind gusted, sending their cloaks flapping against their legs. The stranger, however, wore no cloak, just a long tunic over his breeches, as well as long boots whose tops were held fast to his legs with crisscrossing strips of leather. An odd-shaped hat was on his head, its details indistinct in the dark, as were his features, although he was of average height and build. Despite the lack of a cloak or mitts, the Unseelie looked indifferent to the cold, standing at ease before them.

Brorda put his knife away and folded his arms over his chest. "So then, Unseelie, tell us your purpose here."

"Purpose? You ask much, Ward. I do not know you, Brorda of Bernicia, nor the Lady Nona of the Cymry. Seelie Fey, Healer and Ward, set in time and space, solid as rock. You I do not know." His face turned to Thomas. "But that one, the bright flame of need and bonds, the youngling shepherd, tangled thought and whisper-wind; him I know. More brother than you, merchant. I say, and say again: I know him."

Thomas' heart tripped in his chest at the words. The way he spoke was odd, with a slight singsong to his voice. As he listened he could almost see the things he spoke of, twining in-between the words. It was strange, and disconcerting. He gritted his teeth, trying to ignore it.

Brorda tensed, his eyes intent on the stranger. Beside him, Nona had one gloved hand clenched on her cloak, to keep it flapping, the other resting on the knife at her waist. In both of his companions he could sense a leashed expectancy, a sense that they were gathering their Fey power, ready to bring it to use. *And do what?* Thomas swallowed, trying to calm his tripping heart.

"You have named us, saying you do not know us. 'Tis a strange form of unknowing," Brorda said. "Name yourself, then. Give us that courtesy, at least."

Thomas had experienced the effect of the thrice-spoken name at the Gathering, and earlier this afternoon Brorda had spoken of the power of names among the Fey. *Speaking a name speaks them true. Do not lightly give another that power over you,* he had warned.

This Fey had spoken their names without giving them his own. At the very least, rude. Maybe more than that.

The stranger walked closer to them, stopping a few feet away. An axe and a knife hung from his belt, as did a small bag. The hat on his head was long, bouncing against his back as he moved. It reminded Thomas of the hats he used to wear as a kid, the ones knitted into a long point, with a pom-pom at the end. What hair they could see was dark, but without the light Thomas could not tell whether it was brown or black.

It was hard to tell the stranger's age' his face was unlined, his features mild. The wind gusted again from behind the Fey, bringing with it a faint whiff of putrefaction overlaid by another odour. It was an odd, metallic smell, not entirely unfamiliar to him, but he couldn't place it.

Nona frowned. "Are you injured, sir?"

Injured? Cold realization washed over Thomas. The man smelled of blood. A chill snaked down Thomas' spine, the image of the slaughtered ram rising up in his mind.

The other Fey glanced at Nona, amusement on his face, and then bowed deeply, sweeping his hat off his head and pressing it to his heart. It did, indeed, have a pom-pom on the end. The Unseelie straightened and replaced his hat, adjusting it over his ears.

"I am the Jack," he said to her, and then looked at Thomas. *"Jack-o-lantern, Jack be nimble, Jack be quick, Jack jump over the candlestick. Jack and Jill went up a hill, Jack-of-all-trades, Jack-in-the-box, Jack-in-the-Green. Spring-heeled Jack, if you like. The Jack of all trades."*

The words were odd at first, incomprehensible, until sudden meaning clicked in, and the chill Thomas felt deepened.

Once again, a Fey had spoken to him in English.

35

The stranger smiled again. *"I understand, little shepherd. You think they are your friends. But they cannot travel upon the winds, nor do they understand like I do, wilding shepherd, O youngling flame of fire and need."* His voice was low and rhythmic, its pleasant tone unthreatening. The words wove around him, whispering. *"You need much, do you not? You desire much, you feel much—"*

"Enough!" Brorda said sharply, and Thomas blinked, feeling as if he had just been slapped awake. "I will not allow you to Charm the boy," Brorda continued, his voice hard. "State your business here, Unseelie. I grow tired of your games."

Quick amusement flashed over the Unseelie's face. "But my business *is* games, Ward. Quiet games, sneaky games. The Jack knows them all. The best games, I should say."

"Games that include slaughtering small animals, frightening the humans?"

A small smile played around the Fey's lips, and he dipped his head in acknowledgement. "The best games."

"You reek of blood," Nona stated, disgust filling her face. "Your hat is soaked with it. It stains your tunic and breeches. What is this evil you do in the name of amusement? You presume much, to provoke the humans this far. The livestock is necessary for the winter months. Wish you to bring suspicion upon us all? Or is that your plan?"

The Unseelie threw back his head and laughed, a laugh that deepened the chill in Thomas' blood. *Christ, have mercy.*

"Seelie sheep," the Jack said, his smile changing to a sneer. "Soft and fuzzy and wearisome." He looked at Thomas. *"Come, wilding. I will show you the ways of the wind. Leave these fools. This Ward could no more teach you than a moth teaches the flame. He will be consumed by you. The lady is tasty, to be sure, but both of them too entwined with their Court to be of any use to you. Your pledge is young yet. Come with me."* He smiled, fiercely. *"Don't you want to know how to fly?"*

As he spoke the word *fly* there was a sudden pressure against Thomas' mind, and the word echoed in his thoughts. This Unseelie was a Speaker, too.

"No!" he blurted out, and the pressure disappeared.

The Jack's eyes widened fractionally. He inclined his head courteously. "The youngling speaks." His eyes narrowed, and the pressure returned, sharper and stronger.

The Jack wanted Thomas to go with him, to fly the wind. The desire, born on the Unseelie's *push* into his mind flowed through him in a sweet song, evoking desire and repulsion in equal measure.

Flashes of the demon's touch ricocheted through him, shards of memories from Halloween night.

Thomas stood frozen, panicked spurts of adrenaline coursing through him, as he resisted by instinct the slippery feel of the other's Fey's mind. But he didn't know what he was doing.

He heard a small whimper and saw out of the corner of his eye that Brorda and Nona also stood frozen. Power thrummed in the air around him, and he realized that they were being held in place, prevented by the Unseelie from moving.

Anger flared into flame. "Let them go," he growled through his teeth, through the pressure in his mind. "I'm not going to go with you, *Jack*, I swear to you by the Name of *Christ*—"

Suddenly the pressure disappeared, and Thomas staggered. Brorda fell to the ground and Nona would have too, except that Redcap jumped nimbly between them and caught Nona up in his arms, flashing a grin at Thomas as he leapt towards the crossroads.

Fear galvanized him into motion. He was a couple of steps behind the Jack when the other Fey entered the crossroads. Fey power sparked around the Unseelie, building…

"STOP!" He leapt forward, reaching for the Fey, the word reverberating around them.

The Jack staggered, releasing Nona.

Thomas snatched her close to him, twisting his body to protect her as best he could as their momentum carried them in a tumble towards the ground.

Then everything went away, obliterated in a white searing light.

Thomas floated in a white cloud, devoid of any sensation. Slowly he returned to himself, the white ball surrounding him dissolving around the edges, bits and pieces of himself fitting back into place.

"Thomas!" He heard Brorda's voice from far away. "Lady, can you help him?"

"I don't know," Nona answered. "Christ, give me strength," she muttered and he felt her hand upon his head.

Healing. Bad idea. Another encounter with Fey power would surely burn him into oblivion. He tried to move, felt himself twitch. His word of protest emerged as a groan.

"Wait!" Brorda said. "Thomas, can you hear us?"

The white ball around him was evaporating quickly. He could feel his fingers tingling now and realized that he lay on the ground, the cold seeping through his cloak. He managed to open his eyes.

Nona and Brorda bent over him, their faces framed against the star-bright sky. A white spot right marred the centre of his vision, but it slowly dissolved as he blinked up at them, fading away as sensation returned to his body.

"Slowly," Brorda said as he helped him to sit up. "What happened? Did the Unseelie harm you? He is a powerful Speaker."

"I'm fine," Thomas said, rapidly taking inventory. *I think.*

"Are you sure? What happened?" There was a faint quiver in Nona's voice, and her hand trembled slightly as she brushed an errant black curl from her face.

"A flash, like before, but bigger." Seeing their frowns, he took a deep breath and stood, shaking off Brorda's arm, willing his legs to steadiness. "You didn't see it?"

Nona's frown deepened. "I felt the power, certainly, but there was no flash. At least not that I saw."

Brorda shook his head. "Nor I. He took the Lady Nona, ran towards the crossroads, you yelled, and he disappeared. The next thing I knew, you were on the ground." He frowned. "What did you see?"

Thomas thought carefully before replying, trying to sort through what had happened. "It was a huge white flash, like my head exploded. Like before, when he appeared. But worse."

Brorda frowned. "I suspect it has something to do with the Travelling.

Do you remember this white flash when you Crossed here?"

Thomas shook his head. "No. But I don't remember anything from that Crossing. I hit my head right after, and it's all gone."

"Ah, well," Brorda said, and sighed. He looked back at the empty crossroads. "What are your thoughts on the Unseelie, Lady?"

Nona's lips thinned. "He has a devil, that is certain," she said. "God preserve us." She crossed herself hastily. "The blood. Christ, have mercy." She looked at Thomas. "He would have taken me without your aid."

Thomas flushed at the gratitude in her eyes, but before he could reply, Brorda spoke.

"He is gone. If you are able, let us head back to our beds, and to warmth. Our work is done this night."

"You don't think he's coming back?"

"Nay." His face was grim as he shook his head. "I suspect he took the Lady knowing you would follow, and you proved too much for him. He may be back, but not this night."

Come with me, youngling. The Unseelie's words echoed through Thomas' mind. A chill shivered up his spine. "I don't get it. Why me?"

Nona spoke before Brorda could reply. "You are a Traveller. A wilding. An irresistible combination for one such as him, perhaps." She grimaced. "He spoke words I did not understand. But it seems you did."

Don't you want to know how to fly? Thomas raked a hand through his hair, the Jack's voice echoing through his mind unpleasantly. "It was my language. From home. He wanted me to go with him. I don't know why."

"That is a question we will discuss on the morrow," Brorda said. He let out a breath. "This night is dark enough already. Come, let us keep our thoughts far away from this Jack and his games. Walk softly in the woods. I fear this Unseelie has roused more than us from our beds."

He turned and slipped into the trees, Nona close behind. Thoroughly chilled now, Thomas followed. It took a great effort not to turn around to check behind him.

36

"How did you sleep?" Brorda asked as they walked along the shore, the waves crashing against the sand. "You look weary."

Thomas shrugged, the night's dreams ghosting around the edges of his mind. "I dreamt about him," he said, reluctant to say the Jack's name in the sunlight, an irrational fear seizing him that to do so would be to call the Unseelie to them.

Maybe not irrational. He was learning to trust his instincts.

Brorda grimaced. "I as well," he said. "Unsettling dreams, to be sure."

Sandpipers scuttled back and forth on the beach, expertly avoiding the waves on the shore, their small cries piercing through the sound of the surf. Thomas took a deep breath of the bracing air, trying to dispel the foreboding that had haunted him since he had awakened.

He and Brorda had slipped away from the merchant's tables, leaving Brorda's human cousin in charge of his wares. Nona had been called away again to the sick child. Which was fine with Thomas. His tangled feelings for the Fey girl were a distraction he didn't need.

"What do you think he wanted with me?"

Brorda glanced at him, clearly uneasy, then took a deep breath, letting it out in a cloud of white steam. It was much colder, and despite the sunshine, grey clouds were scudding in from the horizon, looking as if they held snow. "I have heard of this Jack before, tales of the Redcap. It is said he roams the wilds, and that he craves blood. That he drinks it in order to increase his Fey powers because of a bargain he made with the Undying. He dips his hat in blood to stain it red and to strike fear into his victims, and to show the Undying he is doing their work." Brorda hesitated, then continued. "The tales say he is a wilding."

Thomas stopped walking, staring at Brorda. "A wilding?" His thoughts raced over the previous night's encounter. "That's why he wanted me?"

Brorda shrugged, uneasiness filling his face. "Do you think he comes from your time?"

He had spent some time during his restless night thinking over that very question. "I don't think so. It didn't feel like he came from my home, my time. Not really. He just felt…odd."

"Indeed," Brorda said dryly. He took a breath. "You must be careful. It seems to me that last night he was testing you, feeling out your strength." His gaze raked over Thomas again. "He found more than he expected, I think."

Thomas flushed and raked his hand through his hair, still rattled by what Brorda had said. *A wilding? No wonder the Fey are so afraid of me, if that's what they think I could become.* He forced himself to think. "You said last night that you've heard tales about Travellers who can go from place to place, not through time. You think that's what he did?"

Unease filled Brorda's face. "There are tales of the Wild Lands, and of the Fey who walk in them. Solitary Fey, with no Clan or Court. Travellers, perhaps, but perhaps not. But these were tales told by a winter's hearth. Stories to frighten children. As are stories of Redcap. I did not know they were true tales."

Thomas snorted. *Welcome to my world.* He began walking again, hoping the motion would jar some of the scattered pieces of the mystery together in his mind. "If he wanted me, why try to take Nona?"

"To ensure you would follow," Brorda answered. "Your affection for her is noticeable." He glanced at Thomas. "She is pledged to another."

He clenched his jaw, his face flushing. "I know."

Brorda laid a hand on Thomas' arm, bringing them to a halt once again. "Yet there is a more important question. You were able to resist his Call, and so he took the Lady Nona, knowing you would follow. But why did he let her go?"

Thomas frowned, trying to remember those last chaotic moments. "I yelled at him," he said, thinking it through. "You've got a point. Why did that work?"

Brorda's gaze swept over Thomas again. The Ward looked hesitant, apprehensive. "Because mayhap you did more than yell."

He frowned, the sequence of events playing through his mind. Redcap leaping for the crossroads, his own frantic fear, screaming at the other Fey to stop—

Realization dawned. He took a step back from Brorda, the blood draining from his face.

"Yes," Brorda confirmed, watching him warily. "You are a Speaker. Nectan suspected as much, but the events last night confirmed it."

Thomas shook his head. "No, I'm not. I can't be," he said, a cold ball of ice blooming in his stomach.

He yelled at the Jack, flinging the word ahead of him, fuelled by panic and fear. Redcap staggered and lost his grip on Nona—

There *had* been something more, something he had not realized in the midst of it all, would not have remembered except for Brorda's question. That *flinging* of the word had involved more than his voice. It had also included some of his will, his desperation to stop the other Fey spurring an instinctive mental shove that had accompanied his scream.

"The strength of your Gift surprised him, I think," Brorda said carefully, watching Thomas. "He wanted to take you. For what purpose, I cannot guess. But you showed him you will not be so easily Tamed."

The words barely registered. He was a *Speaker?* Able to influence another's will, speak into their *minds?* A choked cry escaped him, and he whirled around to face the ocean waves, wishing they would come and swallow him up. It was bad enough to be Fey, to be a Traveller, but to have *this* so-called Gift? A curse, more like it.

Suddenly, something else Brorda had said sunk in, and he spun around to face his Teacher again. "Nectan suspected?" he choked out, a bright blaze of anger erupting as he remembered the Knowing, the feeling of being laid utterly bare before the king, the helplessness of it.

Brorda held out his hands. "We dared not tell you, not then. We thought—"

"*We?*" Thomas' hands fisted at his side. "You knew, and you didn't tell me?"

Brorda's jaw clenched. "This is not necessary. You must understand—"

Again Thomas didn't let him finish. "I don't understand *anything*, remember? I don't *know* anything, except that I'm stuck here alone, trying to survive. Trying to get home." Another thought struck him. "*Do* you know how I can get home? Or have you been lying about that, too?"

Brorda drew himself up, his clear blue eyes flashing hard as ice. "I have not lied to you. I am pledged to our king, bound to him by my oath. If he tells me not to reveal this to you until I deem the time right, then so be it. It is he that has had the Knowing of you, not I."

"You're all afraid of me," Thomas retorted. "Afraid of the *wilding*, afraid of what I might do, what I might become. You're supposed to be teaching me, yet this is the first time I've seen you since the Gathering. Nona avoids my questions, tells me it's your job to answer them. Nectan suspects that I'm a Speaker, but he doesn't think it a good idea for me to *know*?" A sudden sea breeze whipped the hair into his face, and he raked it back with a savage thrust of his hand. "I pledged to Nectan because I had to. And now you have me, safely on a leash, where you all can watch me. But none of you really wants to help me." He heaved a breath. "What else is there? What else hasn't he told me?"

"You try me, wilding," Brorda hissed, anger flooding his face. "Yes, the Fey are afraid of you. We would be fools not to be. And there are some of us, including me, and the Lady Nona, *and* our king, who are afraid *for* you as well. There is much you don't know, true, and much that can bring danger to us and to you as well if the telling comes at the wrong time." His jaw bunched as he clenched his teeth and then let out a breath. "Have patience. You will learn all there is to learn when it is safe for you to do so."

"Safe? And I suppose *you* decide when that is."

"That is the task our king has given me, yes." He held up his hand to forestall Thomas' angry retort, his gaze raking over him. "Listen well to another of the Rules before you accuse me of treachery and betrayal: *An Untamed wilding must die.*"

Thomas' gut clenched, bits and pieces of Nectan's knowledge fitting together in his mind, coalescing into certainty. "Die?"

"If a wilding cannot be taught, if he or she cannot be Tamed, they must die." His eyes flashed. "And before you ask why, think on this Jack we just encountered, and you will know the answer."

Thomas stared at him, frozen, unable to argue against the other Fey. Who knows what havoc Jack Redcap had brought to human and Fey alike? But that didn't make it easier. His emotions roiled within him, churning like the waves.

He was suddenly sick of it all. He threw up his hands. "Fine. Then just leave me alone. All of you. I don't want anything to do with any of you. I'll figure out how to get home by myself. Or maybe I'll go find the Unseelies. They might be more helpful."

"Thomas—"

But he whirled and stalked away, allowing the waves to drown out any further words the Ward might say.

He half-expected to feel Brorda's hand on his shoulder, but as he strode further down the beach, he realized that the Ward had let him go.

Don't you want to learn how to fly? The memory of Redcap's voice whispered through his mind, and he pushed his hand through his hair again, fighting the echo of horrified desire that accompanied the words.

Maybe I do, he thought sourly. *At least I'd get away from here.*

37

Thomas pulled the saddle strap tight, working as quickly as he could. After a mainly sleepless night, he was eager to get back to the peace of the monastery and have a chance to think things through.

Speaker. He blew out a breath, trying to control the spurt of panic that erupted every time he thought of it. He didn't want this, didn't want any of it. Didn't want to be here, stuck in the Dark Ages, didn't want to be a demon-touched freak, and most especially, didn't want the ability to influence another just by using his mind. But how could he ever stop himself from doing it, now that he knew he could? Worse, last night he had used the Gift unconsciously. What if that happened again?

Despair filled him, and his fingers stilled as he leaned against Missy, his eyes closing as he bent his head and rested his forehead against her solid bulk. *I have to get out of here.*

Missy snorted, and stamped her foot.

"Okay, girl, okay," he muttered, pushing himself away from her. "You're right, let's get going." He gathered the reins in preparation for leading her out of the stable, patting her smooth neck as he did so.

"Thomas?"

His heart plummeted as he recognized the voice at the same time as he felt the familiar response to another Fey, and he sighed, turning his head to see Nona silhouetted in the stable door.

She looked tired, with shadows under her eyes and an unruly black curl lying against her cheek, where it had escaped her head covering. She and Celyn had been gone all morning, seeing to the sick child.

She took a few steps into the stable. "Brorda has told me what happened. I'm glad I found you before you left." She took a breath. "Nectan knows your fear of the Fey, your feelings about this Gift. He thought it prudent to wait before he told you, to allow Brorda to teach you more of the Rule and our ways, to help you accept yourself."

"Prudent. Really. And if Redcap had taken me away, made me like *him?* Because I didn't know, couldn't protect myself?"

Nona's eyes flashed, and she shook her head. "Our king couldn't have known that would happen. He thought you safe, and in the monastery."

Thomas' jaw clenched, another thought striking him with a cold blow. "Did you know, too? That I am a Speaker?" The word choked out of him.

Even in the gloom of the stable, he saw the faint flush on her cheeks. "As to that, I could not be sure," she said. "'Tis often a Gift the Travellers have, but I did not know—"

Anger flared to life again, and Thomas cut in. "And you didn't think to tell me that? To warn me?"

"It was not my place. The king—"

"The *king*. Right. It always comes back to him, doesn't it."

"His duty is to protect his people," Nona said, with some heat. She composed herself with effort. "You are a wilding. He could have killed you where you stood the night of the Gathering. Yet he welcomed you into his Court. And you have pledged to him," she added pointedly. "You must obey him, *trust* him. All he does is for the good of his Court, for *your* good. He will not allow you to become as Redcap, a danger to Fey and human alike. There is too much at stake."

Thomas shook his head, not wanting to accept she could be telling the truth. "I have to get out of here," he said, voicing his thought of a moment ago. "I just want to go home, back to my life…" His throat seized up and he couldn't continue.

Missy whiffed, her big head swinging back, nuzzling at his shoulder.

"And you will still be Fey," Nona said, her voice sharp. "I've told you before. The Fey of your time will find you, Seelie and Unseelie alike. Let Brorda help you. And Nectan. Learn what you can, and when we find your way to your home, at least you will be prepared."

Prepared. Right. He shook his head, suddenly weary. "I'm going back to the monastery. I need to think this through. Let Celyn know."

Nona sighed, then stepped forward and kissed him on the cheek, stepping back quickly. "I will pray that God will give you the peace you seek," she said, her voice husky.

She turned quickly and left, leaving Thomas staring after her, her kiss burning on his skin.

38

Thomas blew on his hands to warm them, the chill in the room stiffening his fingers. He looked around the scriptorium, at the rows of monks bent over their tables, their breath rising in mists above them, and not for the first time he wondered how they could produce such beautiful work with hands that were half-frozen.

Despite the cold, Thomas was glad to be there, helping Brother Donal, the head of the scriptorium. It was a good distraction from the roiled emotions that had plagued him since his return. Today he was cutting a pile of new quills from long goose feathers for the monks so that the work could continue uninterrupted if a quill broke while the monks were transcribing.

There were only small fires allowed in the scriptorium, which also doubled as the monastery's library, in order to protect the precious manuscripts collected there. As well, this building held more windows than the others so that the natural light was plentiful for the monks as they worked, to compensate for the lack of candlelight.

Consequently, the scriptorium was always cold, especially on a winter's day like today. Like the monks, Thomas was bundled in his cloak and a warm blanket, but the cold still pierced and cramped his fingers. He blew on them, rubbing them together to generate more warmth.

Some days the work could not continue because of the bitter cold, but today Brother Jarlath stood at the front of the room, reading slowly and carefully from the Gospel of Luke in Greek, the only other sound the slight scratching of the quills on the vellum as the monks worked.

From here the manuscripts would be taken to other monasteries, both in Britain and beyond to the continent, where the monks from Ireland were slowly but surely establishing the Church's presence once again, now that the chaos of Rome's collapse had faded.

Thomas loved everything about the scriptorium, from the production of the manuscripts to seeing the finished products themselves. The scribes used a beautiful rounded style of letters that they wrote carefully on the lines pricked in the vellum, the words clear and neat. Most of the scrolls were like the one they did today, with not much embellishment.

But the illuminated manuscripts, the ones that were the work of a few selected monks, were stunning works of art. Thomas had been helping one day when Brother Adair worked on a Gospel of Matthew that was destined for a church in Gaul. The manuscript was full of swirling Celtic designs in rich colours, highlighting the beautiful neat lettering. Painstaking hours of work done for the glory of God by one man in this cold little building on the edge of the known universe.

The whole process fascinated him; the pricking of the design on the vellum, the inking of the outlines of the artwork, the production of the ink to colour the designs. Some of these pieces would survive hundreds of years to his time, displayed now in museums, some of the greatest treasures of this era. Thomas wondered at times what Brother Adair would think if he knew.

The other manuscripts stored in the scriptorium were treasures of a different kind: copies of the works of Homer, Aristotle, Socrates, and others, collected by the monks through visits to other monasteries or through judicious trades. The knowledge of the ancients, all knowledge in fact, was valued by the monks even though their Christian faith was at odds with some of the teaching they contained.

Thomas' fingers tingled as the blood began to flow in them again. A sudden longing for a cup of hot black coffee seized him. He closed his eyes, remembering the rich smell of it that had greeted him most mornings. His mother's caffeine addiction was the benign twin to her alcoholism, and she drank many cups a day, especially in the morning. Thomas liked the smell more than the taste—tea was his hot beverage of choice—but a cup of coffee would be a boon for him today.

His sleep had been restless, haunted by the dream that had visited him on and off since his Crossing. In it he walked through the mist, an impression of inevitable doom haunting every step. That was the bare bones of the dream, the part that never changed. Other elements were added here and there—for example, the night before, Redcap's voice had woven in and out of the mist: *Don't you want to learn how to fly?*

He rubbed his face with his hands, trying to send the dream-memories away, to eradicate Redcap's voice. His stomach rumbled. The honey-sweetened porridge the monks ate most mornings had not gone far enough to fill him, and it was a fast day, which meant no lunch would be served. The thought of coffee had triggered memories of breakfasts back at home, and he thought longingly of pancakes dripping with golden butter and maple syrup.

He stopped the thought, but then reconsidered. *What the heck.* Once in a while, once in a very few once-in-a-whiles, he would allow himself a few minutes to think about all the things he missed from his own time, his old life. And right now, it would be a good way to silence Redcap's voice in his head.

Orange juice, he began with relish, sticking with the breakfast theme. *Or even just an orange.* It had been so long since fresh fruit of any sort had been available in the winter-locked north. *Bananas. Any tropical fruit, really. Coke. A Big Mac, a hot dog, ketchup, potato chips, an Oh Henry. Fries and gravy, Kentucky Fried Chicken, pizza.* That one stopped him short for just a moment, envisioning his favourite pizza—pepperoni with fresh tomatoes. *Tomatoes,* he added, and then, *Chinese food, ginger beef, sweet-and-sour pork, egg rolls. Butter chicken, naan bread. Curried lamb. Tacos.* He was on a roll now. The rules he had set for this exercise were that he had he to do it quickly, without thinking too hard; and he had to stop once he repeated himself.

Rice, chicken alfredo, salad, pita bread. A memory of his mother flashed into his head. *I love this stuff,* she said, dipping some pita bread into a bowl of hummus. It was before she had become sick, before her sour live-in boyfriend, Joe, had turned up on the scene. She had been tipsy; nothing new there, but there was something about the way she spoke, her eyes crinkling up at the corners, just *happy*. Looking young and carefree, like he hadn't seen her in a long time. The mom he only rarely glimpsed, the one who got burned out of her for good by the booze and the cancer and the chemo. He got up and hugged her, startling her into a fit of giggles—okay, maybe she had been drunker than he thought, but still, nothing like the miserable wino she became, the one who reached for the bottle first thing in the morning and went to bed clutching it to her chest.

He grimaced. That was the problem with this game; it had the potential to go sideways, the memories sending him into a funk, or worse, into grief that could still ambush him and leave him hollowed out. *Shoulda stopped at pizza.* He took a shaky breath, his throat tight with unshed tears.

The door to the scriptorium opened just then, and a young novice, a boy of twelve or so, popped his head in, scanning the room. He caught sight of Thomas and gestured for him to come.

Grateful for the distraction, Thomas put down his knife and the half-finished quill and hurried over to the door, stepping outside with the boy. Small snowflakes were flying around in the air.

"Bishop Aidan has need of you," the boy said. "He is in his cell." He turned, hurrying away without awaiting a reply.

The bishop had returned the day before from his journey to baptize the *thegn* Sicga. Thomas couldn't imagine what bishop wanted from him, but he made his way to Aidan's cell, curious.

He knocked on Aidan's door, and at the muffled invitation to come in he entered. Aidan was there, his eyes warm with welcome.

Celyn stood beside him. He nodded at him as Thomas came in. It had been a week since he left Bebbanburg after the encounter with Redcap, and Thomas flushed under the Welshman's keen gaze, remembering that he had left in a hurry, not waiting to say goodbye.

"Master Thomas," Aidan said with a small nod.

"My lord bishop," Thomas replied, inclining his head. He looked at the Welshman. "Celyn."

Before Celyn could speak, a knock sounded and the door opened.

Thomas' heart sank as Brother Frithlac, the Sensitive, entered.

Great. Now what?

39

Frithlac's face puckered in a frown when he saw Celyn, but quickly smoothed as he looked at the bishop. "My lord bishop, I praise God that you are returned safely from your journey, glory be to Him."

"Thank ye, Brother Frithlac." Aidan nodded at the short monk. He glanced at Thomas and Celyn. "Come, sit down, all of you. There is something we need to discuss." He gestured at the table, and they complied, Aidan across the table from the rest.

"Father Gaeth has told me of your concerns," Aidan began, his eyes on Frithlac. "I wish to hear them."

Frithlac darted a look at Celyn and looked back at Aidan. "Surely the Lord Celyn has no interest in this business?"

"Celyn may have some light to shed on this matter," Aidan said mildly. "Say what ye will, me son."

A cold chill gathered in Thomas' gut. This couldn't be good.

Uncertainty flickered across Frithlac's face. "But my lord, if you would permit me to speak to you first, I—"

"No," Aidan cut in, his voice mild still, but Thomas saw anger flare briefly in his eyes, and Frithlac flinched slightly. Thomas didn't blame him. There was a backbone of iron in the bishop, and Frithlac had just run into it. "I will not listen to accusations and whispers. Speak your mind, here, in front of Master Thomas, and let us get to the bottom of it."

His lips thinned slightly, but the monk drew himself up, taking a deep breath through his nostrils.

He reminded Thomas of a banty rooster on his uncle's farm, but the faint amusement he felt at the thought was wiped out with the monk's words.

"Very well, my lord bishop, if you insist. I have told you before that this Thomas is a danger to us, but you have refused to listen. But now I have evidence you must not ignore. We cannot continue to harbour Satan in our midst. We must expel him, or we risk this work that God has called us to."

Evidence? Thomas looked at Celyn, but the Welshman's eyes were fixed on Frithlac, a slight frown on his face.

Aidan folded his hands together on the table as he listened with mild interest. Gaeth had obviously alerted him as to the nature of the accusation. "Speak plainly, me son."

"You have heard of the strange events that occurred before you left, the animals killed, the mark of the Evil One on them. It has been discovered that it was this one," he said, gesturing emphatically to Thomas, his thin voice rising in indignation, "this shadow-walker, who has killed them in such an unnatural fashion."

Thomas' heart gave a hard thump in his chest, and then started to beat faster. He had half-expected some further confrontation from the Sensitive since the day on the beach. But this accusation was unexpected.

"Come now, me son," Aidan said, his voice still mild, but there was no mistaking the sternness in his face. "Ye speak foolishness. Why would Master Thomas do such a thing? And why do ye think it was he?"

The monk leaned towards the bishop. "As to why, I cannot guess the ways of the Devil, my lord bishop. But I know it was he. Think on this: Never has such a thing happened before, until he came here. And was not one of the animals killed a sheep, while under *his* care?" He stabbed his finger at Thomas, and then pointed at Aidan. "My lord bishop, your great love for all men makes it difficult for you to discern the truth. Not all are harmless."

The sudden anger that infused Aidan's face was no deterrent to Frithlac, who continued, his voice hard. "We must not let our love blind us! The day the ram was killed, this devil left the monastery, and the killings stopped. He went to Bebbanburg, where that night the smith's goose was killed, its head found on his doorstep in the morning."

He turned to Thomas, triumph blooming on his face. "You cannot deny it! You were seen leaving the Lord Celyn's home late that night, long after any good Christian should have been in bed. You were seen, skulking in the shadows, no doubt looking for another animal to sacrifice to the Devil!"

Silence fell.

I was seen? Before he could stammer out an explanation Aidan looked at Celyn. "My Lord Celyn, this is why I have asked ye here. Can ye tell us the truth of this matter?"

Celyn's lean face was troubled. He glanced at Thomas briefly, then looked back at the bishop. "As to that, he was at Bebbanburg when I came back from escorting the Lady Nona to Master Herewulf's holding, for his wife was having a difficult birth. Master Thomas stayed in my house, yes. But I was ill, my lord. My cousin gave me a potion, and I slept." He paused. "I did not wake until the morn, and Thomas was there when I awoke."

"You see, my lord? The Lord Celyn cannot deny it. It is as I said: the devil's spawn went hunting that night, hunting for something to slake his bloodthirst—"

"Enough, Brother Frithlac!" Aidan's sharp tone startled Frithlac into silence. "Ye will be silent, so ye will."

Frithlac flushed and lowered his eyes.

Aidan eyed him with exasperation for a moment, and then turned to Thomas. "Me son, ye have heard our brother. What do ye say? Do ye be the one responsible for these strange doings? Speak the truth now, before Christ."

Thomas saw no accusation in his eyes, which made him feel worse. In a roundabout way he *was* responsible for bringing Redcap here, but he could hardly confess that. His gut churned. *I didn't kill the animals. That much is true.* "No, my lord bishop, I am not."

"And did ye leave Lord Celyn's house that night, after he fell asleep?"

Thomas' heart plummeted. He looked at Aidan, at his long, intelligent face. He had given him shelter despite the strange circumstances of his arrival, and only shown him kindness since then.

And then there was Celyn, whose face was impassive, but Thomas could see the tension in him. He couldn't lie to these two and live with himself.

"Yes, I did, my lord," he answered, hearing Frithlac hiss in satisfaction beside him. "I went for a walk. I needed to think, and to pray." All of that was true, as far as it went. He could say that much without lying. And he *had* prayed as he walked to meet the others. He shrugged, trying to appear casual. "I do the same here, as you know."

It was true. He often walked at night, enjoying the beauty of the stars and the sea under the moon. The monks thought it odd, but he was glad, now, that he had ignored their subtle disapproval.

Aidan nodded. "Aye, indeed." He looked pensive for a moment, and then took a breath. "This is a difficult matter, for it is the word of one man against another." He turned to Frithlac. "This person who saw Thomas—who is it? Will they come and speak with me?"

Frithlac looked uncomfortable. "I do not know, exactly. It was told to me, who heard it from someone else—" His voice trailed off under Aidan's scrutiny.

"As ambassadors of Christ, we should be above reproach," the bishop said, a hint of censure in his voice. "We should not listen to gossip, or spread its poison." He regarded Frithlac for a moment, and sighed. "Ye are zealous for our work here, and that is good. But take care your passion does not lead you into sin." A muscle in Frithlac's cheek twitched, but his face remained carefully composed as Aidan continued. "Go to the church, and pray for forgiveness. Remain there until I come to give ye your penance. Speak to no one about this."

Frithlac's jaw clenched. "I seek only to protect God's work here—to protect *you*, my lord bishop."

"Aye, but perhaps that is not your job," Aidan said pointedly. "Away with ye now." He stood and extended his hand, and Frithlac rose and bowed over it, kissing his ring. He straightened and stumped to the door in his peculiar hitching gate, leaving without a backward glance.

Aidan sighed and shook his head. "*Far is taninne an abhainn, 's ann is mò fuaim,*" he said under his breath. It was Gaelic, and it took a moment for the sense of the words to emerge. *Where the river is shallowest, it will make the most noise.* The bishop looked at Thomas. "His zeal is great, but misguided. And he is wary of ye, so he is, no matter the reassurances I give him."

Because he is a Sensitive. Because he could be right. I could be a threat to the monastery. Thomas swallowed and took a deep breath. "I don't want to cause trouble. Perhaps I should leave." Panic fluttered at the thought. Where would he go?

"Nay, me son," Aidan said with a firm shake of his head. "God has led you here. And I find that He will not allow me to let ye go, not just yet. Ye have a place here until the time comes for you to go. But we must ease Brother Frithlac's fears, quiet the tales." He regarded him for a moment, thinking. "Father Eata and I have just returned from baptizing the Lord Sicga and his family. On the way back God gave us the opportunity to speak His Word to a family of Picts we came across, poor and desperate they were, far from their clans, and in great need." He frowned. "They live in a strange place, not easily found by outsiders. But they were eager for the Gospel, and indeed, the small kindnesses I showed them had great effect. I baptized them into the faith, but they need teaching, and practical help besides. Father Eata promised to come back, to take them some food and other supplies, and to stay with them until the spring, so he did. I've asked Celyn to go with him, to guard him along the way, as they live in an inhospitable land." He paused for a moment. "If you go with them, it would get ye away from here for a time. And it is not only for your sake I ask. The way is difficult, and it would ease my heart to know Celyn had a companion for the journey back."

It made sense. If he left it would give Frithlac a chance to settle down. *And if Redcap finds me again, at least I won't be here.* He nodded. "I might not be much help to Celyn, but I'm willing to go, if he doesn't mind."

The Welshman lifted a brow. "As to that, I would value your company. I agree with the bishop. It would be good for you to be away from here, to silence Brother Frithlac's tongue."

Aidan looked relieved. "Father Eata is gathering the supplies. Ye will leave when the tide allows in the morn."

Aidan said a blessing over them, and then Thomas and Celyn left. The few flakes of snow that had been falling earlier had multiplied; a thin layer of snow covered the ground now, puffing around their feet as they walked.

Celyn cast an eye at the sky. "It will be a cold journey, I fear," he mused, and then he looked at Thomas. "There must be some unrest among the Picts, to drive this family from their home. And just yesterday, another came to Bebbanburg, a metalsmith, it seems. He says he came to deal with Gaerth, but I don't think he spoke all of the truth." He blew out a breath. "He came from Brudei's court, where Oswy's nephew is fostered. Oswy will soon get the truth from him."

Thomas only nodded, not trusting his voice. *Nectan.* It had to be the Fey King. He must have heard of Thomas' encounter with Redcap from Brorda. Heard that Thomas had discovered his Speaking Gift.

His jaw clenched. All the more reason to leave with Celyn before the Seelie King could track him down. The last thing he wanted to do was to speak with Nectan. As far as he was concerned, the further away he stayed from the king, the better.

40

Arawn snorted and danced under Celyn, his eyes rolling, and Celyn tugged hard on the reins to settle the stallion down. "Easy," he said, absently patting the stallion's neck as he scanned the trees alongside the path. *"Byddwch mean heddwch."*

Be at peace. Thomas eyed Celyn, and seeing the tension in his face, thought the words were as much for the Welshman as for the big black stallion, who had been skittish and fretful ever since they had entered a thick forest of gnarled trees.

Beside him, Father Eata's bay gelding tossed his head up and down, eyes showing white. In contrast Missy stood placidly underneath Thomas, ears pricked but content, and Thomas leaned down and patted her glossy neck, taking some comfort in her calm.

The fact was, the place was spooky. He had felt uneasy ever since he had glimpsed the dark bulk of wood on the horizon, and as they drew closer his unease had only grown, becoming worse the deeper they went into the forest and as the way grew progressively gloomier.

In contrast to Celyn and Thomas, Father Eata sat unperturbed on his horse, seemingly untroubled by the twitchy feeling that the others shared. A feeling that intensified as they stood on the path, as if the trees were crowding closer. Thomas shook it off. "Let's keep going."

"Aye, but we'll have no choice but to stop soon. T'will be dark soon, and we'll have to make camp. I hope we are out of these woods before then." He looked around, but there was no lessening of the bulk of the forest around them, and he exchanged an uneasy glance with Thomas.

Thomas understood his reluctance to stay overnight; the thought gave him the heebie-jeebies. He glanced up at the sky to judge the time, but he couldn't see the pale winter sun through the branches of the thick, twisted trees that crowded over the narrow path.

Like they are gobbling up the light that remains. He shook his head slightly, trying to dispel the disturbing thought. But the image bloomed in his mind: the cold limbs, reaching down, plucking them from their horses, tossing them back and forth like playthings, their clothing ripped and torn, branches skewering them, their blood falling to the ground like rain.

"God have mercy, but there is an ill feel to this place," Celyn said, his face white as he crossed himself, almost as if the disturbing vision was one that he had seen, too.

A sudden breeze rattled the bare branches around them, but the sound did not quite seem to match the feel of the breeze. The rattle was louder than the small whisper of air on their faces would lead them to think, as if the faint breath of wind was magnified among the trees to become a stiff gale.

"Do not fear," Eata said. The priest looked as serene as if he were in the church at Lindisfarne. *"Those who trust in the Lord are like Mount Zion, which cannot be shaken but endures forever. As the mountains surround Jerusalem, so the Lord surrounds his people both now and forevermore."* He looked around. "This *weald* is a strange place; Bishop Aidan and I remarked on it when we came through before. But we came to no harm."

The branches above scraped together in the breeze, and Thomas saw Celyn hunch down slightly in the saddle, as if expecting an attack from above, and realized he had done the same.

Get a grip, he told himself, and straightened, but the branches squeaked again and alarm flared. "We have to keep going," he said, with an apologetic glance at Eata. He met Celyn's gaze, seeing the same skittering panic he felt in the Welshman's dark eyes. "Let's not stop again until we are through."

Celyn's jaw clenched. "Think you," he said. "To ride in the dark, through these woods…" He blanched, his voice falling silent.

Missy tossed her head and whickered urgently as Thomas stepped her closer to Arawn. The stallion swung his head around, but he did not bite. Thomas leaned over to Celyn. "I know," he said. "But I'd rather keep going than stop for the night." His stomach twisted at the thought. He sucked in a breath and let it out, trying to contain his jumpy nerves.

Arawn stomped the ground, as if in emphasis to his words. Somewhere in the deep woods, away from the path, the trees sighed and creaked in the wind, but there was no breeze stirring their cloaks where they stood on the path.

"An ill place," Celyn muttered again, looking around. "Like Gwydion's trees."

Thomas had heard the tale over the hearth fire in Oswy's hall, a story of trees the sorcerer Gwydion had enchanted to fight with him against Arawn, the King of the Otherworld. It had seemed a comical tale as he imagined the trees marching to battle, but now as he glanced at the black branches outlined against the grey sky, it didn't seem quite so funny.

"Old," he murmured, looking around at the tangled woods on either side of them. "The trees are old here."

Suddenly he felt a whisper of something, like an eddy in a slow-moving brook brushing up against him. Something hidden in the depth of the forest, something that caused Fey power to leap to life within him in a sweet rush.

He sucked in a breath, momentarily distracted. *A Thin Place?* The whisper faded before he could track it down, and he let out the breath.

Celyn frowned. "What is it, boy?"

Thomas shook his head. "I don't know. I felt—I don't know," he repeated, his earlier unease returning as the Fey power faded. He felt unbalanced, off-kilter. He wanted to plunge into the trees to search out the source of that whisper, but recoiled from the thought at the same time. "We need to keep going," he said again.

Celyn studied him for a moment, and then turned Arawn's head, leading him back to where Eata sat on his horse. "How much further until we break free of these trees, Father?"

Eata looked around at the featureless twist of trees and shrubs lining the path. "'Tis hard to say, my lord. It continues for some time. The bishop and I stayed a night here on the way. On the way back he wished to leave in the morning after Lauds and so we got through the *weald* before night fell."

Celyn's eyebrow rose. "You had no trouble here overnight?"

Eata shrugged. "Nay. Bishop Aidan said the *caim* and we shared the night watch, even though it didn't seem necessary."

Celyn shook his head slightly, and Thomas understood his bewilderment. The thought of spending a night here was more than he could bear.

They live in an inhospitable land, Aidan had said, and Thomas remembered the uneasy look in Aidan's eyes. And he had made sure that he and Eata didn't spend a night here on the way back. Perhaps the bishop had been more affected than Eata had realized, after all.

The trees rustled deep in the woods, but again, Thomas felt no breeze to stir them.

Celyn glanced at him, a thin sheen of sweat on his brow glinting in the half-light. "Pray God it will not be too long before we are out of these shadows." He squinted ahead, trying to discern the path. It narrowed sharply ahead, quickly dissolving into darkness under the trees in the waning afternoon's light. They would have to ride single file for a while. "Lead the way," he said to Eata. "Thomas will follow, and I'll bring up the rear."

Eata nodded and kneed his horse into motion. Thomas nudged Missy to follow Eata, but Celyn stretched out his hand and caught the reins, halting him. "Be careful," he said, his voice low so Eata could not hear. "Follow close behind, and do not stray." He let out a breath. "God be with us, and may all the saints preserve us."

Thomas took a shaky breath. "Amen."

Celyn touched his sword, his face grim. "If these trees rise up against us, my sword will do just as well as an axe."

That would have been a ridiculous statement in any other place, but there, in that haunted woods with the shadows lengthening around them and the eerie creaking of branches deep in the woods, it gave Thomas some comfort. He nodded and kneed Missy into motion, catching up to Eata before he disappeared around the bend, Celyn close behind.

Aside from those odd creaks and rustles, all was quiet, for the most part. Too quiet, perhaps. No bird song broke the silence, no chatter of a squirrel. They rode in silence, the footsteps of the horses muffled by a thin layer of snow that blanketed the ground. It was cold, but not overly so.

Once, they were startled by a rook's harsh cry, the bird clumsily launching into flight above their heads, and shortly after that, Thomas thought he heard the ghostly lament of wolves from far away. But it quickly faded, and then he wondered if he had heard it at all.

Occasionally the odd whisper that he could feel but not hear teased him, rousing his Fey nature to life. He struggled to keep Missy's nose pointed ahead and to not plunge into the trees in search of the swelling pulse of desire that plucked at him as he rode. It whispered of freedom, of the unrestrained glee of a Gathering, of the freshness of morning and the beauty of moonlight.

Like the Thin Place, but different. Mixed up in the whisper was something dark, something elemental: the absence of law; the loosening of restraint; wild and intoxicating catnip to his Fey nature. He concentrated on the feel of the reins in his hands, Missy's solid bulk beneath his thighs, and Eata's back as he led them along the path.

He wondered if this whole forest was a Thin Place, but soon dismissed the thought. It had a different feel than the oak grove he had Crossed through. He wouldn't be surprised to find one here, though. His mouth went dry at the thought of it. He was not sure he could step into it and abandon himself to the Crossing in the midst of these glowering trees.

As he suspected, once the sun set it all became worse. The darkness magnified the foreboding atmosphere, and he had to focus to keep his imagination from going wild. He found himself repeating the *Kyrie* under his breath. *Christ, have mercy; Lord, have mercy.*

Behind him Arawn erupted once in a while in a shrill whinny that jumped his heart into overtime every time. Celyn's muttered Welsh curses as he fought to control the stallion were eagerly captured by the attentive focus that filled the *weald* every time the silence was breached.

After about an hour of this, when his nerves were stretched to the breaking point, suddenly the path widened and the trees thinned out along the path. Eata stepped his horse out into an open space. Thomas kneed Missy and she leapt into action, startled, with Arawn close behind.

Eata stopped as the others caught up. They were on the edge of a small meadow, the snow a white smudge on the ground, the trees on the far side of the meadow a black silhouette against the dark clouded sky.

Normal trees, Thomas thought with relief as he studied them. The odd atmosphere that plagued them fell away as soon as they stepped out into the open, and he felt himself relax for the first time in hours.

Beside him, Celyn took a deep breath. "Thank the good Christ," he muttered. He glanced at Eata. "How much further from here until we reach the Picts, Father?"

Eata frowned. "It was a couple of hours from the settlement to the *weald*," he said, and yawned. "We should stop and rest before we go further."

"Aye," Celyn said. "We will make camp in the shelter of those trees ahead."

Thomas nodded his agreement. The further away from the brooding mass of the forest behind them, the better. "Let's go."

41

Thomas offered to take the first watch. He was too jumpy to relax enough to fall asleep. Though they had made it safely through the shadows of the *weald,* he couldn't trust his dreams.

He hunched his shoulders under his cloak, poking at the fire. His gaze drifted to the line of trees across the meadow from them, but he quickly glanced away when an echo of the odd feeling that had chased him throughout those woods shivered through him.

He crossed himself quickly. *God, keep us and protect us.* He glanced over at Celyn and Eata who lay stretched out by the fire. Celyn frowned and muttered in his sleep, but Eata slept easily, his face unlined and peaceful. God watched over His own, even here in this wild, untouched place.

His gaze drifted to the *weald* again, and the small frisson of mingled dread and desire danced over him again. Clenching his jaw, he rose and walked around the fire, sitting down with his back to the *weald.* He poked at the fire again, watching the sparks as they whirled upwards. *We made sure to say the caim.* Eata's words came back to him. After a moment, Thomas rose, closing his eyes, searching for the words in his memories of the nights Celyn and he had travelled to Bebbanburg.

His voice low so as not to disturb the others, he said the prayer, turning in a slow circle with his pointed finger outstretched. He felt slightly ridiculous and yet altogether sensible, all at once.

'O Sacred Three, the Mighty Three, amen." His hand dropped to his side as he finished the prayer, and he drew in a breath. As he let it out, he felt a lessening of the fears that had gripped him and he opened his eyes.

He sat down again, feeling more settled, but he still kept his back to the trees.

Celyn shook his shoulder to wake him, but Thomas was already awake. He sat up, raking his hand through his hair to straighten it, grimacing at the thought of what he must look like, with his wild hair and scant wispy beard. Shaving with a knife was not easy at the best of times, and he often didn't bother.

"Father Eata will say prayers for Lauds," Celyn said.

Thomas nodded and got up, stretching. The horses were a dark huddle under the trees next to them. Missy lifted her head, her breath escaping as she greeted him with a soft chuffing sound. A light snow had begun to fall, and it was colder than the day before, but there was no wind. Thankfully. Not only did that make the temperature bearable, but It was a welcome relief from the unrelenting gusts that were the norm on Lindisfarne.

The sun was just peeking over the horizon as the priest began the prayers. Thomas closed his eyes. For a moment he abandoned himself to the sweet rise of Fey power, a cleansing wash of tingling energy that invigorated his tired mind and body. *Praise be. Thanks be to God.* The others said the words, and he felt them resonating through him on the crest of his burgeoning power as the sun rose.

He opened his eyes as the power subsided, and he joined in the service, saying the psalms and prayers from memory as best he could.

They ate a scanty meal of dried fish and hard bread and started on their way. As they rode, Eata described the family they would meet: a man and wife, their young boy, and two other adults—older aunts or something; Eata wasn't clear. It was also unclear why they lived so far from the rest of the Picts, who dwelled further north. All Eata knew was that they had been at their holding for less than a year, and the harvest had been poor. He spoke the Pictish language, but not fluently, and apparently these people were more close-mouthed than most. But they had responded to Aidan, and had accepted Christ, and Eata was eager to mentor them in the faith.

The path they followed towards the holding was little used. Since it led directly into the *weald*, Thomas was not surprised. Most people, human and Fey alike, would instinctively stay far away from those ancient trees. He couldn't imagine anyone would enter it unless they had to. Surely no one could stay long in those haunted trees without being profoundly changed. A Fey would wander its paths, drunk on Fey power and mystery.

But Thomas thought it would be worse for a human. The eldritch power of the forest would wear away the thin veneer of civilization to reveal a ravening and brutal creature of whims and impulses with no restraints.

The snow continued to fall, soft flakes that gathered on their cloaks and puffed up around the horses' hooves, muffling the sounds of their passage. Despite his scant sleep, Thomas felt refreshed. The cold air kept him alert, and he enjoyed the beauty of the snow-clad trees and hills around him.

They had ridden for about an hour when Celyn reined in Arawn. His eyes were fixed on the horizon, above the trees that stretched out in a dark line to the right of where they had stopped. Thomas squinted, and saw in a moment what Celyn had seen: smoke, rising above the trees. It was hard to see: grey against the grey sky, the falling snow a further impediment. After a moment, a small breeze brought a faint whiff of it to their noses.

"This be the holding?" Celyn asked, turning abruptly to Eata.

The monk squinted at the smoke, unease in his face. "'Tis in the right direction—this path curves ahead, past that rise," Eata said, gesturing ahead. He shook his head. "It can be nothing else. No one else lives around here, they told us so themselves."

Thomas looked at the smoke, which lifted to the sky steadily. "Something big is burning." He looked at Celyn. "A bone-fire?"

Celyn shook his head. "Nay, I do not think so. We had better make haste. But be wary. We know not what has happened. Follow my lead." He gathered Arawn's reins and touched his heels to the stallion's side, who responded instantly, starting into a gallop.

Thomas followed, his earlier peace quickly dissolving like the snow on Missy's neck. He couldn't help but feel that something was wrong, and they were heading right towards it.

42

The smell of smoke grew stronger as they rode. Soon it was visible in the air around them, curling through the trees.

Celyn reined in Arawn, putting up his hand, and they all pulled their horses to a halt. "How much further, Father?"

"The trees thin out ahead, and then we will be upon it. It—" Eata stopped abruptly, interrupted by a thin moan which pierced the air. "God, have mercy!"

Celyn pulled his sword out of his sheath. "Follow closely!"

After a short gallop, they broke out of the trees and reined their horses to a halt, surveying the scene before them.

The holding was ablaze. Three structures burned, the flames snapping and crackling, throwing heat into the winter's chill air. A fourth larger structure stood unharmed. There were empty pens where pigs had been and a dead goat lying stiff-legged in a pasture. Small lumps of feathers were scattered around the yard—chickens, dead, their feathers intermittently lifting in the breeze. The air was full of smoke from the burning structures, stinging their eyes and mixing with the steadily falling snow to obscure the details. Thomas pulled up his scarf, to try to filter the smoke out of the air he breathed.

Three steps led up to the door of the untouched building, which was obviously the family's dwelling. A man sat hunched on the bottom step, rocking back and forth. He did not react to their appearance at all. He was muttering, his voice rising and falling, sometimes fading out entirely. It was obvious the man had been there for some time, for some snow had collected on his head and shoulders. There were no other signs of life.

"Uirolec!" Eata cried, scrambling off his horse and running over to the man, who gave no sign that he had heard the monk. Eata spoke sharply in Pictish, but the man continued to stare blankly ahead, his voice an unintelligible mumble.

Thomas scanned the area, looking for the others Eata had said should be there. His looked back at the unburnt dwelling, unease growing within him.

He turned to Celyn, about to comment, and the words died on his lips.

The other man's eyes were fixed on the scene, his face pale. But the look on his face, an expression of mingled dread, horror, and naked grief, froze him to the spot. "Celyn?" he asked uncertainly, fear spiking though him.

The older man ignored him. His eyes were focussed on the ruined holding, but he seemed far away. "*Bu 'ma,*" he muttered, as if to himself.

The language switch momentarily confused him until the meaning filtered through a split second later. *He was here.*

Celyn dismounted, his sword still in his hand, and began to run on stumbling legs through the smoke to the intact structure.

The Welshman's distress was so unlike his usual composure that it was evident that something was terribly wrong. He seemed to know who had done this. But how?

Speculation would have to wait. Thomas quickly dismounted and secured the horses, afraid the fire would spook them. He kept an eye on the others as he did so, worried that whoever Celyn referred to would suddenly appear.

Eata sat by Uirolec, who was still lost in shock. Celyn stalked around the yard, his sword at the ready, searching for the culprit, Thomas presumed, although he thought it pretty obvious that whoever had done this was gone.

He finished tying Arawn to a tree and quickly joined Eata.

The Pict was around thirty years old, with a shock of thick black hair. His face was lined and weatherworn, his cloak frayed and dirty. A string of bright blue beads hung from his hand, clenched in his fist. He did not acknowledge either Thomas or Eata but continued to rock back and forth. Every once in a while he would break out in a tuneless hum, unintelligible words surfacing occasionally. The words were largely unknown to Thomas, as they were in Pictish, but the tune was familiar, one he had heard before.

It was a lively song about a young man who goes to market to secure a worthy present for the maiden he is wooing. It was a fun one, full of the double entendres that the people of this age loved. The contrast to the destruction around them was jarring, so much so because as he sang it, tears ran unceasingly down the man's face.

Thomas glanced at Eata, whose face was drawn with pity and shock. "Has he told you anything?" he asked, softly, so as not to startle the Pict.

Eata shook his head. "Nay, may God have mercy. But his family, his child—" he broke off, his eyes dark with horror and fear.

Thomas swallowed, sharing the monk's fear, and involuntarily he looked at the door to the dwelling, which was shut.

"They are inside." Celyn materialized out of the smoke and snow like a wraith. He spoke harshly, his eyes flat and hard, his sword gripped in his hand.

Thomas' heart jumped. "What is going on? What do you know about this?"

But Celyn ignored him. He stepped up to the man and in a swift movement sheathed his sword and gripped the man's cloak, pulling him to his feet. "Where is he? He's not long gone—tell me which way!"

Eata leapt up with a cry, tugging on Celyn's arm, but the Welshman shook him off.

"Tell me!" Celyn insisted, intent on the Pict.

The Pict, who had been unresponsive, suddenly snapped into awareness, his eyes focussing on Celyn's face. His eyes widened, and he began to babble quickly.

"What's he saying?" Celyn said, looking at Eata, his voice a low growl.

Eata recoiled at the look on Celyn's face.

"*Tell me!*" Celyn roared.

Eata paled and looked at the Pict, concentrating for a moment. "It's— something about—" He shook his head and listened again. Comprehension dawned and horror filled his face. He looked at Celyn. "A devil came riding. He says it over and over. A devil came riding. *Dia Trócaire!*" He crossed himself quickly.

"Celyn!" Thomas said sharply. "Let him go!" He pulled on Celyn's arm. "Celyn!"

Celyn snarled and threw the man down, who landed in a shuddering heap at Eata's feet. Thomas recoiled as the Welshman rounded on him. "Don't stand in my way, boy! He saw him—God's Blood, he *saw* him!"

"Saw *who?*"

Celyn's eyes filled with fury as he stepped closer to Thomas, his muscles bunched and ready.

Thomas swallowed, but held his ground.

"A devil came riding. Think, you—one of your *friends,* perhaps?"

Thomas' blood ran cold at the words. *A devil.* Celyn had seen the demons with their hands on Thomas. *One of my friends? Is that what he thinks?* The words stung, but he couldn't dwell on it. Something was going on here that he didn't understand.

Rage filled Celyn's face, along with something else: grief, deep and raw.

Thomas' heart plummeted, a terrible suspicion hardening to certainty. "You've seen this before."

Celyn's jaw clenched, and he whirled away from Thomas, his fisted hands lifting to his head, and then he turned back.

Thomas' heart twisted. The rage had gone, just like that, leaving only grief etched on Celyn's face in stark lines.

"His family is inside," he said, his voice strained. "See to them. I cannot—" He struggled for a moment, and then whirled away again, his head bowing under some unimaginable weight as he stalked away, and then fell to his knees a few feet away, as if he could no longer stand.

Behind Celyn the buildings continued to burn, adding flying ash to the snow obscuring the scene. A crow *cawed* harshly as it settled on the goat's body, its black shape dark against the white and greys of the scene. Another circled overhead, calling. Soon there would be more. He looked over at the unburnt house, his eyes drawn to the closed door, the chill in his gut blossoming out to encompass all of him.

The Pict had reverted back into his earlier state, fixed and staring, rocking back and forth. He broke out again in the same hum as before, his voice rising and falling, the words seemingly forgotten.

Eata knelt beside Uirolec. He looked up at Thomas, his face grim.

Thomas nodded, then sucked in a breath. He stepped up to the door and opened it; the Pict's lament a background to his thudding heart.

43

Thomas braced himself, knowing whatever was inside was going to be bad, but even so, the horror of what he saw froze him into place.

Celyn was right. The family was there. They were all dead, and hanging in a neat row from the central beam of the house's roof, their clothing stiff with blood. More blood pooled on the floor beneath them, soaking into the wooden planks, the air thick with the metallic tang of it.

Thomas' gaze jumped over them, able to bear only brief snatches of detail. They had been arranged by age, with the youngest, a boy of about three—or two maybe, it was hard to tell—the first in line, the first to be seen when the door opened, followed by a woman—the mother? Two other adults were behind her, women, judging by the clothes, which is all he had to go by as parts of their faces were missing—

Thomas stumbled back out the door and turned and retched, and heaved again and again, until his stomach was empty. As if from a distance he heard Eata's cry as the monk stepped up to the door and peered inside, recoiling in horror after a brief glimpse of the interior.

"*Go sabhála Dia sinn!* Christ, have mercy!" He sank down on the steps, crossing himself fervently, pale and trembling.

Thomas wiped his mouth with a shaky hand, and straightened up. He reached behind Eata and tugged the door shut, careful to keep his eyes averted as he did so. He held his breath until the door was firmly closed, and leaned back against it, its solidity a comfort in a world that had suddenly lost its moorings. He didn't know what else to do. He was unable, for a moment, to do anything at all.

The Pict still rocked and hummed. Thomas' gaze rested on him briefly.

The man had seen *that*—

His thoughts stuttered to a halt, his stomach protesting again, and he swallowed the bile back. Eata looked at him, his eyes reflecting the shock Thomas felt, and sat beside the Pict, putting his arm around him. He began to pray, his voice intermingling with the man's low singsong.

Thomas squinted through the snow and saw Celyn, kneeling in the courtyard, his head bowed. The sight clenched his gut.

He pushed himself away from the door, willing his shaky legs to move. He patted Eata's shoulder in brief comfort as he passed him, fighting down nausea as the scene inside the house flashed through his mind again.

He had wondered about Celyn's family, why he never mentioned a wife, why he was here in Bernicia instead of Gwynedd, in Cymry. Why he never spoke of his past. Now he had a gut-churning suspicion of some of the answers to those questions, and he wished with all his heart that he did not.

Thomas approached Celyn warily. He did not want to impose on the Welshman's privacy, but Celyn knew something about this, it was clear. *God, have mercy. God, help us.*

He assumed Celyn was praying, but he saw that he was wrong. The other man sat back on his heels, as if his legs had simply lost their strength and he had sunk to the ground, unable to continue. His eyes were closed.

Thomas sank down in a squat beside Celyn, feeling helpless and utterly inadequate. What on earth was he supposed to say, to do? "Celyn," he said through the knot in his throat.

The other man flinched but did not open his eyes. His face was drawn, lines etched deeply. He looked older, beaten.

Thomas swallowed down the bile that rose in his throat. "You were right. They are inside."

Celyn opened his eyes, but he did not look at him. "Dead."

Thomas' mouth was dry. A shudder passed through him as he forced the word out. "Yes."

Celyn crossed himself quickly, and then again. "May God have mercy on them," he said. "May God forgive—" His voice choked off, and his hand fell.

The snow fell thickly, muffling the sounds of the crows' calls that were growing in volume as more birds joined the one that busily pecked at the goat. The two structures were burning down, the flames running out of fuel. Whoever had done this had not been long gone. Celyn had been looking for signs of him earlier. But whatever impulse had driven him then had disappeared, leaving the older man empty, kneeling in the snow.

He shivered. Cold had settled within him, matching the declining temperatures outside. A result of fear and the lingering effects of shock, he supposed. It felt like he was covered in an icy blanket.

He clenched his jaw. They could easily die here in the cold if they didn't do something. They needed Celyn. And as much as he was wary of treading on the other man's grief, he had to rouse the man somehow. He had to know what was going on, what Celyn knew, for all their sakes. But he was dreading hearing it, all the same.

"I'm sorry. I don't know what's going on here. Something terrible happened to this man's family, and I think…" He faltered, losing courage. He took a breath and continued, forcing the words through the ache in his throat. "I think maybe the same thing happened to yours, and I'm sorry, so sorry—" He stopped abruptly and shoved his hand through his hair, the snow on his head icy cold on his hand. "Look. Sorry doesn't work. I know. I get it. It doesn't begin to touch it." He took another breath, trying to steady himself. "Tell me what happened, if you want, or don't, if you don't want to. But we can't stay here like this. It's getting colder, and there's nowhere else—" he broke off, unwilling to say the words. His breath escaped him in a white cloud. "We have to help this man. We can't leave his family like that."

"A devil came riding," Celyn said, his voice flat. "A devil." For the first time, he looked at Thomas, who flinched at the bitter darkness in the other man's eyes. "And he has the right of it, he does. This one's heart is black, black as night, filled with bloodlust and wickedness. A ghoul, and not a man." His jaw clenched, his eyes bright with unshed tears. "But even as he is, God uses him as a scythe, a burning ember, an instrument of judgement. A teacher, for at his hand I learned penance; at the sight of his depravity, I learned the depths of my own."

Celyn turned from him and looked at the horses, who were warily watching them from the shelter of the trees some yards away. "Think you, of a young man, full of pride, riding off to war at the side of his brother. His land has suffered under the bloody rule of the Saxons, and he has the chance to make the invaders taste the edge of his sword, to suffer as his people had suffered. This young man leaves his wife and his child, a daughter who is the light of his heart—he leaves them, all the while thinking himself a man, not knowing instead that he is the worst kind of fool."

His fists clenched on his thighs, his gaze fixed on the horses. "Think you of this fool who rides off with tales of glory in his head, and leaves his family behind without a second thought—his wife, his daughter, his mother—leaving them there to face what was to come without his sword to defend them, not hearing the devil himself laughing as he rides away."

Normally Thomas would have welcomed this flow of words from the usually reticent Welshman, but now, with the taste of ash in his mouth and a deep foreboding growing within him at every word Celyn spoke, he had to struggle to keep still, to listen.

"The battle was won, the Saxons defeated, but at a greater cost than he had expected. Killing a man up close, his blood splattering on your face, seeing his soul depart from his eyes with your blade in his gut—the young man began to understand then, see, that the true cost of war is not the blood spilt, the men killed; but the death of his soul, one small part at a time, and he knew that he could not continue, knew that God called him to a different path."

Celyn snorted then, humourlessly, his sudden bitter smile worse than the mask of grief he had worn before. "A fool, then, and worse than a fool, think you! He rode home, eager for the embrace of his wife, the sweet smile of his daughter—" His voice broke, but he clenched his jaw, sucking in a few breaths through his nostrils.

Thomas didn't want to hear it, not with the vision of the slaughtered family still flickering in and out of his mind, not with the toneless voice of the Pict rising and falling behind him in an eerie lament heard through the rioting *caws* of the crows. "Celyn," he said, anguish twisting his heart.

But Celyn continued, ignoring him. "God's path led him to his holding, where the animals were dead, the buildings smouldering; where all lay in ruins except for his house. God's path led him to silence where there should have been the shouts of his family welcoming him home, to the silence that was full of the devil's laughter. And then—"

Thomas had to look away from the pain in the other man's face, and he heard the next words as if from a distance.

"Then he went inside."

44

Silence fell. Thomas swiped at the tears on his face, trying to pull himself together. "I'm sorry," he said, once he was certain he could speak. "I'm so sorry."

He wasn't sure if the other man heard him. Celyn's ravaged face was bleak, his eyes far away.

So much tragedy and sorrow. He felt unmoored by it all. But he had learned at the hands of his own tragedies that time kept on going and life continued, even if everything within you wished it didn't. "The one who did this—do you know who it is?"

The other man sat unmoving, lost in his memories of blood and pain. He took him by the shoulders and shook him slightly, not knowing what else to do, knowing only that he had to snap Celyn out of the grief or he could be lost there forever. "Celyn!"

The Welshman's eyes focussed on him, anger sparking in them. "Leave me!" he snarled, shaking off Thomas' hands. "Leave me be!"

"And do what? Sit in the snow all day? This man needs our help!"

"Our help? God's *Blood*, boy—" Celyn's voice choked off, and he pushed himself to his feet, taking a few staggering steps away, and halted, swaying on his feet. Thomas rose too. He had gotten Celyn moving, but now what? The other man's distress was a barrier he was not sure how to breach. Celyn lifted a hand to his mouth, stifling the sob that shook him and took a ragged breath. "This is my fault, all of it, my fault..."

"What are you talking about? Of course it's not your fault!"

Celyn whirled to face him, his eyes wild, his face distorted in a snarl. "I searched for him, see, but he had disappeared into the wind, ridden it back to hell where he had come. The only thing I learned in my searching was that he was a be-damned *Saxon*. Someone had spotted him, riding to my holding, saw his Saxon blade and his Saxon armour. A *Saxon!*" Celyn spat the word, breathing heavily. "I had left my brother Griffith fighting them, thinking myself too good to soil my blade with their blood. I gave up the search—*gave it up*, think you—and rode back to Griffith's side. With him I had my revenge, and I tell you, boy, I gave no mercy. Mercy had been burned out of me along with my holding, squeezed from me as the rope had squeezed the life out of my sweet Rhianwen."

Thomas wrapped his arms around himself as armour against the images that Celyn conjured up, fighting the urge to tell Celyn to stop.

Tears were flowing down Celyn's face now, but he seemed not to notice. "God left me to it, left me to the blood, and the darkness. The Saxons tasted my revenge, one holding after another. Even as their armies had ravaged our people, so we ravaged them. And I was there, in the midst of it, my blade dripping with blood, more animal than man, at times."

He heaved a few breaths. "Until one day—" He broke off, his eyes pools of bitterness and shame. "One day I saw the face of *my* wife on the woman my brother had defiled, saw *my* daughter in the face of the child screaming for her mother. I came back to myself, and I saw myself for what I had become: no less a demon than the one who had killed my family. Men were returning to their holdings, to their ravaged families, and cursing my name, as I had cursed his." He shook his head, remembering. "I left my brother's side and found my way, eventually, to Hii, where the monks took me in, for Griffith had branded me a traitor and I had no home in Gwynedd any longer."

Celyn closed his eyes briefly, the anger fading from his face, replaced by weary sorrow. He opened his eyes. "If I had kept looking, I could have found him, but finding him was taking too long. I joined my brother and tried to slake my fury on the innocents I slaughtered, not on the one who deserved my wrath. I let him go, and this is the result." He waved a hand at the ruined holding. "It was my hands that did this, just as much as his. And how many others beside?" His hand dropped. "God has brought him back to me, to finish the task I left undone. And I'll not turn away again. He is not long from here. I am going to find him, and I am going to kill him."

He held Thomas' eyes for a moment, and turned, stalking towards the horses, the crows fluttering up at his passage, then settling back down to their feast.

Thomas stood frozen for a moment, trying to gather himself. He couldn't let Celyn ride off, but how could he stop him? He willed his muscles to move and followed, catching up as Celyn began to untie Arawn. "Wait."

But the other man ignored him, and Thomas put a hand on his arm, urgent. "Listen to me just for a moment. Please!"

He had not slept much the night before. That, and the shocks of the morning, had frayed his self-control. And he was desperate to stop the other man, desperate to somehow reach him, and so as he said *"please,"* his Fey power surged up for a moment, throbbing through the word.

It touched Celyn, just for a moment, before he realized what he had done and snuffed it out, struggling to stay in control through the brief touch of pain and grief he had felt raging in the other man.

Celyn turned to him, his face grim. "You'll not stop me, boy," he said, his voice low and hard.

Thomas didn't think Celyn had noticed, the Speaking had been so quick. But it had worked, all the same. He took a deep breath. "I'm not trying to stop you." Justice here was crude, but what choice did they have? There were no jails. Whoever had done this had it coming, in his opinion. "Look. I get it. You want to go after him. Fine. But you're just going to leave us here?" A sudden gust of wind shook the branches above their heads. The snow swirled and danced, and Arawn stamped a hoof, snorting. "The snow's getting worse. Besides anything else, you can't track him in this."

Celyn's jaw clenched. "I have no need to track him. We both know where he's gone."

The weald. The knowledge sprang into his mind. His heart sank. He knew Celyn was right. The man who had done this had gone into that forest, its muttering whispers a siren song this creature of blood and death would not be able to resist. *Had not resisted.* The realization coalesced to icy certainty. This man would be at home in those woods— perhaps it was where he lived. There, or in another forest like it, a place where the wild power of the earth had never been tamed or touched by man. A place forgotten since Eden had been young.

And with a sudden twist of his guts, he knew that this ruined holding would not only reveal Celyn's secrets. It would expose his own.

He couldn't let Celyn go into that woodland alone. Celyn was a Sensitive, open to the power that had its home in the *weald.* In his rawness and grief, Celyn could be caught by it, *changed* by it, just as this killer he hunted had been changed. Perhaps that man had come unaware into it, had heard the whispers of the trees and had listened to them for too long.

A creature of no restraints. He swallowed, remembering his thoughts that morning. It could happen to Celyn—*would* happen to him, if Thomas were not there, his Fey power a buffer against dark pull of the *weald*.

He had to go with Celyn, but in order to help him, to protect him in there, he would have to tell him that he was Fey.

It would take all his strength to enter that forest, to seek out the killer, to shield himself and Celyn from the inherent danger. He wasn't even sure he could do it, *how* to do it. But he knew that he couldn't worry about hiding his Fey nature from Celyn while he did what needed to be done.

"Celyn, stop." His voice was strained, rough.

Celyn had one foot in the stirrup and was preparing to haul himself up, but he turned, his eyes narrowing in anger at the interruption.

There was no way out of this. "Wait. Please." He tried to corral his thoughts. "I'll go with you. It's too dangerous on your own. But we can't leave Eata here by himself, to deal with the Pict, and his family." His throat tightened as he saw the steely anger in Celyn's eyes crack for a moment, saw the river of grief beneath. He forced himself to continue. "You don't have to come in the house. Eata and I will take care of that. But the Pict…we can't leave him alone. Someone has to be with him."

Celyn swallowed, shaking his head.

God, help me. Thomas bolstered his faltering courage and plunged ahead. "The Saxon won't have gone far in this weather. We know where he's going. Please, help me deal with this, and then, when it clears, we'll go after him."

Thomas saw the struggle on Celyn's face, saw his desire to depart warring with his practical nature.

"By all the saints," he said through his teeth, "you try me, boy." His eyes shut, and a tremor ran through him, his fingers clenched in Arawn's thick mane.

Thomas' heart ached, for Celyn, for the Pict. He understood the bitter truth of death, of having to live when those you loved were gone. "I'm sorry. I know. If I could change all this," he waved a hand at the holding, "I would. All of it—your family, the Pict's family, my parents—" He choked for a moment, and then forced himself to continue. "But no one can." He heaved a breath. "The snow is getting worse. It's getting cold.

You can ride off to find the Saxon, and I can't stop you. But you'll leave Eata and I to make that house fit for us to sleep in tonight, and the Pict by himself while we do it. Look at him: he's barely functioning. He needs someone to be with him."

Celyn's eyes opened, his nostrils flaring, the war on his face evident as he looked back at the ruined holding, at Uirolec, lost in his grief.

Thomas put his hand on Celyn's shoulder, and the other man looked at him, his dark eyes haunted and brimming with tears. "You need someone to be with you, too." He held Celyn's gaze for a moment, and then turned, leaving him to make up his own mind.

He had only taken a few steps before Celyn spoke. "Hold, boy." Relief washed over him as the other man joined him. "The ground is frozen. We'll not be able to bury them. I'll gather some wood." He passed a shaking hand over his face, closing his eyes briefly. When he opened them, hard certainty filled his eyes. "But we leave as soon as the sun rises, if the weather allows."

Thomas nodded, standing still for a moment as Celyn began to search among the smouldering ruins, weary relief filling him. *Thank you, God.* This hurdle had been passed. Tomorrow, or whenever the weather cleared and the tasks here were done, he would go with Celyn to the *weald*, and face what had to be faced then. Including telling Celyn he was Fey. But not today. Thank God.

He shook that problem off to think about later and forced himself to move. He joined Eata, who still sat beside Uirolec. "I need your help."

The Pict sat and rocked, seemingly oblivious. But Thomas wanted to be careful what he said, just the same. He spoke softly. "We have to take them down."

Eata paled and crossed himself. "The Lord Celyn...?" He darted a look at the Welshman, who was rummaging carefully through the still smoking remains of the buildings.

Thomas shook his head. "He'll stay out here, keep an eye on him," he replied, pointing with his chin at the Pict. He took a deep breath. "We have to do it."

Eata swallowed but stood up resolutely, and Thomas took heart from the monk's steady courage.

God, help us. Christ, have mercy. Christ before us. He mounted the steps and with a trembling hand, opened the door again.

45

Thomas **woke to** the sounds of Celyn building up the hearth fire and heating water. It was still dark, but dawn was approaching, and as the sun rose, he welcomed the rush of Fey power. The sweet tumble of it washed away his dreams, which had been full of fire and blood. *This is who I am,* he thought, as the sensation faded. *I am Fey.* He let out a breath, struggling, as always, to come to terms with it. At least it would help him in his search for the one who had wrought such destruction. Today he and Celyn would find the man and kill him, and he felt no horror at the thought, not with the memories of Uirolec's slaughtered family and Celyn's ravaged face in his mind. Celyn was right. They had to stop him.

The resolve propelled him through their preparations for departure. While he had no doubts as to their course of action, he wrestled with how and when to reveal his secret to Celyn. Finally he decided that he would wait until just before they entered the *weald*. Close enough that Celyn couldn't leave him and carry on alone, if the conversation went badly.

Although it was cold, sun began to peek through the clouds as they started out. Missy sensed his nerves, and pranced and fought the bit as they rode, their breath steaming out into the crisp morning air. Celyn's face was set in determined lines as he rode beside Thomas, his eyes hard as flint.

Within an hour they came upon a spot near the path where someone had hunkered out the storm. A lean-to had been hastily constructed, a blackened pile of wood and ashes still warm to the touch. Hoofprints led away in the direction of the *weald*.

Their hunch had been right. The Saxon was going back into the muttering shelter of the *weald*. They mounted in silence and continued, more quickly now that they knew he was just ahead of them.

Once the brooding bulk of the trees was revealed around a curve in the path, Celyn touched his heels to Arawn's flanks, forcing Thomas to urge Missy into a gallop behind him, his heart pounding hard now that the time had come.

Celyn pulled Arawn to a halt at the edge of the trees. The tracks they followed led into the woods and disappeared into its gloom. Although the day was bright and sunny, the light was swallowed up in shadow not far into the *weald*. "It is best you stay close to me. I will lead the way."

Thomas had been glad for Celyn's normal reticence as they rode, for there was only one thing that he could talk about, and it was lodged in his throat like a rock. But he had to speak, now. "Wait. I have to stretch my legs, just for a minute." He slid off Missy, ignoring Celyn's impatient look. "And there's something I have to say, before we go in there." He looped the reins over a branch and looked up at Celyn, his heart hammering. *God, help me.*

Celyn frowned, but after a small moment he dismounted and tethered Arawn close by.

Thomas breathed a small sigh of relief. At least now Celyn couldn't go galloping into the trees without him, once he found out the truth. He swallowed and took a deep breath, squaring his shoulders. *Everything will change now,* Thomas thought, with a pang of regret and fear. "I couldn't tell you this before, but I have to now."

Celyn's face sharpened in interest. "Speak quickly, then. The Saxon is getting further away while we stand here."

Thomas raked his hand through his hair. *Just say it, come on.* "You won't find him without me," he said finally. "You will search and search and get lost in there, and probably never come out. But I think—" He checked himself, and continued, more strongly. "I *know* I can lead you to him."

Celyn shook his head, impatient. "Don't be foolish. I am far better at following a trail than you, we both know that."

"No. Not in there. You won't find him, but I will." He swallowed. "Because of who I am. Because of *what* I am."

Celyn's eyes narrowed as he looked at Thomas. Missy whickered softly, and Arawn stomped a hoof. The trees stirred, a faint rattling sound coming from their tangled depths, and then silence fell again.

"When you found me, you said you thought I was a Changeling, taken by the *tylwyth teg* when I was young."

Celyn nodded, wariness creeping into his eyes.

Thomas held the Welshman's gaze, willing him to understand. "That was close enough to the truth to work, but it's not going to work anymore. Not now. Not *here*." He waved at the trees. "I'm not a Changeling. I am Fey." Something in him shifted, and settled, as he said the word. "One of the *tylwyth teg,* one of the *Sidhe.* I didn't know it, not until after I got here, but it's true."

Silence fell around them, the cold light of the winter's day throwing harsh shadows on the ground.

"Have you gone mad, boy?" Celyn said finally, but Thomas saw something pass through his eyes, a flicker of uncertainty. Celyn was a Sensitive. Thomas had not told him anything he hadn't already suspected, even if he hadn't admitted it to himself.

"It's true," he said again. "I wish it wasn't, but it is."

Celyn shook his head, the brief uncertainty gone. "Think, you! This is what they *want* you to believe. The *tylwyth teg* are cunning, so it is said. And they do not like to be made to look foolish. You have escaped them, and it must chafe them." He stepped closer, his face intent. "They want you back, boy. How better to do that than to make you think you are one of them?"

A sudden gust of wind blew some snow up from the ground, and it whirled around them briefly before settling back down. Celyn looked over at the trees, and back at Thomas, a dark suspicion on his face. "It's this *coedwig*, is it not? A faery place if ever I have seen one. I saw it pulling at you yesterday. And today, you wake with this foolish notion?" He shook his head, his face grim. "It is best I go after the Saxon alone. You cannot risk it, I fear."

Thomas shook his head. "I know it's hard to believe—it's hard for *me* to believe, too. I thought I was just like everyone else, until I crossed that meadow and the demons came after me, and then I woke up, here."

Celyn eyed him warily, but he kept silent.

Thomas took a deep breath, and continued. "And that's what I couldn't figure out. People don't just disappear and reappear somewhere else. But I did. The first thing you told me was that I was a Traveller, one who could walk between the worlds. Well, you're right. I am. It's one of the Gifts of the Fey. I learned that here."

"And how did you learn this?" Celyn asked, suspicion in his voice.

Thomas clenched his jaw, casting around for what to say, but he had no choice but to tell the truth. "From Godric," he said.

A grimace twisted Celyn's face, and he spat on the snowy ground. "The gleeman, the harper you tried to run to."

"Yes."

"Of course!" The words came out as a hiss as Celyn's face darkened in anger. "You cannot trust him! *He* is one of the *tylwyth teg,* not you. He has bespelled you with his music and his lies! Can you not see it?"

Thomas shook his head and raked his hand through his hair. "Forget Godric! If it wasn't him, I would have found out from another!" Unbidden, Nona's face rose up in his mind, but he quickly turned away from that thought. He could not betray her, or any of the other Fey.

He looked away, frustrated, and saw the *weald* rising up before him, the shadows shifting in its grey depths, and he swung back to Celyn. "I can't prove this to you, not yet, anyway. I don't know enough. But I had to tell you this today, before we went in there. That place is dangerous, you know it. You *felt* it. Without me, it will destroy you."

Again he saw a flicker of acknowledgement in Celyn's eyes, but it quickly disappeared, and the other man shook his head, impatient. "If you know something of this place, tell me, and be quick. This foolishness has already cost us some time."

Thomas forced his voice to be steady. Celyn could not go in there alone. "It's old. Parts of it have never been disturbed since the Creation. And if you go wandering in there, you will start to forget." His conviction became stronger as he looked over at the trees, heard the faint whispers in the branches. He looked back at Celyn. "You'll forget why you are there, you'll forget who you are. Nothing will matter but the fall of sunlight on the leaves, the whisper of the air through the branches, the shapes of the shadows all around you. And you will follow those shadows, further and further in, forgetting everything but the need to find this man, to punish him, to have your revenge. And soon that is all that will remain; the desire for revenge, the need to punish. The Saxon won't matter anymore. Anyone will do." He swallowed. "I think something like that happened to *him,* too. You have to tread very carefully in there."

Silence fell. Thomas saw that Celyn wanted to reject his words, to dismiss them as fantasy. But he also saw the uneasy glance he gave to the trees, and allowed himself to hope, just a little. Celyn was a Celt, after all. Superstition was part of his blood.

"As to that, what makes you think that you will resist the spell?"

"I might not." He held up a hand at Celyn's impatient look. "But this is your task, your revenge, not mine. It won't affect me the same as it does you. And if I don't have to hide who I am, *what* I am—" he broke off, trying to find the words to explain what he hardly understood himself. "I am Fey. I have some power in there, I think. I think if I listen hard enough, I can find him. I felt him, yesterday, when we were riding through, but I didn't realize what it was, just felt a sense of something wrong, something twisted. I thought it was just the trees, but when we found the Pict yesterday, saw his family—" he swallowed heavily, pushing the image away from his mind. "I thought about it last night. What I felt was *him*. This forest is old, but it isn't deliberately malevolent. The effect it has on people is more the result of who *they* are than the forest itself. I can find him in there. I can lead you to him." He took a deep breath, steadying himself. "But you'll have to help me. You're right; it *did* pull on me yesterday. And today it'll be worse, because I'm going to have to allow myself to be *Fey* in there for this to work. I don't know what that means, what that will look like. I might need you to pull me back. It's a powerful place, and I'm not sure how long I can resist it."

Celyn's face was impassive. Thomas was not sure if Celyn believed him, or if he thought him mad.

Finally he shook his head. "We have more to speak of, boy, but now is not the time. One thing we can both agree on is that the less time we spend in there, the better it will be. But he is getting further away as we speak, and I will not allow him to escape, not again." Thomas heard the cold certainty in Celyn's voice. "Lead me to this man, and I will protect you, I swear it before God and all the saints." He let out a breath, deliberately unclenching his fists. "But we will pray first, for as God is my witness, never has the path ahead been more confused."

Thomas nodded, relief coursing through him, chased by anxiety over what was to come. He knelt beside Celyn on the snowy ground, his breath escaping in white mists as he followed Celyn's lead.

Then they crossed themselves, rose to their feet, and mounted their horses, the brooding trees closing around them as they entered the *weald*.

46

As soon as they entered the forest, the muttering branches fell silent, untouched by the gusting breeze they had felt before they had entered. The only sounds were the muffled pace of the horses' hooves and the squeak of the leather in their saddles as they rode.

Moss hung down from the huge twisted trees in places, and ivy twined its way up the gnarled trunks in others. Like yesterday, it was hard to see past the path they were riding upon, even though the sun had been shining as they entered the woods. Shadows deepened just a few paces to either side of them, allowing only the vague outline of trees and bushes to be seen. Last night's snow dusted the branches, and it dropped sometimes on Thomas' cloak when they rode close enough to brush by them.

But he hardly felt it, struggling as he was with the ambient power of the forest, which pulled at his Fey power. Yesterday by force of will he had been able to ignore it, but today he could not if he wanted to track the Saxon.

The presence of the other man was like a whiff of something rotting coming to him on the breeze, but he only experienced it when he allowed his Fey power to respond to the *weald*, rising up within him much as it did at sunrise and sunset each day. But unlike those times, it did not subside but flowed through him in a rush of sensation, making his fingers tingle and his blood sing, and he would get scared, and pull back.

It was like he was standing at a door, holding his shoulder against it to keep it shut against a force that was pushing from the other side, and every once in a while he would let the door open, just a bit, and then would have to shove the door shut again, to keep from being swept away.

But it was at those moments when the door was open that he could sense most clearly the stink of the Saxon and could adjust their way through the trees, paths opening up under Missy's hooves where there had been no path a moment before.

All of this occupied so much of his attention that it was hard to spare a thought for Celyn. The way was narrow, forcing them to ride single file at times, and he had to remind himself to listen for the sound of Celyn following behind.

It was one of those times when he had been wrestling with shutting the door, finding it harder to do the deeper they went into the trees, that he realized Celyn was no longer behind him.

He drew on the reins and hauled Missy around, his heart in his throat, and let out a breath as he saw Arawn standing some yards behind, Celyn sitting still upon the stallion. "Celyn!"

Arawn started, and Missy whinnied at the same time. Celyn snapped to attention then, and he shook his head, touching his heels to Arawn's flanks to catch up. His face was pale, his forehead shiny with a sweat.

"You can't stop," Thomas said, alarmed at the sight of him. "Keep following me. Don't think about him. Just follow me. And pray. That might help."

Celyn swallowed and nodded, and after a moment, Thomas turned Missy back and urged her to keep going.

He heard Celyn following, and let out a breath. After a moment he also heard Celyn's voice, muttering a prayer as they continued, the words drifting up through the trees like smoke. It was one of the litanies of the monks.

Have mercy on us, O God, Father Almighty.
O God of hosts.
O noble God.
O Lord of all the world.

The words followed Thomas as they rode, an anchor in the shifting shadows.

Sometime later, Thomas pulled Missy to a halt. The path was wider here, and Celyn was able to bring Arawn up beside Thomas's mare. It was hard to tell how much time had passed. The trees blocked the sunlight, leaving only an eerie sense of timelessness in its absence.

Thomas scanned the trees on either side. He could feel the Saxon, the stink of him getting stronger and stronger. He opened the door to his power, riding the sweet surge of it, and narrowed his gaze on a tangled patch of underbrush. But now he could see a faint path that led into the deeper woods beyond. And he knew the man they sought had gone that way.

"We are getting close, but we'll have to walk a bit," he said, glancing at Celyn. The man was looking at him oddly, but he swung off Missy and tied her to the huge ash that was by the path. "Come on."

But Celyn remained in the saddle, looking down at him with wary reserve.

What is wrong with him? "Time to go," he said again, impatience colouring his words. "You have to—" he checked himself, realizing suddenly that his Fey power wreathed his words, that he was on the verge of Speaking into Celyn's mind to compel him to do his bidding.

The cold shock of realization cut off the power, and he took a deep breath, chilled. "We have to be out of here before it gets dark," he said, flattening his hands against his thighs to stop a sudden tremor. *Get a grip, Tommo.* "Before sunset."

"Then why not ride?" Celyn's eyes narrowed as he studied him.

Had he noticed that surge of power? *Hopefully not.* Thomas shoved aside the thought and shook his head. "We have to go through here." He gestured at the forest that rose up beside him.

Celyn squinted into the trees where Thomas had indicated, and sudden comprehension flooded his face. He dropped off Arawn and peered more closely, and looked back at him. "He went this way?"

He nodded. "He's down there along that trail. I don't know what he did with his horse. We'll have to be careful."

Celyn's lips thinned. "As to that," he said, "I agree. This man is dangerous, we know that much. He likes the taste of blood." His jaw clenched. "And perhaps he knows we're coming."

Thomas considered the thought. "Perhaps. But I don't think so."

"Why not?"

Thomas shrugged again, and confidence filled him as his Fey power surged again. "Just a hunch," he said, unable to help the fierce smile that suddenly bloomed. "But I'm feeling pretty good about my hunches right now."

Celyn drew back at the look in Thomas' face. "*Man duw,*" he muttered under his breath, crossing himself quickly.

"Follow me," Thomas said, a fierce glee filling him at the knowledge the chase would soon be over. He let his worries fall away as he embraced his power, stepping into the tangle of trees that crowded the faint game trail.

He hardly heard Celyn plunge in after him.

47

Thomas strode along the trail, his heart lifting in the thrumming joy of Fey power. It was hard not to abandon himself to its sweet drawing pull, but his sheer fright at what might happen if he did kept him from embracing it entirely. That, and Celyn's presence. The Welshman would be lost if Thomas did not protect him from the *weald's* lambent power. He was sure of that.

Just how to protect him was another matter, but Thomas didn't dwell on that thought. It was dangerous for him, too, here in the wild embrace of the *weald*. It would not take much for him to abandon Celyn and go further in, to explore the hidden places of the woods, to see what happened when he allowed his power free rein.

But when he began to think that way, when the fall of moss off a branch or the solid bulk of an oak's spreading canopy caught his eye and fired his imagination, he forced his eyes away from it. As it had been at the Gathering, his mind and heart teetered on the edge between his human and Fey nature, and he wasn't sure which way he wanted to fall. But his time in the monastery had settled many prayers and psalms into the deep places of his mind where he did not have to think about them, and they rose to his mind now, whenever the pull of the *weald* threatened to overwhelm him.

And so he alternated between embracing wild Fey joy and surrendering to God. Sometimes he could not tell the difference.

Their mission also helped to keep him focussed. The sense of the other man's presence grew stronger the deeper they moved into the trees. He could barely contain himself from breaking into a run.

But he was hindered by the fear that the man they pursued was Fey. The disturbing memory of Jack Redcap skittered around the edges of his mind as he followed the game path, pushing past brittle shrubs and low-hanging branched. *The best games.* The Jack's words haunted him, along with visions of the slaughtered ram and flashes of Uirolec's family.

Was Redcap a wilding? Driven by impulses he could not control, his untrained power sending him into madness? Was that to be his fate as well? Those questions checked his surrender to his Fey power more than once.

As he pursued the stench of the one they sought, however, the conviction fell upon him that the Saxon was not a Fey. He couldn't explain why, but he began to breathe easier even as he sensed them coming closer and closer to their quarry. He hoped he was right. To meet another Fey in this place, one who had killed like this one had, one who had Gifts Thomas could not understand, would be something far beyond whatever meagre powers he could bring to bear.

Finally the trees opened up ahead into a small clearing, and he stopped, his heart pounding. The Saxon was close.

Celyn was a few paces behind, and for a moment Thomas was alone at the edge of the clearing. Deer tracks crisscrossed in the snow, and the faint trails of mice. And over them all, plain in the new snow, were the Saxon's tracks. They led across the clearing and disappeared into the trees across the way. He felt the wrongness in the air, the stink of the man they sought, and knew they would soon catch up to him.

He turned as he heard Celyn approaching behind him, and the words he was going to say died on his tongue.

Celyn held his sword as he stalked towards Thomas, his eyes glittering fever-bright. Thomas saw at once, *felt,* with his Fey-sense, that the Welshman had succumbed to the forest's spell, his grief and anger sparking the *weald's* power to life, consuming his restraints and leaving him with only one thought in his mind: to kill the Saxon. And if Thomas stood in his way, Celyn would cut him down with no thought. He would leave him there with his life's blood pulsing out of him, and would then find the Saxon and cut him down, too.

And would take his place in this *weald*, lost in a fevered dream of blood and revenge.

Thomas saw it all clearly, his blood freezing in his veins as Celyn marched towards him, vicious anger distorting his face as he raised his sword and swung it, two-handed.

Thomas ducked and spun away from the sword's deadly edge, and dodged again as Celyn roared in rage and came after him, quick on his feet. Thomas saw there was no thought in the Welshman but to destroy and kill.

"CELYN! NO!" Thomas threw the command at Celyn much as he had thrown a similar one at Redcap, his power sparking to life in desperate instinct, twisting away again as the sword's keen edge whistled past his ear.

He felt the power connect, felt it break through the siren song of revenge that was urging Celyn on, felt a brief touch of Celyn himself, his grief and rage, and then the power snapped back, singing through his veins.

Celyn froze, the sword lifted, his breath coming in deep gasps as the brightness faded from his eyes, distress filling his face. "Thomas?" he said, lowering the sword. His face twisted, and he threw his sword away, covering his face with his hands as he sank to his knees. "Merciful God, forgive me!"

But there was no time to go to him. Suddenly he sensed a looming darkness, a sharp *stink,* and for the second time in as many minutes he dodged away from the keen edge of a sword that arced towards him.

The Saxon stood behind him, his face twisted in a snarl. The man had made it look as if he had gone ahead and then had doubled back, in order to ambush them. Thomas yelped in fear and Celyn's head snapped up, and with a low growl he dove for his sword as the Saxon charged at Thomas again.

In his skittering backward flight, grasping feebly at his Fey power but unable to concentrate on anything but the sword as it whistled towards him, Thomas stumbled over a tree root, which likely saved him, for as he fell back the sword whistled over him, just where his head would have been, and then Celyn's sword clashed with the Saxon's blade in a metallic clang.

The Saxon was a large man, heavily muscled, with unkempt dark hair. He wore no armour, and despite the cool temperature, he wore no shirt under his tunic. With a high, keening cry he spun and advanced on Celyn, his sword glittering in the winter morning's light, his eyes wild and crazed.

Thomas scrambled to his feet and watched, helpless, as the Saxon hacked and thrust, driven on by madness and fury, lost in a blood-soaked nightmare. Celyn nimbly parried every stroke, spinning and ducking, his face set in resolute lines of fury and purpose.

Despite the Saxon's bloodlust, Celyn was the much superior fighter, obvious to even Thomas' untrained eyes. In a matter of moments his blade had torn the sword from the Saxon's hands, and the other man was weaponless and stumbling. Celyn advanced quickly, seeing his advantage. The Welshman was not under the spell of the *weald* again, but the long years of pain were etched on his face as his sword lifted, along with a resolute purpose.

Thomas knew he could not let it happen, not here. The power that thrummed through the *weald* was neutral, and likely undetectable to most humans, except for those like Celyn and the Saxon, who were Sensitives. For those, the power would inflame their deepest desires, whether they be innocent, or dark. It was dangerous, but not to everyone.

But Thomas knew that if Celyn spilled this man's blood here, it would not only be Celyn who was at risk.

The power that saturated this forest would change into something dark. The whispering voices of the trees would speak to all who entered, Sensitive or not; would drive them to pursue those passions at any cost to themselves or others. Killing this man here, allowing his blood to soak into the forest floor, would curse unknown numbers of others to that dark fate.

And for a Fey to hear the call of the *weald*, and to enter it, unawares…

Thomas sprang into motion, grabbing Celyn's sword arm. "No!"

The Saxon swayed on his feet, his face twisting into bitter rage. "Finish it!" he roared, stepping towards Celyn, slapping his own chest once, and again. "Do it, ye thrice-cursed coward! Or is your blade too dull, and you a mewling child? Come on, man, do it!"

Celyn's face flushed with anger at the Saxon's taunts, and he tore his arm from Thomas' grasp, his muscles bunching as he prepared to swing the final blow.

"Celyn!" Thomas grabbed his arm again. "No! You can't! Not here! Please!"

The Saxon swung to him, his eyes pinpoints of dark hatred, his hands fisting at his side as he began to stalk towards him. "I'll kill you, you bastard, you sucking pig; kill you and carve you, make you scream and beg and piss your breeches, cry for your mamma, and when she comes to save you, I'll kill her too, long and slow-like, and you'll watch and *beg* me—"

"ENOUGH!" Celyn roared, cutting off the Saxon's low rumbling threats, once again shaking off Thomas' grasp and tackling the man. In one swift motion, he pressed him against a tree, his sword's edge under the Saxon's chin, the other hand fisted in his tunic at the neck. "Silence, 'ere I cut your tongue out!"

The Saxon struggled, but could not free himself. He spat at Celyn, his eyes contemptuous, and Celyn snarled, pushing the sword up higher, forcing the man to lift his head up high to avoid the sharp edge.

God, help us. Thomas gathered his thoughts, raking a hand through his hair. "Not here," he said again. "Not now. Not like this."

Celyn glanced at him quickly. *"He deserves to die,"* he said, in Latin, and continuing in that language. "He killed my wife, my mother, my child. And the Pict's family, and who knows how many others. And you ask for mercy? He has not shown any, and I'll give him none."

The Saxon's eyes narrowed, and Thomas saw that he had not understood, which is likely what Celyn wanted.

Mentally switching gears, he replied in the same language, hoping the words were coming out right. "I understand." He took a breath. "But you feel the power of this place. A moment ago you nearly killed me because I stood in the way of your revenge. But you were able to stop yourself in time." Celyn's eyes narrowed, and Thomas wondered if he had felt that moment, too, when Thomas had Spoken into his mind, had silenced the *weald's* siren song. He thrust the thought aside, and continued. "If you kill him now, *here,* that power will call to you again, and you won't be able to stop it."

Fear and anger warred together in Celyn's face, and Thomas took another step closer, pressing home his point. "You know I'm right," he said. "And there's a part of you that doesn't care. But I do, and I won't let you do it."

He drew on his power then, deliberately: allowing it to fill him, ready to stop Celyn in any way he had to. They stared at each other for a moment, and then he spoke again, trying a different angle. "Uirolec needs to see the end of this, just as much as you do. It might help him."

Thomas prayed Celyn would relent. His only other option was to use Fey power to stop him, and that was the last thing he wanted to try. Especially since he didn't know how.

Celyn's eyes narrowed, fear flashing through them. "Truly, you are one of them? Speak the truth before God." The words were spoken softly, his eyes intent on Thomas' own.

Thomas swallowed, his throat tight, and then he nodded, once.

Celyn held his gaze a heartbeat longer, and then turned back to the Saxon, whose eyes widened as Celyn pressed him harder against the tree. "I will kill you," he said softly, in the language of the Saxons, his voice a deadly threat. "Today. But not yet. The man whose family you killed yesterday will see your death as well. Don't mistake this delay as mercy. You will be dead ere the sun sets. Think you on that, and prepare."

"Coward," the Saxon growled, struggling against Celyn. "Bastard born cur, stinking—"

His words were cut off by a swift blow from Celyn, and his head snapped back against the tree, blood flowing from his lip. He shook his head, a bloody grin blooming on his face. Madness bloomed in his eyes, and something else—a flash of longing for the freedom that death would bring, its cold embrace the only way out of the nightmare the power of the *weald* had wrought in him.

Pity sparked in Thomas, but he squelched it, thinking of Uirolec, and of Celyn, and of the nameless others this man's bloodlust had destroyed. The woods had beguiled the Saxon, it was true, but he had made choices as well. "Enough."

The Saxon turned to him, his sneer fading as he saw Thomas' face.

"That's enough. It's over." Thomas held the Saxon's eyes for a moment, and then he looked at Celyn and nodded.

They tied the Saxon's hands in front of him, the other man strangely docile now, but Celyn kept his sword out, ready if the Saxon turned violent again. They retraced their steps on the game trail and found the Saxon's horse hidden further down the main trail.

The man mounted with little grace, his bound hands fettering him, and Celyn tied him to the saddle. He looked over at Thomas. "Let us leave this place, quickly." His eyes roved over Thomas, fear sparking in them, quickly suppressed as he turned to Arawn and mounted the stallion, holding the rope that led to the prisoner's horse in one hand.

Thomas mounted Missy. He closed his eyes, briefly, the Fey power stretching to life inside him as he turned his attention to it, and opened his eyes, looking back along the way they had come. The way out would open before him, if he just followed his instinct.

The contaminating stink of the Saxon had been muted. He still felt it like a burr in his side, but it was no longer pervasive. The *weald's* power was quiescent now, thrumming on the edges of his senses, barely felt. He nudged Missy into motion, his emotions as tangled as the trees around them. What would Celyn do, now that he knew the truth? He let out a breath. The consequences could be dire, but he was not sorry for it, remembering again the Welshman advancing towards him with his sword raised, bloodlust in his eyes.

Because he was Fey, because he was a Speaker, he had been able to snap Celyn out of the spell the *weald* and his longing for revenge had woven on him. And because he was Fey, he could lead them out of these woods.

I am Fey. His chin lifted.

For once, the thought did not bring despair.

48

"My son," Eata said, looking up at the prisoner, "because of the foul deeds you have done, your life is forfeit. In the name of God and of Oswy, king of these lands, you will be hanged from the neck until dead. Will you not repent of your sins and seek God's forgiveness?"

The Saxon sat on his horse with his hands tied behind him. A noose lay around his neck, the rope tied to a large branch of a spreading oak tree by the road at the edge of Uirolec's holding, visible for all to see as they passed by. Celyn stood to the side of the horse's hindquarters, a switch in his hand, his face shadowed and grim.

The man snarled and spit, causing Eata to take a hasty step back. He looked up at the Saxon, smoothing the anger from his face.

"Very well. May God have mercy on your soul," he said, crossing himself, Celyn and Thomas following suit. Uirolec stood unmoving, as he had since they had brought him out of the hut, his eyes open but unseeing, still in shock. The sight of the Saxon, their explanations, had done nothing to rouse him.

Celyn looked up at the Saxon. "For Muireann, Brude, Cadha, and Eara, whom you slew here in cold blood and with no pity. And for Blodwyn, my mother, Eleri my wife, and Rhianwen, my daughter. You will go to your death with their names in your ears, and you will know that I, Celyn of Gwynedd, have had my justice."

The Saxon sneered, and Celyn brought the switch down hard on the horse's hindquarters. The horse squealed and jumped forward, and the Saxon was left dangling, his neck broken in a clean snap.

Thomas supposed he should feel some pity but a cold satisfaction filled him instead. The swinging body brought to mind Uirolec's family, hanging from the rafters. This man would harm no other innocents, and he could only be glad for it.

Eata stepped forward and fastened the notice he had printed neatly in both Anglic and Latin onto the Saxon's breeches, a sign for those who could read. *Murderer. Hung here in the name of God and of Oswy, King of Bernicia.*

He stepped back and looked over at Celyn, who had corralled the Saxon's horse. "It is done, my son. May God give you peace."

Celyn looked up at the body, taking in the sight as if he were memorizing it. Then he turned away. "The sun goes down. It is best we get back."

They walked in silence back to Uirolec's holding, Eata guiding the Pict by the elbow, leaving the Saxon's body swinging in a slow circle in the gathering shadows of dusk under the tree.

There had been no opportunity for Thomas to speak to Celyn about what had happened in the forest, and so as Eata led Uirolec back to the house, Thomas walked with Celyn to the paddock with the Saxon's horse.

Celyn glanced at Thomas but stayed silent as he began to undo the girth straps on the horse's saddle.

"I'll help you." Thomas began to work on the bridle, trying to figure out what to say. But every word died on his tongue, so they worked together in silence, setting the tack aside when they were done.

Celyn undid the lead rope while Thomas opened the gate, and the horse tossed his head and trotted through it to join the others, who whinnied sharply at the stranger.

Celyn swung the gate shut and began to fasten it with the rope, and Thomas took a deep breath. *Now or never. Just say it.* "I told you about me because I had to. I couldn't do what I needed to do, in the trees, and hide it from you. But you can't tell anyone. It has to stay secret." He held Celyn's gaze. "Not anyone—not even Aidan."

It was full dark now and hard to see Celyn's face. But when he spoke his voice was mild, and Thomas let out a breath he did not know he had been holding. "As to that, I have given you secrets of my own I would have you keep, as well."

Thomas opened his mouth to respond, but Celyn continued.

"I have told no one else of my sins. Not even the bishop, as much as he presses me. And yet I spoke of it to you." He shook his head. "Aidan tells me that he thinks God wishes you to be *periglour* to me."

Periglour. Soul-friend. Thomas frowned. *Really?*

"As God is my witness, I did not understand him. But it seems we have both borne each other's secrets, and shared much that we cannot tell to others. And so perhaps he is right." His jaw clenched. "I confess, I do not know what to think about what you told me. Whether it be true or no, I cannot say, but I—" A horse squealed suddenly, interrupting him. He blew out a breath and clenched his jaw briefly, his eyes hard. "Know this. I will not allow harm to come to the bishop or God's work on Lindisfarne through my silence. If it means breaking my word to you to protect him, I will do so."

Thomas let out a breath. It was more than he could have hoped for. "I understand." He heaved a sigh, the weight of his impossible circumstances crashing down on him again. "Look. I would leave now, if I could. I just don't know how to get home. But as soon as I figure it out, I'll be gone, I promise."

"You speak foolishness, boy. There is no need for that," Celyn said with some asperity. He laid a hand on Thomas' shoulder. "You saved me in the forest. You were right: I would still be there, wandering in its depths, lost to blood and madness, if not for you. And you led me to the Saxon and freed me of my vow to revenge my family. Whatever means it took for you to do it, I am grateful. I will not forget it."

Thomas' eyes pricked. He was glad the gloom hid the flush in his face.

Celyn squeezed his shoulder, briefly, and then dropped his hand. "Come," he said, not unkindly. "Father Eata will be saying the prayers, and I think we both could use them, no?"

Thomas nodded, relief washing over him that this terrible day was over. They walked side by side to the dwelling, the stars pricking the sky above, the snow ghosting around their feet, the darkness hiding the worst of the disasters the Saxon had wrought upon this place. He wondered for a moment what Uirolec would do now, how he would cope.

Like we all do, he thought, weariness falling upon him as he stepped with Celyn into the dwelling, to the sound of Eata's voice lifting in prayer. *One day at a time, and the best we can.*

49

"There is more to this story," Nona said, her eyes flashing. "There is something different about you, and I would know what it is."

Thomas' heart sank as he shrugged off his cloak and hung it on the peg beside the door. Nona had lit the hearth fire, and the welcome warmth seeped into him as he considered what to say. She had been present yesterday when they had brought Uirolec back to Bebbanburg in the driving rain, and had heard the story of what had happened when they reported to Oswy in the hall.

Not the whole story, of course. And her eyes held more than a hint of speculation when she had quickly glanced at him before he and Celyn had left the hall to return to Celyn's home. They intended to take the Pict to Lindisfarne, but the weather was too foul for travel and Uirolec needed some time to rest.

He had managed to avoid her thus far, but she had been waiting for him at Celyn's house after lunch, and his heart sank. He had a feeling she was not going to be happy about all that conspired in the *weald*. Looking at her now, with her arms crossed at her chest as she waited for his answer, almost tapping her foot in impatience, he knew his intuition was right.

Unfortunately he had not come up with a strategy as to how to tell her what had happened. And as always, her presence set him off-kilter. He raked his hand through his hair, wondering where to begin. *God, help me.* There was no easy way to do this. He stepped past her to the fire, holding out his hands to warm them. The rain still drummed down outside, the chill in the air going right to his bones.

"Tell me," she urged, her eyes narrowing as she searched his face.

He sighed. *No point beating around the bush.* He turned to face her. "The *weald* was a place of power, or something. Somehow the Saxon had been corrupted by it. I think he was a Sensitive—I mean, it had the same kind of effect on Celyn."

"Celyn?" A thin edge of alarm coloured Nona's voice. The windows were shuttered against the rain, enclosing them together in the half-gloom. They both spoke softly, for this conversation was one that no human should hear. "There are ancient places in the world, where Fey and human alike can be entranced, 'tis true. This Saxon, he resided in these woods?"

"I'm not sure. Maybe."

"And you and Celyn went in there to find him." She sucked in a breath. "That was foolish. You, a *wilding*—"

The word pricked him. "I didn't have much choice. Celyn was going in after him. I had to go, too. I had to protect him."

"And how did you think to do that?" She swept her gaze over him, her voice sharp. "You had no sword, no way to use your power—" She shook her head slightly, impatient. "What did you do?"

"I could feel the man there, smelled him like a rotten stink. I couldn't let Celyn wander around in the trees too long. I had to lead him to where the Saxon was. And I only could do that if I wasn't worried about hiding from him what I am." His heart took a thump in his chest as he turned to face her, the words spilling out. "I told him I was Fey. I had to."

"You *told*—" She stared at him, shocked, and then sat down abruptly on a stool pulled up to the hearth, as if her legs had given out. "God have mercy, Thomas, what have you done?"

He sat on the chair. "I didn't have a choice. The power in there worked on Celyn, too. It fed his desire for revenge, possessed him. He tried to cut me down in my tracks in order to get to the Saxon. I had to stop him somehow."

Nona's chest rose up and down as she sucked in a breath. Her face was pale, her eyes glittering green as her gaze speared him. "How?"

Thomas flinched. "I used the Speaking Gift. Somehow. Like I did when Redcap tried to take you. He swung his sword at me, and I panicked. I don't know how I did it, but I felt our minds connect, and then he snapped out of it."

"Snapped—?" Her voice rose, on the edge of panic.

"He was himself again, I mean. The Speaking worked. Thankfully, because that's when the Saxon attacked us. If Celyn had killed him in the midst of his bloodlust, in that place—" The memory flooded back, fear piercing him anew, and he leaned forward, willing her to understand. "He would have been lost there, no different than the man he killed."

But it was as if she hadn't heard him. "He knows you are Fey." She closed her eyes briefly, her face white. "You have no idea—"

"I'm sorry. I didn't want to tell him. I didn't know what else to do."

Nona opened her eyes and stood up. "I must go." She swept by him and grabbed her cloak.

Thomas jumped up. "Wait!"

She ignored him, the door slamming shut behind her as she left.

Oh for Pete's sake— His jaw clenched, and he swung around and slapped the table, hard, the sting of it sharp as he sat down. *I had no choice.*

It was true, but the thought brought little comfort.

50

"Ye be off again, Master Thomas?" Father Gaeth stopped in his tracks, his arms full of scrolls.

Thomas hid his impatience as he mounted Missy, tamping down the urgency that bubbled up. He forced himself to answer the Prior cordially. "Yes, just for a few days."

He had no idea if that was true or not, but it didn't matter. There was no time for a long conversation. He had been waiting all day for the tide to recede and now that it was safe to travel, he had to get on his way. "I'm going to Bebbanburg, to visit the Lord Celyn."

"Ah. I am taking these records to the bishop. I'll tell him straightaway," Father Gaeth nodded briskly. Thomas was glad it was the Prior that he had run into. Gaeth was always in a hurry to go somewhere or do something. Most of the others were content to meander and dawdle, no matter that their Rule urged punctuality and efficiency. And they especially loved to indulge their curiosity over what everyone else was doing, and when, and why.

"Thank you," Thomas said, gathering up the reins.

Father Gaeth nodded, but instead of hurrying off, he paused, a slight frown on his face. "Are ye sure ye must leave now? T'will be full dark by the time ye get to Bebbanburg." His shoulders shifted in an uneasy movement. "Perhaps it'd be best to travel by day."

Thomas studied him, suddenly alert. Something in the Prior's voice echoed the fear that had been chasing him all day, since Nectan's voice had speared through him like a bolt of lightning during the Matins prayers. *Come now, all Seelies. Come!*

The Call held an undeniable urgency and a sense of immediate action to it as it faded, and had been repeated off and on all day. The Seelies were to meet at a cleared field close to a holding around three miles from Bebbanburg village, at one hour past dusk. Time enough to make it if he left *now*.

He stuffed back his impatience, forcing himself to focus. It was odd to see the normally stoic Prior uneasy. "What do you mean, Father?"

Gaeth shook his head slightly. "I dinna know, my son. But these last few nights, there's been something—a feeling in the air. Like something's watching, or something's coming." One shoulder lifted again. "Brother Seamas says that the dogs have been restless, snapping at shadows. Ye will remember the chickens, cut up as they were, and the ram—" He broke off, swallowing.

"Yes," Thomas replied, careful to keep his voice neutral. It was over a month since Redcap's visit, and although there had been no sign of him since, speculation as to the cause of the animals' odd deaths still ran rampant in the monastery. Some of it, thanks to Frithlac, was still aimed at him.

The monk smiled faintly. "Me ma would say the Old Ones are walking," he said, and shook his head as if to dispel that thought. "Foolishness, perhaps. But still, it will be dark soon. Can ye no wait until the morrow?"

The Old Ones. One of the names the Irish Celts gave for the Fey, along with *Sidhe*. What would Gaeth say if he knew Thomas himself was an Old One? He forced himself to smile. "No. I must go." Seeing the other's frown, he added, with sudden inspiration, "It's the Lady Nona's birthday. I promised the Lord Celyn I would come. Don't worry. I'll be fine. But I must leave now, while the light holds."

"Ah. Well, go with God then, Master Thomas. And send the Lady the bishop's best wishes. He will pray a special blessing for her tonight."

Thomas suppressed a twinge of guilt for his lie, and nodded. They would need Aidan's prayers, no matter the reason. "Thank you, Father. I will."

He had just reached the wet sand left behind by the tide's retreat when the alarm echoed in his head again, as it had in regular intervals throughout the day. *Come. Come now, all Seelies!* Spurred on with fresh urgency, he touched his heels to Missy's sides and bent his head over her neck as she surged into a run, clumps of mud and seaweed flying up behind him.

Something's watching. Something's coming. A chill touched him. Gaeth's words described the exact feeling that had been haunting him all day.

And every instinct he possessed screamed at him that each powerful thrust of Missy's legs brought him closer to that *something*.

Thomas reined in Missy as he squinted at the silhouette of Bebbanburg. The king's hall was dark against the grey twilit sky. There was no alarm evident around the town, nothing amiss at Oswy's fortress that he could see.

Whatever threat prompted Nectan's alarm was likely a Fey matter, then, not one involving the humans. The thought was no comfort. Aside from whatever danger awaited, there was Nectan himself to deal with. He had much to speak to the king about, but he would prefer to do it in private. And he wasn't entirely sure he wanted to go haring to Nectan's side like a dog to its master, no matter his pledge.

For a moment, he hesitated, torn between continuing and turning back to the monastery, leaving the Fey to their business.

He took a deep breath. It was tempting, but he couldn't do it. Whatever Nectan's purpose was in Calling the Seelies together, it was bad, Thomas had no doubt. And Nona wouldn't have turned away from the king's Summons. She would respond to the Call.

There hadn't yet been the chance to mend the rift between them. Thomas had hoped to give her a little time to cool down and then go and see her, try to make things up. Nectan's Call had interfered with that plan. Despite the awkwardness between them, Thomas couldn't leave Nona to face whatever danger was coming while he huddled at the monastery, no matter how distasteful he found the thought of seeing Nectan again.

More than distasteful, he had to admit. He was frightened of the king, of his power, and the hold he had over him. He had gone over and over that pledge in his mind, yet he had always come to the same conclusion, that there was nothing else he could have done. But it rankled him all the same. The Knowing had been bad enough. What else would the king require of him? And would he require it this night?

Anxiety made his heart trip in his chest. He had to go, both for Nona's sake and because of his pledge. He could only hope that whatever this crisis was, it would be over quickly.

The peace of Christ fill me, the power of Christ aid me, the presence of Christ be with me evermore. The prayer brought some peace, and he started to turn Missy towards the small rutted track that branched off from the main road and led towards the meeting place.

And froze, the hairs on the back of his neck prickling as an eerie, wailing howl touched his ears, so faint that it was a mere suggestion of a sound. Missy whinnied sharply, her head coming up as her muscles bunched beneath her. Thomas had to react quickly to keep her from bolting, but she reared and plunged for a moment until he could calm her enough to get her to stand still.

He gathered the reins in one hand and leaned down to pat her quivering neck, trying to calm his own heart as well. The horse responded to his touch, but her eyes still rolled white and she blew a steaming breath through her nostrils, her foot stamping once. "Easy, girl," he murmured. He couldn't blame the horse for her reaction, for he felt much the same himself. *What was that?*

His blood froze as the sound came again, and Missy trembled, violently. *Something's coming.* Thomas fought down his fear as he wheeled Missy in a tight circle, trying to determine where the sound came from. He heard the dogs of Bebbanburg responding, barking and howling frantically in response as the eerie sound ghosted through the night.

He whirled Missy around again as it faded out. As far as he could tell, the track that led towards the meeting place of Nectan's Seelies would also lead him towards whatever had made that sound.

The calls rippled through the night again, slightly louder. *Wolves? No, dogs. Hounds, on a hunt.*

A sudden gust of wind snatched away the faint, eager sound. But its temporary cessation did nothing to ease the sickening dread building in his gut. Those were no ordinary dogs, that much he knew. The sound of their howls was enough to curdle milk. He had a moment's shuddering sympathy for whatever was being hunted, and thrust it aside. He would find out, soon enough.

The Call flared to life in his mind, more urgent than before. *Come, now!* But he didn't need the prompt. Those beasts were headed this way. No matter his complicated feelings towards Nectan and the other Fey, he would rather face this threat together with them than by himself. At least with them he might have a chance.

He gathered the reins and touched his heels to Missy's flank, and she burst into motion, her hooves beating a steady rhythm beneath him as he leaned over her neck and urged her on.

51

The howls speared intermittently through the air as Missy galloped down the faint track, her legs stretching out under her in powerful thrusts. But soon they came to some trees that crowded on either side of the path, and Thomas had to rein her in to a walk.

As the sun dipped towards the horizon, the wind picked up, bringing with it a few icy flakes. They had not gone long before Thomas realized he would not be able to ride much further. The howls were closer now, and louder, and every time Missy heard them, her head reared up and she tried to bolt. Soon Thomas' arms and legs were aching from the strain of keeping her pointed down the path.

Thomas didn't blame the horse. The eerie wails were having much the same effect on him. They scraped against his nerves and wormed into his brain, bringing with them echoes of nightmares and visions of every bogeyman he had ever contemplated. And it grew worse by as the sun sank towards the horizon. It was as if his Fey power amplified the effect of their cries.

One particularly long sustained bout of howls dragged him into a place in his head reserved only for his most desolate thoughts, and everything else faded away into darkness. He was alone with his worst fears, which were bearing towards him on black wings of despair, carried by the sound of the hounds. *The darkness is yours you are alone you are nothing you will fail you bring the darkness…*

Time slowed, and stopped. He tried to break away from the accusing voice, but there was nowhere he could go that the howling storm could not reach.

COME! The Call erupted through the darkness with as much the same effect as being dashed in the face with cold water. He snapped back to himself just in time to realize that he was slipping off Missy's back. He made a frantic attempt to grab at something, anything, but it was too late. He hit the ground hard, Missy's squeal loud in his ears.

The breath was knocked out of him, and he could only gasp ineffectively for a couple of moments. Thankfully the howls had stopped or Missy would have bolted. But she simply stood there, looking back at him bemusedly. It was full dark now; the Call that had broken through the dreadful spell of the howls must have been timed with the surge of power as the sun went down.

He took a trembling breath as he struggled to his feet. *Christ, have mercy.* He grabbed Missy's bridle and leaned on her solid bulk, grateful for her presence. *Get a grip,* he told himself sternly, taking a stronger breath. A quiver ran through the horse, and he patted her neck. "Easy, girl," he said. She nickered softly and turned her head to breathe on him. Thomas rubbed her forehead, his heartbeat slowing, and she whickered softly in his ear.

A sudden thought struck him, and he quickly stripped the horse of the saddle and blanket and vaulted onto her back. He sat for a moment, allowing Missy to get used to it, but he could feel a difference in the horse immediately, could feel the muscles relaxing under her skin. He breathed in deeply again and clucked his tongue. Missy responded and stepped ahead, her breath steaming out.

An ululating howl shivered through the dark trees, and Missy started, but not as badly, even though the cry was louder, closer than before. And Thomas weathered it better, too. The contact with the horse helped him as much as it did Missy. It restored him, gave him back a piece of himself that the fear had leached away.

"Atta girl," he murmured. "Go easy. We can do this together." He threaded his way through the trees as quickly as he could make Missy move. As the vicious howls seared through the night, he prayed under his breath for whoever was being hunted. It was bad enough to hear the sound of their eager cries. To know that you were the one they sought would be infinitely worse.

Thomas urged the mare into a canter wherever he could. Time was running out. The hounds were getting closer. Finally Thomas broke through the trees into a large field covered with stubble that crunched under Missy's hooves.

A group of Fey stood in the middle of the field with their backs to him, about ten yards away, facing the trees that lined the clearing on the far side. Not as many as were at the Gathering, but this emergency had come quickly. Only those in the immediate area could respond in time.

Thomas scanned the group. Nectan was conferring with Domech, who stood with his sword at the ready beside his king. Brorda's tall form was easy to see, and then Thomas' heart gave a jump as he saw Nona standing beside the Ward.

The rest he recognized from the Gathering: a couple of the musicians and another of Nectan's guards, as well as Strang, the sour-faced Fey. They all were armed, with swords or axes or bows strung tautly, facing the far end of the field. Even Nona held a short knife at the ready.

Nectan turned, and although the light was dim, their eyes met across the field. *Wilding.*

Tension and fear thrummed through the word. Fear at what was to come, fear of *him*. A warning was woven through it as well, a reminder of his pledge of fealty. Thomas swallowed as he hurriedly dismounted and wrapped Missy's reins around a nearby branch, his stomach fluttering with nerves.

He joined Nona and she glanced at him, her face pale. She opened her mouth to speak, but the howls erupted again, the eager sound filling the night. The creatures were close now.

"What *is* that?" he choked out.

"The Hunt!" Before she could say more, another eerie howl rippled through the night, and Thomas flinched in reaction, a few scattered exclamations erupting from the other Fey.

A bugle's bright cry rose sharply above the sound of the hounds, and Thomas raised his hands to his ears instinctively to muffle the sound. It scraped and jangled against his nerves even more sharply than the sound of the dogs.

"He is close, my king! We must prepare!" Domech said, his face white.

"Take your places!" Nectan commanded, his voice tight with strain. "The Hunt comes. Gather your courage and be ready for my command!"

Some of the Fey melted away into the night, ringing the field, lifting bows and swords, intent on the gap in the trees where the hounds would appear. Nona, Brorda, and Domech stood with Nectan, who turned to Thomas and gripped his arm, his amber eyes fierce. "Dinna be foolish, now, wilding! Remember your pledge! I've no time to tell ye—"

But his words were cut off. Thomas heard Missy whinny sharply, the other horses joining in as they stamped and pulled frantically at their tethers.

The air was filled with the sound of the bugle and of the hounds' frightful cries, which reverberated around the trees, bringing with them a terrible weight of doom and destruction. All around him Thomas could feel Fey power gathering, the silent forms around the clearing shimmering like starlight in the gloom.

Brorda caught his eye, and Thomas saw grim desperation in his face. "Thomas—" he choked out, but then a horse broke through the trees, carrying two riders, and there was no time for anything else.

The horse was labouring, white foam flying from its mouth as the rider urged it on. The man holding the reins was Fey, his form glimmering in the dark, but the figure clinging to his back was human, a female with long hair that streamed out behind her as the horse flew towards them. Thomas' eyes touched on her, and then snapped back to the Fey, seeing the power shining brightly within him, the leashed energy of it. The rider turned in the saddle to look behind him. With a sickening lurch in his gut Thomas saw the black outline of an arrow sticking out of the man's upper back.

Beside Thomas, Nectan held a sword at the ready. Brorda hefted a *seax*, and Nona held her knife out, rigid with tension. Thomas drew his knife as well, the feel of it in his hand steadying him. *God, help us.*

The adrenaline coursing through him made everything crystal clear, all the details popping out in stark relief.

The horse flew past the shadowy trees, getting closer with every stride of its powerful legs.

The faint moonlight revealed the rider's face and Thomas froze, an ice-cold spike piercing his heart. Everything fell away, and even the appearance of the hounds as they broke through the trees, huge and dark, baying in their unnatural tongues, could rouse him.

They didn't matter, not anymore. Nor did it matter that the Huntsman was finally revealed, charging out from the oaks on a horse the colour of ashes, wearing a helmet sprouting deer's horns.

Thomas barely felt the howling wind that preceded the Huntsman, a wind that shook the branches of the trees and tore at their cloaks, causing them to stagger in place, fighting to stay upright.

It was all just a distraction. The only thing that mattered was the man who rode pell-mell towards them.

The man being chased by the Huntsman was someone he would have known anywhere—even here, at this impossible time and place.

The man on the horse was his father.

52

The horse bore down on them, the hounds on its heels and the Huntsman's bugle splitting the night in an unearthly wail.

It can't be—

For a moment he convinced himself that he was wrong, that the uncertain moonlight was playing tricks on him, but as the rider drew closer, his doubt vanished. It was his father. There was no mistake.

My father is alive. My father is Fey. These two thoughts filled his head, careening around in a wild flurry. Both of them carried so many implications that he couldn't begin to catalogue them all. He whirled to face Nectan, a terrible suspicion hardening into certainty as the king looked at him, and Thomas saw it confirmed in his eyes.

Nectan knew. Knew that it was his father riding for his life with the hellhounds snapping at his horse's hooves, had known all along that his father was here. *Alive.*

The howling of the hounds and the vicious whip of the wind made it impossible to be heard, even if Thomas could force any words out. Nor was there any time.

The panicked squeal of a horse ripped through the hounds' cries and Thomas spun back to see the horse carrying his father tumble to the ground, an arrow protruding from its hindquarters. His father landed heavily some ten feet away from them; the woman rolled and scrabbled over to where his father lay motionless.

Thomas' attention snapped to the Huntsman, seeing him clearly for the first time. He was Fey, glowing in the moonlight with Fey power, shadowed by something dark that twisted and writhed, almost but not quite mirroring his every motion. The oily grace of it caused Thomas' skin to crawl. He had seen that same motion before, surging towards him across a field last Halloween. *A demon.*

"Christ, have mercy!" Nona gasped.

Nectan pulled his sword out and took one step towards the two on the ground, but froze as the Huntsman yanked his mount to a shuddering halt and leapt off it, striding towards them.

Thomas couldn't have moved if he'd wanted to, the shock immobilizing him as surely as if he were bound in chains. *My father is alive. My father is Fey. He's alive.*

The hounds surged around the two on the ground, obscuring them from view. Nona gave a low cry and lurched forward in a half step, but Domech stopped her, his hand grabbing her arm.

She swung on him, but he shook his head once, his eyes hard. "Nay, Lady, not yet, or ye will die, and all of us with you! Patience!" he hissed.

Eyes flashing, she glanced back at the scene in front of them, and then, chest heaving, she stepped back. Nectan's sword glittered coldly in the moon's pale light. A slight tremor passed through him, and his voice reached them in a low mutter, but Thomas couldn't concentrate enough to hear what the king was saying.

His attention was focussed on the figure on the ground. *A Fey.* Thomas could see the power in his father, felt the Fey-sense that sparked up and down his nerves when he looked at him. There was no mistake.

The injured horse thrashed and squealed in terror, the dogs barking and snarling, scenting blood. They slunk away as the Huntsman strode through them, milling with excited whines around his ankles. He motioned quickly with his hand, and suddenly the dogs turned away from the two on the ground, and leapt upon the horse.

Nona gave a cry and turned away, a shudder rippling through her as the ravening pack attacked the defenceless creature. The horse's thin scream cut off abruptly, leaving only the wet sounds of tearing, and the snarling of the hounds.

The other horses panicked, lunging and neighing in a piercing cacophony from where they were tethered around the field. But even that noise didn't mask the human woman's voice as the Huntsman drew his blade as he advanced towards the two on the ground.

"NO!" she screeched, throwing herself over the prone man, who still lay motionless. With one swift motion the Huntsman leaned down and grabbed her by the arm that she had raised to protect them. The instant he touched her, she went limp, Fey power surging around her, and then he tossed her aside as if she were a rag doll. She lay still where he had flung her, a few feet away, one arm outstretched on the ground beside her, long hair obscuring her face.

The Huntsman skirted the prone figures as he walked towards them, his sword dangling in his hand loosely. He stopped in front of Nectan, and the howling wind suddenly ceased, leaving only the sounds of the hounds snapping and snarling at one another as they feasted.

The horned helmet the Huntsman wore had faceplates that curved over his cheeks, obscuring his features, other than a long jaw and thin lips defining a wide mouth. His eyes were visible as well, but when Thomas caught a glimpse of them, he wished they were not.

They were not clear as glass as he had been accustomed to see in a Fey. They were dark, full of shadows and clouds. A glimpse was all he could take. He took a shuddering breath and closed his eyes, scrambling to pull himself together.

God, have mercy. Christ, have mercy. O Mighty Three. Christ, have mercy. Thomas clung to the words like a drowning man would cling to a rope. But then the Huntsman began to speak, and his eyes snapped open, his concentration shattered.

Who is it that defies my Hunt, that rings me here, that stops my blade? Name yourself, and prepare, for I will have my prize ere this night is through.

He spoke softly and not entirely out loud. Thomas heard the words in his mind as well, echoing in a half-beat behind, just as the demon-shadow was a half step behind the Fey's movements.

He tried to block the haunted voice from his head, to push it away, but it was like grappling with fog.

Nectan raised the tip of his sword slightly and lifted his chin. When he spoke, his voice was steady. Thomas had no idea how he managed it. His own voice was stuck in his throat, strangled by fear. "You know who I am, Hunter."

Behind the horned man, the dogs continue to feed, the carcass juddering under their onslaught. The coppery smell of blood hung heavy in the cold air. The Huntsman regarded Nectan for a long moment.

Nectan, King of the Seelies, Speaker.

Nectan trembled at the power the Huntsman wove through his words. But the power was woven lightly. The Huntsman was merely playing with the king, showing his power but not wielding it fully. Nectan stood his ground, and the other Seelies, too, kept their weapons drawn where they were stationed around the field, not a movement among them even as the Huntsman swept his gaze over them in a slow, wide circle before turning again to the king.

And the others I could name, indeed. But one.

The oily feel of the words sliding through his head was so unpleasant that Thomas almost did not understand him, but then the creature's eyes locked on him, and the meaning suddenly slammed home.

The Hunter looked back at Nectan. *You wish a trade then: my prey for this flame of fire.* The Huntsman cocked his head, considering. The air around them grew colder. Thomas could see the vapour of Nectan's breath, but from the Huntsman, nothing. But were his lips even moving? It was hard to tell. *I do not wish it, not this time, Seelie King.*

Thomas scrambled to understand. Nectan meant to hand him over to this creature in return for his father? Is that what his pledge would require of him?

I will take my prize and depart. I am Called. The Huntsman nodded once, as if the matter were settled, and moved as if to turn aside.

Nectan's hands firmed on his sword. "No. Ye willna take him."

Thomas saw the fire of Nectan's power filling him and his own power sang to life in response, a sweet storm within him. The rest of the Fey were drawing on their power too, and they shone like stars fallen to earth around the clearing.

His heart hammered so hard he could hardly breathe.

The Huntsman turned back at Nectan's words. *This one is not pledged to you.* He inclined his head towards Thomas' father. *And there be none of his blood to claim him. He is mine.* He stepped forward, lifting his sword. *You risk much, Seelie. You cannot win a fight against me. My blade will drink your blood, if you so wish.*

Behind the Huntsman, Thomas' father began to stir, and Thomas' heart lurched in his chest, the sight breaking his paralysis. He stepped forward to stand beside Nectan, gripping his knife. "You're wrong. *I* am of his blood. He is my father." His voice wavered a bit, but he lifted his chin, cold sweat pooling under his armpits, willing himself to stand still, even though everything within him wanted to run away. He heard Nona's stifled gasp behind him as he continued. "You can't have him."

The ghoulie eyes slammed back to him again. *Name yourself, Fey.* Slight curiosity coloured the voice. *This one is Matthew MacCadden, yes, a Fey of bright power. Power you share, I see. But do you share his name, Traveller? Tell me. I would know.*

The compulsion to blurt out his name, the desire to obey, shot through him. But he could not give this creature his name, and along with it, power over him. *Jesus.* He collected himself, willing his voice to be steady. "I'm his son, and I claim him. That's all I'm giving you."

The Huntsman considered that for a moment, his head cocking slightly to one side. Thomas' jaw clenched as his gaze swept over him again, fighting the insidious pressure to give in. And then, the pressure withdrew, and the Hunter spoke again. *In which Court do you stand, Traveller? Think well before you answer, for I will hear the lie on your lips, and you will answer for it*

Traveller. How did this creature know? He thrust aside the speculation, trying to ignore the clamouring desire that beat through him to tell him everything, to let the Huntsman *Know* him—He took a shuddering breath, grasping at self-control. *Christ Almighty.* "I am Seelie, pledged to Nectan, King."

Silence fell, broken only by the dogs' fierce snarls. The roused power of the Gathered Fey snapped against his nerves like electricity. Would they fight for him, too, if the Hunter took him?

After a long moment, the Hunter spoke, his voice echoing unpleasantly in Thomas' mind. *You have the right. The claim of blood and the presence of your Court is surety. I leave my prey to you, firefly. His blood be on your hands.* He nodded once, formally, and Thomas nodded back, willing himself to breathe again.

The Huntsman turned to Nectan. *This one is barely Tamed. You may rue the day you took his pledge.* He slid the sword into the scabbard, his Fey power shimmering and swirling, mixing with the dark shadow that slid around him in an oily pool. *The Hunt is not easily turned aside. It is fortunate my hounds have fed; else I would have given them one of your Fey to satiate them in payment for your arrogance. But know this: I will not forget.*

The king gave the barest of nods to the other Fey, his sword still raised, rock steady in his hands.

The Huntsman turned on his heel, his cloak flowing around his ankles. A faint smell of corruption wafted over them. He turned back after taking a couple steps. *I will gather a human this night as payment to my lord, and your Court will not interfere.*

The muscles moved in Nectan's throat as he swallowed, and then nodded again.

The dark Fey lifted his bugle from where it lay across his chest and gave a piercing blast that rang out among the trees and vibrated Thomas' bones. The hounds leapt up as one and scrabbled over to their master, bloody muzzles shining black in the night.

The Huntsman leapt upon his mount and whirled it around, a great wind once again roaring out from the motion, causing Thomas to turn his head and close his eyes against the swirling debris of branches and dead leaves it flung against them.

When he opened his eyes, the Huntsman and his hounds were gone, and the wind ceased abruptly, as if it had never been.

Thomas stood frozen in place a half-second more, then stumbled over to where his father struggled to rise. He fell to his knees beside him, Nona close behind. His father was on one knee, his head bowed as he braced himself against the ground, the arrow sticking obscenely from his back. He lifted his head and their eyes met, and Thomas' heart lurched in his chest again.

His father. Alive. Clear grey eyes, eyes that matched his own, met his.

"Tommo," he whispered, joy and pain lancing across his features. A trickle of blood dripped down the side of his face from an abrasion on his temple. "Son. Thank God you are safe." His eyes fluttered, and Thomas had to catch him before he fell flat on his face on the cold ground.

53

Thomas **froze in** shocked immobility, his arms full of the impossible weight of his father. *Tommo. Son.* The familiar voice echoed in his head, much as the Huntsman's had earlier, and he had just as much success in keeping it out.

"Let me see!" Nona sank to the ground beside him, giving him a few more moments to gather himself as he eased his father to the ground. His father had some sort of knapsack strapped to his back, with a bulky, hard object in it. They had to cut the strap on his injured shoulder to remove the bag, and then moved aside his father's cloak and bloodstained tunic to reveal the injury. The arrow was firmly planted in his father's upper back, in the shoulder.

A wave of nausea swept over Thomas at the sight, his brain kicking into gear in a sudden spurt of panic. Men died from injuries like this in this time. "Can you Heal him?"

Nona glanced up at him quickly, but then bent over his father, examining the injury. "We need to get the arrow out. Can you do it? I will aid you."

Thomas stuffed back his roiling emotions and nodded. He gritted his teeth as he gripped the arrow's' shaft, willing his queasy stomach to settle, trying to steady his shaky hands.

Behind him, the rest of the Fey gathered around Nectan, their voices a low murmur, but he had no attention to spare for them.

Nona bowed her head and placed her hands on his father's back on either side of the shaft, and closed her eyes. She began to pray in a low voice, and at the same time Thomas felt the prickle of Fey power as she called it to life. He sucked in a breath and pulled as gently on the arrow as he could.

Whether it was Nona's Fey power or just dumb luck, the arrow slid out of his father easily, blood flowing freely as it did so. Thomas threw it away in disgust.

Nona peered at the wound and then bent down and sniffed at it. She straightened up. "Good. It is not poisoned, thank the good Christ. We must bandage him and get him somewhere warm, where I can make a proper poultice." Her eyes met his. "If God is merciful, he will survive."

Thomas nodded, the fear that squeezed his heart easing slightly. He helped her staunch the flow of blood, using his father's cloak as an improvised bandage.

Nona's hands stilled as they shifted his father and the moonlight struck his face. She sucked in a breath. "Your father," said, her voice shaky. She glanced up at him. "You've never told me of him."

His mother had always remarked how much Thomas looked like his father, but Thomas hadn't realized it until now, when he saw him again with an adult's eyes, bathed in the moonlight. They shared the same facial structure, the same thick black hair. And his eyes. *Fey eyes.*

"He died when I was nine years old," he said, unreality stealing over him as he looked down at the body on the ground again. "He walked out and never came back. There was an accident; he was dead…or so we thought. But he must have been *here*—" His throat seized up, disturbing speculations crowding through his mind.

"A Traveller's path is a strange one indeed," Nona said. She took a breath, shaking her head as if to clear it. "Come, we are almost done. Help me finish."

As he helped her, the first shock fading, his mind began to kick into gear. All those years they had mourned him as dead, but his father had been here. *He was alive all the time.* His mother's face flashed through his mind, and a spark of anger flared into life.

Brorda squatted down beside them. "Thomas," he said, hesitancy in his voice.

The sight of the other Fey was tinder to his anger. "Did you know?" he asked, rising to his feet. "About my father, that he was here. Did you know?"

Brorda rose as well, wariness filling his face.

Thomas' fists clenched. "Don't lie to me, *Teacher*. Did you know?"

Brorda held his gaze steadily. "I knew of the Traveller who was living in Dál Riata, but I swear, until this eve I did not know it was your father!"

"Mother of God!" Nona looked up at Brorda in shock. "He is *that* Fey?"

Thomas stared at her, seeing the dismay flooding her face. A memory flashed from the night of the Gathering. He had looked for Nona before they left, and had seen her in conversation with the king, her face raised to his in urgent appeal, the shake of Nectan's head in reply. He had dismissed it as a Fey matter at the time, and had been too shattered by the night's events to want to know more.

He also remembered Brorda, the discomfort on his face when he had asked him, repeatedly, about how to Travel, how to get home.

"You both knew." Icy certainty filled him. "Maybe not that my father was here. But you knew of a Traveller, someone who could tell me how to get home. Why didn't you tell me?"

Nona rose smoothly. "We could not," she said, her chin lifting as if she dared him to contradict her.

The Gathering. The Knowing. Thomas' anger flared white-hot, as his earlier suspicion snapped all the pieces together. Nona and Brorda had not told him because they had not been given permission.

54

He whirled around, looking for Nectan, and saw him standing in the midst of the Fey about ten feet away, watching them. The swirling Pictish design on his face gave his face a sinister cast in the moonlight. As their eyes met he crossed his arms on his chest, his mouth set in a grim line.

Thomas' anger coalesced into fury, and he started towards the king, his fists clenched.

But he did not get far. Brorda grabbed him, restraining him as scattered cries rose up from the rest of the Fey.

Thomas ignored them all. "You knew he was here, all the time!" he snarled at Nectan. "At the Gathering, you barged into my head and found out everything about me. But you kept this from me, you didn't tell me —" his words choked off as he struggled against Brorda's iron grip.

"Thomas!" Brorda's voice was sharp in his ear, and he grunted at the effort of holding Thomas back. "Take care how you speak to your king!"

Thomas heaved against Brorda but could not release the other's grip.

"Let him go, Ward." Nectan's voice rang through the clearing. "This must be done."

Brorda looked over at the king, startled, but at Nectan's affirming nod, he looked back at Thomas, a warning in his eyes. "Be careful, wilding," he said, his voice low, and released him.

Thomas shook Brorda's hands off and stalked over to Nectan, whose Fey power wreathed his form in a shimmering nimbus.

Domech stepped in front of the king, his sword in hand, forcing Thomas to a halt.

Nectan stepped forward. "Nay, Domech. I dinna need your blade."

Domech almost spoke, but then stepped back, throwing Thomas a hot look of warning.

The other Fey had lifted their weapons as well. A low, rumbling growl erupted from behind him. He whirled around, fear spiking through him, the hounds fresh in his mind. A large dog stood there, hackles raised, sharp teeth bared as the growls rumbled through its throat. Thomas recognized it from the Gathering. One of the musicians was Wolf Clan, and this, his dog. It had been friendly enough that night, but now Thomas could only see fury in its eyes.

From above he heard the shrill cry of a falcon, suddenly piercing the night.

Beyond the dog his father still lay on the ground, next to Nona and Brorda who stood frozen in spot. *My father is here.* The thought was a sharp knife in his mind, its edge honed by betrayal. He whirled back to the king, but before he could speak, Nectan held up a hand.

"Hold, wilding," the king said, his voice low and laced with thrumming power. "I am your king, and I have your pledge."

"My *king?*" His own power leapt to life, the wild, sweet shock of it lending his fury a keener edge. He was sick of being manipulated, kept in the dark, sick of this whole place. "Not for much—" He was going to say *longer* but in the blink of an eye Nectan was upon him, and he was flat on the ground, the king's knife in front of his eyes. Nectan's clear amber eyes glowed with Fey power, his face distorted by a snarl as his mind slammed into Thomas. For a split second nothing existed but the implacable will of the Seelie King and his white-hot anger. Then Nectan's presence inside him was gone and Thomas' heart kicked to life with one slow thump.

"I *am* your king," Nectan said, his voice low and throbbing with emotion and Fey power. "The next time ye raise your power against me will be your last. This I swear to ye, Thomas mac Caden, Traveller, Speaker, and wilding, under this moon and sky and before this Court. Ye dare defy me, and ye will die."

The words fell into the hollow place inside of Thomas, shimmering with Fey power, the Speaking of his name causing a shudder to ripple through him. For a moment he felt dislocated, lost, the shocks of the night too much to bear, but then everything snapped back into place, and he found he could breathe again, albeit with some difficulty, since the king's forearm was under his chin, pressing him to the ground.

Nectan's eyes burned above him as he waited for Thomas' acknowledgement.

Despair filled him. Once again he had no choice. As much as he wanted to let go of his Fey power and see what would happen if he did, the king had just shown him that he could stop Thomas just as easily as swatting a fly. Fury surged through him, but he corralled it, barely, clenching his jaw and managing an awkward nod. Nectan held his gaze a moment longer, and then pushed himself upright.

Thomas rose slowly, trying to pull himself together, his stomach churning. For the life of him he did not know what to do next.

"Now ye will ask for my forgiveness, wilding," Nectan said, his voice tight. "And ye will tell this Court that you wilna do such a thing again."

Thomas eyed the Fey who ringed him, their weapons raised, suspicion and fear in their eyes, and he looked back at the king, who stood as before, his arms crossed on his chest, his eyes hard. *An Untamed wilding must die.* The Rule snaked through his mind, and he lifted his chin, his hands fisting at his side.

He didn't have a choice, not if he wanted to live, but it didn't mean he had to like it. "Forgive me, my lord king," he said, almost choking on the words. "It will not happen again."

"You have taken leave of your senses!" Strang stepped forward, his bow held in his hand, his eyes hard as he faced the king. "You must kill this wilding, now! He defies you, and yet you let him live? And this Fey, the one we risked our lives for tonight, this is his father? What game are you playing?"

Nectan looked at him coolly. "Ye would have the Hunt take a Fey who has Called to us for help?"

Silence fell. Strang's face twisted in disgust, but he did not speak, and Nectan continued.

"I am king over the Northern Seelies, a king of the Fey. I canna allow one of the Blood to be taken by that foul creature, to be used as he wished, nae matter who he be. What destruction would come of it?"

Strang's eyes flashed. "We could not have stopped him if this wilding had not been here, not without great cost to us." He turned to the other Fey. "See what risks our king takes, ponder his actions this night, and tell it to those who were not here. He protects the wilding and this Traveller who has refused us, and puts the rest of us in grave danger. Think on this." He looked around at the Fey, as if memorizing each one, then clenched his jaw and stalked away, the other Fey parting to let him pass.

Nectan lifted his chin. "Be at ease, my people. We have saved one of the Blood from the Alder King's foul hands, and no harm has come to us.

That is what ye must think on, and tell to your kin. We have done well this night." He looked around the circle at them. "But ye all heard the Huntsman: he will take a human this night, and we canna interfere." His eyes flashed in anger. "T'will mean trouble for us, to be sure. Go to your homes now, and prepare."

Thomas looked at the other Fey. Their expressions ranged from doubt to outright hostility. Clearly Nectan's support from his people was not as unquestioning as the king would want. Not that Thomas cared. He had no love for the king himself.

Nectan turned to a slight Fey, who had a shock of white hair. "Horse Lord, this Fey and the woman will need care. Can they stay with you until they have recovered?"

Thomas recognized him; it was Torht, the bone carver, one of the Fey he had met at the Gathering, and had seen a time or two, around Bebbanburg village.

Torht inclined his head, his pale hair white in the night. "As you wish, my lord king. And the Healer as well." He turned to Thomas. "You may come as well, Traveller."

Thomas didn't need his invitation. He would go with his father whether anyone wanted him to or not. But it didn't hurt to be gracious. Especially as Torht had spoken kindly to him. He nodded. "Thank you."

"I will see them safely there, my lord king," Brorda said.

Nectan nodded. "We will join you soon. But I will have words with the wilding first. There are things he needs to hear that are for his ears only." He looked around at the others. "The rest of ye go now in peace and in the brotherhood of the Seelie Fey."

The Fey glanced at one another and began to put their weapons away and gather their horses. Some glanced at Thomas, fear and suspicion mingling in their eyes.

Nectan looked at him. *See to your father, and then we will speak.* He turned to speak to Domech, dismissing Thomas.

His mouth twisted at the brush of the king's mind, wishing he had a way to block it.

He walked back to where his father lay unconscious and squatted down beside him, his emotions a tangled ball. He laid a trembling hand on him, feeling his solid warmth underneath his hand. *My father is alive. My father is Fey.*

Eyes burning, he took his hand away, blowing out a breath that ghosted white, no longer certain of anything at all.

55

"**Thomas,**" **Nona said,** kneeling beside him, her face a pale oval in the moonlight. She shook her head. "I had no choice. Our king would not allow me to tell you of this Traveller, not until you had learned more of our ways. And he was right to do so. Some information can be dangerous if it is given at the wrong time." Her eyes held his for a moment, and Thomas knew she spoke not only of Nectan, but also of Thomas' decision to reveal his true nature to Celyn. "Think you! I did not know he was your father. Word had come to the Southern Seelie Court two years ago of a Traveller living in the North who refused to pledge to either Court. We were warned to stay away from him. It was thought he would not stay long. Travellers rarely do. As time went on talk increased, as to why he had come, why he lingered." She paused. "He must have been waiting for you."

Thomas clenched his jaw and raked a trembling hand through his hair, trying to pull himself together, to make some sense out of the whole mess.

He forced his tangled thoughts away from his father and focussed on Nona. Just moments ago he had experienced the wrath of the Seelie King, the wrath reserved for those who defied him. As much as he wanted to, he couldn't blame Nona, nor Brorda for that matter, for not being willing to go against the king's wishes. Especially not for him, a wilding.

"All right," he said, his voice rough. "He told you not to tell me. I get it."

Relief blossomed on her face. "Truly, I am sorry."

He swallowed, trying to ease the tightness in his throat, trying to think. "I don't understand—" Words failed him for a moment, all the things he didn't understand clamouring for attention. He tried again. "The Huntsman. Who is he? What was this all about?" His lips thinned. "Or is that something *else* you can't tell me?"

Her face tightened at his barb. "There's nothing else our king has forbidden," she said, with a touch of ire. "As for *who*—" She shrugged slightly. "The Alder King, some name him. The Leader of the Wild Hunt. No one knows from whence he came, or how."

"He's a Traveller?"

Nona frowned. "Perhaps. Likely. There are places that are outside of time. Places the Fey go only at great peril to themselves. It is said he travels through the Wild Lands, and likely through time as well. The stories of him come to us from long ago." She grimaced. "You saw the shadow of the demon on him?"

"He was possessed."

Nona shook her head again. "As to that, I think not. He is using the power of the Undying, to be sure, but he is not consumed by it." Fear flashed over her face, and her lips thinned. "'Tis a mystery I do not wish to think upon."

Thomas had to agree. The memory of the demon-shadow coiling around the Huntsman made him slightly queasy. "He's Unseelie?"

"They do not claim him." Her eyes slid away from his.

The realization struck him like a blow. "Another wilding. Like Redcap." *No wonder they're all afraid of me.* He shook his head. He couldn't think of that now. "But why was he chasing my father? What did he want with him?"

Nona frowned. "I do not know. Humans are usually the prey of the Wild Hunt. Not the Fey. We are not such easy prey, as you saw this night."

"And the humans he catches? What happens to them?"

She lifted one shoulder, unease on her face. "They disappear."

Thomas remembered the horse, torn apart by the hounds, and suppressed a shudder. Just then, as if conjured by their conversation, a distant wail of a bugle drifted over the field, brought in on the night breeze.

"God, have mercy," Nona breathed. "We must cease this talk, lest we bring him upon us." She crossed herself quickly.

Beside them, a low moan arose from the woman who still lay prone on the ground. A young Fey man had been tending to the woman, and he looked over at Nona as the bugle's call faded. "Healer, would you come and aid me? She is Charmed, I think, but, 'tis no normal Charm."

Nona glanced at Thomas quickly then rose and stepped over to where the woman lay, kneeling down beside her. Thomas' father was still unconscious but looked comfortable enough, so Thomas joined her, wanting to get a closer look at this human who had been with his father, who had tried to protect him from the Huntsman.

She was slim, with curly dark hair that tumbled around her in wild abandon. She had high cheekbones and full lips, her lush beauty evident even in the shadowed night. She looked to be in her twenties, scarcely older than Thomas himself was, he realized, his gut clenching.

Nona examined the woman quickly, frowning as she closed her eyes and laid her hands on her for a moment. Thomas felt a brief surge of Fey power, and then the Welsh girl opened her eyes. "Yes," she said to the other Fey's questioning look. "She has been Charmed. But as you say, 'tis different."

Thomas frowned. "What do you mean, 'different'? Can't you wake her up?"

"As to that, I believe we could," she said slowly, "but I don't think it would be wise. The Alder King has caught her in a dream, and I fear she would not be able to leave it if we were to force her awake now, before it has run its course. The dream would become a waking dream, one she could never escape from. It is a trap he has set for her—for us."

The other Fey nodded. "An Unseelie trap," he said with distaste. "To do good results in harm." He glanced at Thomas quickly, and then away. But Thomas saw the accusation in his eyes all the same.

Nona looked at him, apologetic, but Thomas shook his head. They could think what they wanted. Not much he could do to stop them, after all.

Brorda appeared beside them, looking down at the woman with wary curiosity, but, after a quick glance between them, shifted his shoulders, shrugging off the questions he obviously wanted to ask. "We must go," he said. "The Hunt may yet come back. His words cannot be trusted."

As if to emphasize his point, the breeze shifted again, bringing with it the ghostly howls of the Huntsman's hounds.

"Sounds like they are further away." Thomas stood, listening for the sound, but silence fell again.

Brorda shrugged, distaste on his face. "For now." He sighed, and laid a hand on Thomas' shoulder. "Our king wishes to speak with you. I will take your father and protect him as if he were my own," he said. "Do you know the way?"

Thomas nodded. He had been to Torht's holding a time or two with Celyn or the monks. It was not far.

Brorda dropped his hand and let out a breath. "Our king told me only today of your father. We would have told you earlier, if the tides had not prevented you from coming sooner." He sighed again. "*Ne mæg werig mod wyrde wiðstondan.*"

Thomas recognized the quote; it was from a poem that he had heard more than once over the tables in Oswy's mead hall. *No weary mind may stand against the* wyrd. The pagan Saxons, like Brorda, held a fatalistic view of life, wrapped up in their idea of *wyrd,* an inexorable process that connects everything, a web on which everything hangs together.

It is not your choice, but God's, that brings ye here. Aidan's words came back to him, and he grimaced. *Wyrd* or God, either way, he found himself here against his will. *All comes from God's good hand.* He had heard Aidan say that more than once, too. *Right.*

He looked down at his father, his jaw clenching. All those years when he would have given anything to see his father again, and now, here he was. And maybe he would finally get some answers to the questions that plagued him. If his father survived.

He helped Brorda lift his father onto his horse. The Ward sat behind him, encircling him with his arms as he held the reins so that the unconscious man would not fall off. Nectan's cousin, Domech, did the same for the woman. Nona found her horse and mounted as well.

He found the bag that his father had been carrying and passed it up to her, to take with them.

"I'll come as soon as I can," Thomas said. "Thank you." If the Huntsman returned, he had some confidence that Brorda would not leave his father to the hounds and ride away, which is more than he could say for Domech, who eyed him coldly, distaste plain on his face.

"I will see him safely to the bone carver's holding." Brorda lifted a hand in farewell and turned his horse, the others following. Thomas watched until they were swallowed up in the darkness of the trees.

He stood still for a moment, trying to collect himself. He shook his head. *This has got to be the strangest night of my life.* All those years his family had thought his father dead, and yet he had been alive, here, in this time. His mother's face flashed through his mind, and his brother's, the grief that had lingered through the years still echoing through the empty space within him that his father had left behind.

He blew out a breath and raked his hand through his hair, looking over to where Nectan stood waiting, his arms crossed over his chest.

Nectan's gaze met his, the king's eyes hard and unyielding. Thomas' jaw clenched, with all the ways the king had deceived him flashing through his mind, sparking his anger afresh. He needed answers, and he would get them before this night was over.

56

"I have nae obligation to explain myself to ye," Nectan said as Thomas reached him. "The good of the Seelie Fey is always my first concern, not the needs of one Untamed wilding."

"One Untamed wilding who pledged himself to you."

"And that pledge holds me here," Nectan said, the edge to his voice razor-sharp. "Your father gave me no such pledge, yet I have risked the lives of my Court for him this night. For the good of all the Fey. Do not forget that, wilding."

Nona had been right then. Thomas frowned, trying to put the pieces together. *What game are you playing?* Strang's question of a moment ago was a good one.

Nectan continued, giving Thomas no chance to reply. "I received word two years ago of a Traveller of great power who lived in Dál Riata, near the monastery at Hii. Your father," he added, in case Thomas missed the point. "I went to see him, but he refused to pledge to the Seelie Court." His eyes hardened at the memory. "There was much he wouldna tell me. I was certain he was Unseelie, until I learned he had also refused them as well." He shook his head. "Travellers are not common amongst the Fey. We are uncertain of their ways, but a Traveller never stays long outside of his own time. So we watched your father, and waited for him to leave. But he didna go."

He gave Thomas a hard look, as if it were his fault. Thomas didn't know how to respond. For all he knew, it was. "The Unseelies watched him too. But he kept himself away from the Fey, even married this human woman ye saw tonight, a Sensitive who is niece to Eachan of the Horse

Clan."

Married. The word lanced through his heart, and Thomas had to force his mind away from it in order to keep listening as the king continued.

"And then came word of your arrival, and ye came to the Gathering." Nectan stopped, eyeing Thomas up and down. "There ye were, full of power, untaught. A wilding. And it was clear that ye be his son. Ye be much like him in looks."

"It was all a test," Thomas said, realization sweeping over him. "Whether I would pledge to you or not. And the Knowing—you wanted to see if my father had sent me to you, or if I knew of him. You thought he was plotting against you or something." His fists clenched, and he deliberately relaxed them, trying to keep his anger under control. "But after that, after you shoved your way into my head, you knew I had no idea my father was here. You knew I thought he was dead. Why didn't you tell me?"

"For your own sake," Nectan replied with some heat. "Think, for once! He has said nothing of his origins, or why he is here. He refuses to pledge to the Seelie Court, to any of the Fey. And he left ye as a wilding, with none of the Fey to guide ye!"

The sting of those last words clamped Thomas' mouth shut against the response that had sprung to his lips. His father *had* left him. There was no denying it.

Nectan pressed home his argument. "I dared not send ye running to his arms, not before ye had the chance to grow in your power, to know what it is to be Fey. To give ye a chance to stand up to him, if he meant harm. Once I thought ye ready, I planned to tell ye."

"So what happened here tonight? Why not just let the Huntsman kill my father, if you're so afraid of him? You saved his life. Why?"

The king drew up to his full height, disgust on his face. "I wouldna let another Fey be captured by the Hunt, whether he be Seelie or Unseelie, nae matter our differences."

The steel in his voice left no room for questions, but again Thomas had the niggling feeling Nectan was not being completely honest. He shook his head, weary of trying to figure it out. "So how did you know he was in trouble?"

"He Called to me this morning, when he knew the Hunt was after him. I sent a Summons to all the nearby Fey. And they came."

"This morning? So he must have been close enough—" His words cut off as another realization washed over him. "He was coming to see me."

Nectan nodded in agreement. "Aye," he said. "If the tides hadna prevented your arrival, I would have prepared ye."

Thomas snorted. "Right. You'll forgive me if I don't believe you."

Nectan raised his chin, his eyes cold in the moonlight, his Fey power bright. *He's afraid of me. They're all afraid of me.* So why bother allowing him to live? Why force him to pledge to the Seelie Court? *What's really going on?*

"This is what I think," he said finally. "You had no intention of telling me about my father, not until you could twist the circumstances to fit whatever plan you are hatching. But the Hunt forced your hand, didn't it? If it wasn't for that, you would have found some way to keep us apart until you thought I was *Tamed* enough to meet him."

He took a step towards the king, whose eyes flashed once in warning, his Fey power a bright force around him. Thomas uncurled his fists; he had no intention of taking the king on in a fight he could never win, even though every fibre of his being ached for it. "I have the Huntsman to thank for bringing my father to me. Not you. I won't forget that." He took a breath, trying to control his simmering anger. "I pledged to you. Because I did not have a choice, not because I wanted to. Just keep that in mind. And know this: as soon as my father recovers, we will be leaving this flea-bitten century behind. Until then, keep away from us."

Nectan's eyes narrowed. "I will do what my duty requires, as will you."

Thomas clenched his jaw against the words he wanted to say. He turned on his heel and stalked away, his shoulder blades twitching, expecting to feel a knife buried between them with every step.

But no such blow came. When he reached Missy he leaned his head against her comforting bulk for a moment, trembling with the after-effects of shock and anger, his thoughts awhirl.

Missy whinnied, loud in his ear, and was answered by another horse. He looked up and saw Nectan on his horse, fading into the trees at the edge of the clearing, leaving him alone without a backward glance.

Alone. The black wings of despair circled around him, beating on him mercilessly. He had always been alone, had always been different from everyone else. Even among the Fey, he was separate, an outsider. He clenched Missy's mane, her solid presence a comfort. *He was waiting for you.* Nona's voice floated through his mind, and he shook his head, his heart constricting.

It was too much to think about; he couldn't put the pieces together. He undid Missy's tether and pulled himself up onto her back. He turned her head into the trees, looking for the spot where he had abandoned the saddle. Only the occasional rustle of an animal in the woods, and once, the hoot of an owl far above, disturbed the quiet of the night as he saddled Missy and retraced his steps back.

The clearing was empty but for the carcass of the horse. He gave Missy a wide berth around it, but even so, her eyes showed white as her head tossed up and down when she caught the scent of blood. His gaze slid away from the sight, but despite his best efforts, flashes of memory seared through his brain. The horse, falling to the ground, the gruesome sight of the hounds attacking it, the tall figure of the horned Huntsman striding towards them.

The darkness is yours you are alone you are nothing you will fail you bring the darkness—

He shook his head, willing the dark thoughts to flee, but they circled around him, snapping at his will, and he had to draw the mare to a halt, immeasurably weary all of a sudden. He was tired of being alone, misunderstood, mistrusted. And he couldn't shake the impression that had haunted him since the day he woke up here, the feeling that came to him in the night, in his dreams.

That he was walking in the mist towards something of great importance, something he couldn't see, his doom gathering around him, drawing closer with every step.

The wind whispered through the trees. *You are alone.* The words cut through his heart, and he fisted his hands around the reins. He looked up at the sky, at the wheeling stars above, the crescent moon stabbing the inky velvet.

God, help me. That prayer had been on his lips from his first moments here; at times it had been the only prayer he had. But one thing the monks had taught him was that when you had no prayers of your own, sometimes you could use another's.

The path I walk, Christ walks with me. He closed his eyes. "I'm not alone," he muttered, opening his eyes, his voice breaking the silence of the clearing. "Not alone."

His father was here. Hope flared, fragile and uncertain, but real nonetheless. A light shining at the end of a long tunnel. He had been longing for someone to show him how to get home, had been praying for it. Now, in this impossible manner, his prayer had been answered.

Once my father recovers, we will be leaving. His words, spoken to Nectan in anger, came back to him now. *We will be leaving.* Emotion surged through him, making his throat ache with the effort of keeping it at bay, and he swallowed. "Come on, girl, let's go," he said, and lifting the reins, he touched his heels to her flanks.

Missy surged into motion beneath him, and he leaned down over her neck and gave her full rein, as eager as she was to put this night behind them, to leave the questions behind.

Home. I'm going home.

57

The echo of the hounds' eerie cries faded from Wulfram's mind. He opened his eyes, clenching his jaw against the rage that filled him.

The thrice-bedamned *Seelies* had thwarted his plan. His lip curled in disgust, thinking of Nectan standing defiantly before the Huntsman, the others ringing the glade around him. Matthew would be dead, if not for their interference.

How on earth had they known? And why had they come to the other Traveller's aid? He knew for a fact that Matthew had refused Nectan just as decisively as he had Raegenold.

But be that as it may, here he was. The Huntsman had failed; *he* had failed. And now the boy and his father were reunited.

Disaster.

His crow had seen the whole thing, but unfortunately it couldn't transmit the conversation between the Huntsman and the young Traveller. The birds didn't understand human speech.

Now what?

Matthew will surely tell the boy about him and his plans. That could be catastrophic.

Wulfram clenched his fists at his side, trying to think. He let out a breath, trying to calm himself. He had never been one to wallow in indecision or regret. What was done, was done. Now he had to figure out what to do next.

He thought for a moment, and then it came to him.

He had wanted the father dead, out of the way. But perhaps he had sprung the trap too soon. Matthew could be the perfect bait to bring the boy to him.

It would be trickier, granted, but it could work. He could figure something out.

He had to. His plan, and the future of the Fey, depended on it.

END BOOK ONE

ACKNOWLEDGEMENTS

Thank you for your purchase of *Wilding: Book One of the Traveller's Path*. I hope you enjoyed reading Thomas' story as much as I enjoyed writing it. I would love to hear your thoughts on the book. Please leave an honest review at the online retailer through which you bought it. More reviews mean better rankings on the online sites and helps other readers discover it, so leaving a review will be a tremendous help to me. Thank you so much!

If you want to learn more about the world of seventh-century Anglo-Saxon England, or more about my writing, check out my blog, *The Traveller's Path*, at **lasmithwriter.com**. *Bound: Book Two of The Traveller's Path* is coming soon! To be kept up to date with publication news and be the first to know about anything related to *The Traveller's Path* books, sign up for my newsletter at my blog. As a thank you for signing up, you will get a BONUS short story featuring Godric, one of the Travellers from *Wilding*. You can also follow me on Twitter @las_writer and on Facebook at my L.A. Smith author page.

There are so many who have helped me in my writer's journey to get to this point. Mentors, teachers, and friends. I hesitate to start saying thank you in fear that I will miss someone. But a few must be mentioned.

First of all, thank you to authors Matthew Harffy and Edoardo Albert, who graciously read an earlier draft of this novel and gave me wonderful endorsement quotes. If you want to read more books about Anglo-Saxon England, both fiction and non-fiction, look up both of these writers. You won't be disappointed!

To my wonderful family and friends, who have encouraged me over the long years of writing and self-doubt, thank you. You have no idea how much your support has meant to me. Some of you have read this book more than once and given me great feedback. You've made this book better.

Finally, endless thanks to my husband and children. Over the time I've been writing this book my three children have grown up around me and left our home on adventures of their own. Through it all they have always been a source of strength and support. My husband has read the manuscript more times than anyone else and somehow has not gotten sick of it. He has been my biggest cheerleader, and I couldn't have written this without him. Mark, Josh, Luke and Sarah, I love you more than I can say. I'm so glad I'm travelling the path of my life with you all.

To God be the glory.

ABOUT THE AUTHOR

L.A Smith lives in a small town in Alberta, Canada. She loves drinking tea, walking her dog, knitting, and writing. Not necessarily in that order, and not necessarily all at once.

You can catch up with her on Facebook at L.A. Smith, on Twitter @las_writer, and on her blog at lasmithwriter.com

Made in the USA
Middletown, DE
20 July 2019